RETURN OF
AN ANGEL

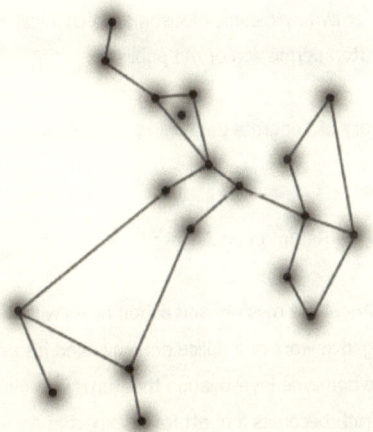

BY

R. TAYLOR

ARTWORK BY SANDY DOBBS

Library of Congress Cataloging-in-Publication Data

Taylor, R.

Return of an Angel / by R. Taylor

Summary: Return of an Angel is a mystery and action novel with a NEW twist! Return of an Angel follows the investigative work of a police detective and his partner in New York City who investigate a routine homicide investigation that turns into more than what they bargained for—and the truth becomes a quest for unexpected answers.

The first of a trilogy, this book includes a flavor of comedy, romance and drama providing a unique reading experience. The integration of personalized astrological charts located in the back of the book, gives readers a complete descriptive portrayal of the story's characters that's never been done before. Clues included in these charts offer an additional element to deducing the story.

ISBN: 978-0-615-26112-6 Hard Cover
ISBN 978-0-578-00150-0 Paperback

[1. Characters —— Fiction.   2. Precincts —— Fiction.]

Printed in the U.S.A.

First American Edition, 2008

Acknowledgements

Special friends who have supported me during the completion of this trilogy are; Marjorie D., Bruce H., Julie H., Julie K., Joan M., Rick M., Maria M., Teddi K., Bobbi S., and Sherry S.

While Melanie Jean G. encouraged me to transform my potential script for *N.Y.P.D. Blue* into a novel, Kelly Lee C., my beautiful, charming, elegant, inspiring, intelligent, and humorous daughter, shared her exceptional writing talents with me.

Sherry D. K.'s NewYork information brought the city to life for me, while Sandra MacTavish S., the first to read my unedited manuscript, became extremely helpful with her homeland knowledge of Scotland.

Marc S. G., my spirited Sagittarian son's childhood antics—including his Rock and Roll years as a drummer—not only provided me with years of laughter, but also supplied me with enough information for many other books.

Illustrator and Artist, Sandy D., provided priceless assistance.

An exceptional recognition for the wonderful authors, filmmakers, and actors of detective / crime films; *Boston Blackie, Charlie Chan, The Falcon, Sherlock Holmes, The Lone Wolf, Miss Marple, Perry Mason, Mr. Moto, The Saint, The Shadow, The Thin Man, Dick Tracy, Philo Vance,* and *The Whistler.* Also included, are those wonderful Film Noir films, too many to mention here. My earlier television inspirations also include; *Columbo, Miami Vice, Homicide, and N.Y.P.D. Blue.* Today, there are so many wonderful detective orientated productions that "my honorable mention" list would be endless.

Reviews:

"I found **Return of an Angel,** the first book of **THE ROAA TRILOGY,** engaging from the start," **says Mark Massagli, President Emeritus of the American Federation of Musicians of the United States and Canada**. "A modern day mystery, with action, romance, comedy and intrigue all rolled into one great story. If you love good cop stories, classic music, and unusual characters, then this distinctive read is for you!"

"A wild and wonderful ride with colorful characters," **says Jeff Sturges, Musical Composer for TV Series; Murder She Wrote, Walker Texas Ranger, Simon & Simon, and T. J. Hooker**. "This novel has all the ingredients for an awesome movie and the music referred to in the book is very impressive. Taylor has a marvelous method of picking the correct background music for her characters and story situations.

"What a wonderful experience and enchanting read," **says Teddi Kessie, Owner and Founder of The End Result**. "Each locale is described so interestingly and every character is defined in a colorful way. Having clarity and humor, one can "see" everything so clearly. This book has such an unusual format. The illustrations throughout the book are wonderful, and the Astrological Charts led me to visualize the characters at a deeper level. I loved this book—it was a joy to read."

"I found this first book wonderfully exciting and enjoyable," **says Jana Sutter, Physical Therapist and First Place Nevada Silver State Body Building Competition Winner**. "I couldn't put it down. Its cliff-hanging ending held me in a delightful suspense. If you are a fan of the Lethal Weapon and Die Hard films, you will love **Return of an Angel**."

Dobbs's Biography:

Artist Sandy Dobbs had aspirations to be an artist ever since high school. He continued his art education in college by taking traditional art classes, which included studies in oils, charcoal, pastels and other mediums. After college he moved into the computer art medium working for a leading digital gaming company. Later he taught art and computers for the public school system. Creating artwork and enjoying time with his family are his main pursuits. You can find more of his latest artwork at: http.//darksandman66.deviantart.com/

INTRODUCTION

ROAA takes place in the year 2002. It is a fictional, mystery novel about two homicide detectives in New York City—their, fears, desires, weaknesses, addictions, and personal relationships. The main characters—Billy Cavanaugh and Archie MacTavish—experience, action, romance, comedy and intrigue.

Blue-eyed Detective Billy Cavanaugh was born December 3, 1965 in New York City. His blondish brown hair frames his face in a flattering way and his five foot nine slender body, boyish smile, and charismatic personality, makes him very appealing to the opposite sex. Due to the harsh circumstances of his childhood, this detective carries a lot of emotional baggage and experiences flashbacks of being raised by his single mother in the San Fernando Valley of California. His childhood existence takes a dramatic turn in Los Angeles, when a LAPD homicide detective saves his life. The flashbacks not only deal with his youth, but also include his alternate life as a famous rodeo bull rider. Loving Classic Rock, he smokes Marlboro cigarettes, drinks Budweiser beer and J & B scotch. Because of where he has made his home, MacTavish often refers to him as "Brooklyn."

Born in Scotland on September 15, 1936, dark-humored widower Detective Archie MacTavish is a romantic—making him quite the ladies man. His moustache and well-groomed, short, silver-gray beard frames his slightly balding head. His tasteful wardrobe, Scottish accent, and striking, twin-like resemblance to the actor Sean Connery, have allowed humorous situations to develop in his life. Financially secure, MacTavish has made a very lucrative living as an artist for over forty years. His paintings hang in some of the wealthiest homes throughout Europe. This alternate income allows him to wear designer suits and clothes. He loves the nightlife and enjoys his liquor—Johnny Walker Red scotch to be specific. Having a great admiration for Engelbert Humperdinck, he is often humming, singing, or listening to his music.

Opinions expressed, and discussions engaged by my characters are utilized for the sole purpose of defining their fictional personalities. They are not, in any way, intended to undermine any government, organization, people, place or thing.

The astrological charts section—found in the back of the book—is designed specifically to support my fictional characters. Their biographical charts, according to my personal studies, have been formulated to their birthdays and are intended to be brief and condensed representations of each character's existence and personality traits throughout their lives. Although I have explained their personalities briefly throughout the book, the edited charts reveal a more personal side of their being, and can be researched at any time during the reading of the book.

೮ාೞ

RETURN OF
AN ANGEL

LADY IN GRAY

The city of New York was experiencing its first fierce afternoon rainstorm after a long and icy winter. Amidst the towering wet buildings in Manhattan were several hotels. In one of those hotel rooms, a naked, thirty-six year old Billy Cavanaugh was sitting up in bed—smoking a cigarette and listening to the song *Love To Burn*. Mesmerized by the ferocious wind outside, he watched as it forced unrelenting raindrops to splatter against the hotel windows. Lying next to him was a dark haired companion—face down in the pillow. Cavanaugh took one last puff off his cigarette before putting it out. Getting up, he walked across the room to a chair where he had left his clothes the night before. Grabbing his blue jeans off the back of the chair, he slipped into them, turned around, and zipped them up. A bolt of lightening flashed across the windows as he walked into the bathroom and leaned on the sink. Staring blankly into the mirror, he turned on the water and splashed it up on his face. Shaking his head, he ran his damp fingers through his hair and dried off with one of the hotel towels while walking back into the bedroom. Sitting down on a chair, he pulled on his designer western boots and slipped into a blue pullover sweater. Walking over to the nightstand, he quietly opened the top drawer and picked up his personal belongings; a cell phone, watch, wallet, 9mm Glock, and an NYPD shield. Subsequent to holstering his gun, he removed a hundred dollar bill from his wallet and slipped it thoughtfully under his companion's pillow. Leaving the room, he put on his raincoat and hurried down the hallway towards the stairs. After reaching the staircase, he hastened down the steps and headed out through the lobby. Pulling out a pack of Marlboro's, he lit one up and walked fearlessly into the downpour. He stood quietly on the curb as he hailed an oncoming cab, and after it came to a stop, quickly climbed in.

"19th precinct in Manhattan, you know where it's at?" said Billy, shaking the rain off his head and wiping his face with his arm.

"Piece of cake," the driver responded, glancing at his passenger in the rearview mirror as he drove away. "Hey, I know you. You're Kid Cavanaugh."

"You got me," Billy smiled, looking out at the rain drenched streets.

Smiling enthusiastically, the driver said, "I saw you ride in Austin. You rode a bull named Original Sin. Man...I thought that bull was gonna be inscribed on your tombstone."

"That seems to be the only ride everyone remembers." laughed Billy, recalling his rough ride and being hurled into the air like a rag doll in the midst of a menacing tornado.

"So how many buckles do you have now?" smiled the driver.

"Three," said Billy, as he cracked open the window and tossed his cigarette out.

The cab driver glanced at him in the rearview mirror and said, "So, you a cop now?"

"Detective," replied Billy, rolling up the window.

"I didn't know that. I read somewhere you had a ranch. Still got that...your ranch?"

"What," Billy laughed again, "are you writing a book or something?"

The cab driver, focusing on the oncoming traffic and glancing again into his rearview mirror said, "Nah, I used to have a ranch...lost it in my last divorce. The woman wiped me out. Now she lives on the ranch in Wyoming and I drive a cab in New York."

Feeling sympathetic for the cab driver's loss," Billy said, "Hey, I didn't mean to—"

"Forget it," the driver interrupted humbly, "you should see some of the farm animals I get in this cab. Compared to them you're a lamb." The two men laughed as they continued conversing about rodeos and the rainy weather.

Suddenly, Cavanaugh's phone rang. Looking at it, he recognized that the call was from his partner, Archie MacTavish.

"Mac, what's going on?"

"We picked up a homicide and the captain's calling you in on this." MacTavish was in the precinct parking lot, sitting in his Lexus. Reaching under his seat, he pulled out a scotch-filled silver flask. After removing the top, he took a drink and said, "Where are you?"

"Pulling in as we speak, and heading right for you," said Billy, as the cab pulled up alongside MacTavish's car.

Laughing, the cab driver said, "Next time you ride Kid, try to pick a domestic neutered bull."

"That *would be* a better choice," smiled Billy, as he reached into his jeans and paid the fare. "Thanks for the ride."

Trying to avoid the rain, Cavanaugh hastily left the cab and joined his partner. "Five more minutes and I would have been heading for home," he said, wiping the rain off his face as he jumped into the passenger seat. "My car's in the precinct lot."

"Sorry," said Mac, as he placed the flask under his seat. "I know what its like to be called in on your off time."

"You'd better get some breath mints in your mouth before we hit the crime scene," suggested Billy.

"Well it's nice seeing you again Brooklyn," Mac mocked, as he drove away.

The dreary April day had provided the city with its most recent murder in Manhattan. Police units were already on the homicide scene when the two detectives arrived. After MacTavish parked the car, Cavanaugh hurriedly jumped out—leaving his door open. He quickly ducked under the yellow plastic crime scene tape, moving towards two police officers holding black umbrellas.

"HEY CAVANAUGH, IT'S RAINING YOU KNOW," Mac yelled, as he walked around his car and slammed the passenger door shut. "Been spending too much time on the ranch," he mumbled under his breath. Pulling his designer raincoat closed over his stylish Armani suit and tie, he hastily approached his partner, who was already questioning the

4

officer standing under an umbrella. With his head bent down, he said, "So what have we got here?"

"Dead male in his sixties," said Billy, leaning down and peering under the plastic cover. "Crime Unit been here yet?" he blinked anxiously, trying to ward off the wind blown rain falling on his face.

"Not yet," said the officer, who was sharing his umbrella with MacTavish. "Why don't you guys take this umbrella, I'll take cover with my partner." Handing MacTavish the umbrella, the officer walked away and joined his fellow officer.

"This was no robbery, nothing's been taken," said Billy, as he examined the well-dressed victim. "His watch, wallet, money, ID, credit cards—they're all here."

"Looks like a hit," said Mac, while protecting his partner from the rain with the umbrella.

Looking up, Billy replied, "Good deduction Sherlock."

Suddenly, something across the street caught Cavanaugh's eye. Perspiration replaced the rain on his face. As he slowly rose to his feet, his wet eyes fixed on a woman emerging from the crowd and entering a nearby building. Her unexpected appearance filled him with nervous apprehension and his heart dropped like a rock. Shaking, he staggered forward and fell into MacTavish's arms.

Glancing across the street, Mac made light of the incident and said femininely, "This is so sudden dear; maybe we should get a drink in the Village first?" He quickly recognized the seriousness of the situation when Cavanaugh became weak and pallid. "You okay Kid?"

Breaking away from his partner's grip, Billy wiped his face with his coat and said, "Yeah...I'm fine."

"Well, you don't look fine," Mac argued back. "Maybe you should go to the car—take some time out."

"I said I'm fine!" Billy insisted, stepping past his partner and staring at the office building where the woman entered. "Can you cover this while I go check something out?"

"What the hell is going on," said Mac. "You nearly pass out, and now you want to go for a damn walk in the park. Look up in the sky; it's a downpour for Christ's sake!"

Pointing to the building, Billy said irritably, "I need to go across the street."

Stepping in front of Cavanaugh, and blocking his view of the building, Mac said, "Have I missed something here?"

"What are you talking about?" snapped Billy, ducking back under the umbrella that MacTavish was holding.

"Does this sighting of yours have anything to do with the man lying here at our feet?" Mac said heavily.

Chokingly, Billy answered "No."

"Then would you mind telling me what the hell this is all about?"

Billy gave a disgruntling sigh and said, "I think I saw my mother going into that office building."

"Okay," Mac replied softly. "I have a mother too, but I sure as hell don't stop a criminal investigation if I see her walk into Bloomingdales."

"You don't understand Mac; it can't be her."

Overly concerned with his partner's behavior, Mac said, "You look ill Kid. Listen, backup's on the way. When they get here we'll let them take over and get you a drink at the nearest bar."

6

"IT CAN'T BE HER!" Billy said hotly. "I must be losing my mind. Mac...my mother? She's dead. She died when I was fourteen."

In the short time the two detectives had worked together, Cavanaugh had never mentioned his mother.

"Now I really need a drink," Mac mumbled, as he thought about the dead woman who came back to life.

After watching and hearing the whole episode between the two detectives, one of the police officers walked over to them and said, "Excuse me, would one of you detectives want to tell me what the hell is going on, because this body's about to float down 5th Avenue if we don't do something about it now!"

"Yeah," replied Billy defensively, "and what's your suggestion Officer...what the hell is your name?"

"Ford," he replied. "Officer Robert Ford."

MacTavish quickly intervened and pushed his partner aside. Leading the officer away, he said, "Ford, my partner's not feeling well. He took a bad fall off a horse last month. You see he rides in rodeos in his off times. Crazy, I know. You see, he fell off the horse and landed on his head. We all thought he was okay, you know, recovered? But I guess not. Bear with me here and forget what you heard. I didn't understand any of it either; he was like this when he first fell off the horse. Best thing we can do is not to upset him. I'm going to take him to the hospital. My guess is they'll probably re-admit him. Why don't you go ahead and do what needs to be done? You think you can take care of this until our back-up gets here?"

"Sure, I'll take care of everything," Ford replied, taking back his umbrella. Glancing past MacTavish, he saw another detective unit driving up to the crime scene. "Looks like your back-up is already here," he said, pointing at the arriving car.

Turning around, MacTavish was relieved to see his fellow detectives. "It's Keaton and Matthews—they're with us."

Blonde, blue-eyed Detective Vickie Keaton, on the surface appeared to be shy, but could also be extremely forward and aggressive—the latter was the side she projected when doing her job.

Detective Marc Matthews, her partner, was an out of shape, thirty-seven year old redhead, who by choice, happened to be stuck in the 60s era. Twenty-five pounds overweight, his head led the way when he walked and his red hair was thick and always in disarray. The out of style clothes he wore often looked like he had slept in them. His mentor was Lieutenant Columbo—the fictitious television detective played by the actor Peter Falk.

Cavanaugh was standing in a trancelike state—staring at the building across the street when Mac approached him and said, "Get in the car Kid, replacement troops have arrived and we're leaving."

Climbing into the car, Cavanaugh's eyes once again locked on to the high-rise building that his mother supposedly walked into.

Leaving his spaced out partner, MacTavish turned around and rushed towards their back-up mumbling nonsensical words.

"What's going on Mac?" asked Vickie, rolling down her window and handing him an umbrella that he quickly opened.

"Yeah, is there anything we can do?" Marc inquired.

"The Kid's not feeling well; do you think you two can finish this up for us until we get back to the station? It'll be greatly appreciated. They're in the process of removing the body," he said, glancing at the crime scene. "Those two officers holding umbrellas have a list of the witnesses. Apparently, nobody wanted to hang around in this downpour. Just take care of what's left here and start the paperwork for us when you get back to the precinct?"

"Sure, no problem," Vickie responded sympathetically. "Does he need a doctor?"

"No, he'll be all right, he just needs to get out of this downpour." Looking up at the rain as it fell from the dismal sky Mac replied, "We both do."

"You two go ahead," said Marc, leaning across Vickie. "He's probably got that flu that's going around. I had it myself last week. Don't worry; we'll cover this for you."

"THANKS, I OWE YOU," Mac yelled, as he hastily got into his car and tried to appease his young partner. "You know Kid; there are a lot of people in this world that resemble someone else. I saw a show on television Friday night about everyone having a twin somewhere."

"Give me a break," Billy argued, "when do you ever watch TV on Friday nights? Friday nights you're at the bar, and television would definitely interfere with your week-end socializing."

"At the bar...that's where I saw it."

Cavanaugh raised his eyebrows in disbelief and replied, "Yeah right."

"For God's sake Brooklyn, it's a regular monsoon out there. With the rain and sweat in your eyes, how can you be sure of what you saw?" Looking at his partner, MacTavish saw the frustration and confusion building up and quickly changed his approach to the situation. "Maybe she was one of those twins, or someone that just looks like her."

"Mac, it's not like that. As a kid I had this psychic connection with my mother. Whenever she was around I could feel it. It didn't matter where I was; I always knew when she was there. I'd get this weird feeling, and there she'd be...as if she'd materialized in front of me."

"Are you trying to tell me you're a psychic, or have you just been overdosing on the *X Files*?"

"Mac...all I know is I haven't felt that way since I was fourteen, and when the feeling came today well, it knocked the wind out of me. Then seeing her...or at least I thought I did. I could have sworn it was her." As he watched the rain bouncing off the windshield wipers, he sighed, "What's happening to me...am I losing my mind?"

"Where did you see her last?" said Mac. As Cavanaugh pointed to the building that he saw the woman enter, MacTavish peeled his car out backwards and spun it around. Honking and having some near misses with a few taxis, he made a u-turn and pulled up in front of the high-rise. "Just promise me one thing Kid," he stipulated, "that you won't be on one of those psychic hot lines exposing my personal life."

Cavanaugh didn't absorb what his partner was saying; his mind—and not for the first time—was elsewhere. As he stared out the passenger window, his thoughts and fears swirled through his mind like a giant typhoon. In the midst of his mental tropical storm, the lady in gray, and his mother, swirled around him calling out his name. It was MacTavish's voice that diminished the storm in his head and brought him back to reality.

"Let's go find that lady," said Mac.

Even though the wind had subsided, the steady rainfall didn't deter MacTavish from getting out of his parked car and leading the way towards the building. As he approached the entrance, he noticed Cavanaugh wasn't with him. Turning around, he saw him still sitting in the car. Rushing back, he opened the passenger door and said, "Would you care to join me inside?"

Snapping out of his trance, Cavanaugh got out and hurried past him. Following him into the building, MacTavish mumbled something about being a fish out of water and needing his scotch without water.

A nostalgic look of pre-WWII permeated the lobby. The dimly lit area had a film noir atmosphere and held a mixed odor of dampness and mildew. The walls were covered with a chestnut brown woven cloth that resembled bamboo. On each side of the entrance were three lights with half moon copper bases hanging on the walls. Inside the copper bases were glass light enclosures, designed to represent a giant frosted tulip. Leading up to the reception desk was a large oriental rug on a brown octagonal tile floor that dated back to the 1930s. The mahogany reception desk was inlayed with black marble. On top of the desk was an antique, bronze lamp. Its dark green glass shade gave the room a mysterious aura.

"Classic, but not un-familiar," Mac mumbled, as he trailed behind his partner—examining the lobby's décor.

A young security guard, showing very little confidence in himself, sat behind the desk. His awkwardly tilted body had a slight twitch and his left hand arched slightly across his chest.

Believing him to be slightly autistic, Cavanaugh approached him sympathetically. Showing his badge, he gently started the conversation. "Hey, how you doin?" Glancing at the guard's badge, he said, "Franklin, that's your name?"

"Fr-ra-kl-lin...Ja-mm-es," the young man stuttered. "Wh-at-t...do you-u wa...want?"

"It's okay," Billy continued, "don't be scared. We're police officers. See, here's my badge." As he moved closer, the guard's eyes began twitching as he unsteadily backed away.

Glancing down at the marble desktop, Cavanaugh got distracted as he noticed a hairline crack along the right edge. "Can't be worth too much with that crack in it," he thought.

MacTavish observing his partner's lack of concentration, quickly moved forward and intervened. "We're looking for a lady who came in here about twenty minutes ago. She's about—" Suddenly, Mac realized he couldn't give the description of his lady in gray. "Brooklyn, you want to help me out here?"

Cavanaugh found great enjoyment when his partner jumped into a conversation he couldn't finish, like diving into a pool before checking to see if there was water in it—which MacTavish once did on a three-day scotch binge. If the pool hadn't been full of dead leaves he'd probably be dead.

Smiling, Billy said, "Blonde hair up in a twist, black raincoat over a gray suit—carrying a black umbrella and black briefcase."

"Did you forget about her silver earrings?" said Mac.

Ignoring his partner's sarcasm, Billy said, "Forget about the earrings Franklin, did you see where the woman went?"

Unsteadily, Franklin held on to his chair and sat down at his desk. "No, laa-dy," he stuttered. "I hav-ent seen no...one since...the r-ain...st-started."

Cavanaugh's smile slowly left his face. His stare quickly turned insistent, and his eyes took on a steely glint of determination. Staring sternly into the boy's eyes, and with a hint of irritation in his voice, he leaned towards him, as raindrops dripped off his coat and onto the desk.

12

"Look, let me run this by you again. A blonde in a gray suit came in here twenty minutes ago...well...now its thirty-five minutes ago. And we," Billy argued, pointing to MacTavish and himself, "want to know where she went."

MacTavish realized his partner was overreacting, and once again intervened. Wedging himself into Cavanaugh's space, he pushed him away from the desk and the trembling guard. Standing with their backs to him, he said, "Now take it easy Brooklyn. Maybe this woman changed her mind and walked back out."

"No," said Billy, moving away from his partner. "She did not come out!"

MacTavish backed up and pointed to the front door. "It only takes a few minutes to walk out of here. How the hell can you be sure she's still here?"

"If she did in fact walk out, why didn't he see her walk in?" Billy said irritably, pointing at the guard.

Pulling him away, Mac said quietly, "For God's sake, look at him. Maybe he took a piss, maybe he fell asleep...let it go." Grabbing his partner by the shoulders, he repeated his words sternly, "It's time to let it go."

As Cavanaugh glanced back at the guard, he nodded yes and reluctantly agreed to follow his partner's direction.

MacTavish turned around and approached the nervous guard. "Look Franklin, it's been a tough day. My partner's dog died today and he's not quite himself—had the dog since he was a child.

As the guard gave Cavanaugh a very sympathetic look, Billy sighed and mumbled, "Here we go again."

"You see, he and the dog were very close," said Mac, as he pretended to wipe a tear from his eye. "They went everywhere together—for years they were inseparable."

"Oh, for Christ's sake," Billy declared, as he stepped away from them and looked up at the ceiling with a questioning expression and thought..."why me?"

Ignoring his partner, MacTavish continued his dog tale. "He got up this morning and there was the dog, lying on the pillow next to him, dead—poor thing passed away in the night. So you see, it's not you he's upset with...it's all about the dog." Removing a tissue out of his raincoat, he blew his nose.

"Its...ok-kay," the guard replied with great sensitivity.

"We're both sorry for not acting appropriately," said Mac, as he gave his partner an indisputable look. "We are sorry, aren't we Detective Cavanaugh?"

Knowing the limits of MacTavish's patience, Cavanaugh faced the guard and replied with a half smile, "Franklin, I'm really sorry."

"It's...o...kay...n-now," Franklin said, waving goodbye.

"My dog died?" Billy questioned, as MacTavish guided him towards the exit.

"He's a sensitive guy. I figured he needed something he could relate to."

As the detectives approached the front door, Franklin spoke out. "Ex-cuse-m-ee?"

The two detectives stopped and turned around slowly. "...Yes," Mac responded softly.

Franklin stammered and sighed, "Th-the d-dog...wa...hat....k-k-kind...was-s it?"

14

Cavanaugh, cynically rolling his eyes at his partner, proceeded anxiously through the front door.

"POODLE, IT WAS A POODLE," Mac hollered out, measuring the dog's size with his hands over his head as he left the building.

The lobby became eerily silent. Looking up slowly, the security guard's demeanor slowly transformed. He stood erect and watched the two detectives running towards their car. Grabbing a towel, he wiped down the wet desk, and without hesitation, tossed the towel into the trash can. Removing a pack of Marlboro lights out of his jacket, he lit one up. Whistling, he reached for his cell phone and made a call. "Yea it's me," he said without a stutter, "I believe I'm off duty. And by the way, toss this desk, our visitor noticed the crack."

Outside, the two detectives were still in disagreement. "My dead dog is a poodle?" said Billy, opening the car door and shaking his head.

"Was," Mac said getting into the car. "Was a poodle."

Cavanaugh let out a sarcastic sigh and looked out the window.

"Look I didn't think he could relate to you having a Pit Bull or Doberman. Your attitude was forceful enough," said Mac, as he drove away.

"Mac, you never cease to amaze me."

"I hear that quite often from people who are close to me."

The two men became silent as MacTavish tried to focus on the difficult driving conditions. Cavanaugh's thoughts however, were elsewhere. Hypnotized by the windshield wipers and the rain, his mind traveled back to a more carefree time in his youth.

ଛୀଔ

SUMMER OF '75

...It's the summer of '75 in Southern California's San Fernando Valley. Nine years old Billy Cavanaugh is riding his black bike along the Los Angeles Wash.

About the size of two car lanes in width, the LA Wash is a runoff for excess water to avoid flooding in the city—the slanted cement sides create a tempting place for kids to ride their bikes and skateboards. These usually dry washes can have five feet of rapid moving water in minutes—sweeping away everything in its path. Although it's a restricted area with "No Trespassing" signs posted along its borders, the signs are often ignored by the kids.

Young Billy has a hard time with rules and boundaries. He enjoys the excitement of being someplace where he isn't supposed to be, like today, when he's surfing the slopes of the wash on his dirt bike. He is wearing worn out blue jeans and a white t-shirt with a logo that reads FATBURGER.

Cavanaugh recalled the tee shirt and the local burger stand on Normandy Avenue—a favorite place he often went with his mother. He looked forward to those weekend outings. "God, those burgers were good," he thought, remembering the oversized burgers that were made with fresh ground beef, grilled onions, and cheese. As he recalled the fresh lettuce leafs, tomatoes, mayonnaise, mustard and pickles that topped them off, his mouth began to water. Being nine year old, it was a very exciting time and place—celebrities who would often pull up in their Cadillacs and limos to buy the mouthwatering burgers—his mind quickly drifted back to that day in the wash.

...he flips his bike on the edge of the wash, and tumbles into six inches of water that is draining slowly down the wash—the dirty water is cooling and saturates his clothing. Picking up his bike, he heads up the side of the wash.

When he finally arrives home, his mother is not impressed with the condition of his clothes and says, "Billy, you need to get out of those wet clothes. Billy Cavanaugh...do you hear me? And how many times have I told you to stay out of the wash? You have no idea how dangerous it is down there."

It was now MacTavish's voice Cavanaugh heard.
"...Earth to Brooklyn. Are you there mate?"

Still looking out of the wet windshield of their squad car, Cavanaugh came back to reality and said, "Sorry, I guess I spaced out."

"As I was saying," said Mac, "we both need to dry out. Let me rephrase that. You need to dry out...I need a drink."

Outside, the weather began clearing up. Only a slight drizzle remained when MacTavish's cell phone rang. "Mac here." Pausing, he whispered, "It's Rollins. Yes captain...right now he's very wet."

The captain of the 19th Precinct was Al Rollins, a charismatic Black man in his sixties—his sparkling smile gave a look of true happiness. The father of twin boys, he had been married to the same woman for over fifteen years.

"Don't worry about your homicide, Matthews and Keaton have it covered," said Rollins, "they're doing the paperwork now. Tell me about Cavanaugh, how's he doing?"

Glancing over at his partner, Mac said, "He's seen better days. The Kid's cold, shivering, and running a bit of a fever, thought I'd take him to my place."

"Keaton told me how sick he was," Rollins continued, "and Matthews went on and on about the flu he thinks the Kid has. That being the case, you two need to stay away. I don't need anybody else coming down with this crap. I got enough people out as it is."

"I understand," responded Mac.

"Just make sure he takes it easy."

"I'll do that Captain—and thank Matthews and Keaton for us," Mac replied as he disconnected the call.

"Does this mean we're off?" said Billy.

"Off until Monday."

"Good old Marc," smiled Billy, as his mind drifted away from the lady in gray.

"He can be very beneficial at times," said Mac, as he turned onto the Sunrise Highway and headed for his home in Islip, New York.

MacTavish, and his deceased wife Catherine, inherited the Islip property back in '53 from her aunt when it was nothing but woods—the 1953 beautiful birch forest had been slowly replaced throughout the years by a concrete city with stores, parks, homes and restaurants.

MacTavish built a spectacular home there in '54—more extravagant than homes being built now. Everything about his three-story home spoke of elegance, including a closed-off loft, with a huge skylight and lots of windows.

The loft was where Mac's alter ego as an artist took over. Most of his artwork can be found in the art circles of Europe and selling for as much as $300,000. A famous celebrity living in France recently paid $286,000 for one of his paintings.

The MacTavish home was set back from the street behind a large security gate with sensor lights. Beyond the gate was a large lawn—framed by an old fashioned English garden. A winding path led up to a 1890s circular porch that surrounded the house. On the left side of the porch hung a wooden swing; to the right were two white wicker chairs. Lilac trees bordered both sides of the porch, while giant rose bushes braced themselves against the tall security fence. Giant elm trees provided a blanket of shade for the house and yard—the backyard, a lavish floral garden, reflected Catherine's love of flowers—many of which were reproduced in MacTavish's paintings.

Far behind the house, stood a four-car garage where Catherine parked her car. She didn't believe in having gasoline and carbon fumes anywhere close to the living quarters.

MacTavish however, always parked on the street in front of his home and continued to do so, even after her death.

It was no longer raining when the detectives pulled up in front of the MacTavish residence. "Home sweet home," said Mac, as he opened the car door and stepped out.

As Cavanaugh got out of the car, he tossed his head back, ran his fingers through his damp hair, and followed his partner up the walk to the security gate. "This is the only part about coming to your house that I'm not thrilled about."

"Aw c'mon, she's my baby girl. Actually, she's gotten quite attached to you," Mac replied, unlocking the gate.

As they entered and walked up the winding path, Billy nodded and said, "Yeah right, then why do I get the feeling that every time she sees me she wants to knock me down to the floor and rip off all my clothes?"

"I'll have none of that Kid," said Mac fiddling with his key as they approached the front door.

"None of what?"

"Leading her on the way you do," insinuated Mac.

Cavanaugh tilted his head over his partner's shoulder and said, "Just open the fucking door."

As MacTavish opened the door, an unfathomable silence greeted them. Walking in, he turned on the light; leaving Cavanaugh to close the door behind them. Removing his wet trench coat, he hung it up on the hand carved oak rack next to the door and called out, "Honey, come say hello...Billy's here." Looking at his partner he said, "Take off your coat before you ruin my Persian rug."

Cavanaugh removed his raincoat, hung it up, and walked cautiously into the living room.

"Maybe she's in the kitchen," Mac sighed, leaving his partner alone in the living room.

As Cavanaugh glanced over his shoulder, he saw her staring at him from the hall closet, underneath the staircase. With glowing eyes, her body pushed the door open and crept towards him.

"IN HERE MAC," Billy yelled out with great apprehension. "I THINK YOU—" But before he could finish the sentence, a huge, honey colored Rotweiller, Wolf, Golden Retriever mutt mix, knocked him to the floor and stood over him growling and licking his face at the same time. Pinned to the floor, Billy hollered out loudly, "I FOUND HER MAC."

MacTavish walked back to the living room smiling. Being intentionally oblivious to his partner's condition, he sauntered over to the dog and patted her on the head. "Aw...there's my girl. Are you playing with my partner?" he said condescendingly.

"Mac," Billy threatened, with a growing irritation towards the dogs' behavior.

"Okay girl," laughed Mac, as he reached down and gently pulled on her. "Come on, let him up."

"Why does she do that?" Billy said, getting up and brushing himself off.

"She's a very demonstrative lady. Which if I may add," said Mac, focusing his attention on Honey, "is exactly how I prefer all the women in my life. Let's go girl, a trip outside will do you good."

MacTavish escorted her through the kitchen and into the huge backyard where she quickly squatted to pee. "AND STAY OUT OF THE MUD," he yelled. As he turned to re-enter the house, Honey bolted past him—galloping through the kitchen on a quest to find the young detective.

Seeing Cavanaugh on the couch, the dog jumped up and plopped down next to him. Just inches away from his face and staring at him with a lethal glare, growled in a low menacing tone.

Facing straight ahead, Billy tried to ignore her and called out, "Mac...I may have to shoot your dog."

MacTavish moved towards the couch and sat down next to her. "You have to be more sociable Kid," he said, ruffling the dog's chin.

Cavanaugh looked over Honey's head and gave his partner a stern look.

"Come on girl...let's get you some dinner before you start chewing on the Kid. Save him for your dessert," laughed Mac, as Honey jumped down and followed her master back into the kitchen.

"These are the times when I believe I have a psychotic partner bordering on homicidal tendencies," snickered Billy joyfully.

"GET OUT OF THOSE WET CLOTHES," Mac yelled out, "YOU'RE STARTING TO MILDEW AND HONEY'S ATTRACTED TO MOLD."

Cavanaugh smiled as he headed for the stairs. Sitting on the plush carpeted steps, he removed his wet leather western boots and proceeded up the wooden staircase. As he reached the top of the landing, his pullover sweater was off and he was undoing his jeans. Reaching MacTavish's bedroom, he dropped his badge, gun, cell phone, and watch on the dresser.

Entering the massive bathroom, Cavanaugh slipped out of his jeans and stepped into the shower. Six different showerheads were placed throughout the massive glass stall—adjusting the one over his head, he turned the other five off. Turning the water on, he stepped in and closed the huge sliding door behind him. With both arms stretched out, he leaned on the front of the stall letting the torrent of water rush over his head and down his muscular body. His mind drifted to another time and another shower—recalling that April of '77 evening as if it was yesterday.

...Eleven-year-old Billy is taking a shower in his mother's rented Tarzana, California home.

"Billy, you need to hurry up, we can't be late," Kelly says to the closed door of his bathroom.

It's a twenty-minute drive from their home to The Afterglow—a small jazz club on Ventura Boulevard where his mother is singing tonight, and because of her longtime friendship with the owner, her son is allowed to sit in one of the private booths that's always reserved for celebrities.

Between waiting on tables and doing extra work in films and television, Kelly Cavanaugh finds time to do the thing she loves best—singing. She has never yearned for stardom, for it's the freedom of not having ties to a nine-to-five job that she relishes. Her blonde hair, beautiful smile and fantastic figure, never fails to turn heads when she walks into a room. Tonight she is wearing a black, long sleeve, low cut, and full-length jersey dress—the mid-thigh side-slit on her black dress reveals a pair of great looking legs.

Jumping out of the shower, young Billy grabs a towel, quickly dries off and slips into his jeans. After putting on a light blue sweater, he brushes his hair and rushes to his room where he pulls on his cowboy boots. Hurrying into the living room, he sees his mother waiting for him.

"Okay Billy, show time!" Kelly says joyfully. "Let's do it." As they walk out of their Tarzana home, she stops abruptly and says, "These high heels ain't for running sweetheart, I forgot my make-up bag. Would you run and get it for me, it's in my bedroom. Please hurry."

He was abruptly brought back into present time. "Can you hurry up," said Mac, "I'm hoping you're done in there. Honey has rolled in the mud and she desperatcly needs a shower."

"I'm out," Billy replied, turning off the water. "Just let me grab a robe." Slipping it on, he opened the door.

MacTavish rushed past him—struggling to hold his very muddy and slippery dog. He quickly sat her down in the shower and closed the glass door.

Honey immediately began to shake off the mud, spraying it everywhere.

"Now I see why you have all those showerheads," Billy smiled.

"They do come in handy," said Mac, re-adjusting all the showerheads. "Will you be kind enough to shut the door? I have a dirty blonde to bathe," he said, as he stripped off his clothes and joined Honey in the shower.

Cavanaugh closed the door behind him and went to the guest bathroom. Leaning on the marble sink, he stared into the mirror—expecting some answer from his mirrored image. "What the hell happened today? Maybe I'm losing it," he said, as he stared into the sink—losing all track of time.

Fifteen minutes had passed when MacTavish's elaborate sound system—playing an Engelbert recording of *The Way It Used To Be*—brought Cavanaugh back into present time. He walked slowly into the guest room and the walk-in closet that contained some of his clothes. As he slipped into a pair of jeans and a brown, long sleeved sweater, MacTavish poked his head in the doorway and startled him.

"Christ, you're as bad as your damn dog."

"How much longer are you going to be?" said Mac anxiously, stepping into the room fully dressed. "I see you found the clothes you left here four months ago."

Brushing past them both, Honey jumped up on the queen-sized oak sleigh bed that Cavanaugh had slept in.

"Not long, I'm just about ready," Billy replied, heading for the duffle bag that contained his personal items.

"I'll be downstairs," said Mac. "Keep an eye on him Honey."

Lifting her head off the pillow, the dog gave Cavanaugh a small, rolling growl.

"MAC!" snarled Billy.

"Just kidding," laughed Mac, as he approached the top of the staircase. "HONEY, LEAVE HIM ALONE AND LET HIM GET DRESSED." Proceeding down the hand-carved oak staircase, he sang along with the music... *"so play the song the way it used to be...before she left and changed it all to sadness."*

Upstairs, Honey had snuggled herself into a large ball on the bed, pulling the multi-colored satin quilt around her body. As Cavanaugh stood at the foot of the bed and glared at her, she felt his energy. Opening her eyes, she looked at him. Words did not have to be spoken for she knew what his determined look meant. Jumping off the bed, she quickly left the room. Reaching out with his hand, Cavanaugh slammed the door shut behind her.

In the hallway, Honey looked around and made a decision. She trotted off to her master's room and jumped upon his king-sized bed. Before settling down to sleep, she fluffed up the down pillows with her giant paws.

Back in the guest room, Cavanaugh snatched up his snakeskin boots and walked down the hall to revisit his partner's room.

Lifting her head off the pillows, Honey watched suspiciously as Cavanaugh put on the watch he had left on the dresser earlier. Giving him an intimidating stare, she began to growl.

"Oh knock it off, it's my watch," he said, grabbing the rest of his things and leaving the room.

Sitting down at the top of the stairs, Cavanaugh put on his boots and mulled over their outing. "...Mac's usual Friday evening out. This is his opportunity to help me forget what happened today. Maybe I do need to get out and get over it."

"Are you ready?" inquired Mac from the bottom of the staircase.

"Let's do it," Billy answered, as he descended down the stairs.

MacTavish removed his black leather coat from the hall closet and tossed Cavanaugh's brown leather coat over to him.

"Is Honey ok?"

"Yeah...she's in your room asleep," Billy replied, slipping into his jacket.

"Then let's go. There's women out there in them there hills pardner," responded Mac, using a western drawl.

26

Smiling, Cavanaugh set the security alarm and followed his partner out of the house—just as Engelbert's song ended with ... *"she will always remember the way it used to be."*

౞౨౮ౢ

THE BLUE MAGNOLIA

The rain had given the city a breath of refreshing dry crisp air. Standing on the front porch, Mac took in a deep breath and said, "What say we get something to eat. I think it's about time I introduced you to The Blue Magnolia."

"Sure," said Billy, as they walked down the front steps and made their way through the gate towards MacTavish's black Lexus.

"You drive," said Mac, tossing the keys to his partner.

Cavanaugh opened the driver's door, slid in behind the wheel and started the car. As he drove towards The Blue Magnolia, MacTavish turned on his CD player and sang along with another Engelbert hit. ..."*they say you've found somebody new, but that won't stop my loving you* —" He wondered what connection MacTavish had with his obsession of Humperdinck's music? Between Engelbert's and Jerry Goldsmith's music, he hadn't heard him playing anything else. He, on the other hand, preferred Classic Rock music—Bad Company, AC DC, and Lynard Skynard were a just a few of his favorites.

The Blue Magnolia was a small, dimly lit jazz/blues club that served everything from baked ribs to sweet potato pie. The club revealed its location with a vertical neon sign that was shaped like a magnolia— flashing white and then blue. Walking through the door made one feel like they were in an old film noir flick. The interior booths, tables, and a mirrored bar, resembled a nightclub from the early 1930's era. Single white magnolias were placed in small, round, clear vases on blue tablecloths that covered each table.

The club's live entertainment consisted of a local blues band with other musicians randomly sitting in. In between sets, the club played musical tracks from the early forties to the blues and jazz artists of today.

Driving through the city traffic, Cavanaugh glanced over to his partner, who had fallen asleep in his black designer clothes—a silk tie, and shirt, tailored slacks, and leather jacket. "He'll definitely have some heads turning when he walks in," thought Billy.

MacTavish's Sean Connery look and Scottish brogue usually captivated all of the women wherever they went.

"If I didn't know better," smiled Billy, "I'd swear I was driving the actor."

Cavanaugh occasionally teased his partner about looking like his would-be-mentor and recalled a time when they had to investigate a suspect living in a low-income neighborhood.

...After knocking on the apartment door of the suspect's last known address, an elderly Black woman, with a very hostile attitude answers, "What do you want?"

Billy, showing his shield said, "I'm Detective Cavanaugh, and this my partner Detective MacTavish ma'am. "We're looking for a Robert Peterson. We need to talk to him."

Scowling, she slowly gives Cavanaugh the once over—examining him from the top of his head right down to his cowboy boots. Turning to MacTavish, she gives him a deadly stare, and while pointing a shaky finger at him, says, "And who the hell are you?"

"I'm Detective Archie MacTavish," he answers politely.

Squinting at him she says, "The hell you are. You ain't no detective. You're that big actor...Sean Connerfree. I've seen your movies. What the hell do you want with my grandson?"

"We're making a movie and we need him to drive a car off the Brooklyn Bridge," says Mac irritably. "Now, can you tell me where he is?"

"He ain't here! Ain't seen him for three weeks," she replies rudely to MacTavish, while winking at the young detective.

Cavanaugh is about to burst out laughing. He pulls a precinct business card out of his pocket and hands it to her. "When you see him, please tell him to call us."

Gently, the old woman takes the card out of Cavanaugh's hand and says softly, "Now you cowboy...you're kind of cute."

"Have a nice day madam," says Mac, pulling his partner away.

As they begin to walk down the hallway, the woman yells out, "HEY YOU...MR. CONNERFREE?"

Cavanaugh, turning his back to the both of them, leans on the wall and tries to suppress the laughter he's about to let loose.

MacTavish turns around slowly. Reluctantly, he acknowledges the old woman. "Yes?"

"WHEN'S THAT MOVIE COMING OUT?"

"What movie is that ma'am?" Mac inquires, with a confused look.

"THE ONE WHERE MY GRANDSON'S GONNA DRIVE OFF THE BROOKLYN BRIDGE?"

Cavanaugh looses his self-control and heads down the hall roaring with laughter.

"Just tell him to call the number ma'am. And my name is Detective Archie MacTavish."

"YEAH RIGHT! THE HELL IT IS!" yells the woman, as she slams her door shut.

MacTavish turns around and slowly walks down the hall to where his partner is wiping the tears of laughter from his eyes. "You think that's funny?" he says, pushing past his partner and proceeding down the hall.

"No, I don't think it's funny," says Billy, "I think it's fucking hysterical!"

"Enough!" says Mac, walking down the stairs.

31

Cavanaugh couldn't resist ribbing his partner, as he imitates the old woman's voice. "Sorry Mr. Connerfree. I didn't realize you were that famous actor. Is this what you do when you're not filming?"

MacTavish, taking an unsuccessful hit at his partner, watches as Cavanaugh ducks and runs into the street laughing.

"Life is never boring with Mac around," thought Billy, as he continued driving towards The Blue Magnolia.

When MacTavish woke up, he knew by the look on his partner's face that he had experienced a flashback. "You leave the scene again Kid, where did you go this time?"

Smiling, Billy said, "I was just remembering the Shawn Connerfree incident." MacTavish gave his partner a discourteous glance as they searched for a parking space. "Hey, I thought it was funny," said Billy, as he found an open spot and parked.

"You would," Mac replied sarcastically, getting out of the car.

As they walked in the direction of the club, the neon flickering flower welcomed their arrival. Once inside, the two detectives walked through the crowd to an open round booth that was facing the stage and bar.

It was a lively night at The Blue Magnolia. Breaking through the crowd, was a very short Black woman in her late sixties, wearing a red sequined dress. Her husky voice laughed out, "Hey baby," as she sauntered over to MacTavish and gave him a hug.

"LUWANDA," Mac yelled happily. "Bobo here with you?"

"Bobo and I have an agreement. I don't pick up a gun and go to his job and he don't put on a dress and come to mine!"

MacTavish laughed as he introduced his partner, "Luwanda, this here's my partner, Billy Cavanaugh."

"Pleasure to meet you detective."

"Same here," said Billy.

"And will I have the pleasure of hearing you sing tonight?" Mac questioned.

"Tonight I'm singing just for you sugar. What's your choice for the evening?"

"The choice of the evening is Johnny Walker my dear, but you can sing anything your little heart desires. And your preference would be—"

"Make mine a double Tennessee Whiskey on the rocks. I'm on. Got to go," she interrupted, as she made her way to the stage—the band playing a blues rendition of *Born Under A Bad Sign*.

As the two detectives slid into the booth, MacTavish recognized the famous blues guitarist who was sitting in with the band and singing a duet with Luwanda.

"Quite a woman there," said Mac. "Her husband is a hell of a detective in the One Five precinct."

"That crack she made about her husband wearing a dress, was she serious?"

Mac nodded yes. "Just keep it to yourself. He's not a transvestite, just enjoys dressing up like a woman sometimes. Luwanda even helps him with his wigs and make-up...been doing it for over twenty-five years."

One of the two white waitresses working at the club was an attractive raven-haired woman wearing a white, 40's style pantsuit. She had a very exotic and seductive look about her. The way she slowly

33

walked towards the two detectives reminded Cavanaugh of someone sultry he had seen before.

"Hello Mac...the usual?" she said, in a low and sexy tone.

"The usual, and give the Kid a beer."

"In case you haven't noticed Mac, he's no kid," she said, as her hair fell forward, and covered one of her eyes.

As she leaned across the table and placed two napkins down in front of them, Cavanaugh couldn't help but look at the curvaceous full breasts that hung loosely in her outfit.

Addressing the young detective, she said humorously "I'll be right back detective...that's if you're through with your observations."

Billy looked up at her and said, "Excuse me, but have we met before? You do remind me of someone."

"Roger Rabbit's wife...I get that a lot. I was a redhead until that movie came out. Mac remembers...don't you Mac?"

"I could never forget," he answered seductively, visualizing her with red hair.

"And you changed it because—" Billy inquired.

"I got tired of the damn rabbit jokes," she interrupted, as she turned around and walked away slowly—knowing that the young detective was watching her every move.

Laughing, Billy said, "She even walks like—"

"Like who," interrupted Mac.

"Jessica Rabbit."

"She is definitely one hot woman," said Mac, as he sang along with the guitar player, who was still singing *Born Under A Bad Sign*. *"A big legged woman gonna take me to my grave."* Stopping abruptly he said, "You ever had a big-legged woman Kid."

"Yeah, your Mama."

Laughing at his partner's attempt at humor, MacTavish said, "You know why I like you Brooklyn...because you're so much like me. Ah-h-h, and here comes our beautiful waitress with our drinks."

As she placed their drinks on the table, MacTavish pulled out a fifty-dollar bill and tossed it on her tray. While focusing on Cavanaugh's eyes, she placed his beer on the table.

Looking back at her, Cavanaugh didn't realize she was still holding the bottle when he placed his hand over hers. "Oh, sorry," he said, removing his hand.

"Nothing to be sorry for, it felt pretty good," she smiled, slowly picking up the fifty-dollar bill and sliding it down between her breasts.

Cavanaugh couldn't help but center his interest on the cleavage that held her tips.

"Thanks Mac," she said—her eyes still focused on the young detective, while Cavanaugh's eyes remained glued on her breasts.

"Alex, you need to lighten up on my partner," said Mac.

Suddenly, Cavanaugh broke loose from his fixation on her breasts and looked at his partner—believing that another prank was being pulled on him. His mind jumped to the conclusion that standing in front of him was a transvestite. Biting his lower lip, he shook his head and assumed it was another one of his partner's practical jokes.

Quickly perceiving Cavanaugh's wrongful conclusion, MacTavish decided to run with it—believing it to be more of an educational lesson than a prank. "Why not?" he thought. "After all, the Kid needs a lesson in *wrongful perceptions before getting all the information.*"

"Alex?" said a shocked Billy, looking back at the voluptuous waitress.

"Short for Alexis," she smiled, then turned around slowly and sauntered away.

"Mac...is it Alex, or is it Alexis?" challenged Billy.

"I don't get your drift mate."

"Is Alex a she or a he?"

"Oh for Christ's sake Kid, what the hell does it matter—transvestite or female—as long as she's great in the sack?"

"I can't believe you didn't give me a heads up," said Billy, as Alex walked past—pausing for a moment and giving him a wink. Embarrassed by her flirtation, Billy dropped his head on the table and said, "I don't believe this. A transvestite thinks I have the hots for her...for him! Good Lord, Mac!"

"Lighten up Kid, Alex is a woman. I called her from the house before we left. Did you think she was a psychic? The woman's not ever seen you before and yet she knew what you're brand of beer was."

"And Luwanda's husband?" said Billy with hesitation.

"Now that's a true story and not to be repeated," Mac replied. "Bobo is a cross dresser. You know Kid, jumping to conclusions before you review all the evidence and circumstances could lead you to a lot of false accusations. You need to ask questions before leaping to unverified conclusions."

"Something I really need to work on," Billy thought, knowing his partner was right about one of his personal shortcomings. He quickly dismissed it from his mind, as he and the other customers applauded Luwanda and the band.

"My friend Otis here is going to take the stage while I take a break," said Luwanda, while another famous guitarist joined the band singing *Everyday I Have The Blues.*

As Alex walk by their booth, MacTavish grabbed her arm and threw another fifty-dollar bill on her tray. "Sugar, give Luwanda a double Tennessee on the rocks."

"Will do...and thanks," she said flirtingly.

Watching her walk back to the bar, Mac sighed, "Awe, to be thirty again."

"From what I've seen, you seem to get plenty of action for your age," said Billy, drinking his beer. "Being thirty again could kill you."

"My boy, if I were your age, I certainly wouldn't be sitting here with me. I would have been out the door with Alex before we ever sat down."

"Well that's the difference between us," said Billy gravely. "Sex is not a revolving door for me."

"That sounds a bit judgmental. I've known you for what...two years now?"

"Sixteen months," Billy sighed.

"Okay, I stand corrected, sixteen months. I haven't seen you date or even flirt with anyone."

Cavanaugh knew he hadn't shared any of his private love life with his partner, nor did he want to right now.

"I don't have any time in my life to settle down," Billy said defensively.

"I'm not talking about settling down. I'm talking about getting laid. There is a difference you know."

"Can we talk about something else?"

Mac leaned back in the booth and said confidently, "Well at least I know you're not Gay."

With a surprising and surrendering attitude, Cavanaugh smiled, picked up his beer, and said, "Okay, how do you know I'm not Gay?"

MacTavish adjusted his jacket, and giving him a side profile, said, "Because you never hit on me."

Cavanaugh, having a mouthful of beer, sprayed it out on the table—choking and laughing loudly.

"What the hell is so funny?" said Mac, as Cavanaugh wiped off the table with some napkins.

Drying his mouth and looking around, Billy said softly, "Maybe it's because...the only thing to come out of your mother fucking closet besides your Armani suits, is your dog."

MacTavish grabbed a menu off the back of the booth and as he opened it said, "You can say whatever you like about me, but never degrade my dog. Shall we eat...what sounds good?"

"Fried chicken," said Billy without hesitation.

"Fried chicken it is," Mac agreed, as he threw the menu back behind him and waved to Alexis.

"What else can I get you two?" said Alex, bringing them another round of drinks.

"Two hens please."

"Two hens it is," she replied. Pausing, she directed her words to Cavanaugh. "You're a very good sport detective."

"Yeah, well when your partner's a nutcase, you kind of expect things like this."

"We haven't been formally introduced. I'm Alexis. I've known Mac a long time. He used to frequent another place that I worked, until it was burned down...BY THE TOONS," she laughed loudly.

"It's nice to meet you Alexis," chuckled Billy.

"I'll be right back with your food."

Cavanaugh watched as Alexis turned around and swayed her way across the room towards the kitchen. Her sense of humor about the characters in *Who Framed Roger Rabbit* was a captivating characteristic that he found extremely attractive.

MacTavish knew there was a side of his partner that could fall in love quickly. Concerned about the type of woman that he would pick, he said, "You know Brooklyn; I believe when you finally fall for somebody, you're going to fall hard. Hopefully, it won't be the wrong woman."

Cavanaugh looked down at the table and then out into the lively club. He thought about the long distance relationship he was now in— the one MacTavish knew nothing about. "Maybe there's nothing wrong with that," he said solemnly.

"I just hate to see some woman fuck with your head."

"He hit the nail on the head," Billy thought, realizing that his recent and long time relationship had been a roller coaster ride from the very beginning, which involved several split-ups and affairs during that liaison. The anger he carried from those episodes was now deflected towards his partner. "I'm not training for the fucking Olympics Mac," he said heatedly. "Trust me…I'm doing just fine."

"Just make sure you have a net under you," said Mac, putting his hand on his partner's shoulder to calm him.

As Alex walked up with their place settings, she observed Mac's affection for his partner and smiled as she approached them. "You didn't tell me you two were an item," she teased. "There's a hotel right down the street if you need to get a room."

Grabbing her arm gently, MacTavish pulled Alexis down so that her breasts were in his face—smiling coyly he said, "If I was thirty years younger, I could show you who the item would be."

"I've been hearing that for ten years now," said Alex, as she pulled away. "The truth is; brunettes don't turn you on."

"Ah-h-h, you know me well Alex," Mac grinned.

"That I do," she smiled, as she walked away.

Glancing across the club, MacTavish focused in on a beautiful redhead wearing a low cut and provocative turquoise dress that revealed her large breasts and covered an incredible built body. As she sat down at the bar, he stood up and removed his jacket.

"You will have to excuse me," said Mac. "They're playing my song."

On stage again, Luwanda had begun to sing *At Last*—an old blues standard that she dedicated to MacTavish.

"Enjoy the moment," thought Billy, as he watched his partner lean over the redhead's shoulder and whisper in her ear. Helping her up, he gently placed her arm through his as they walked gracefully towards the dance floor. Suddenly, Cavanaugh had a momentary fantasy of the two of them living in the days of King Arthur.

...MacTavish is King Arthur and the redhead is Lady Guinevere. Both are wearing royalty clothes of the era as they walk together through a castle.

Cavanaugh could tell by the expression on the redhead's face, that MacTavish could have her for the rest of the night if he wanted. "These two have definitely spent some intimate times together," he thought, while watching them dance. "I got to hand it to him; he sure knows how to win them over. Is there any woman he can't seduce? Probably not...damn he's good!"

After reaching for a piece of cornbread and taking a bite, Cavanaugh stared at his beer. His mind drifted back to his childhood and life on the road with his mother—remembering one occasion vividly.

...The swift Amtrack train moves in and out of the California Pacific Coast shoreline as it travels toward San Francisco—just passing Santa Barbara.

Young Billy's mother is sitting across from him—wearing cuffed blue jeans, a tight white tee shirt and Hawaiian print wedge sandals. Her nails and toenails are painted pink and her long blonde hair is piled on top of her head.

Looking at her he reflects, "I have a really cool mom. But sometimes, she can really piss me off."

Kelly glances up from the script she is reading and says softly, "Are you okay?"

"Yeah," Billy answers, looking out the window.

"Hey," she says, touching his arm to get his attention. "We'll have lots of fun, I promise. This is only a three-day shoot and we have our room for a week. We'll explore the city, ride the trolleys, go to Chinatown and eat at Fisherman's Wharf...we'll even go to Alcatraz. How's that sound?"

"Yeah, Mom, it'll be great." he agrees, as he continues staring out of the train window.

Kelly returns to reading her script. She makes a good living by picking up small acting parts here and there. This new film has her playing a waitress in a diner. The serial killer mystery—slash detective movie—is being filmed in the Bay area.

Young Billy could care less about his mother's job. He tries to be interested in the trip, but his mind drifts back to the friends he left behind. Living in Tarzana has been the longest time they've resided anywhere. As the train moves closer to San Francisco, he yawns as he continues staring out of the window and across to the Pacific Ocean Coastline.

Sitting in The Blue Magnolia, Cavanaugh yawned as he recalled his mother humming an old Billie Holiday recording of *As Time Goes By*. Blinking at his beer, he shook his head and came back to present time; it was now Luwanda who was singing the same song. He looked at his watch. Almost eight o'clock and the chicken dinner in front of him was half gone. "Funny," he thought. "I don't even remember eating it." Getting Alex's attention, he waved his empty beer bottle for her to bring another round and watched as she placed the order with the bartender. Leaning back into the booth, with his head against the tufted blue leather, he focused in on his partner—still dancing with the redhead. After the song ended, he watched as MacTavish escorted the redhead back to the bar.

"Well?" said Billy, as his partner approached him.

"Well what?" Mac questioned, sliding into the booth and patting his perspiring forehead with a napkin.

"Are you bringing her home?"

Taking a swallow of his scotch, Mac said, "With you there? You must be kidding. I'll get with her another time."

"Look, I can always take a cab home," smiled Billy, fiddling with his Budweiser bottle label.

"To be honest, I'm really not in the mood tonight," said Mac, eating his dinner.

Cavanaugh, giving sly smile, looked down at his beer and said, "Did you forget to get your Viagra refilled?"

"I don't need any fucking Viagra," said Mac abruptly, pointing his fork at his partner. "I've already had a very exhausting day." Looking at Cavanaugh's half-empty plate, he said, "I take it *you're* finished!"

"I don't even remember eating it," said Billy nodding his head.

Giving his partner concerned look, MacTavish stopped chewing his food. "You sure you're okay?"

"Yeah, I'm good," said Billy, recalling how his mother would come alive at The Afterglow. Smiling, he thought about how similar the circumstances were. Only now, he was with Mac. "I was just thinking about my mother. This place reminds me of a club in LA she used to sing in."

"Interesting," said Mac. "And what kind of music did she favor?"

"Blues," Billy replied. "She did a lot of background vocals for the R&B recording people and appeared with different groups in Vegas. She also did imitations; Billie Holiday, Ella Fitzgerald, Etta James...you'd have liked her Mac, even though she wasn't a redhead."

"And your father?"

"I don't even know who he is," sighed Billy. "All she ever said about him was that there were severe complications in their lifestyles and she just couldn't go along with the choices he made in life."

As Alexis arrived with their drinks, she said, "I take it you guys all through here."

"Yes," said Mac, slipping her a hundred dollar bill.

"Thanks again," smiled Alex, picking up their dishes and giving Cavanaugh another wink as she walked away.

"Shall we call it a night?" said Mac, checking his watch.

"Yeah, I'm beat. It's been a long day." Leaving his unfinished beer, Cavanaugh grabbed the car keys off the table and followed his partner past the bar.

As MacTavish passed behind the redhead, he patted her on the ass—and without missing a beat, kept walking towards the exit.

Cavanaugh noticed her smiling in the bar mirror and thought, "He's probably the only guy in town that could get away with that."

Outside, MacTavish shrugged his shoulders as they walked to the car and said, "Well that was lovely."

As Cavanaugh pressed the remote to release the car door locks, he gave his partner a sly smile.

"Now what?" said Mac, getting into the car.

"Last chance," said Billy, as he climbed into the driver's seat and put the key into the ignition. "You sure you don't want me to go home?"

"Just start the fucking car," said Mac.

"You sure?" Billy laughed.

"Do I have to drive this fucking car?" Mac said arrogantly.

"I just want you to be sure," said Billy, as he drove away.

"For Christ's sake Brooklyn, are you ever going to shut up?"

"Well, I just thought—"

"I could always play my *Music From Scotland* CD," Mac interrupted harshly.

"You're right, quiet is good. Oh God...fucking bagpipes at two in the morning," Billy mumbled softly.

"I heard that," said Mac, as he put in a film soundtrack CD of one of his favorite composers, Jerry Goldsmith. Closing his eyes and listening to the music of *Medicine Man*, he had but a fleeting thought about the lady in gray.

ഔറ

FROM SCOTLAND TO MONTANA

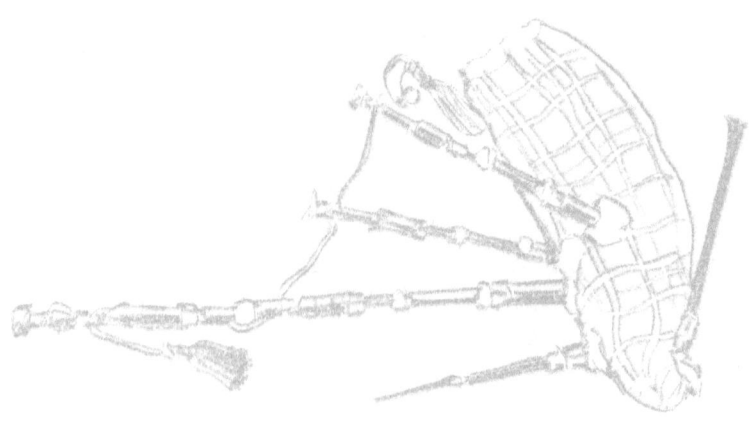

It was Saturday morning at MacTavish's home. In the spare bedroom, Cavanaugh was sprawled out face down on the bed. A pillow covered half his face, while his left leg was wrapped in a down quilt.

...In his dream state, the redhead that MacTavish danced with last night enters the guest bedroom. He watches from his bed as she slowly unzips her dress and lets it fall to the floor. The beautiful naked woman moves closer and gently slips under his bedcovers. She crawls on top of him and licks the right side of his neck—her lips, moist and inviting. As she moves her mouth across his lips to the side of his face, her hair brushes across his face. He is very aroused as she continues moving from side to side across his body, her hair flowing across his face. Suddenly, he can't breathe. Her hair is suffocating him. Unable to move or breathe, he feels like he is dying.

Panic stricken, the young detective opened his eyes to find Honey lying on top of him, licking the side of his neck. "What the fuck? Okay, move it," he said, pushing the dog off of him by rolling her over until she fell on the floor. Getting out from under the covers, he looked down at his erection and said, "Christ...I get a fucking hard on from a dog. Are you sure Mac didn't put you up to this?" As Honey stretched out on the floor and closed her eyes, he said, "Well I'm glad *you're* satisfied." Pushing the covers out of his way, he sat on the side of the bed—stretching and scratching his head. "I guess it's time to get up and head for the park."

The word park brought Honey to full attention; she lifted her head and watched as the young detective walked into the closet and put on a pair of sweats. Grabbing his socks and tennis shoes, he sat down with his back to her. Tying the last lace on his shoe, he gave her a fleeting look and said, "Well, are you just going to lay there? I'm going for my run, if you want to go, then you need—" But before he could finish his sentence, she was out the bedroom and down the stairs. Walking to the top of the stairway, he saw her sitting at the front door— the leash hanging loosely in her mouth. Rushing down the stairs, he approached the security alarm and turned it off. As he unlocked the door, she pushed past him. Galloping down the steps, she trotted over to one of the giant elm trees in the yard—sniffing and peeing while Cavanaugh did some leg stretching.

"Okay girl, let's go," said Billy, fastening the leash to her collar. As he led her through the security gate, a warm sun peeked in and out of the white clouds that hung beneath a bright blue sky. He began jogging, while she trotted alongside. Their destination was a familiar neighborhood park. Suddenly, Honey picked up the scent of the park, and like a trail horse heading back to the stables, made a beeline for it. She quickened their pace into a full run, forcing Cavanaugh to keep up.

"I guess this is where we pick up speed," Billy assumed, dodging puddles and parked cars. Reaching the park, he led Honey towards the damp grass. Once there, she came to a dead stop and took a long pee. Cavanaugh bent over to catch his breath—sweating and panting heavier than the dog. "Good girl, I needed that," he said, regaining his breath and leading her to a nearby bench. While enjoying the freshness of their surroundings, he gave her neck and ears a good scratch. They strolled briefly around the park before heading back to her home.

The refreshing morning air gave the young detective a sense of tranquility. He liked this area of the city—a quiet neighborhood, accented by beautiful homes and wonderful landscaping.

On the walk home, Honey made her presence known by ignoring the barking of the neighborhood dogs—surprisingly, she was quite calm and friendly towards them. As they approached the MacTavish's home, she pawed anxiously at the gate—sensing that her master would be making breakfast and that always meant a few bacon strips for her. Once inside the yard, Cavanaugh removed her leash and watched as she bolted across the lawn and up the steps—waiting impatiently to be let inside. He quickly caught up to her and opened the front door. The smell of hot coffee, eggs cooking, bacon and biscuits, permeated the air. Barreling in and running towards the kitchen, Honey almost knocked her master over when she rushed in.

"You two are back I see," smiled Mac. "How was the run?"

"Great! She gave me quite a workout," said Billy, looking at her sprawled out body—her face submerged in a ceramic water bowl.

"Great timing," said Mac, as they both walked into the living room. "Everything's just about done."

"I'll be down as soon as I shower," said Billy, taking off his shoes and rushing up the stairs—two steps at a time.

"MAKE IT QUICK, YOU DON'T WANT YOUR BREAKFAST TO GET COLD," Mac yelled out, as he turned on his giant television screen. After a few minutes of channel surfing, he settled on *The Discovery Channel*. Turning around, he walked back into the kitchen and finished scrambling the eggs. Pouring them into a hot skillet, he tossed them until they were perfectly cooked. As he divided the food onto black china dinner plates, he gave Honey quick look and said, "So you gave him a good run did you?"

"She always does," said Billy, as he walked in wearing pajama bottoms and a white tee shirt—grabbing the orange juice container out of the fridge, he filled two glasses.

"No. No orange juice for me," said Mac.

"Too late...already poured them."

"Grab those biscuits out of the oven and let's eat," Mac said hurriedly, as he moved into the living room with the plates and juice filled glasses on a tray. Cavanaugh pulled the biscuits out of the oven, dumped them into a breadbasket, and joined his partner who had already settled down on the couch. As they both began to eat, MacTavish tossed a piece of bacon to Honey, which she quickly devoured.

"I've turned on *The Discovery Channel*...if it's alright with you?"

"Yeah, sure," Billy replied.

Cavanaugh respected his partner for his intellectual abilities and deliberated the thought, "...probably one reason why women are so easily drawn to him."

Scotland appeared on the television screen in front of them. It was a documentary film about the North Sea Coast—north of Edinburgh. The screen showed a beautiful and serene seaside village called Aberdeen.

"Look, that's where I grew up," smiled Mac.

"I had no idea you grew up at the beach," Billy laughed, downing his first glass of orange juice.

"I'll have you know that Scotland is an incredibly beautiful country," Mac defended.

Raising his arms in a surrendering manner, Billy replied, "I never said it wasn't. I just didn't realize you were a beach guy. I thought you ran around the Highlands in a kilt." MacTavish picked up a dishtowel off his tray and threw it at his partner. "Okay, okay," smiled Billy, ducking and laughing. "I'm sorry. I didn't know you were so damn sensitive about your country."

"Look Kid, my life as a boy wasn't easy, but I learned a lot as a child. My grandpa and granny on my mother's side ran some whiskey stills. My father, a fisherman by trade, taught me a lot about life and I have some wonderful memories living there. It was a beautiful place until the oil companies came in and started drilling—ruined the whole damn environment. Our fish were never the same. When I was a teenager, my parents moved us to Kinghorn—a hundred miles from Glasgow. Now there was a beautiful city by the sea."

"So you are a beach guy," said Billy, as he downed the second glass of orange juice.

"You got to be joking. July and August never gets above seventy degrees. And it rains every fucking day."

"So much for the sunny beach," laughed Billy.

MacTavish saw an opportunity to get his partner to open up about his younger life and took it. "And what about you Brooklyn...where did you spend most of your youth?"

"Here and there. My mother and I moved around a lot."

"You know," said Mac, "yesterday was the first time I heard you mention your mother." As a veil of coldness fell over Cavanaugh's face, MacTavish quickly realized that he had hit an open wound and took their conversation in another direction. "Its okay, why don't you tell me about the ranch in Montana?" said Mac, picking up the dishes and walking towards the kitchen. "You never did tell me why you rode wild bulls."

Cavanaugh shook his head and smiled as he finished off a piece of toast. Picking up his dishes, he and Honey followed MacTavish into the kitchen. For a brief moment, as he slipped his dirty dish into the sink, he disregarded his partner's interest in his life and handed Honey a leftover bacon strip. After rinsing off his hands, he felt very relaxed as he opened up and talked about his childhood. "When I was fourteen, I moved to this ranch in Montana right after my mother died. Evidently, she had made some kind of arrangement with this guy Harrison in case something ever happened to her. Since I had no immediate family, the arrangement was that he would raise me. He didn't want me jammed up with the system, foster homes and all that crap, so the two of them had worked it all out. I think my mother always wanted me out of the big city...I was a wild and reckless kid."

MacTavish continued listening, as he cleaned the dishes in the sink. He was sympathetic for his partner not having a father in his life.

"For a long time," Billy continued, "I thought maybe Harrison was my real father. We had a long talk about it when I was sixteen…he wasn't. Evidently, he and my mother had been friends since high school. They always kept in touch and ended up buying the ranch together. I'm half owner of that spread. Harrison never married and has no living relatives, so it'll be mine someday. It's really a great place. I love it there. For a fourteen year old kid from LA, it was quite a culture shock—that lifestyle really settled me down. My new outlets became riding, roping, skiing and ice hockey." Cavanaugh finally felt comfortable talking to MacTavish about his life. The only other person that knew anything about him was Harrison. Putting the dishtowel down, he leaned up against the black marble countertop and continued sharing his childhood history. "Harrison said my mother would occasionally see him on the rodeo circuit every now and then. He said he met me at a rodeo when I was about five, but I don't remember. Hell, I don't even remember going to a rodeo as a kid. He's a great guy Mac. There's nothing I wouldn't do for him."

"Did this Harrison know your father?"

"He said he didn't. My mother…she said my father kept his distance from us. Personally, I don't think she wanted him around me at all. She didn't hate him or anything like that, but whenever I asked about him, she said it was complicated and not something I should pursue or talk about. I got the impression I was the result of her first affair."

"So this guy Harrison," said Mac soothingly, "he's been like a father to you?"

"Yeah…he's been pretty amazing. My mother, she did the right thing," Billy said sadly, as he thought about her. "I'm glad she made that decision. I really lucked out—had a fairly good life as a kid. The day of her funeral, Harrison gave me a letter that explained her plans for me. It was as if she knew—"

Feeling his partner's discomfort, MacTavish offered him a cup of coffee and said, "Its okay Kid, here you go."

Cavanaugh paused telling his story and took a sip of the coffee. "She was a firm believer in astrology—studied it for years," he continued. "Evidently, astrological charts can reveal everything about you."

Sensing that his partner was contemplating the idea that his mother knew her future, MacTavish quickly changed the subject. "Did she ever tell you what your father's last name was?"

"How did you know Cavanaugh was my mother's maiden name?" said Billy, looking suspiciously at his partner.

MacTavish knew he could resolve a lot of the personal issues that his partner was having because of his own personal experiences. It was a moment of indecision that quickly departed from his thoughts.

"With the feelings your mother appeared to have had about your father," said Mac, as he finished cleaning up the kitchen, "I seriously doubt that she would have given you his name."

"You're probably right. Her letter...I carried it around for a long time until it just fell apart," he sighed, as they walked back into the living room. "Anyway, living in Montana, I learned rodeo riding from Harrison. Competition came easy and I really enjoyed doing it...still do."

"I'm glad you shared all that with me," said Mac. "It puts my mind at ease to know there's someone else looking out for you. In fact, I'd like to meet this Harrison sometime."

"Yeah," said Billy. "Maybe we can get you up on a pair of skis."

"I'll have you know, I was quite the downhill racer in my time."

Over time, Cavanaugh had learned that MacTavish could fabricate a lot of untruths convincingly. Believing this was one of them, he had a visual picture of him on skis—slipping and sliding all over the place. Stretching his arms above his head he yawned. Grabbing the remote, he sat down on the couch. "I may have to take a nap. I feel like I could sleep for a week."

"Go for it," said Mac, as he grabbed his car keys and jacket. "I need to get some groceries and run a few errands. Honey's almost out of food. Take it easy, I'll be back shortly."

"Okay," said Billy, as he heard the door close behind him. Flipping the channels, he came across the annual rodeo trials. After watching them for a few minutes, he stretched out on the couch and fell into a deep sleep.

Honey trotted up to him and got close to his face. Staring at him and getting no response, she slowly backed away and sprawled out on the floor beneath him, where she too fell asleep.

ഔൠ

Secrets Of The Armoire

Asleep on MacTavish's couch, perspiration rolled off Cavanaugh's forehead. Restlessly, he dreamt about his childhood in Tarzana, California.

…His mother is standing over him. "It's okay," he hears her saying. "You're just running a little temp, you'll be alright." She opens a small homeopathic bottle of pills and says, "Just put four of these tablets under your tongue. Guess there's no school for you today kid. Sorry we can't go anywhere, but if you'll feel better tomorrow, we'll take a run down to Venice Beach." Pulling a blanket up over him, she gently kisses him on the cheek.

Cavanaugh drifted off into a deeper sleep—sleeping soundly until the television woke him at eight o'clock that evening. Looking around, he yawned and rubbed his eyes. Except for the television that was still on, the house was quiet—the lights were on and the curtains had been drawn shut.

"Mac," said Billy, glancing around the living room. "Honey," he called out. Not getting a response, and realizing that the channel on the television had been changed; he knew that his partner had returned home and picked up the dog.

A movie classic, starring Sean Connery, was playing on TV—the hairpiece Sean was wearing made him look exactly like MacTavish.

Cavanaugh looked intensely at the screen and said, "What did you do Mac, climb into the television set?" Imitating *The Twilight Zone* series theme song, Billy sang, "*Do-do-do-do-do-do-do-do*. Suddenly, his singing was interrupted when he heard his partner opening the front door.

"Thought you might be hungry," said Mac, carrying a giant pizza and closing the door behind him and Honey.

"Sure," said Billy. "I feel like I slept the damn day away."

"Well, you were a wee bit tired," smiled Mac, as he put the pizza down on the large oak coffee table. Hearing his favorite actors' voice, he said, "I see our man is giving another excellent performance."

56

"Our man," laughed Billy, as he got up and headed for the kitchen to get plates. "I never thought of Sean as *our* man. What do you want to drink?" he asked, opening up the fridge. "*I'll have a tall scotch and don't forget to put in a splash of water,*" he said in synchronization with MacTavish's voice. "Why do I even ask?" he said under his breath, turning to the sink and picking up the Johnny Walker Red bottle. Opening the half filled bottle, he emptied it into a tall crystal glass and finished it off with some bottled water. Grabbing a beer out of the refrigerator, he yelled, "SMELLS GREAT." Walking back into the living room, he yawned and said, "Damn...I feel like I could sleep for a week."

"Pull up a seat," said Mac, passing two slices of pizza over to his partner in exchange for his scotch filled glass. "The food will wake you up."

"Anchovies? You and my mother would have gotten along great," said Billy, as he bit into his slice of pizza.

"Really," sighed Mac.

"Yeah, she loved them—in pizza and Caesar salads. One major problem for you though...she wasn't a redhead."

MacTavish coughed and started choking on the pizza slice he had just bitten into. As he bent over, his eyes watered up.

Billy hit him on the back and said, "Do I need to do the Heimlich maneuver?"

"No," said Mac, swallowing more scotch. "I'm okay and no maneuvers. A damn anchovy went down the wrong way." After taking a few deep breaths and another mouthful of scotch, he said, "And as far as dating women who aren't redheads, I do date them. I've learned to compensate."

Cavanaugh stopped eating and gave him an inquisitive look. "You know, I'm probably going to regret asking you this," he said, drinking his beer. "And just how do you compensate?"

"Wigs."

Raising his eyebrows, Billy repeated, "Wigs?"

"Wigs," confirmed Mac.

"I should have figured that one out," Billy groaned, finishing his slice of pizza.

"I'm quite serious. I give them a wig to put on. None of them have ever objected to wearing one. In fact, most of the ladies thought it was quite romantic."

"Sure Mac," Billy said in a skeptical tone.

"You don't believe me?" said Mac, getting up and walking into the dining room where he opened the armoire's double doors. Inside, were several expensive and beautiful red wigs.

As Cavanaugh got up and approached the armoire, he began to smile. His smile quickly turned into loud laughter. "Mac, you never cease to amaze me."

"I really don't see anything humorous in this."

"Oh c'mon, you really ask a date to wear one of these?"

"Only if they don't have red hair," Mac substantiated.

"Okay, I knew I shouldn't have asked," said Billy, as he turned around and walked back to the couch. Sitting down, he watched as his partner closed the armoire doors.

"You know Kid; there are a lot of men out there with much stranger behavior. You don't see any whips and chains here do you?"

Smiling, Cavanaugh picked up the remnants of pizza and plates and headed for the kitchen.

Honey immediately got up and followed him. She knew the young detective would give her the leftovers and she had her eye on a half-eaten pizza slice.

As he entered the kitchen, Billy mumbled quietly, "No, you're right, I don't see any whips and chains, but then I haven't been in your basement either."

"I HEARD THAT," Mac bellowed out.

"Ears like a fucking elephant," he whispered to Honey, tossing her the half-eaten pizza slice which she immediately wolfed down. "Fish eaters, I'm surrounded by fish eaters," he said, grabbing another beer and walking back into the living room.

"Find something to your liking," said Mac, as he tossed him the remote. "I'm going up to take a shower. It's been a very long day."

"It seemed pretty short for me."

As MacTavish climbed the stairs, he stopped and leaned over the railing. "How about a movie Brooklyn, are you up to it?"

"You don't have to baby sit me Mac, I'm fine."

"Let me rephrase the question. Are you up to a fucking movie you little prick?"

"Yeah, sure," smiled Billy.

"Then would you let Honey out? I'll be down in a few."

"C'mon girl, it's time to tease the neighbors," said Billy, picking up his cigarettes and lighter. As he walked the dog towards the kitchen door, she began to whine. "Hold on hold on," said Billy, unlocking the door and watching as she bolted down the steps and into the yard. Smiling, he recalled one of his favorite Cary Grant films, *Arsenic and Old Lace*—a comedy about two elderly aunts who were killing off homeless men and burying them in the cellar. Turning on the porch light, he yelled out, "NO MORE THAN ONE BODY TONIGHT, CAUSE WE'RE RUNNING OUT OF SPACE IN THE CELLAR." As he lit up a cigarette, he still couldn't understand why he was so tired and tried to shake off the feeling of wanting to go back to bed. 'Maybe I am coming down with something—last time I felt like this I was thirteen," he contemplated, while having a flashback of spending the night with his high school pal Chris and their experimentation with downer drugs. Finishing his cigarette, and leaving Honey outside, he headed inside and up to the guest room. Getting a change of clothes out of the closet, he heard his partner call out.

"I'm done Kid, it's is all yours."

MacTavish left his bedroom wearing a grey silk print shirt, matching tailored slacks, and expensive grey designer shoes. Walking down the stairs, he began singing; *"Please release me, let me go..."*

As Billy quickly headed to the master bathroom shower, he mumbled, "What is it with those Humperdinck songs? I should bring over some of my AC DC or Metallica CD's. Having second thoughts, he said, "Maybe not, it would probably give him a stroke."

Meanwhile, in the backyard, Honey was busy playing with a neighbor's cat. Suddenly, she heard her master singing. Her interest in the cat was gone as she ran up on the back porch, sat down, and began to join in with her master—howling like a coyote under a full moon.

"I'm coming," said Mac, as he approached the kitchen. "Okay girl, that's enough," he said opening the door. "Get inside before we have more cops showing up here." After securing the door, he proceeded to give Honey some fresh bottled water in her basin. While reorganizing some things in his kitchen, he saw a familiar Renaissance pinky ring hanging on one of his dish brush scrubbers. Smiling, he removed it from the brush and held it in his hand. As he ran his fingers over the amethyst stone that was embedded in the silver design, his mind flashed back to earlier that day when the owner of the ring had visited him. After putting it safely into a rose vase that sat on the window sill, he washed his hands and was drying them on a kitchen towel when Cavanaugh walked in.

"Are you ready to go?" said Billy.

"Hang on while I turn on the wee one's show. Here you go girl," said Mac, turning on *Animal Planet.* "Maybe they'll do a rerun of that new show you love...*Dogs Gone Wild on Spring Break.*"

"Very funny," said Billy, as he walked over to the hall closet and removed both their jackets.

"I thought it was quite good," Mac claimed, as he set the house alarm and closed the door behind them. Throwing Cavanaugh the keys, he said, "You drive."

"Where are we headed?" said Billy, as they approached Mac's Lexus.

"The Mall Theatre," replied Mac, as they got into the car and began to drive away.

Looking in the rearview mirror, Cavanaugh smiled as he saw Honey poking her face through the living room drapes. "I was just thinking, the way you are about redheads, I'm surprised you didn't end up with an Irish setter."

"What, me a Scot with an Irish dog? You must be joking. However, I suppose I could give her a tint job," he said, turning on his CD player.

Humperdinck's *Winter World Of Love* was playing. Cavanaugh didn't mind listening to the song. It reminded him of a wonderful relationship he had with an older woman named Jennifer in Montana. He thought about the times they went ice skating. Although he was the better skater, he didn't care—keeping her from falling was half the fun. She was so beautiful," he remembered, as he listened to the words of the song.

"...*that as the snow lay on the ground, we found our winter world of love.*"

Warmheartedly, he continued driving to the theatre complex.

It was nearly midnight when the two detectives left the theatre.

"Not a bad flick," said Billy, as they walked back to their car.

Taking a deep breath, Mac sighed, "Could have been better."

"And you're going to tell me how."

"Well if you must know...instead of Donald Sutherland playing the part of the romantic crook, it should have been Sean Connery."

"How the hell could I have missed that?" laughed Billy, as he unlocked the car doors. "I wonder if you'd feel the same way if you looked like Sutherland. You know Mac, it's a good thing you're a detective and not an executive producer. You'd have Connery in every film that came out."

"And there'd be a lot better films made because of it. Nothing against Donald mind you, he's another Scot who has chalked up some wonderful roles. Why do you challenge me in conversation Kid, when you know you can't win," he said, opening the car door and climbing in.

"Someday I'll know," moaned Billy.

"Know what?"

"Know when to keep my mouth shut."

"It's okay Kid; you're playing with a master here. Hang around long enough and you might develop the same art of controversy."

"There's gotta be another life out there somewhere," said Billy. "Sometimes I think I'm leading parallel lives in the Universe and for some reason I'm stuck in this one. Where to Mr. Connerfree?"

"That's good," said Mac. "See, you're learning already. Now drive the fucking car."

Cavanaugh smiled as they headed for another one of MacTavish's hangouts called The Crossroads.

When they arrived at the club, Cavanaugh found an open parking place on the street and took it. After leaving the car, the two men quickly walked towards the club. When they entered, another Engelbert hit was playing through the speakers. MacTavish sang along loudly; "...*if you loved me, really loved me—*"As he finished the song, a round of applause came up from the crowd. Bowing politely, he waved humbly to the customers.

"Great! The one thing he doesn't need is encouragement," Billy mumbled.

The bartender had already poured MacTavish a scotch and water, when Cavanaugh ordered a beer.

"So Brooklyn...you told me your mother was a singer. Are you musically inclined?"

"She was the singer in the family," he answered, picking up his beer. "I play a little guitar and I—"

"You...play guitar?" interrupted Mac, in a mocking way. Suddenly, he spotted an old friend at the bar. "CORRINA," he yelled over his partner's shoulder. "I'll be back in a few Kid. I want to see how she's doing."

63

Cavanaugh turned around to see a petite brunette in her late 30's, sitting at the end of the bar. He smiled at her then turned back to drink his beer. "Yeah, I play a little guitar and sing, but no one seems to give a fuck."

Looking at himself in the mirror behind the bar, he stared hypnotically into it. *Take It To The Limit*—the song playing in the background was a familiar Eagles hit. The images of the crowd in the mirror started to cloud up as if they were in a dense fog. As Cavanaugh continued to stare deeply into the mirror, the mist began to clear and a different group of people were present—customers from an earlier era in time. He watched with great intensity as he observed another scene out of his childhood.

...His mother is on the stage and laughs at something the guitarist whispers in her ear. "Kelly's going to do her version of one of my favorite songs," he says into the microphone, while starting to play the song *Pride and Joy*.

Young Billy is sitting in a booth eating a burger and fries. He'd smile at her now and then while she was singing, but it's the food in front of him that held his main focus.

Cavanaugh snapped back into reality when the bartender asked him if he'd like another beer.

"Yeah, uh...sure. Add a scotch and water to that for my partner."

"You got it," the bartender answered, as he poured their drinks.

Cavanaugh pulled out some cash from his pocket and laid it on the bar. Glancing into the mirror, he caught his partner watching him. MacTavish raised his drink in a toast of thanks, while laughing at something Corrina whispered in his ear. Cavanaugh lifted his beer in acknowledgement. Suddenly, it was his mother smiling back at him in the mirror. As she faded out, MacTavish's face reappeared. Once again, Cavanaugh realized how much his partner reminded him of his mother. "He would have loved my mother," he thought. "Now that would have been a hell of a combination, what an overwhelming thought. Too bad he's only into redheads." Laughing, he remembered the armoire. "HELL...ISN'T THAT WHAT THE WIGS ARE FOR ANYWAY?" he said loudly.

"Excuse me," said the bartender, "were you talking to me?"

"No," Billy replied, a bit embarrassed. "No. I was thinking out loud...sorry."

The bartender acknowledged him with a nod and walked away.

Meanwhile, MacTavish had made his way back to his partner and was standing behind him. Placing his hands on Cavanaugh's shoulders, he asked, "What's going on?"

"Nothing," answered Billy, as he ordered another round of drinks. "So tell me about Corrina."

Sitting down, Mac took a swallow of his scotch and said, "Her father was a cop in the One Three Precinct. He was killed in an alley. They never did find out who did it. Now she works in the D.A.'s office... she's a good kid. And you?" he said, changing the subject. "I've been watching you, and for a while you weren't here with the rest of us. Where did you time travel off to this time, the past or the future?"

"Into the past."

"Really? I was hoping it was the future and you could give me the name of the next Kentucky Derby winner."

"You know," smiled Billy, "I realized tonight that you're a lot like my mother. You two have a lot of similarities—except for the wig thing."

"Cute cowboy, what's say we leave this place? There's a blonde at home waiting for me." As he threw a twenty-dollar tip on the bar, he asked the bartender, "Are we straight with you?"

"Yes," he replied. "And thanks."

MacTavish waved goodbye to Corrina as they made their way through the crowd and out the front entrance. Standing outside, Mac shrugged his shoulders and said, "A bit chilly, don't you think?"

Billy yawned as he unlocked the car and said, "Yeah...well summer will be here soon enough."

"You okay?" said Mac, as he got into the car. "You want me to drive?"

"Nah, I'm good...just really tired, I'm looking forward to seeing that bed."

"Then home William, the lady of the house awaiteth."

"Oh I can't wait," said Billy driving away. "Let the games begin. I wonder where the Yeti will be hiding this time."

The two men laughed as they talked about the dog and Cavanaugh's referral to her as The Abominable Snowman.

When they arrived at MacTavish's home, Cavanaugh could barely keep his eyes open. As he took his jacket off, Honey gave him a warm welcome. "I'm gonna hit the sack," he yawned. "Before I pass out right here."

"Go on," replied Mac, "I'll see you in the morning."

Cavanaugh walked upstairs and barely got out of his clothes before passing out in the bed.

Meanwhile, MacTavish had already let Honey outside and the two of them were heading up to his room. "Time to call it a night," he said to her, as they walked into the bedroom and quickly retired.

It was Sunday morning and MacTavish had already taken Honey for her run. Returning from the park, he had showered and dressed. Entering his kitchen, he poured a cup of coffee. Silently, he made his way through the house and up the stairs to the guestroom where his partner was still sleeping. Knocking on the door he said, "Are you up Kid?"

"I am now," responded Billy, lifting his head from underneath a pillow and looking at the clock on the nightstand—it read 11:30. "C'mon in."

"Thought you might need this," said Mac, entering with the cup of coffee and handing it to his partner.

"Thanks, guess I really slept in," Billy yawned, while propping himself up against two pillows.

"I was thinking we could head over to your part of town for brunch," said Mac. "Are you up to it mate?"

"Sure, but what about Honey's run?"

"She and I did that earlier. Get dressed, I'll meet you downstairs," he said, turning around and walking towards the door.

"Mac....thanks for the coffee."

Holding on to the door, MacTavish glanced back at his partner. "Just get your ass in the shower so we can go. I'm exceptionally hungry," he said, closing the door behind him.

Cavanaugh climbed out of bed and grabbed a blue robe from the closet. He slipped it on while heading for the shower.

Downstairs, MacTavish was straightening up the house. He was heading for the kitchen when he noticed that the armoire doors were slightly open. He walked over to it and put the glasses he was carrying on the floor. Bending over, he looked into the armoire where the wigs were kept. On the lower shelf was a long red one laying flat. He pulled it out slowly and held it to his face. Gently, he placed it next to his lips, and then put it back on the shelf with the utmost care. Closing the doors, he picked up the glasses and walked back into the kitchen humming. After rinsing them off and putting them into the dishwasher, he opened the kitchen door.

"Come on Honey, you have one more outing before I leave." Walking outside, he stood on the back porch and stared into the backyard. Glancing over to the side gate, he remembered someone beautiful that had walked through his yard. While he reminisced about that special love, he and his dog stood quietly for the next ten minutes.

Suddenly, a tapping on the kitchen door window startled the both of them. Cavanaugh was observing them through the glass.

"And where were you, past or future?" said Billy, opening the backdoor.

"In the present, right here on this porch. Are you ready to leave?"

"Yeah," said Billy. "Let's go."

As soon as Honey heard the front door lock, she poked her head through the window drapes until her owner's car was out of sight. Satisfied that they were gone; she trotted up to her master's room and climbed on top of the bed, sniffing the pillows and sheets. Jumping off the bed, she trotted back downstairs. Walking over to the armoire, she sniffed the doors. And after giving a brief whimper, settled down by curling up in front of it.

ॐ

RETURN TO PARIS

Detectives Cavanaugh and MacTavish were driving on the Bell Parkway. Their destination was Emmons Avenue in Sheepshead Bay, a location that was also known as Brooklyn on the Bay. The area was filled with high-rise apartments, condominiums and homes on the water with their own private boat docks. It was the place Cavanaugh called home.

Approaching the famous Strip of Seafood Restaurants, Mac said, "Well Kid, where shall we eat?"

"How about Neptune's Grotto?" replied Billy.

"Fine with me," Mac replied, pulling into the Grotto's parking lot.

The restaurant resembled a huge underwater cave with waterfalls flowing down on both sides of the opening. The rushing water ran into a small lagoon and underneath a bridge that led up to the fluorescent blue lighting that illuminated the entrance. Above the waterfalls was a circular, glass-enclosed restaurant that emerged over the entryway and the bay. The entrance reminded one of an underwater cave with its crusted walls of rock-like formations, shells, and nets that accentuated the rocky décor. Built in aquariums, filled with colorful tropical sea life, were encased in the rocky formations.

As Billy led the way through the entrance, he saw the hostess and mumbled "Oh no." The hostess, a cute little redhead, was wearing white shorts. Her outfit resembled a 1940's modified, sailor uniform.

Hearing Cavanaugh's disgruntling mumble, Mac said, "Something wrong?"

"We came here for lunch and we'll probably be here through dinner," Billy said softly, as he made a head gesture toward the hostess.

Entranced by her, Mac sighed. "The day is just beginning, and if I choose, it could turn into an incredible evening."

"Can we just eat first?" said Billy, as they approached her.

"I'm Joan," she smiled. "Welcome to Neptune's Grotto. Two for lunch?"

"Exactly what I had in mind," Mac answered flirtatiously. "Now I just have to get rid of my friend here so we can be alone."

A bit embarrassed, she said, "This way please," and led them through the restaurant. MacTavish started to follow her very closely.

"Any closer and she can file harassment charges," Billy whispered, tugging on his partner's arm. "Can you keep your dick in your pants long enough for us to eat?"

"Hold it," Mac responded, as he stopped abruptly and pulled a quarter out of his slacks. "Heads it's sex, tails it's food." Flipping the coin up in the air, he watched as it fell in his hand. Raising his arms up in a surrendering mode, he replied, "Food it is."

"Its way too early for this," Billy sighed. "I need a beer."

"I can get you a cocktail waitress from our Starfish Lounge," said Joan, seating them at a table overlooking the bay.

Billy, aware that his partner might make a move on the hostess, interjected with, "Yeah, that'll be fine. Please send one over."

MacTavish checked out her legs as she walked away. "My God the wee one is desirable."

"Are we talking safe sex here? I mean, all the women I see you hit on—"

"A gentleman never talks about his sexual encounters. I will however tell you that I'm very particular."

"Particular? Right! I've seen you hit on everything from hookers to transvestites. Just how many particular women are you in bed with?"

"My dear boy, that lady last night was not a transvestite. And in response to your last question...the number is, none of your business."

"Yeah, well I ain't buying the Alexis story. You have a way of telling the truth, then throwing out an alternate story when it's really the first damn story you told that's the truth."

Mac, imitating Groucho Marx, said, "You know me too well Kid. I'll have to start changing my routine."

Cavanaugh gave him a concerned look. He knew that his partner was attracted to one night stands with redheads. Although the topic of safe sex was never brought up, he felt the need to inquire about it. MacTavish not only represented the father he never had, he also liked having him for a partner and didn't want him to die pointlessly.

"Mac, please tell me you practice safe sex."

"Always," he answered abruptly.

Cavanaugh leaned back in his chair and said, "You answered way too fast."

"Well not exactly always," he replied nonchalantly.

"Not always?"

"Let me explain..." Mac paused, and debated whether or not to continue. He decided to move forward with his story. "I practice safe sex with every partner except one. Someone I've known for a long time. Let me start at the beginning. I'd been married for five years to a wonderful woman that I met in England."

"Catherine," said Billy.

"Yes," Mac sighed. "At that time, I had just begun to work for British Intelligence. I always had an interest in art, so at first, my painting began as a hobby—a way to relieve the stress of my work. To make a very long story short, I met Catherine at a gallery showing where I was displaying some of my paintings. She took an interest in my talent. Her family was very wealthy and the woman made me an offer I couldn't refuse—she became my backer. One thing led to another and we were married. Don't get me wrong, I really did love the woman. She was an incredible wife and I do miss her. Catherine was, and is responsible for my very lucrative art income."

As the cocktail waitress approached, she interrupted MacTavish's story. Seeing their waiter behind her, the men quickly ordered their drinks. As she walked away, the waiter stepped forward and asked, "Are you gentlemen ready to order?"

"Yeah, I think so," said Billy. "Mac, you ready?"

"I am," he replied, looking up at the waiter. "I'll have the salmon steak, baked potato, and a salad with blue cheese dressing."

"And I'll have the Mahi Mahi sandwich with fries," Billy added.

Cavanaugh knew bits and pieces about his partner's love life, but now, for the first time, MacTavish was going into great detail and he wondered why. His curiosity had a moment of suspicion, but he quickly discouraged the thoughts. When the waiter left, he encouraged MacTavish to continue his story.

"It was our five year wedding anniversary and we decided to go to Paris," said Mac. "It was noon when we checked into the hotel. Catherine stayed in the room to freshen up, while I went to find an anniversary gift for her. I bought her everything from clothes to perfume. I was heading down the Rue Mouffetard, weighed down with all of these bags and boxes, when one of the boxes slipped away from me. I reached down to grab it, and out of nowhere, this little longhaired Chihuahua wrapped his leash around my feet. He kept running around my ankles barking. I'm trying not to drop the other bags and boxes and at the same time, I'm trying to get away from him. Spinning around, I bumped into his owner and fell to my knees in front of her. I looked up into the face of the most beautiful redhead I had ever seen in my life," he said. As the cocktail waitress approached their table and served their drinks, Cavanaugh reached into his jeans for cash and paid her. After she left, he listened as MacTavish continued his story.

"She was quite a vision," said Mac, taking a swallow of his scotch and water. "Every thing went out of my head; my life, my marriage...everything. There I was on my knees, with her apologizing and laughing at the same time. The woman was absolutely marvelous. As she helped me to my feet, I began to laugh with her. It was as if the world had stopped and we were alone. I don't know how long we stood there staring at each other. I wanted desperately to kiss her. She was the most beautiful creature I'd ever seen—an angel looking into my eyes. We knew instantly that we couldn't walk away from each other."

"And your wife?"

"I loved Catherine," Mac sighed. "She was my wife and I'll always love her—no matter whom I'm with."

"And this woman you met in Paris?"

"The love of my life, my soul mate," said Mac, as he thought about her.

"Don't leave me stranded here, what happened?" said Billy, drinking his beer.

Hesitating before he took another swallow of scotch, MacTavish took a deep breath and continued his story. "I'll try and explain the best I can. If you've never experienced this kind of love Kid, it may be difficult to understand." Taking another swallow of scotch, he slowly moved forward with his story. "It was like a volcano erupting. We became two different people in another time, perhaps in another era. I can't explain the ecstasy of just being with her in a crowd of nameless people. I wanted to pick her up and carry her away from everything around us. We both knew this was the love of a lifetime. Some people never experience this kind of love Kid, they are the unfortunate ones. It's a relationship neither party will ever forget, even if they separate." Looking at his drink, he paused again and looked out at the bay.

Cavanaugh sensed that his partner was having a difficult time talking about this relationship, so he waited in silence for him to continue.

"I'm getting away from the story," said Mac. "Oh yes...Paris. We walked back to my hotel. I gave the concierge my bags and boxes and wrote a note to Catherine explaining that I would be back later. And that's when I began my double life." Seeing the waiter approach, MacTavish became silent.

"Would you like refills on your drinks?" the waiter asked, bringing their food.

"Sure," replied Billy.

"I'll let our cocktail waitress know," said the waiter, as he turned and walked away.

"You know what really amazed me," said Mac, as he started to cut his salmon. "That beautiful redhead saw my wedding band and never once asked me about Catherine. Being with that woman for those two weeks was the most magical and exciting time of my life."

"Wait a minute," said Billy, while eating his sandwich. "You left your wife alone for two weeks?"

"What kind of man do you take me for," Mac replied, slightly offended.

"You really don't want my opinion...at least not until you finish this soap opera," smiled Billy, as he continued eating his lunch.

"When we left my hotel," said Mac, "we walked and talked all the way back to where she was staying—24 Rue Lamarck—the L'Ermitage Hotel. It was a wonderful three-story hotel with twelve rooms—been there since 1860. The rooms opened up to a terrace garden filled with singing birds. It was a perfect place for an intimate rendezvous. That first afternoon together was spent in her room. I've never experienced such incredible love."

MacTavish paused as he thought about their exotic lovemaking and gathered his thoughts. He speculated about what he should, and could, tell his partner.

"I don't know if I should be so explicit with you about our lovemaking."

"Be explicit," smiled Billy.

"You're sure?"

"Yeah, I'm sure. Continue."

Cavanaugh was confused by his partner's sudden shyness. This behavior was so unlike the Archie MacTavish he knew.

MacTavish, however, disregarded Billy's inquisitiveness and decided that some of the explicit details should definitely be avoided. Pausing for a moment, he reminisced about that very first encounter with his redhead.

"I knew I loved her from the first moment I saw her," said Mac, "and I knew I always would. That night, I went back to my hotel, picked up those packages from the concierge, and went up to my room. Catherine smiled when I walked into the room with all the gifts and asked me if I was happy. I told her I was on cloud nine. Now here was another woman in my life who never wanted answers. So I alternated my days and nights with each of them. Red and I rented sailboats, walked in the fabulous gardens of Paris, went dancing in the evenings and spent a lot of time talking."

"Red...her name was Red?"

"It was the nickname I gave her," said Mac. "That name became very special to both of us. So where was I? Oh yes, Catherine. My wife and I went to all the historical places and art galleries. She had a lot of friends there to visit, which gave me a lot of free time. And when Paris was over, a part of my soul stayed there. All the years Catherine and I were together, never once did she ask me about Red. I always felt she knew—from that very first day that we arrived in Paris. You know," he sighed, looking out at the boats that were sailing into the Bay, "I wonder now if I ever could have made a choice."

"Maybe they both knew you couldn't make that decision and that's why it was never brought up," Billy replied. "You know, a lot of men would have found yours to be the perfect marriage."

There was so much of his life with Red that MacTavish wanted to share with his partner. He decided to continue as best he could, for he had gone too far to turn back now.

"I guess in a way it was...for all three of us," said Mac. "It had only been a few days after Catherine and I came back to the States when I became restive. I couldn't think about anything except Red."

"Whoa, you're over my head here. Restive?"

"According to Webster," Mac began, "the definition is impatient, edgy, restless, and the feeling you're giving me right now Brooklyn— agitated.

"Sorry," Billy smiled.

"Finally," continued Mac, "I made some excuse to Catherine about going to London on art business and flew back to Paris. Carrying dozens of flowers, I rushed back to that wonderful little hotel and ran up the steps to her door, yelling out her name. I opened her door and found the room empty. The manager told me she had gone back to the States."

"Was she French?" asked Billy.

"No. She was from the East Coast—an all American girl, born and raised in USA."

"So what happened after Paris?" Billy inquired, as the cocktail waitress brought them more drinks.

MacTavish pulled out twenty dollars and handed it to her. As she began to give him change, he waved her away.

"I didn't want to fly back," Mac continued. "My mind was bouncing off the walls. I needed time to reflect on my life and everything that had happened, so I decided to find the nearest travel agent and take a ship back. When I arrived at the travel agency, the woman told me they had nothing sailing for two weeks. She stared at me for a few seconds and told me to hold on. After making a quick call, she came back with a big smile on her face. Said there was a cancellation on some Celebrity Cruise ship—a passenger was getting off at Rouen—there would be a space available if I wanted it. So I rented a car and drove an hour and forty minutes up to Rouen. I couldn't get her off my mind. What can I say, I was obsessed with her. I figured a nice long boat ride would take my mind off of her."

"And did it?"

"No. And I had no idea what I was getting into. I thought a Celebrity Cruise might offer some enjoyable entertainment."

"Was there a problem?"

"Oh yes, a big problem...that boat was filled with celebrities."

Confused, Billy said, "I don't understand."

"The passengers were the celebrities," said Mac.

"No!" Billy replied, with an unexpected look of surprise.

"Yes. Every star you could imagine was on board. So here I am on the gangplank, trying to get up to the ship, when a steward spots me struggling with my bags and runs down to greet me. Grabbing my bags, he tells me how glad he is that I have joined the other celebrities and welcomes me aboard."

"He thought you were Sean Connery?" Billy said humorously.

"Evidently. I tried to explain who I was, but the idiot snickered and tried to pacify me by telling me about other actors on board that were using incognito names."

"Were you able to straighten it out?"

"The more I tried to explain, the more he humored me. I wanted to throw the little shit over the side. As I followed him to the stateroom, I finally realized why I got on board. The gal at the ticket office must have thought I was Connery traveling incognito and that's why she gave me the damn ticket."

"So what did you do?" smiled Billy.

"I needed a way home so I went along with it. I figured I'd just hide out in my cabin. What else could I do? With all those damn actors on board I couldn't risk someone exposing me in the middle of the ocean. I don't do well in rowboats. JAWS made quite an impression on me."

Cavanaugh tried hard to suppress any amusement in Mac's tribulations, but he couldn't help letting his laughter slip out loudly.

MacTavish gave him a very unsympathetic look and said, "You know it amazes me how you find great humor in my tragedies."

"Sorry Mac," said Billy, choking on his food. "You gotta admit, it's a very funny story."

"It wasn't a tragedy Mac; you got to play your mentor again."

"Great," he responded flippantly, "I need another drink. This time I need a double."

Cavanaugh found it difficult to keep a straight face. Smiling, he waved at the waitress and pointed at his partner's scotch. "Go on," he said, encouraging MacTavish to continue. "I can't wait to hear the rest of this."

"As the steward and I moved through the hallway, I can't tell you how many actors I passed. Thank God I never worked with them."

"You mean Sean never worked with them," Billy corrected, as he tried to be serious. However, his smiling eyes revealed the humor he was experiencing as he listened to MacTavish's high seas adventure.

"Can I finish my damn story?" scowled Mac.

"Sure, go on," said Billy.

"I knew then I was in for one hell of a boat ride. Entering my cabin and dismissing the steward with a substantial tip, gave me the feeling that I'd better stay put if I didn't want to swim home."

"So, did you stay put?" said Billy taking a swallow of his beer.

"You must be joking. After two days and nights of hearing the laughter and music, I was ready to take a shot at going up on deck. I had cabin fever and needed to get out. That night, I decided to make my move. I left my room quietly and moved along the corridor to the outer deck. There were lots of famous people milling around—talking, smoking, eating, and the best part, drinking. I made my way over to a bar that was set up on the dimly lit deck and ordered a drink. As I began to pay for it somebody smacked me on the shoulder. When I turned around I came face to face with an old actor's familiar Irish face, and I knew I had worked with him."

"You mean *Connery* had worked with him," interjected Billy.

"Who the fuck is telling this story?"

"Sorry," smiled Billy.

"I figured Harris new I was a phony and the game was over," Mac continued. "But instead, he looked right at me and just glared into my face. I don't know how long we stared at each other, before he moved real close to my nose and asked if I had a fucking facelift. And then he wanted to know the name of the damn doctor who did it."

Cavanaugh tried to contain his laughter by placing his left hand across his mouth and casually pinching his nose.

"You gotta admit Mac; this really is a funny story. Maybe we should submit a screenplay. Should we go for film, television, sitcom, or miniseries?"

MacTavish ignored his partner's humorous attempt at comedic standup and gave him a look of dissatisfaction. "Do you want to hear the rest of this story, because I can stop right now."

Cavanaugh desperately wanted to hear more of his partner's seafaring voyage and encouraged him to continue. "Please go on," he said seriously.

"I made my way over to a small secluded lounge," said Mac. "It was dark inside, so I figured I'd hide out, have a few drinks, and go back to my room. As I entered, I could hear Engelbert's music being played."

"I suppose all that excitement got your mind off Red?" said Billy.

"That's exactly what I thought!" he answered excitedly, while finishing his scotch.

"So then what happened?" asked Billy, as he reached into his jeans for his money and paid for another round of drinks.

"I entered the lounge and made my way to a secluded corner. I thought if I kept my head down, everyone would sense that I wanted to be left alone. Listening to the music brought Red right back into my head—along with Paris and all that went with it. I'm standing there, looking at the floor when the orchestra began playing *After The Lovin'.* Well that damn song just about did me in. I lifted my head and made my way through the lounge. Something made me look up to the stage. One of the background singers looked exactly like Red.

MacTavish paused as he remembered how she looked in that beautiful turquoise gown and how her red hair illuminated the stage. "As I moved closer through the crowd, Red turned and saw me moving towards the stage. She still wasn't sure who I really was."

"Are you sure she didn't think you were Connery?"

MacTavish gave his partner a frustrating stare and continued telling his tale. "As I got closer, she looked into my eyes and realized it was me. After the song ended, her entire face brightened up. Whispering something into the musical conductor's ear, she turned to the orchestra for acknowledgement and began to sing the song *Unforgettable.* As she walked off the stage, her eyes locked on to mine and she reached for my hand. The woman was more beautiful than I remembered. We danced while she sang to me. When the song ended, everyone applauded. One of the other background singers came up and took the microphone out of her hand. It was as if she knew we needed to be together. We kept dancing and holding on to each other, as if letting go would make one of us disappear."

"Destiny," Billy interjected.

"I often thought about it being that," responded Mac. "What were the odds of ever seeing her again? I decide to take a fucking boat back to the States and there she is."

"My mother would have said it was Karma—past life lovers, metaphysical soul mates. A lot of people believe in that stuff."

Dropping his head, MacTavish thought about the similarities that Cavanaugh and Red had in their metaphysical belief systems. Tears welled up in his eyes. Glancing out at the bay, he paused for a moment, then quickly cleared his throat and continued his story. "You know, she said the same thing to me that night. I remember her saying that no matter where we are, we'll always find each other so we can be together—even if it's only for a few hours. As we walked out on the deck, I began to tell her of my search—explaining how that one fleeting thought brought me to that ship and her. It was then she told me it was our Karma. Out there in the moonlight, she began to tell me the story of her life. Who she was, where she came from, and what lay ahead for her."

"So who was she?"

Avoiding his partner's question, MacTavish once again looked out at the Bay and said, "I kept my arms around her for fear she'd vanish. Later we went to my cabin and once again time stopped for us. It became our honeymoon voyage."

"You really loved her," Billy said softly.

"Still do," he answered, looking back at his partner.

Cavanaugh leaned across the empty luncheon plates and said, "Wait a minute, just how long has this been going on?"

MacTavish knew he could go no further with his story. Once again, he looked out through the window that faced the bay.

"Mac..." said Billy, apprehensively. Waiting for a response, he leaned back in his chair and stared at his partner.

As the waitress approached their table, she said, "I see you're all through here," and quickly cleared the table.

"Yeah," answered Billy, "seems like we're through in a lot of ways." After the she left, Cavanaugh remained focused on his partner. He sat silently for a few moments before trying again to get a response to his question. "You know Mac; you always said we had to be honest with each other. No lies, remember?"

"I remember," Mac answered, his eyes fixed on the bay.

"Then why the hell are you shutting me out now?"

"Some things are better left alone," Mac said softly.

"And you wonder why I won't open up to you?" said Billy defensively. "You're always telling me I need to expose my deep, dark secrets...bring them out into the light, and don't be afraid to talk to—"

"Yes," Mac interjected.

"What?" said Billy, leaning across the table.

"Yes I still see her," Mac replied strongly, as he turned away from the window and confronted his prying young partner.

"Then why—" Billy began, only to be cut off once more by his partner.

"Did you ever think that this relationship is so sacred and personal that I don't really want to discuss it with anyone? You are the only one who knows about her. You know more than my wife ever knew."

"But if you still see her—"

"It's complicated" said Mac, getting up and tossing a fifty-dollar bill on the table. "And you are never to repeat what I've just told you. Is that clear mate?"

As Cavanaugh stood up, he tried to figure out why his partner told him so much. And now, without any explanation that made any sense, was clamming up.

"Mac, you're single now," he said, as they walked towards the exit. "Why do you care who knows?"

Mac pulled him aside and said, "It's my personal life Brooklyn! Did you not hear me? This conversation, not any part of it, is never to be repeated. Got it mate?"

Cavanaugh, trying to process everything his partner had told him, backed off. Knowing he had pushed Mac to the limit, he realized it would be futile to keep debating about it. Besides, he was tired and had enough emotional problems of his own going on.

"Okay, you have my word," sighed Billy. "I may not agree with you on this, but I'll keep your secret."

Mac's mood softened as he said, "I appreciate that. Now can we just go?"

"Yeah," said Billy.

"Good," Mac responded, as they walked out of the restaurant in silence. Once outside, he took a deep breath of the fresh, brisk air and said, "It's great to be here near the water. I can understand why you live here."

As they walked towards the car, Cavanaugh pulled a pack of cigarettes out of his jacket and lit one up. His eyes were focused down at the pavement as he thought about Mac and Red. His curiosity got the best of him. Climbing into the driver's seat he asked, "Are you ever gonna tell me where she lives?"

"In time Brooklyn, but not today," replied Mac, tossing his partner the car keys.

Putting his seat belt on, Cavanaugh looked at the steering wheel and tried to make light of the whole situation. "Does this mean the boat story is over?"

"Just drive the fucking car," said Mac.

Smiling, Cavanaugh knew that someday he would know more about Red, but it would be on Mac's timetable not his. His intuition told him that this would not be the last time he heard about the infamous Red.

₧₧

HAVE GUN
WILL TRAVEL

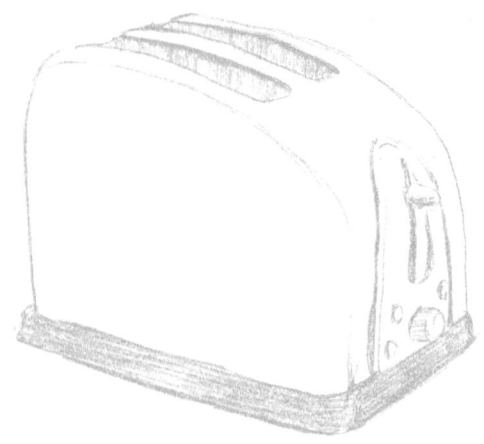

Cavanaugh and MacTavish had arrived at the One Nine and were walking up the stairs to the Detective Bureau when Captain Rollins came barreling out.

"Be back in a few," said Rollins, stepping down past them.

"Everything okay?" Mac inquired.

"Yes," Rollins said tensely. "I'll fill you in when I get back."

"What do you think?" questioned Billy, nodding towards Rollins, hastening towards the front entrance.

Glancing over his shoulder, MacTavish watched Rollins leave the precinct. "Don't know," he said, shrugging his shoulders. "I guess we'll find out when he gets back."

As they approached the receptionist's desk, Cavanaugh observed there was a new replacement. "Where's Alisun?" he inquired, addressing the stranger sitting at her desk.

"On her honeymoon Detective Cavanaugh," the new male receptionist answered. "She got married Saturday, so I'm filling in."

"Finally!" said Mac, moving past his partner. "She's only been talking about it for the last four years."

Staring at the receptionist, Billy asked, "Do I know you?"

"Well...yes you do. I mean we do...know each other," he answered clumsily. "We were in the Academy together."

Still staring at the young man, Billy said, "Yeah, you're Clifford, right?"

"You remembered," the enthusiastic young man smiled.

"So how's everything going?"

"It's going," Clifford replied. "I'm hoping this works out...until Alisun gets back of course."

"Well I guess we'll be seeing each other, I mean since you'll be working here and all," said Billy, moving away. "Welcome aboard."

"Thanks," answered Clifford, as he watched the young detective walk away.

MacTavish, observing Cavanaugh's conversation with Clifford, was curious about their talk. Looking across his desk as Cavanaugh pulled out his chair, he said quietly, "What was that all about?"

Billy, placing his hands on his desk, leaned over towards his partner and whispered, "We were in the Academy together. He couldn't make the grade, there were some problems."

"What kind of problems?" said Mac, sitting down.

"Seemed like a good guy," Billy whispered. "Just wasn't cut out for the rough stuff—too sensitive. Couldn't shoot anybody if he had to." Glancing at the entrance, he saw Detectives Keaton and Matthews walking in and stopping to welcome Clifford to the precinct.

"Feeling better Kid?" said Marc, entering the bureau and taking off his coat.

"Yeah, I do," said Billy. "And thanks for covering our homicide. What have you got so far on Kingman?"

"There's no suspect," responded Vickie, sitting down at her desk. "We have a few witnesses, but they only saw the guy falling down. Nobody paid much attention in that downpour."

"What we do have is a sixty-three year old victim named Larry Kingman," interjected Marc. "His ID says he's from Cleveland. We ran his plates through the Ohio DMV—confirming that he was an Ohio resident."

"When we checked with Cleveland PD," said Vickie. "They didn't have any missing reports on the guy."

"In his wallet," said Marc, "was a business card from Security Providers, also Cleveland based. I called and left a message on their voicemail. Meanwhile, Forensics is working on a medical report for us," he continued, as he sat down at his desk. "They've been really busy. Our M. E. got called out to the Bronx on a special case and this flu business...it took a lot of people out," he said, using a decongestant spray up his nose. "The squad is really struggling to cover the overload." Opening his desk, he grabbed several cold pills and swallowed them with the help of his bottled water.

"Anybody know where's Rollins was rushing off to?" Mac inquired, as Keaton walked towards them.

Leaning over Cavanaugh's shoulder, she looked across to MacTavish and said, "Personal business. He's meeting some people from Miami." Walking back to her desk, she quickly changed the subject. "Cleveland is supposed to be calling me back after they check out Kingman's home address."

"So who's going to Cleveland?" Billy laughed, with a subtle smirk on his face.

Looking at Cavanaugh, Mac said stubbornly, "Well, it won't be me Brooklyn. Oh no! I am *not* going to Cleveland. Let them come here. I'm not leaving the state of New York! No! No fucking Cleveland," he mumbled to himself, while keying in on his computer.

The following morning, Detective MacTavish was sitting next to his partner on a flight bound for Cleveland, Ohio.

"Are you sure you don't need a drink?" said Billy, staring out the passenger window.

The two detectives were high above the city of New York, when MacTavish finally responded. Slightly agitated, he turned to his partner and said, "Why is it Brooklyn...whenever I don't want to do something, and you're involved, I somehow fucking end up doing it. Can you answer that?" Without responding, Cavanaugh picked up his Coca Cola and drank it. "Am I going to get an answer to my question?" Mac said heatedly. Just as the young detective made an attempt to speak, Mac cut him off and said, "And if you tell me it's Karma, I will permanently leave your ass in Cleveland!"

Billy nodded and replied softly, "You were the one who said we needed some time to relax and get away from my undocumented visions."

"In New York! Not in fucking Cleveland!"

"What the hell is so bad about Cleveland?" said Billy. "Why not look at it as our vacation?"

MacTavish couldn't believe what his partner said. Quickly, he straightened up in his seat. "Vacation? When one wants a vacation they go to the Bahamas...to Mexico...or the south of France. Not to fucking Cleveland!"

"Okay, okay," Billy said quietly, "So it's *not* a fucking vacation! I was just trying to make it some-what enjoyable."

MacTavish looked at him inquisitively and said, "How long were you on that Montana ranch before you saw civilization?"

Cavanaugh sighed as he laid his head back against the seat, realizing he couldn't change his partner's ideas about their destination.

Ignoring his partner, MacTavish said, "I guess if all you see is cows and horses growing up, Cleveland could very well be the highlight of your life."

Cavanaugh closed his eyes and smiled as his partner stopped the flight attendant to order a scotch and water. As the plane moved smoothly above the clouds, MacTavish glanced through an art magazine, while Cavanaugh slept uninterrupted until they reached their destination.

A few hours had passed when the plane finally landed at the Cleveland Hopkins International Airport. Inside the terminal, MacTavish and Cavanaugh were headed towards passenger pick-up with their luggage. Walking outside, they looked for the Cleveland detectives who were meeting them.

Approaching them were two smiling men, who looked like characters out of a Mafia based movie. Both men appeared to be in their late fifties or early sixties. One very short man appeared quite jovial and outgoing—laughing and grinning as he walked. His partner however, was the exact opposite—quiet and reserved in nature.

Mac leaned over to his partner and whispered, "I hope no one's got a contract out on us. I've seen guys approach their hit with those same smiles."

"You know who those guys look like?" frowned Billy.

Unimpressed, Mac said, "They do bear a strong resemblance to De Niro and Joe Pesci."

"You guys from the One Nine?" said the taller man.

"That would be us," smiled Mac.

"I'm Detective Gambino...Ricco Gambino."

"And I'm Louie Petticelli," said the shorter man cheerfully.

As both men extended their hands with a welcoming handshake and a hospitable demeanor, Mac said, "It's a pleasure to meet you both."

"Yeah, same here," smiled Billy.

"How are things in New York?" said Ricco.

Smiling, Mac said jovially, "Actually, we've just arrived from the Bahamas."

Cavanaugh shook his head and gave a dissatisfied sigh. "Christ, here we go again," he thought.

"Don't we all wish," replied Ricco.

"Your captain said you had a real sense of humor Mac," laughed Louie, as they walked away from the terminal.

"Really?" said Mac. "Are you *sure* he said it like that?"

"Well, to be exact," smiled Louie, "he said; *your sense of humor at times, leaves a lot to be desired.*"

"Now that sounds more like our captain," Mac scoffed. "I do have one question though...you two ever get shot at by the good guys?"

Laughing, Louie slapped MacTavish on the back and made him fall forward a few steps. "You're a fucking riot Mac, you know that?"

Cavanaugh found the situation very humorous—immediately liking Detective Petticelli. Not too many people could get away with smacking his partner on the back. MacTavish, on the other hand, wasn't offended. There was something about the little guy that emanated harmless fun and he sensed it.

Approaching his car, Ricco unlocked it and tossed the keys to his partner. "Try to ignore Louie," he said, getting into the passenger seat. "He means well. Just don't encourage him."

"I'll try not to do that," smiled Mac, as he and Cavanaugh climbed into the backseat.

Louie slid into the driver's seat and started the car. As he drove away from the airport, he looked into the rear view mirror and said, "You guys ever been to Cleveland before? It's a fun place."

Cavanaugh, trying not to laugh, looked over at his partner with a questioning expression.

"No. But I've been told it's a great place for a vacation," Mac responded critically.

"Cleveland...for a vacation?" said Ricco, as he turned back and faced MacTavish. "If you wanna a vacation you go to the Bahamas or the south of Italy. You don't come to fuckin' Cleveland."

"Finally, someone who thinks like I do," said Mac.

"Hey, I'd come here for a vacation if I didn't live here," beamed Louie.

"You gotta excuse Louie," smiled Ricco. "He didn't get out much as a kid. He's from a small village in Italy where goat herding was considered the recreational sport." Looking at the little guy, he said, "I still haven't figured out how I ever ended up with you as a partner."

Louie turned his head and looked back at the New York detectives. "It's Karma," he grinned. His response triggered laughter from Cavanaugh which quickly caused him to choke.

"You okay?" said Ricco.

Smacking his partner hard on the back, Mac responded. "He's fine."

"This is where you'll be staying," said Louie, as he pulled into the Ritz Carlton Hotel on West 3rd Street.

"Very impressive," said Mac, stepping out of the car in valet parking.

"After you get settled in," said Ricco, "we'll meet you in the bar and discuss the case."

"Sounds great," smiled Mac, as they all entered the hotel.

"We've checked you in," said Ricco. "Just give them your name and get your key card—City's picking up the tab." Leaving them in the lobby, Ricco and Louie headed for the hotel lounge.

As the New York detectives approached the front desk, they set their bags down on the floor. "I believe we have a room reserved...MacTavish and Cavanaugh?" said Mac.

"We were expecting you gentlemen," smiled the hotel representative. "Welcome to the Ritz Carlton. You have a two bedroom two bath suite; here are your key cards. Do you need help with your luggage?"

"No thanks, we've got it covered," Billy answered, grabbing the cards off the marble counter.

MacTavish picked up his bags and followed his partner towards the waiting elevator and stepped inside. As the doors closed behind them, Cavanaugh pushed the button that would take them to the eighteenth floor.

"Well, what do you think about our new co-workers?" said Billy.

"Haven't formed an opinion yet. However, one of them does remind me of someone I know."

As the elevator doors opened on their floor, MacTavish led the way down the hall corridor. Approaching their suite he said, "Let's see, 1812 should be right about here." After unlocking the door, he entered the suite and said nonchalantly, "Not bad."

"Not bad? Are you *kidding*?" said Billy, in awe of the suite and its view of the city. "This is great!"

"They have to give you some incentive to come to this city," Mac responded coolly, as he entered one of the two private bedrooms and began to unpack his clothes. Removing his weapon, he inserted a magazine and clipped his gun to his slacks. Glancing up, he noticed his partner still inspecting the rooms. "I hate to interrupt your tour Brooklyn, but we've got a couple of Italians with weapons waiting in the bar."

Cavanaugh grabbed his gun, loaded it, and followed MacTavish out the door. "You think Ricco's related to the Gambino family?" he probed, as they walked towards the elevator.

MacTavish gave his partner a questionable look and said, "I don't think that subject is open for debate. Unless of course, you're planning an early demise."

96

"Oh yeah...point taken," Billy replied, as they stepped into the elevator.

Downstairs in the cocktail lounge, Louie was conversing with Ricco, who was sitting across from him. "We gonna take them out to the Kingman house?" he asked, as he played with the beer in front of him.

"If they wanna go," replied Ricco, taking a swallow of his scotch on the rocks. "And I'm sure they will."

"They seem like really nice fellas," said Louie. Suddenly, his eyes lit up. "Ricco, check this out, they're the Nicefellas and we're the Goodfellas. Getting very animated, he said, "Huh, huh? Get it? Nicefellas, Goodfellas?"

"Louie, we have new lives now. Why are you bringing up all that old shit?"

"I was talking about the movie!" Louie retaliated loudly. "It was a joke!"

Looking over Louie's shoulder, Ricco saw the New York detectives standing in the doorway. As they made their way to the booth, he whispered, "Our Nicefellas are here."

"You guys get settled in okay?" said Ricco.

"Yes, and we appreciate the extra effort," replied Mac, sitting down next to him.

"What are you guys drinking?" smiled Louie.

"I'll get them" said Billy, as he turned around and walked towards the bar.

"What have you got so far on this Kingman character" Mac inquired.

"Your victim had a house out in Shaker Heights. It appears he didn't have any family—no wife, no girlfriend," said Ricco.

"No boyfriend either," grinned Louie.

MacTavish gave the little guy a somber and quizzical look, while Ricco, ignoring his partner, continued with his report. "Seems like the guy had no personal life, and nobody seems to be looking for him."

Cavanaugh returned with the drinks and sat down next to his partner. "Did I hear no one is claiming our victim?"

"Yes," said Mac. "No wife or girlfriend. And most important, no boyfriend."

Ricco laughed, as MacTavish raised his drink in a toast to Louie.

"I must have missed something here?" said Billy, looking confused.

"Yeah, it was something Louie said. But don't let it bother you," Ricco replied, "he's my partner and I don't get half of what he says. Any idea where you guys want to begin?"

"The house," Mac resolved quickly.

"Okay then," said Ricco, "we're ready if you are."

After finishing their drinks, the men got up from the table. As they left the lounge, MacTavish and Ricco walked ahead of Cavanaugh and Louie, who were lagging behind.

"You and Ricco been partners long?" questioned Billy, as they all made their way through the extravagant lobby.

"We been working together a couple of years now," said Louie. "We've known each other since high school. You and Mac, how long you two been paired up?"

"Sixteen months."

Catching up to their partners, they overheard MacTavish questioning Ricco about the case. "...We don't have any record of any kind of employment or retirement on our victim. We were hoping you guys had something."

"We have nothing before his last position for eight years," said Ricco. "A CEO for a corporation called E. D. Y.'s Security Providers—a phantom corporation."

"Great," Mac replied, as they all walked outside.

"From what I understand," alleged Ricco, "this guy had company ID on him when you found him."

"Yeah, it was in his wallet," Billy confirmed, as the valet drove up with Ricco's car.

As they all approached Ricco's waiting car, Cavanaugh and Louie got into the backseats, allowing MacTavish to sit up front with Ricco.

"Have you guys done a profile on this guy?" said Mac.

"Should be on my desk this afternoon," answered Ricco, as he started the car. "It's coming from our high profile division in Miami."

"We're sure this guy's a victim, right?" said Louie.

"Nothing's ever for sure when you're dealing with unusual circumstances," Mac responded. "We had pouring rain that destroyed DNA, a massive crowd scattering in all directions, very few witnesses, and four people who heard nothing, but saw him fall, that was it."

"Not much to go on," said Louie.

"What about Kingman's personal life and his neighbors?" said Mac.

"We covered the whole block," Ricco quickly responded. "It seems this guy was a very private individual. According to his neighbors, he traveled a lot, was cordial and polite, but kept his distance."

"Was he a Canadian?" Louie asked excitedly.

The other detectives were puzzled by the little guy's question. You could tell by their expressions that they didn't know how he came up with the victim possibly being Canadian.

"Louie, why would you ask that?" Mac inquired.

"Canadians," he smiled, "they're very polite and cordial."

Cavanaugh laughed at Louie's antics, while MacTavish's expression was one of total confusion. Looking over to Ricco, he asked, "Does he do that a lot?"

"Unfortunately, he does," replied Ricco.

They were still discussing the case when they arrived in Kingman's neighborhood—one of the higher priced areas of the Cleveland suburbs.

"I take it the grounds are maintained by a professional service," said Mac, as they pulled up in front of Kingman's house.

"Anybody talk to the gardener?" said Billy, looking at the recently cut lawn.

"Yeah, the company is called GreenScape," Louie answered. "Practically everybody on the block uses them. Sam's the gardener who works this area. Payment was always paid a year in advance by mail. We got the same story from Sam that we got from the neighbors. When they saw Kingman, he was very polite and quiet." As they all got out of the car, Louie took a deep breath and sighed, "Definitely Canadian."

As they walked towards the house, Ricco observed that MacTavish had an overly concerned look. "Something wrong Mac?"

"The nice quiet loner phrase makes me a little uneasy," he responded in a hushed tone.

"Yeah, me too," said Ricco. Walking up the front steps, he continued his summary of the house. "No security gates or barred windows, just your standard house alarm. All these homes have them. If this guy was a hit, he certainly wasn't expecting it—not the way this house is set up."

"We can also rule out a romance gone bad and any family members looking for their inheritance," Louie interjected, as he distributed the latex gloves he had in his jacket.

"Ricco," said Mac, pulling him aside." Was there a meaning behind Louie's statement?"

"Mac, I gave up trying to understand his off the wall statements years ago. It was the best advice my psychiatrist ever suggested," smiled Ricco, unlocking the front door and escorting the three detectives through the entrance and into a very conservative home.

"Have you guys gone through everything?" said Billy, putting on his gloves and glancing around.

"We thought we'd wait for you," Ricco answered.

"Let's get to work," said Mac, removing his jacket. "I presume your team has dusted for prints?"

"This morning," said Ricco.

"Up or down," Mac asked.

"We'll start down here," said Ricco, taking off his overcoat.

"Looks like we're going up Kid," said Mac, walking up the stairs with Cavanaugh following closely behind. Once upstairs, the two detectives made their way into a large master bedroom. Off to the left was a den, which MacTavish studied cautiously before searching it. "This place is too neat," he said softly, observing a computer in the bedroom den. "That might be of some help Brooklyn, why don't you check it out? If you find anything relevant, download it into your home computer and make copies. I've got a funny feeling about all of this."

When it came to his partner's intuition, Cavanaugh didn't question it. He had found him to be very accurate on previous occasions. "Piece of cake," he responded, sitting down at the computer.

MacTavish scrutinized everything. He started with checking out the multiple walk-in closets. "AN OBSESSION WITH CLOTHES WAS NOT ONE OF KINGMAN'S ADDICTIONS," he yelled out, "IN FACT, I'D SAY HE DIDN'T SPEND MUCH TIME HERE AT ALL." While going through the drawers, he noticed that everything seemed to be in its place and very neatly organized. An intense look grew on his face as he walked back to the desk where Cavanaugh was reviewing files. Opening the computer desk drawers, he carefully examined its contents. Closing the last drawer, he slowly stood up and asked, "Did you find anything?"

"Yeah," said Billy, as he opened up the computer's hidden system. "E. D. Y. Security Providers was part of his password. Now why would anyone use the name of the company that he supposedly worked for as the password? Evidently he had nothing to hide."

"Or...he had everything to hide. I think you need to get everything downloaded, and I mean everything."

"No problem...it's gonna take awhile."

"Great," Mac responded, grabbing Billy's shoulder. "I'm going downstairs to see how our Italian actors are doing."

"Oh God," Billy mumbled; "Now I'm working with an all-star cast. *Detectives on Tour*, watch for it on your local network—airing in September." He laughed as he set the download into operation. Getting up, he walked over to the mirror and studied his facial features— displaying several different profiles in the mirror. "And who do I look like, Kiefer Sutherland, Sean Patrick Flannery...Stephen Dorff? Oh for Christ's sake, I really do need a vacation!" Leaving the room, Cavanaugh headed down the hallway. Reaching the stairs, he saw the three detectives standing at the bottom of the staircase—discussing the interior of the home.

"I don't like it," said Ricco. "It's too fucking neat."

"This whole house is way too organized," Mac agreed.

"Very good deductions," said Louie, leading the way into the immaculately kept kitchen. "Everything in here...none of it has ever been used. Opening a drawer he said, "Check this out; four knives, four forks four spoons, four dish towels. And here," he continued, pulling out drawer after drawer, "One can opener, one spatula. One, one, one!" he repeated, showing them each utensil. "I don't know, but they *sure as hell* look brand new to me."

"Even the coffee maker is brand new," Ricco pointed out, picking it up and sniffing it.

Turning the toaster upside down, Louie shook it and said, "See, nothing...not a fucking crumb. This guy didn't live here, nobody did."

"You're right," Mac responded, as he looked around the kitchen. "Visited perhaps, lived here...no."

"Want my guess?" said Billy, staring at his fellow detectives. "It's been swept—cleaners would be my guess."

"Very good Watson," Mac replied. "That would explain the facade?"

"Hey what's a facade?" questioned Louie.

"It's a phony house," Billy responded. "It's like a movie set. You know, fake—not real."

"Oh-h-h," Louie smiled, as Ricco looked at his watch.

"Brooklyn you've got it," said Mac. "It's a fucking set! We were looking at this as if it was real and it's not."

103

"You mean they were making a movie here?" Louie said seriously. Bewildered by Louie's statement, the three men turned around and stared at him. "WHAT?" he said awkwardly.

Ricco leaned towards the New York detectives and said, "You guys need to remember that he does that a lot. I'm telling you, learn to ignore it or it'll drive you fucking crazy."

Cavanaugh, realizing he had to close down the computer, said anxiously, "I need to go back upstairs."

"He downloaded all the data," said Mac, watching his partner run off.

"SO KINGMAN NEVER REALLY LIVED HERE!" interjected Louie loudly.

Smiling, Ricco looked at his watch and said, "Four and a half minutes. He's actually getting better with the ear, brain, mouth connection."

"How the hell did he ever pass the written test to be on the force?" Mac whispered, leaving the house.

"Don't ask," said Ricco, "Let's just say it took a long fucking time."

Cavanaugh rushed down the stairs and joined the other detectives outside.

MacTavish had an eerie feeling about being in the home. He felt a breeze of relief once Louie secured the house and they all walked towards Ricco's car. Opening the car door, he got into the front with Ricco, while Cavanaugh and Louie quickly climbed into the back.

"Feel free to use the precincts' computers," said Ricco, acknowledging Cavanaugh in the rear view mirror. Louie can get you set up with all that when we get back.

"Thanks. I appreciate that," Billy replied.

"You guys like Italian food?" asked Louie. "We thought you might join us for dinner."

"Great," Mac grinned. "We'll join you on one condition. In the restaurant...we get the chairs against the wall."

Cavanaugh understood his partner's humorous insinuation that Ricco and Louie previously had Underworld affiliations. They all laughed, remembering the old gangster era when mobsters would sit with their back against the wall so that they could keep an eye out for anyone who might want to kill them.

"You are one fucking funny guy Mac," said Louie, leaning forward and smacking him on the back. His hit shoved MacTavish slightly forward in the passenger seat.

"Louie, lighten up on the body hits," said Ricco.

"Oh yeah, sorry, I get carried away sometimes."

"Its okay Ricco," said Mac. "I like him."

"Who likes who?" Louie said nervously.

Cavanaugh appreciated Louie's sense of humor. He saw an opportunity to mess with the little guy and took it. "Our president," he smiled. "They say he got a new Secret Service agent who he really likes."

"Oh that's nice," said Louie. "Cause I always thought he hated those fuck-ups."

One by one, the detectives started laughing. Their uncontrolled laughter quickly filled the car.

ಐಚಿ

W. A. S. P.

Arriving back at the precinct, Ricco and Louie were the first to enter the building, with the New York Detectives following closely behind. They moved passed a busy sergeant talking on the phone at the front desk, and a uniformed cop trying to calm an angry couple who were arguing with each other about their stolen car. Ricco led the way down the hall and through a set of double doors. After scanning his handprint and speaking his name into a minuscule microphone, the large security doors opened.

"Whoa!" exclaimed Billy.

Ricco and Louie looked at the young detective with puzzled expressions.

Seeing their confusion, Mac whispered, "Horse term, he's a rodeo bull rider."

Smiling, the Cleveland detectives led the way into the sophisticated, hi-tech operations center.

"This is some setup you have here," said Mac.

"We like it," Ricco answered, as he sat down at an elaborate high profile set-up that was connected to a space satellite system.

In the center of the room, six self-contained units formed a half-moon facing a desk that contained a large electronic headboard— hanging above it was a giant plasma video screen that had the ability to show images from any location in the city. It was capable of zooming in and out of any objective that the camera locked on to—displaying all locations simultaneously.

"Not only can we screen all of Cleveland; we can view other cities and any locations in the state," said Ricco, as he rapidly viewed Ohio.

Overcome with the systems' precision and secretive operations, Mac said, "I'm impressed!"

"Oh there's more," said Ricco, inserting the accessible data for New York.

Stunned by the aerial shot, and watching as people hurried past his Manhattan precinct, Mac said, "That's our precinct on the screen. Christ, it's Big Brother."

"To a certain degree," explained Ricco. "Governments have been using it for their own personal purposes for years. Our system is more advanced than anything they have. What I'm showing you is just the tip of our iceberg. Those people going in and out of your precinct are being televised via satellite. And unlike our government, we don't view anything of a personal nature."

"Yeah," smiled Louie, "like watching a hot babe taking a shower. We can't do that."

MacTavish raised his eyebrows and looked at Cavanaugh, who was trying desperately not to laugh. As he thought about the government's hidden involvement of using satellites, he said, "That part is pretty fucked up—"

"See," interrupted Louie, "Mac agrees with me. It's pretty fucked up when you can't lock on to a hot babe in a shower." Grinning from ear to ear, he walked over to MacTavish and looked up at him. A few moments of silence prevailed as they continued staring at each other.

Looking down at the little fellow, Mac replied very slowly, "I was referring to Ricco's statement about the illegality of our government using this kind of technology for personal reasons."

Frozen in time and staring into MacTavish's solemn face, there was at least ten seconds of silence before Louie responded with a half smile and sighed, "Oh-h-h..."

While Cavanaugh and Ricco tried to stifle their laughter, MacTavish brought the conversation back to a serious nature. Looking at the screen, his face tightened as he said, "Can you get into our precinct?"

"No," Ricco answered. "Only Miami can authorize those actions. Any unauthorized actions will get you shut down."

"Then you've never seen the inside of our precinct?" said Mac.

"No, but Miami has," said Ricco, observing MacTavish's discomfort. "Mac, you look a little uncomfortable with our program. I understand, I felt the same way when I was first introduced to all this."

"I'd like to know why Miami is keeping tabs on us," Mac responded sternly.

"It's not like that," explained Ricco. "For years, people suspected that the government was using stealth radar and satellites to watch the world. Mention assassination in your home or on your phone lines and you've got FBI agents watching your every move. This Agency has one goal; to get this country back to its original principles by deterring crime. We track serial killers, help out in child abduction cases, and reveal terrorism threats. When a lead comes in we get locations, names, and faces for printouts. Local law enforcement is then given subtle information to where the perps might be. We're like the overseers of our states. We don't even get involved unless it happens in our precinct."

"So who set all this up?" said Billy.

"This Agency was founded by an ex-FBI agent who found out more than he was supposed to," responded Ricco. "He walked away with microfilm data on a lot of illegal government activity that was blamed on innocent parties. This guy decided to put things right by developing a system far superior to what the Feds or any other agency has. Our system has been in operation for over a year, and ninety-five per cent of our current cases in Cleveland are closed."

The New York detectives were stunned by Ricco's statement. Never in history has a precinct had such a high percentage of closed cases.

"Very impressive," said Mac. "But why show us all this technology?"

"You're putting one of these systems in our precinct," Billy quickly interrupted.

Looking at MacTavish, Ricco smiled and said, "The Kid is good."

"Learned everything from me," Mac boasted.

Turning away from his partner, Cavanaugh rolled his eyes as he walked around the room and studied the futuristic technology.

"New York will be the third location," said Ricco. We have four total.

MacTavish moved slowly around the room—eyeing the transformation that had taken place he asked, "Why so long to get into New York?"

"Headquarters had a hell of a time clearing your precinct," smiled Ricco. "Yours has been the most difficult precinct. It's a big job to organize the right precinct and personnel. Yours took a lot of overhauling, that's why you've had five captains in the past two years and many of your co-workers got transferred out."

"That does explain all the changes," said Mac.

"And all this time I thought it was my partner's charming manner that sent everyone away," smiled Billy.

"So this is how you recognized us at the airport?" said Mac, glancing around.

"Yeah," smiled Louie, reaching up and placing his hand on the tall detective's shoulder. Louie, being much shorter than Mac, gave one the impression of them being cartoon characters. After posing for a few comical moments, MacTavish's face displayed a look that made Louie slowly remove his hand.

"This homicide provided a good cover," said Ricco. "We were trying to figure out how the hell to get you here for a vacation."

"Don't tell me Miami had a guy killed to get us here?" smiled Mac.

Louie smacked him on the back and laughed. "I love this guy. He's a fucking riot. No Mac, we don't go that far...unless we have to," he whispered seriously. Louie paused for a brief moment, and then laughed again. "I'm only kidding!"

Mac, trying to overlook Louie's humorous exhibition said, "You talked about one, two and three, who is number four?"

"New Orleans," Ricco answered, scratching his ear lobe.

"What gave you the idea that we'd go along with all this?" Mac inquired.

"That's the same fucking question Ricco asked when the guys from Miami talked to us about Cleveland," laughed Louie.

"Everyone who's been asked to join this team has been highly profiled," explained Ricco. "If there was anything, I mean the slightest thing about you that was doubtful; you would have been taken off the list and transferred out. We wouldn't even be having this discussion if we didn't believe you'd be a part of this organization."

Smiling, Mac looked over at his partner and said, "Are we in Kid?"

"Yeah, I'm definitely in," Billy smiled, as he thought about being involved in a futuristic law enforcement operation.

"I believe you got yourself a couple of new trainees," replied Mac.

"Welcome to the World Agency Surveillance Patrol," Ricco said. "We call it WASP.

"Okay, here's the layout," said Louie, pulling up a chair. Programming the computer with great speed, his screen revealed a detailed survey map of the 19th Precinct. "See, you guys think you're getting a new boiler/ac unit and re-piping system. Displaying his remarkable ability in using the system, he said, "What you're really getting is this...Gentlemen; The New York WASP Headquarters."

MacTavish and Cavanaugh stared at the screen—fascinated with the technology that they would soon have at the One Nine. "When will the work be done?" Billy asked.

"In about two weeks," answered Louie.

As Billy moved closer to the screen, he said, "That's why those guys have been working around the clock."

"Our crews work fast and efficiently," said Ricco. "At some point, you and Cavanaugh will get a two week training vacation in Miami. The system itself is really simple; we're giving you a crash course, Louie had everything down in about five days."

"Yesterday," began Billy, as he recalled Rollins rushing to leave their precinct, "Detective Keaton mentioned visitors from Miami...the Agency?"

"Yes," said Ricco. "Your captain's in charge of getting the job done on time."

"I understand the concept," Mac alleged, "but exactly what goes on here?"

"Let's use a kidnapping scenario, this system tracks them when they hit our state," Ricco explained. "Once we lock on to them, we notify other law enforcement. We use the anonymous tip method—never claiming credit for any capture. Too much information can raise a lot of questions and defeat our purpose."

"Why not start the tracking sooner?" said Billy.

"Good question," responded Ricco. "Maintaining a low profile is not as easy as you think. If we start crossing borders, we start stepping all over each other. As you continue to use the system, you'll see the down side of universal usage without individual monitoring. Eventually, every state will have the same set-up.

"We *are* infringing on some civil rights here," said Mac. "There are a lot of people out there who wouldn't welcome these interventions."

"That's why we have certain limitations," Ricco answered.

MacTavish looked at a simulated map of the United States that covered half the wall. Studying it, he imagined what could be done throughout the country and sighed, "Not enough agencies."

Walking up to him, Ricco placed his hand on his shoulder and said, "All in good time Mac."

"What happens when somebody dies or retires?" Mac inquired.

"The Agency moves in another trained detective," said Ricco.

"Planning on an early retirement?" smiled Billy.

MacTavish gave his partner a cynical look and once again re-focused his attention on Ricco. "Is the whole precinct aware of what goes on here?"

"No. That's why there's no Agency access except for those who are coded. The precinct believes it to be just a security failsafe for cold case files and open cases. Miami wants to get its precincts set up first with basic crews. Clearing the rest of the staff is left up to the captains and lead detectives." Ricco leaned down and opened a locked drawer beneath one of the desks. Inside were two small leather pouches. He handed one to MacTavish and the other to Cavanaugh. As the New York detectives reached into the pouches, they each pulled out a silver WASP symbol. "Attach them to the back of your shield," said Ricco. "They're magnetized. If you lose them, let Miami know immediately. They have the ability to self-destruct them."

"And these are safe to be next to our bodies?" Mac inquired, while handling the pin.

"Yes, very safe," Ricco smiled.

"I lost mine two weeks after I got it," laughed Louie. "So I called Miami to tell them it was gone. Then I remembered that it was on my dresser. When I went back for it I only found a small pile of ash. Miami told me it was a harmless type of futuristic alloy they got from an undisclosed hanger in Nevada."

Cavanaugh smiled deviously and said, "Hanger 51 I'm guessing. Isn't that out where the government keeps aliens?"

"Yeah," Louie said excitedly. "That's the place. Cool huh?"

"I feel like I'm in the middle of some sci-fi movie," said Mac.

"You'll get used to it," Ricco grinned. "Right Louie?"

"Yeah," said the little guy. "Only I felt like I was in an episode of *The Twilight Zone*." Simultaneously, the three men looked at him and burst out laughing. "WHAT?" said Louie, as he closed down the system.

"It looks more complicated than it is," said Ricco. "You don't have to be a rocket scientist to figure it out. Now let's go get some dinner."

"Sounds good to me," Mac replied, following Ricco out of WASP. "I need some water to clear my head."

"We got some bottled water over in the corner," Louie smiled.

Walking next to him, Billy leaned in close and whispered, "Not that kind of water."

"I know, I know" whispered Louie. "Ricco always says he needs his rocks. Sometimes, when he's really upset, he'll say he's gotta get his rocks off."

Laughing, Cavanaugh put his arm around Louie's shoulder and said, "In those situations, I think your partner is referring to something else."

"Yeah...I know," Louie responded shyly.

"Louie, you're okay. You keep me laughing and I like that."

"Thanks Kid," the little guy said happily.

As the four detectives approached the front desk, they could hear voices coming from the lobby entrance. Two hookers were talking to a detective and a police officer.

Louie, wearing a big smile, winked at both prostitutes. "Business as usual," he said to Cavanaugh, as they all walked out of the precinct.

Forty minutes later, the detectives reached the lavish Italian restaurant. Reminiscent of Old Italian architecture, the two-story villa, with an adjoining patio, had a second floor open balcony with a lakeside view. Ricco drove up the circular driveway to the entrance, where a half-dozen, Italian young men were parking customer cars—four of them rushed over and opened all the car doors for the detectives.

"Wait till you see this fuckin' place Kid!" Louie said excitedly.

As they all walked up the steps that led to the entrance, a well dressed man, wearing a black suit, opened the door with a warm welcome—establishing that he and Ricco were well acquainted. The two men laughed and spoke in Italian as they all entered the dimly lit bistro. The host grabbed some menus and led the detectives through a dark corridor, where a large rustic sign hung over the walkway—it read *Little Italy*. Crates and barrels were stacked up against the walls. Some of the crates next to the ceiling seemed to teeter on the brink of falling. Small, wooden antique tables and chairs accented the room and photographs of gangsters, peasants, and landscapes hung on the surrounding walls. The detectives were led through two swinging doors into a lavish dining room where they were greeted by a distinguished man of seventy nicknamed Pepe.

"Welcome to Caruso's Mr. Gambino, we were expecting you and your party. Will you be dining here in Mama Mia's, or upstairs in Giuseppe's Garden?"

"It's up to our guests," said Ricco, acknowledging the New York detectives. "Formal or informal?"

"Informal is good," Billy replied. "We're not really dressed for formal."

"Kid's got a point," said Mac. "Let's go upstairs."

"This way then," smiled Pepe, leading the detectives towards a quaint wrought iron elevator.

"This is my favorite place," said Louie, as they were slowly taken upstairs.

The elevator opened up to a World War II setting. Broken rafters and creaking beams appeared to be falling from the restaurant's bombed roof. Above the rafters, stars twinkled in a falsified darkened sky. War photographs and posters were pasted randomly on the cracked and simulted collapsing walls. Lit candles, inside old empty wine bottles, were scattered on tables throughout the restaurant. In the background, classical Caruso recordings were playing.

Looking at the creative decor, Cavanaugh almost ran into a peasant dressed waiter.

"Look out!" Louie yelled, pulling him out of the way.

"Oh, I'm sorry," said Billy, smiling at the waiter. "I got sidetracked looking around."

"No problem, it happens a lot," the waiter responded. "GINO, THESE PEOPLE NEED A TABLE," he yelled across the room.

A small balding man, with a handlebar moustache and carrying menus, ran over to the detectives. "Sorry," he said, in a heavy Italian accent. "I shoulda' grabbed you when you got outta the elevator. We so busy tonight. But then...we busy every night," he said with a jolly laugh. "Table for four. This a-way Mr. Gambino." As the jovial little man led the men to the back wall that was stacked with sandbags and a private table, the mouthwatering aroma of Italian homemade pasta and pizza followed them. "The table you requested...with two chairs against the wall," Gino laughed, as a waiter brought their drinks.

Smiling, Mac pulled out one of the mismatched wooden chairs and said, "You do know that I was joking."

"Yeah I know," Ricco grinned. "Actually, it was Louie's idea."

Cavanaugh sat down and looked at his surroundings. As he glanced at the World War II photographs on the wall, one photograph drew his attention—the landing of soldiers on the beaches of Normandy. A cold chill ran throughout his body. He felt as if a ghost had walked through him. He tried to rid his mind of the fear and sadness that momentarily overtook his psyche. And yet, something about the surroundings troubled him. The same kind of chill happened several times when he was a child. He recalled his mother telling him that he had encountered a ghost and tried to shake away the feelings he was experiencing.

MacTavish observed his partner's uneasy attitude and quietly got his attention. "Something wrong Kid?" he whispered, leaning over to him.

"No. I just got a chill," said Billy, faking a smile.

117

Cavanaugh didn't want to explain the eeriness he was sensing and the possibilities of a ghostly encounter. As the waiter brought their drinks, the young detective downed the glass of scotch in front of him. Gradually, the ghostly feelings dissipated as he joined the other detectives in discussing their work, WASP, and women—not necessarily in that order.

⁎

ROCK STEADY

Upstairs in the Ritz Carlton Suite, MacTavish, wearing a white hotel robe, had poured himself a glass of scotch. He and Cavanaugh had arrived back at the hotel about an hour ago. Crossing the room with glass and bottle in hand, MacTavish sat down on the couch and turned on the television.

Cavanaugh, wearing a navy blue tee shirt and jeans, walked out of his bedroom and went to the refrigerator. After grabbing a beer, he joined his partner in the living room.

"Well, what do you think about all this," said Billy, as he sat down on the couch, placing his bare feet up on the coffee table.

"It's a bit overwhelming and a hell of a lot for one day. I suggest we forget about all this surveillance stuff and focus on our Mr. Kingman. I don't like all these damn distractions." Refilling his glass of scotch, he said, "We need to get back to New York."

"Who do you think the cleaners were?"

"Who the hell knows," replied Mac. "There are a hundred different agencies out there with that capability...why is the question we should be asking? There's got to be information out there somewhere that'll help us find out about this Kingman guy. We do need that autopsy report. Try to get it from New York first thing in the morning. Let's see what Vickie and Matthews pulled together. Just don't like it," he said, finishing his drink. "Don't like it at all. Oh well, tomorrow's another day. I'm going to bed. Oh by the way, while you were in the shower, Ricco had a rental car delivered to us."

"See you in the morning," said Billy. Concerned, the young detective looked down at his beer. He knew, whenever his partner got those feelings they were not to be taken lightly. Sinking back into the plush couch, he remembered a time last year when MacTavish had that feeling once before. As he looked out at the Cleveland skyline, he recalled that specific experience.

...It is autumn in New York City. Horse drawn carriages are being driven up and down Fifth Avenue. In Central Park, a sixty year old photographer is murdered in broad daylight while photographing people in the area. No one thinks it unusual, believing he's getting better angles for his camera when he slowly collapses on the grass. His local address and studio is in an old warehouse district in the One Five precinct. As they research his history, they find him to be an average guy with no priors. The investigation is going nowhere, and it looks like it's heading for the cold case files. MacTavish, discontent with that decision, decides that he and Cavanaugh should take a look at the victim's loft, even though the detectives from the One Five have previously checked it out.

...As they pull up to the desolate warehouse, MacTavish stares at the building. Cavanaugh identifies the look of nervous tension on his partner's face and says, "What?"

"Don't know," says Mac with a foreboding expression. "There's something strange about the building...just don't like it."

"You have some reservations about going in?" Billy asks.

"Oh what the hell, let's go," says Mac, as he opens his car door and proceeds toward the front of the building.

"This Austin guy, was he the only resident?"

"Yes," replies Mac. "The One Five said he used this space for both his studio and living quarters when he was in town."

As they walk cautiously toward the entrance, MacTavish inserts the key and unlocks the outside door. Inside is a second door with a numbered security pad. Reaching into his pocket, he pulls out a piece of paper with numbers on it. "Evidently there's a silent alarm, so we need to get it right the first time," Mac says quietly, as he enters the coded numbers which releases the lock. Proceeding up the stairs, he lets Cavanaugh lead the way. Halfway up, he grabs his partner's arm and says, "Listen!"

"And just what am I listening for?" inquires Billy curiously.

"Just listen," Mac sighs. "You hear that?"

"I don't hear nothing," says Billy.

"Anything," Mac says. "Anything, I don't hear anything."

"Oh for Christ's sake, now you're correcting my English?"

Giving his partner a push up the stairs, Mac says, "I don't like it mate…way too quiet."

Billy stops abruptly. Turning to his partner he gives him a maddening look and says, "Of course it's quiet. It's a fucking warehouse and the only person that was using it IS DEAD!"

MacTavish stares ominously at his partner as he gives him another push up the stairs. At the top of the stairwell is one more locked door.

"Got another key?" asks Billy humorously.

"No," Mac quietly responds.

"Well it's got a fucking lock," Billy says abruptly.

"Nobody said anything about a damn second key."

Billy throws his hands up in the air and says, "What the fuck, let's see if it's open?"

As he begins to open it, Mac yells out, "STOP," and grabs his partner's arm—holding it tightly in place. Leaning around him, he looks into the loft and says, "Kid, without moving your arm, I want you to slowly and carefully look into the loft."

His motionless hand locked on the doorknob, Cavanaugh cautiously leans over to look inside. Several wires are rigged to the door and connected to a timer—dynamite and a bottle of nitro-glycerin are attached to the timer. "Mother fucker!" he replies wide-eyed, as the clock on the timer begins to tick down from 10:00.

"Close the door gently," says Mac, as perspiration begins to accumulate on his forehead. "It's on a timer. If we get the door closed easily, it won't trigger an immediate explosion."

"Then what?" asks Billy, releasing his hand from the doorknob.

"WE RUN LIKE HELL. GO! GO!" Mac shouts, as he pushes his partner down the stairs. "WE GOT LESS THAN TEN MINUTES TO CLEAR THE BUILDING."

Running down the stairs as fast as they can, Billy yells out, "THE KEYPAD AND KEY—WE DON'T HAVE ENOUGH TIME. FUCK IT, THERE'S ONLY ONE WAY OUT." Grabbing his partner, he shoves him back up the stairs and says "UPSTAIRS," pointing up to the window which is three feet below the booby-trapped door.

MacTavish stops abruptly and stands firm. "YOU'VE GOT TO BE KIDDING. THAT'S A THREE STORY DROP!"

Billy pulls him toward the stairs and says, "ITS OUR ONLY WAY OUT. LET'S GO!"

MacTavish feverishly follows his partner up the stairwell and says, "WHEN THIS IS OVER, I'M SERIOUSLY GOING TO REQUEST A NEW PARTNER, ONE WHO ISN'T STUNT ORIENTATED."

Reaching the window, Cavanaugh quickly uses his gun to break through the glass. "Okay, it's now or never," he says, climbing into the doublewide window frame.

Reluctantly, MacTavish grabs his partner's hand and climbs out on the ledge next to him. "It's a little high don't you think?"

"Not as high as we'll both be when this building goes up," replies Billy."

"Then why don't we just wait, BECAUSE THE JUMP WILL PROBABLY KILL US."

"NOW," Billy yells, as he pushes his partner out of the window and jumps out behind him.

They land in a loose mound of sand next to a large cement mixer. After sliding down the sand, they crawl a few feet to stabilize themselves, and begin running to their vehicle.

"Get down behind the car, that should get us far enough away," says Billy.

As they fall down behind the trunk of the car, MacTavish peers around to the front of the vehicle and looks calculatingly at the building. "We've got a problem mate," he says, turning back to his partner.

"And that is?" Billy asks robustly.

Wiping the perspiration off his forehead, Mac says, "We're not quite far enough away."

"And just how do you know that?"

"I was in British Intelligence, trust me, I know."

Looking at his partner, Cavanaugh's mouth drops open as he makes a gasping demand. "Give me the damn car keys."

"Why?" says Mac defiantly.

"I need the fuckin' car keys!" Billy says firmly, as he reaches into his partner's pocket and removes them. "When I start backing the car out, you start running behind it. With me in front of you, the car will protect you from the blast."

"Are you crazy?" says Mac, watching his partner run and climb into the driver's seat. "YOU ARE CRAZY!" he hollers out, standing up behind the car.

"RUN," yells Billy. As Cavanaugh starts the engine and floors the gas pedal, MacTavish takes off running. "FASTER!" Billy yells out, as the car's back bumper lightly touches the back of his partner's legs. "MOVE IT!" Both of the men move into high gear. MacTavish is rapidly running away from the speeding car that Cavanaugh is driving backwards when the warehouse blows up. Stopping the car, he throws his body across the front seat and covers his head with his arms. The car shakes violently, while debris from the explosion flies everywhere. Luckily, the car is far away enough not to get damaged. Fire is consuming the building, as Cavanaugh quickly leaves the car to check on his partner. Pulling out his cell phone to call 911, he yells out, "MAC, YOU OKAY?" Walking behind the car, he finds his partner lying on his stomach with his arms crossed over his head. "Mac?" he says softly, leaning down to check on him.

MacTavish slowly lifts his hands off the top of his head and says, "Run...RUN!" he repeats louder in an angry voice, as he gets up.

"I thought it was a good idea," says Billy.

MacTavish's bobbing head reminds Cavanaugh of one of those old dashboard ornaments with the wobbling heads—a bobble head. He begins to smile at the resemblance Mac has to that ornament, and tries very hard to contain his laughter, while his partner becomes more animated with every word.

"YOU...YOU THOUGHT IT WAS A GOOD IDEA? YOU...ALMOST RUNNING ME OVER WAS A GOOD IDEA? Let's re-evaluate this scenario," says Mac, brushing himself off. "You barge through an open door that triggers a bomb. You...run me through a window where I almost land in a cement mixer. Then," he says dramatically, "you, if I may point out, not being the designated driver, take the keys from the designated driver, gets into the car, backs it up with me behind it, AND TELLS ME TO FUCKING RUN!"

Looking at him, Cavanaugh could no longer retain his laughter and begins to laugh loudly.

MacTavish, finding no humor at all in the situation, gets closer to his partner's face and with a quiet politeness asks, "Brooklyn...is there something funny about all of this?"

Cavanaugh stops laughing and tries hard to keep his composure—silently he believes that it's fucking hilarious. "No. It's not funny," he lies.

"You're sure?" asks Mac, as he tries to look his partner in the eyes.

Despite the seriousness of the situation, MacTavish looks wildly funny. Covered with soot and dirt, his jacket is hanging off his right shoulder and is ripped in half. A disarrayed tie is hanging off the back of his neck, and his left pant leg is torn up to his thigh. One of his socks is hanging down over his shoe, while the other is still up over his calf—it is far from his usual neat appearance. Suddenly, sirens from advancing fire trucks interrupt their conversation. Fire trucks and police cars are everywhere in the surrounding area. Cavanaugh finds relief in the oncoming traffic and manages to restrain his laughter.

"Did you call them?" Mac asks. Cavanaugh nods yes. "That was before you knew I was alive right?"

"Oh c'mon Mac, I knew you could outrun my driving."

"Really," he responds says arrogantly.

A police car with two officers inside pulls up along side of them. Staring at Mac's appearance, they too begin laughing. "You two okay? You need the Paramedics?" one of the officers asks.

"No, we're okay," Billy answers.

"EXCUSE ME!" Mac interrupts, "DO I LOOK LIKE I'M FUCKING OKAY?"

"Call the paramedics," says Billy.

"WE DON'T NEED THE FUCKING PARAMEDICS," Mac interjects angrily.

Cavanaugh turns to his partner with a confusing expression. "Maybe you ought to go to the hospital, you don't look that great. You could have a concussion."

"I DON'T HAVE A FUCKING CONCUSSION," Mac yells, "ALTHOUGH, I WOULDN'T MIND GIVING YOU ONE RIGHT NOW."

The two officers in the police car stare and smile at the haggling detectives. One of the officers, leans out of the window, points to the burning warehouse and says, "When you ladies decide what you're gonna do, we'll be over there."

As they drive away, Mac gives them the finger. "I'LL DRIVE!" he says gruffly. "After all Brooklyn, I am the designated driver and my running for the day is over, if you get my drift!"

As Cavanaugh walks around to the passenger side of the car and climbs in, he can't help but smile at his partner's comical appearance.

After starting the car, MacTavish steps forcefully on the gas pedal, causing the car to fishtail as he drives away.

"Don't we need to tell those cops what happened?" says Billy.

"Fuck 'em!" snarls Mac.

"The captain won't be happy about us leaving," Billy says softly.

"Fuck him too."

"Okay," Billy agrees, as he raises his hands in surrender.

Mac looks at his partner and asks, "Are you okay with this?"

"Yeah, fuck 'em all."

Suddenly, Mac hits the brakes hard—forcing his partner forward in his seat.

"What the hell?" says Billy.

"Where do you come off with that attitude?" Mac asks.

"You just said—"

"I know what I said," Mac interrupts, as he pulls over to the curb and parks. "Call the One Five. Tell them where we are, and let them know we're waiting here."

"Should really be calling the ambulance," Billy mumbles, as he makes the call, hoping the police officers Mac flipped off won't be the unit that'll respond.

Luckily it wasn't, Cavanaugh recalled, as he slowly came back to present time—rehashing the case that went into the cold case files. Finishing his beer, he couldn't help but remember MacTavish's words, *don't like it* as being some sort of foreboding danger. "Maybe it was his partner's intuition or some sort of clairvoyant gift he had. Maybe it wasn't anything more than expert police training," he thought, throwing the empty beer bottle into the trash.

It was almost midnight as Cavanaugh made his way to his room, hoping for a restful night's sleep. Entering and sitting down on the edge of the bed, he picked up his cell phone and made a call. "Hey, it's me, how are you doin?" As he lit a cigarette, he listened intensely as the party on the other end questioned him. "No, I'm not with anyone. I'm alone. Look, if this is how our conversation is gonna go, I'll just hang up. I've had an extremely crazy week and I certainly don't need you jamming me up with empty accusations." Shaking his head, he looked up at the ceiling and said, "Look, we're both tired. Let's just forget this whole conversation. I'll call you later." Disconnecting the call, he removed his clothes and climbed into bed. "So much for having a restful night," he mumbled as he put out his cigarette and roughed up his pillow.

ജ

Dream On

In his hotel room, Cavanaugh had an extremely restless sleep. Swirling images faded through his sleeping mind, while blurred visions of his childhood re-surfaced.

...An amusement park quickly turns into a carnival setting with a Ferris wheel and a merry-go-round. People are laughing as they walk toward a live, wagon wheel pony ride. On one of the harnessed ponies is a small blue-eyed boy with blonde hair wearing a cowboy hat, tee shirt, jeans and western boots. It is six-year-old Billy. He is smiling at his mother who is holding a camera and waving back at him from the observing crowd. She snaps a picture of him and smiles, "Hold on tight Billy, and don't let go..."

Revolving waves of streaming clouds washed away the carnival scene and Cavanaugh's dream moved forward in time—revealing a much older child. It was a night to remember—one that changed his life forever.

...It's a cold January night, and young Billy is thirteen. He is standing outside a neighborhood convenience store in North Hollywood. A lit cigarette is hanging from his lips as he checks his watch—it's a little after midnight. His three schoolmates, Jerry, Sandy and Chris are with him on this adventure. The boys laugh and talk about what they can rip off in the store, while Jerry tries to convince them not to go in.

"Look, if you guys wanna go in, then go," says Jerry. "If we get caught my dad will kill me. I'm not going to do this. I'll wait out here."

"Suit yourself," answers Billy, as he flicks his cigarette into the street and leads his two friends into the store.

Once inside, Chris and Sandy break away from Billy and go in a different direction. Picking up a magazine, Billy looks through the large glass window at Jerry, who is pacing nervously in front of the store.

A '92 Chevy with its lights off drives in and parks on the far side of the parking lot. The car sits quietly for a few minutes before the doors open and four men step out. Pulling stockings over their heads and putting their guns inside their jackets, the four men move rapidly toward the store.

Jerry, watching the car and his friends at the same time, gets an icy feeling when one of the men gets out of the car with a gun in his hand. Seeing the armed man, he panics, and starts waving frantically to his friend inside. Billy laughs as he watches Jerry jumping around erratically in front of the window. Suddenly, and without looking back, Jerry takes off. Billy doesn't understand what's going on until he sees the men walk into the store. Believing a robbery is about to take place, he quickly ducks down in one of the aisles—with paralyzing fear, he thinks about his stupid choice. "Jerry tried to warn him. Now his friend is safe and he is trapped."

Two of the four men grab the owner and quickly escort him to the office, while the third man heads down the aisle toward Sandy and Chris. The two boys continue walking down the opposite aisle, oblivious to what's happening. As the third man comes up behind the boys, he shoves them up against the dairy case. "LISTEN GOOD, he says, giving the boys a dark and threatening look. "You kids need to forget everything you saw here. Go home and don't say anything to anybody, because we know who you are. You have a choice. Keep your mouths shut and live to finish high school, or end up mutilated and buried alive in a DEEP, DARK hole with snakes...LOTS OF SNAKES," he threatens, pointing his gun at them.

"We don't see anything do we?" Sandy asks Chris.

"No...nothing," says Chris shaking.

"Then get your puny asses out of here before I change my mind and take you out to my car to play with my pets...MY SNAKES."

The two boys rush toward the fourth man who is guarding the entrance. Before letting them pass, he aims his gun at the two boys in a threatening way and says, "Bang bang." Trembling, Chris and Sandy rush past him through the door.

"Are we clear?" the third man asks.

Watching the boys run down the street, the fourth man turns around, takes off the stocking, and shoves it into his jacket. "All clear," he answers.

The third man moves down the aisle to where young Billy is hiding and says, "Are you sure those kids won't go for help?"

"Are you kidding?" the fourth man says, joining his partner. "They were pissing their pants on the way out. Don't worry, they can't identify us."

"Oh fuck," Billy visualizes. "I am so dead!"

"Let's go to the back and take care of this so we can get the hell out of here," says the third man. "Did you lock the front door?"

"Yeah, after the kids ran out. Those little fucks sure can run," he laughs.

"Then let's get this over with," the third man replies, as they walk swiftly to the office.

Billy prays to be invisible and thinks, "Don't let them see me. Oh God, please don't let them see me." By some miracle, he realizes he is safe. Hearing the office door close behind the men, he takes a deep breath and creeps around the outside aisle until he gets in front of the window. Looking around the corner at the manager's door, and realizing it could open at any minute, he knows he has to get out of there. "Okay," he says to himself. "I gotta a make a run for the door. Just remember it's locked. I need to move fast. It's now or never. Might end up with a bullet in my back, but what the fuck, I just need to go!" Creeping quietly toward the door, he unlocks it and opens the door. Unfortunately, his feet trigger the entrance chime alarm on the carpet. He rushes through the door and as he runs past the store window—catches a glimpse of one of the men coming out of the back office. After bolting into the alley behind the store, the youngster jumps a few fences and runs past several houses before finding a hiding place. Two houses away, he hears a dog barking. "Please, no dog, no dog," he whispers, as his body freezes with fear behind some large hydrangea bushes and tall hedges. Falling to the ground, he curls up into a ball. Suddenly, he hears two men running in his direction.

"The dog," one of the men says, as they run ahead to where the barking dog is.

Billy hears a strange voice yelling at the two men.

"HEY, WHAT THE HELL ARE YOU GUYS DOING IN MY YARD?"

"Sorry," one of the men answers. "We lost our dog, thought yours was ours. Sorry."

"GET THE HELL OUT OF HERE BEFORE I CALL THE POLICE," the neighbor yells.

As the two men walk past the yard where Billy is hiding, he hears them talking.

"Goddamn it! This wasn't supposed to go down like this. We need to get back and finish what we came for." Their voices fade into the night as they leave and head back to the convenience store.

Billy takes in a deep breath of relief. "What the hell do those guys have to take care of?" he wonders. "Maybe they're after the money in the safe. God, I can't believe what just happened." Fear overwhelms him as his eyes fill with tears. Wiping them away with his jacket sleeve, he ponders, "If only I was home in my bed. Why did I sneak out earlier to be with my friends? And why didn't I leave when Jerry wanted to? Big mistake." Fretful by his near death experience, his eyes get heavy, and under the camouflage of the bushes he drifts off to sleep on the cold damp ground.

In the Ritz Carlton Hotel room, Detective Cavanaugh had a few moments of restful sleep before his mind drifted back to that time he fell asleep in the bushes. His dreams flashed to the next morning where he was still asleep in a stranger's backyard.

...The alley that leads to the backyard Billy is hiding in, is nothing more than a driveway where people set out their trash for pickup. It also serves as the entrance to their backyards and garages. The sound of trashcans banging, and the racing motor of the trash truck, wakes the cold, and still fearful teenager up. He pulls himself up out of the bushes, brushes himself off, and leaves through the wooden backyard gate. Walking down the driveway, he passes the garbage truck that woke him up.

"How's it goin?" one of the men asks, as he empties a trashcan.

"Okay," says Billy without stopping.

Heading for home, he realizes that this was the longest night of his life and one he'll never forget. As he approaches the house, he makes his way into the backyard. Slowly, he opens his bedroom window. The climb back into the house is easy, for this is not his first escape and return. As he begins to undress, he remembers the many times before he has snuck out. "Those days are over," he mumbles. "What if those guys had killed me, how could I explain that to my mother? Of course you couldn't explain you idiot, you'd be dead." After putting on his pajamas, he climbs into bed. Happy to be home, he turns over and quickly falls asleep.

In the Ritz Carlton suite, perspiration covered Detective Cavanaugh's face. His dreams jumped to the following day when his mother woke him up.

…"Billy, I'm making breakfast," says his mother, through his closed bedroom door. "Pancakes and bacon, are you up for it?"

"Yeah, I'll be out in a minute."

"Well hurry up before they get cold," Kelly replies, returning to the kitchen.

"Okay," he says, yawning and throwing off the bed covers. After pushing his fingers through his shoulder length hair, he jumps out of bed.

Heading for the kitchen, he says, "It sure smells good Mom." Walking up behind her, he puts his arms around her waist and hugs her.

"I get all this for pancakes and bacon?"

"Yeah and Mom…" he says sitting down, "I love you."

Putting the spatula down, she walks over to him and places her hands on the back of his shoulders. "Okay...what do you want?"

"Nothing," he replies while eating.

She pulls out the chair next to him, she sits down. "Okay, then tell me what you did."

"I didn't do anything." he says with a mouthful of food.

Putting her right hand on his forehead, she says, "You're sick and running a temp."

"MOM, THE PANCAKES!"

"Oh my God," she says, running into the kitchen to save the burning flapjacks.

Billy stops eating and looks around the room. "I'm so lucky," he says with tearful eyes, "I almost lost it all. What a dumb move."

Kelly returns to the table with some homeopathic pills in her hand. Seeing the tears in her son's eyes, she becomes compassionate and says softly, "Here take these when you're through eating. You are so pale; one would think you spent the night outside in the bushes."

Choking on his food, Billy contemplates, "She has no idea, if she only knew…"

"William Cavanaugh, you need to go back to bed," she says firmly. "And you can forget about school tomorrow."

"Yeah, I am pretty tired. Thanks for breakfast," he says, as he slowly walks back to his room and turns on his TV. Climbing back into bed, he's glad to stay home and shut the world out.

Spending the next two days at home, gave Billy a bit of relief. Watching TV, he can't find anything about the 7-11 robbery. "Maybe they changed their minds," he ponders. "Things just didn't figure out." Denial starts to set in, as the youngster wants to believe that his night of terror never happened.

…When Billy went back to school, he finds it to be a typical Wednesday. "Looking around he thinks, "Everything appears to be the same…everyone running, laughing, and yelling as usual." As he enters the building, he spots Jerry walking toward his locker. Running after him, he has to push his way through a group of boys before catching up. Reaching out, he makes a grab for Jerry's arm.

Frightened by the cold grip on his shoulder, Jerry jumps forward and shouts alarmingly, "WHAT THE FUCK?"

"Easy," says Billy, as they walk through the hall. "It's just me."

"Christ! I thought they got to you. When you didn't show up Monday; I went to the office to find out where you were. They said your mother called in saying you had the flu."

"I'm okay. You need to try and calm down."

"Look," Jerry continues, "I'm sorry I left you guys. I just got so scared when I saw those guns."

"It's alright. Sandy and Chris...are they okay?"

"Yeah," Jerry answers in a calmer voice. "Chris pissed all over himself when he got out of the store, and Sandy went ballistic—talking to himself for two days. His parents sent him to the psych hospital 'cause he kept mumbling "my life is over, my life is over." So his doctor put him on Ritalin. Now he doesn't say shit. Just walks around with a glazed look in his eyes."

As Billy laughs, Jerry quickly joins in. Both boys begin to see the humorous side of their scary experience. "It's funny now, but it sure wasn't when it happened," says Jerry.

"Have you heard anything about the store?"

"No," answers Jerry. "My mom and I drove by it on Monday. It seemed normal. It was open and everything. Why are you asking?"

"Doesn't it seem weird? Four guys with guns take the owner to the backroom and there's nothing about it on the news?"

Jerry shrugs his shoulders and says, "Maybe they don't want the publicity."

"What?" Billy inquires curiously.

"Well some places don't report robberies for insurance reasons. My mom said it had to do with increased insurance rates."

"Look, its over," says Billy, as he put his arm around Jerry's shoulder. "Thank God we're all okay. What say we forget about ripping off stores, we should leave that to the big guys."

"Yeah, I'm for that," sighs Jerry.

"We better get inside," says Billy, as they rush into their first class.

Detective Cavanaugh's dream raced forward to later that day when school was over and his mother was there to pick him up.

…"Got some major grocery shopping to do," Kelly tells him, as he jumps into their car. "I thought you might consider helping me?"

"Sure Mom. We need to get some more Rocky Road ice cream. We're out."

Their shopping only took about twenty minutes. Outside, Billy pushes the cart quickly ahead and stands on the back of it for a ride. After loading the groceries into the car, he climbs into the passenger seat and says, "Cool Mom, that went fast."

"Damn!" she says driving away.

"What Mom, what's wrong?"

"Forgot the damn milk, we'll have to swing by the 7-11 on the next block."

Suddenly, Billy realizes it's the same store he and his friends were at Saturday night. The idea of going anywhere near that store frightens him.

"Mom, it's okay. I don't…need any milk," he responds nervously, while trying to discourage her from going there.

Looking at him suspiciously she says, "You drink milk like its water, and now you don't want any?"

"I'll go get it on my bike later," he says anxiously.

"Don't be ridiculous. We're right around the corner," she says, driving down the alley and taking the same route her son took on Saturday night—passing the very yard he fell asleep in.

Recalling his night of terror, Billy rolls his eyes and looks out of the window. "Fuck!" he mumbles, as he looks at the very Hydrangea bushes that were protecting him.

Arriving at the store, Kelly pulls into the lot and parks. Reaching into her purse, she pulls out a five-dollar bill and hands it to her son.

"You want me to go in?" he responds, with an inappropriate attitude.

"Never mind, I'll get it. Teenagers! Will I ever get through these years?" she says, slamming the car door shut.

The four minutes she was gone seems like an eternity for Billy—his mind racing to what could be going on inside the store. Finally, he sees her approaching the car.

Opening the car door, she sees that her son is extremely nervous. "Are you sure you're okay?"

"Yeah I'm fine," he answers softly. Turning away, he stares out the passenger window. Everything seems distant and faraway. He hears her talking, but her words are fuzzy and faint. "Who were those guys, and what the hell happened to the owner Saturday night?"

After arriving home, and dropping the last bag of groceries on the kitchen counter, he says "I need to lie down."

"Go on, I can handle it from here. You look tired. Thanks for the help," she smiles. "I'll let you know when the food is ready. Maybe you should take a nap."

"Sure," he responds, as he turns around and walks slowly to his room. As he lies down, the teenager contemplates telling his mother the whole story. "Yeah right. Probably get shipped off to some military school until I'm eighty-four," he thinks, as he slowly drifts off to sleep and once again dreams about the Saturday night getaway.

He wakes up to his mother vigorously shaking his shoulders. "NO. LEAVE ME ALONE. STAY AWAY!" he yells out.

"Billy, it's me."

Opening his eyes, he sees his mother standing over him. "Sorry, I must have been dreaming," he said shakily.

"You better lighten up on those vampire movies," she smiles. Leaning toward him, she gives her imitation of Dracula's voice. "Or the Count 'vill bite you on the neck and make you his slave."

"Okay Mom, I'll lighten up on the movies if you lay off the Transylvanian accent."

"Dinner is served and Igor needs to be fed his flies," she goes on.

Standing up, he pushes her gently out of his room and sighs, "Okay Countess, let's eat."

The aroma of rigatoni, Italian sausage and fresh baked bread filter through the house.

"Grab the salad, it's in the fridge," Kelly says to her son, as she sets up their food on TV trays. Sitting down on the couch, they begin to watch one of Billy's favorite Christopher Lee's vampire movies.

It is a little after eight o'clock, when their dinner ends and his mother yells out from the kitchen. "Billy, could you run out front and give the trees some extra water?"

"Sure Mom," he responds, as he gets up and heads for the front door. Flipping on the outside light, he steps out on the porch and walks to the side of the house where he unwinds the hose and turns on the water. As he begins to water the trees, he glances up the street and sees a car parked about three houses away. It's dark, but a lit cigarette inside the car catches his attention. Easing back behind one of the large bushes, he stares at the car curiously—feeling that someone in the car is there to watch him. He quickly finishes watering, rolls up the hose, and casually walks back into the house. Flipping off the porch light, he quickly races through the kitchen—scurrying toward the back door.

"Where are you going?" his mother asks, while cleaning up in the kitchen.

"Be right back Mom," he says, closing the door behind him.

"Teenagers," she sighs, while loading the dishwasher.

Once outside, Billy runs alongside the house—darting in between trees and bushes. He lowers his body to the ground and hides in between two large bushes where he can't be seen. Silently, he watches as the car starts up and moves slowly down the street towards his house—pausing briefly under a streetlight. Billy sees two men in the car and recognizes one of them. "Christ," he says, "it's the guy from the 7-11. Oh my God they've found me. I am really fucked!" He remains very still until their car is out of sight, then runs into the back yard and re-enters through the kitchen.

"Well Billy, are you done with your nightly romp?"

"I thought I saw a rabbit in the yard," he says, as he hurries past her.

"Billy?"

"Yeah," he answers, looking back at her.

"Did you find it?"

Staring at her with an inquisitive look he says, "Find what Mom?"

"The remains of my last victim?" she answers in her Transylvanian voice. Looking at her, he wonders what the hell she's talking about. "Go," she says, "get ready for bed—you and the rabbit." Switching off the kitchen light, she walks away mumbling, "I really don't know how many more years of this I can take."

"I HEARD THAT MOM," he replies, walking back to his room. "No rabbits," he says to himself, "just a couple of rats." The teenager feels uneasy as he sits down on his bed. "What to do?" he mumbles. "His mother could also be in danger, something has to be done." He pauses for a few minutes, and then makes a life-changing decision. Leaving his room, he yells out nervously. "MOM...WE NEED TO TALK!" Walking into the dining room, he grabs her wrist and pulls her to the couch. "Sit down...please?"

"Billy, you've been acting very weird. What the hell is going on?"

The youngster walks over to the drapes and peeks out at the clear and quiet street. Turning back to his mother with great apprehension, he says, "I'm going to tell you something...and you've just got to believe me. As unbelievable as it may sound, just tell me what I need to do...okay?"

"Okay," she replies calmly. Knowing that her son has never lied to her intentionally, her intuition tells her this isn't some trivial matter. "Tell me what's going on?" she says calmly.

Billy sits down across from her and begins to tell his story—conveniently leaving out his cigarette smoking episode.

Kelly's face is still as she listens to the terror her son has experienced; the fear he felt inside the store, and then in the alley, how he slept in the bushes and then made his way home the next morning. Her face softens with compassion and love for her son.

With tear-filled eyes, he tells her about the men who have been staking out their house. "Mom…I'm so scared. I don't want them to hurt you." As he finishes his story, the thunder outside signals some welcome rain.

Kelly reaches out and pulls him into her arms and says tearfully, "Oh my God, you've been carrying this thing around for days now." Slowly, she pulls away from him and grabs the phone. "You're right, we have to do something and we need to do it right now. Who knows what these guys have planned. It's not just about us; your friends could also be in danger. It'll be okay…we'll get through this. No matter what happens, I promise, I won't let anyone hurt you," she says, while calling the police. "I'll always protect you."

The rain beats heavily on the one-story home, and the wind propels sheets of water against their front window as Billy walks back over to the drapes and once again peeks out. He can't even see the street because of the torrential rainstorm. Closing his eyes, he worries about his mother and his friends. Suddenly, his heart begins pounding hard, and perspiration surfaces on his forehead. His vision is blurry and everything becomes foggy and dark. He vaguely remembers losing consciousness and hitting the floor.

"BILLY…BILLY," his mother yells out.

Cavanaugh's mother's voice became deeper and began to sound more masculine. It was now MacTavish's voice he heard in the Ritz Carlton Hotel suite. Looking up, he saw his partner.

"Goddamn it Billy, wake up!" said Mac, shaking him to get a response.

"Okay, okay. I'm awake," he replied, as he sat up in the bed.

"You're soaking wet... and you kept yelling, *"They're here, they're here."* I think the whole mother-fucking hotel heard you." Suddenly, the hotel phone rang. "Well I knew that was coming," said Mac, picking up the phone. "Yes...no, no problem," he responded, as he walked into the living room. "We're quite all right. My partner had a bad dream. He has them occasionally."

As MacTavish began to tell another one of his fantasy stories to the hotel's desk clerk, Cavanaugh listened to the one-sided conversation. He could only imagine what the other person was saying.

"Was in the war you know," said Mac. "Yes, a flashback of Viet Nam. Oh you were...so you understand?" Pausing, he listened to the manager on the other end of the call and then said, "Yes, it was brutal over there; lots of men have those reoccurring nightmares. Well, I think he's done for the night; he only has one of these every three, or four months. We apologize for the inconvenience. What? Oh yes, he does look a little young for being in Nam. Well, if you can keep a secret I can explain, he's had a facelift. Yes, it does look quite good. I agree—very natural looking. Yes, we will, and you have a good night too."

"What was all that about?" said Billy, walking into the living room wearing a hotel robe.

"That was the front desk," Mac replied. "Three people called in about your screaming. They thought somebody was killing you—

probably thought it was me. I've had a few rough dreams Kid, but never that bad. Let's get some coffee." As they walked into the kitchenette, Cavanaugh watched as his partner poured two cups. "Here," Mac said, handing him one.

Taking the coffee, Cavanaugh headed towards the window. "It's stopped raining," he said, looking out over the darkened city.

For a moment, MacTavish stared inquisitively at his partner. "I don't remember it ever starting."

"Oh yeah...it was raining in my dream," remembered Billy, recalling how those vivid memories of his childhood had caused him many restless nights and dreams in his lifetime.

"Look," said Mac, "we all have dreams, but then we wake up. You seem to carry your dreams into reality and I'm getting a little concerned. How about telling me what this last dream was about."

Cavanaugh felt the need to talk about his nightmares. As he sat down near a window and looked out at the city, he said, "It started in California, where my mother and I were living. I had these three school buddies, Chris, Sandy and Jerry—we considered ourselves a kind of LA Valley gang."

"Even The James Gang had more than four participants," interjected Mac, trying to lighten the situation.

Billy gave a slight smile and replied, "Yeah, well we were only thirteen." Cavanaugh started telling his story—all the way through, and up to his fainting episode. ..."my mother called the paramedics and they took me to the hospital. I woke up the next morning to find her asleep in the chair next to my bed. I didn't remember anything after hitting the living room floor...doctors said I was experiencing some kind of post-traumatic shock." Taking a sip of his coffee, he said, "There were two

L.A.P.D. detectives that needed to be filled in on what I'd witnessed. They wanted to talk to me as soon as I was up to it. One was a young guy named Rob Walker, the other detective, Lee Granger, was a lot older."

Mac gave him a cynical look and said, "Kind of like us?"

"Not exactly," said Billy. "You're a lot older than Granger was."

"Continue your story," Mac said abruptly.

"I told them everything that happened. My mother said she worked something out with Granger so I wouldn't get jammed up in Juvenile Hall, but it was Walker who inspired me to become a cop. He spent five months guiding and directing me."

"Sounds like you were pretty attached to this Walker fella."

"Yeah, he was a great guy, Billy responded. "There's a part of me that tries to be like him. I remember him telling me how brave I was by coming forward and how I probably saved a lot of lives by doing so. He said my observations and reactions under stress would benefit me if I ever decided to be a cop, and what I did in that store was exactly what an unarmed cop would have done in the same situation. He helped me understand my fears about calling 911 and explained that my decision to follow through was the right thing to do."

"He was right you know," replied Mac sensitively.

"Yeah, I finally realized that. He also said I'd make a great detective someday." As MacTavish stared at his partner in silence, Cavanaugh waited for some sort of compliment about his current status as a detective. One never came, so he addressed the situation. "You know Mac, you always have something to say and now you're quiet?"

"You're referring to the remark about you being a great detective?" alleged Mac.

147

"Yes," Billy laughed.

"Well, perhaps someday you will be."

Billy nodded his head and said, "I'm curious...exactly what category do you put me in?"

"Very good," Mac smiled, "great is usually attained after one's demise. There's very few of us great ones still living."

"Do you want me to finish my story, or have you figured it out Sherlock?" smiled Billy.

"By all means Watson, continue. Although I suspect the convenience store owner's wife had put out a hit on her husband. The hit men were probably paid a very substantial amount to make him disappear. I imagine the money was conveniently left in the office safe."

"$150,000...and how did you know all that?" questioned Billy.

"Deduction my dear man," Mac gloated. "Pure deduction by a great detective."

"Don't be looking for a compliment, cause you ain't dead yet," laughed Billy.

Standing up, Mac bragged, "Ah, but someday I'll be immortalized with the other great ones. And now, perhaps we should get some breakfast before we meet our hosts."

"On one condition Sherlock...your ego doesn't join us," said Billy as he walked back to his room.

MacTavish poured another cup of coffee and walked into his own bedroom. Getting dressed, he called out, "Exactly how did Walker die?" A cold silence fell over the suite, as MacTavish gave a sigh and grabbed his forehead. "Damn," he thought.

Cavanaugh walked slowly into his partner's room and said, "I never mentioned that Walker was dead."

"Didn't you?" Mac said nonchalantly.

"No, I didn't."

"Hm-m-m, I don't believe *you did.*"

"Then how did you know he was dead?"

"Well being the great detective that I am," Mac began, "and the attachment you had for Walker, it would have continued to be a close relationship if he were still in your life. And if he were alive, you would have told me about him. That relationship could only have been severed by his death."

Impressed with his partner's deductions, Cavanaugh decided to talk about Walker's death. "It was five months after my stay in the hospital. Walker and I had become very good friends. He had taken me down to Alvarado Street for some Mexican food. Afterwards, we walked over to MacArthur Park and talked about school and what I needed to do to become a cop. There weren't a lot of people around, and the park was fairly quiet that day. As we walked around the lake talking, we approached a man and woman embracing. Suddenly, this guy made eye contact with me. For a moment it seemed as if time had stopped—everything was moving in slow motion. I jerked into Walker, telling him the man behind us was the fourth man...the same man I saw at the 7-11. As we turned around, the man already had his gun out and aimed at me. Walker reached for his gun, but I guess he knew he couldn't get it out in time. He yelled no and threw his body in front of me. I'll never forget that cry, never," Billy sighed, as he walked over to the window and looked out. "Everything happened so fast," he continued, "I fell behind him, trying to hold on to his body. He told me to grab his gun. I was crying as I reached for it, but I couldn't get it out of his holster. Two patrolmen appeared out of nowhere and started chasing the shooter. I started yelling that he had shot a cop. One of the officers' stopped, took aim and unloaded on the guy—knocking him into the lake. The other officer was on his radio. I heard the words none of us ever want to hear...officer down. I sat there holding him, trying to get him to talk to me. I knew he was gone, but I just couldn't stop talking to him. One of the officers pulled me up and held me in his arms. Paramedics came, but it was too late, he was gone. As I looked down at his body and saw his blood all over me, I knew I had to be a detective."

MacTavish saw the tears in his partner's eyes and got a little teary-eyed himself. As Cavanaugh turned to look out the window, he tried to console him. "I want you to know that I wouldn't want anyone else to be my partner. I trust you with my life, and that's a trust I haven't given to many people."

Billy, still focused on the city, said, "How many?"

"What?" said Mac.

"How many?" Billy repeated.

"What do you mean how many?" Mac replied defensively.

"Seems like an easy question," said Billy, as he turned around and faced his partner. "How many have you given your trust to? One, two, three, twenty, forty...how many?"

"Oh for Christ's sake,'" said Mac, irritated with his partner's questioning. "What's the point of how many?"

"The point is...how many?" Billy smiled. "Am I the only one?"

"Of course you're not the only one you little fuck."

Cavanaugh laughed and changed the topic of their conversation. "Okay then, I guess we better head out."

"Christ," said Mac looking at his watch, "I lost track of the time."

Cavanaugh lit up a cigarette as he walked out of his partner's room—leaving him to finish getting dressed.

It was seven-thirty when the New York detectives walked out of their suite and headed for the elevator.

"So Mac," said Billy, as the elevator doors opened. "Am I the only one?"

MacTavish ignored his partner's persistent nagging and followed him into the elevator.

Looking straight ahead, Cavanaugh pushed the lobby button and declared adamantly, "I knew it."

"Knew what?" Mac snapped back.

"That I'm the only one," Billy replied smugly, as the elevator doors closed.

෨෬

An Irish Touch

MacTavish and Cavanaugh had pulled into the Cleveland Precinct parking lot just as Ricco and Louie were rushing out. Rolling down the passenger window, Mac said, "You two look like you're on the way to a fire, I thought maybe we'd all head back out to the Kingman house."

"Boy, you are good," said Louie. "How'd you know there was a fire at the Kingman house?"

MacTavish remembered what Ricco told him, and realized he best ignore Louie's question and not respond.

"They know how the fire started?" asked Billy, as he drove away.

"It was reported as a gas leak explosion this morning," replied Ricco, leaning forward.

"Was that before or after the cat jumped over the moon?" Mac said wittily.

"There's a cat involved?" said Louie.

MacTavish ignored Louie's nonsensical question and remained focused on the topic of the explosion. "Gas, I didn't smell any yesterday. Did anybody smell gas?"

"I didn't smell a thing." Louie responded defiantly.

"You know Mac; I tend to agree with you. Something about this case definitely smells fishy," replied Ricco, looking out his window.

"Alright, it's me...sorry," Louie surrendered, as he rolled down his window.

Confused by Louie's statement, MacTavish and Ricco turned to look at him, while Cavanaugh focused on the little guy in the rearview mirror.

"I'm sorry," Louie said, "it was that fish stew I had last night. It gave me a lot of gas." As the three men broke out into simultaneous laughter, Louie yelled out. "HEY, FUCK ALL THREE OF YOU!"

"Louie, Louie," Ricco interjected, trying to explain the reason for their laughter. But the more he looked into his partner's face, the more he laughed.

"It's okay Louie," Mac intervened, "apology accepted."

"Thanks Mac," Louie answered quietly. "You're not only psychic—you got class too.

Looking back at him, MacTavish was puzzled about the psychic remark.

"You know...the fire?" said Louie.

Still staring at him, MacTavish remained silent and waited for a clearer explanation.

Louie looked at him and with a big sigh said, "When you pulled up at the station this morning you asked us if we were going to the fire."

As Cavanaugh and Ricco started to laugh, Mac turned away with an unsettling expression and sighed, "Why me?'

"What...what I say?" Louie asked, glancing at the other detectives.

"One thing you are Louie, is very entertaining," said Mac.

"Hear that Ricco, I'm entertaining, and Mac should know because he's psychic."

"Are you beginning to understand Mac?" smiled Ricco.

"Yes," he acknowledged, "Be careful how I phrase my sentences."

"That's it," said Ricco. "Otherwise, this could go on all day. Trust me; I had to learn the hard way. However, like you, there are times when I still forget."

"This ought to help my gastric overload," said Louie, as he tossed some antacid tablets into his mouth.

MacTavish and Cavanaugh tried not to laugh, while Ricco fiddled with his ear—struggling to contain his own laughter.

It was a little after nine when the detectives arrived at the Kingman home. The smell of smoke permeated the area. All that was left of the home was water soaked debris and charred beams.

"Christ," said Mac, "they didn't leave much. I'm assuming this was no accident," he continued, looking at the red and yellow plastic crime tape that secured the scene.

"Unfortunately, I was kind of hoping it was," Ricco answered, "The fucking paperwork is going to be a bitch."

Leaving the car, the four detectives walked across the street and ducked underneath the colored crime tape. They approached the front of the house with MacTavish and Ricco leading the way.

Waiting for them was a fireman who could have passed for Santa Claus—complete with bushy eyebrows, moustache and beard. Rather than having a pure white beard, his was more of a salt and pepper mix. As the detectives approached, he walked toward them and said, "You must be from the downtown borough."

"Yeah, I'm Detective Gambino. My partner here is Detective Petticelli." Pointing to the New York detectives, who were putting on latex gloves, he said, "These guys are from..." Ricco was about to say, "The Big Apple" when he saw Louie's gleaming, jokester's face. He looked like a hungry dog waiting for the mouthwatering bone his master was about to throw him. "Detectives Cavanaugh and MacTavish are from New York City," said Ricco, revising his statement. "The owner of this house died while he was in their city."

"Murdered?" the fireman asked.

"Looks that way," answered Ricco, as he looked at the debris around his feet.

"Well it's starting to make sense now," the fireman said.

"Excuse me?" Mac interjected, "what makes sense?"

"Somebody went to great lengths to make this look like an accident," Waldo answered. "Twenty-five years on the job, and if it wasn't for that guy over there," he said, pointing to a man on his knees and deep in rubble, "I'd have written it off as an electrical malfunction."

The man he pointed to was a rugged-looking man in his early forties, with jet-black hair and sapphire blue eyes. He was wearing a khaki jacket with multiple pockets that were filled with small notebooks, containers and vials—hiking boots accentuated his worn out jeans.

"Who is he?" said Billy.

"Name's Shawn O'Hara, he's in charge, I've worked with him before," Waldo responded.

"A good old Irish bloke," Mac smiled.

"Good isn't the word," defined Waldo. "If I were a criminal, I sure as hell wouldn't want him on my ass. I don't believe I introduced myself. The name's Thornhill...Waldo Thornhill. I was nick-named after a cartoon character in Mr. Magoo—my father was a big fan."

"I think you were fortunate," Mac grinned. "He could have been a Tweety fan."

"You're right there," Waldo laughed. "Believe me, I've thought of all the possibilities; Porky, Pluto, Daffy, Goofy... I figure Waldo ain't that bad. Excuse me a moment," he smiled, checking his pager. "I need to call in a report." Turning around, he went back to his vehicle.

The four detectives walked across the fire debris to where O'Hara was absorbed in separating remnants left over from the fire. As the detectives moved closer, they saw him putting ashes into one of his containers.

O'Hara was intensely involved labeling his vials and making notes in his notebook. Without looking up, he spoke in a strong and soft Irish brogue. "Well what do we have here? Four detectives, two from New York—please do not fuck up my investigation by trampling through what's left of the evidence."

"And exactly what is your evidence?" asked Mac.

Still ignoring the detectives, Shawn said, "Aw, the New York detective knows this wasn't any accident."

Startled by O'Hara's abrupt behavior, Mac spoke forcefully. "Look, I asked you a simple question and I would like the courtesy of a simple answer."

Putting the vial and notebook into one of his pockets, O'Hara slowly got up. Without looking at the other detectives, he lifted his head slowly until his eyes locked on to MacTavish. "I don't believe you're a simple man," he said firmly. "You're much too complicated for simple questions and simple answers. You Scots are always in a fucking hurry. I suggest you slow down a bit, because whoever swept this house expected you and your partner to be in it when it was imploded. A neighborhood cat that climbed through an open window saved your life. The feline triggered a wire that was attached to a detonator that was connected to the front door." Stepping back, O'Hara reached down and picked up a trash bag. "What's in here could've been you and you're friends," he added, tossing the bag to MacTavish.

Looking inside, MacTavish pulled out a flattened piece of matted hair imbedded in concrete. "What is it?"

"It's what's left of the cat," Shawn answered sharply.

"Hey Mac," said Louie, "I guess you let the cat out of the bag." Looking into the bag, Louie whispered, "Sorry Puss, your mother should have made you learn your life numbers. Nine means retirement from investigative encounters."

Meanwhile, Cavanaugh, looking amidst the debris, started to pick up something up from the ground. His movement caused O'Hara to yell out, "DO NOT PICK THAT UP!" Too late to ignore the request,

Cavanaugh already had it in his hands. "Has your partner got a hearing problem Mac?" Shawn asked with a quiet strength.

"What the—" began Billy.

Giving him a steely glare, Shawn interrupted and said, "This is not fucking *Treasure Island* Detective Cavanaugh, and you're not here to hunt for buried treasure. My investigations, my island...do you not get it mate?"

Cavanaugh thought O'Hara's attitude was a little intimidating, so he raised his arms in a surrender mode. "My apologies," he said as he placed the piece of debris back on the ground.

"Detective MacTavish, you remember the warehouse last autumn?" said Shawn. "You and your partner were close to hearing those heavenly bagpipes. You were in a hurry then too."

"Actually it was my partner who was in a hurry," replied Mac. "And how did you know about that?"

"Yeah," Louie challenged. "How'd you know about that?"

"Let's take a walk," said Ricco, pulling Louie back by the sleeve of his jacket and leading him to the other side of the house. Cavanaugh decided to join them—leaving his partner alone with the Irishman.

"You were saying?" Mac inquired.

"I take my job as an arson investigator very seriously," said Shawn. "Cases like this one usually have a deeper meaning. You've been involved in two, deliberately set explosions. A rather unique coincidence don't you think? Where I come from, you know who's responsible for the bombings and why they are executed."

MacTavish pondered on how and where O'Hara got his information. "There may be more to this case than just two homicides," he thought.

"You might want to rethink these two situations," Shawn advised, as he made memos in his notebook. "Now I need to get back to work."

MacTavish's expression softened, as he began to agree with O'Hara's idea of rethinking the homicides. He also realized that he and the other detectives had stormed the area like a bunch of raw recruits. "Look, we were wrong and I apologize for our rough intrusion," he said softly.

As the three detectives returned, O'Hara knelt back down on the ground and filled more vials with charred debris, he said, "Apology accepted *Rob Roy*. Do me a favor and take *The Three Musketeers* out of here; I have a lot of work to complete."

MacTavish grabbed his partner and acknowledged him as one of the Musketeers. "Let's go Athos." After moving forward a few feet, he stopped abruptly and turned back to the opinionated Irishman. "I guess this means that high tea is not an option?" Not getting any sort of response, he turned towards the street and said, "I didn't think so."

As the four detectives walked towards their car, Waldo rushed over to them and said smiling, "Sorry, I should have given you a heads up on O'Hara. He's got a bit of an attitude."

"I never met an Irishman that didn't," said Mac, glancing back at O'Hara.

"We'll send you guys a copy of the report after he completes his investigation," said Waldo, as he walked them to their car. After saying goodbye, the four detectives got into their vehicle and drove away.

As their vehicle reached the corner, O'Hara slowly looked up and watched as the car turned the corner and disappeared. "You're not stupid Detective MacTavish," he said quietly to himself. "If you and your partner move cautiously, we just might solve this case before the two of you end up dead."

Inside the car, Cavanaugh was the first to speak. "Well that was interesting. Who the hell is that guy?"

"Don't underestimate him," answered Ricco. "We've heard about him, but never really worked one on one with him."

Turning back to look at Ricco, Mac said, "What's his history, I'm sure he has one."

"Oh yeah," answered Ricco, "Besides being a member of WASP, he's got a hell of a past. An ex-Green Beret, he fought with the Irish Republic Army in Ireland then ended up in Beirut working with Special Forces. The guy has an incredible knowledge of bombs and weapons. He can practically look at an explosion site and tell you who, why, and what time.

"Very impressive," Mac responded with a smile. "That would explain his cordial attitude."

"So why is he working with us?" inquired Billy.

"Personal reasons," Ricco replied. "Who knows, nobody's ever gotten close enough to find out what those reasons are. I made some calls when we took our walk. He's been with the Agency since they opened shop and has a reputation of being a recluse."

"You'd have to be carrying all that baggage," said Mac. "You wouldn't know who the hell to trust."

Smiling, Billy said, "You think his attitude has anything to do with him flying solo?"

"I really like him," said Louie. Surprised by Louie's sincerity, all three detectives turned and looked at the little guy. "What?" said Louie. "So I like the guy, he tells you like it is and doesn't hold anything back.

There's no guessing about what he's thinking. How many guys do you know like that?"

"You're right Louie," replied Mac.

A sudden silence befell the men as they looked out at the city. In the silence hovering over the car, Louie grimly said, "Those kinds of guys...you either like them or you shoot them."

"Louie," laughed Mac. "I'm beginning to develop a deep attachment to you."

In the back seat, the comical detective had a worried look. Moving closer to Ricco he whispered, "Is he hitting on me?"

"No Louie, he's paying you a compliment."

"Okay...good!" Louie answered quietly. "Cause I got a little worried."

Simultaneously, MacTavish began a conversation with his partner in the front seat. "When we get back to the hotel I need to call and see how Honey's doing?"

"Yeah, I'm sure she misses you," said Billy. "Probably should check in with our squad too."

"That's nice," Louie replied, as he moved even closer to Ricco. "Mac's got a honey."

"Louie, you're sitting very close to me, are you hitting on me?"

"ME?" said Louie, stunned at the thought. "NO!"

"Then how about moving the fuck away from me," said Ricco.

Louie slid back over to his side of the car and looked out his window. "Why the fuck would I hit on you?" he mumbled.

Cavanaugh and MacTavish smiled at each other as they listened in on the Cleveland detectives haggling.

Ricco turned abruptly to Louie and said softly, "What the fuck did you say?"

"Me," Louie questioned? "I didn't say a fuckin' thing."

"Hey," responded Ricco, "I'm not crazy, I heard what the fuck you said."

"Well, if you heard what the fuck I said, then why the fuck did you ask me what I fucking said?" Louie debated.

"Hey, I'll ask you what the fuck I want to ask you, whenever the fuck I want to, wherever the fuck I want to," Ricco responded loudly. "So fuck off you little midget."

Louie paused for a moment. His mind appeared to be calculating something. "I think I got more fucks in than you," he smiled.

Recalling the conversation in his mind," Ricco said, "No. I believe I had two more fucks than you."

Mimicking the previous conversation, Louie began counting on his fingers. "You're right," he laughed, "Seven to five."

Ricco gave a little smile and said, "What can I say, I'm good."

MacTavish looked over at his partner who was about to question what happened and quickly intervened. "Trust me on this one Kid, just drive."

೮೦೧೩

SOAPS

VERSUS SOAPBOXES

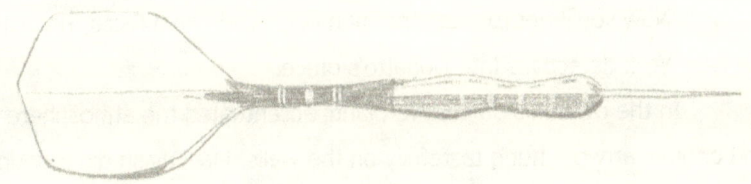

It was mid-morning when the four detectives arrived back at Cleveland's downtown headquarters. Moving past two police officers who were arguing about baseball and the upcoming opening season, they saw Officer Frank Marino at the front desk—listening to an elderly woman complain about gangs invading her neighborhood.

"Hey Frankie, we're back!" Louie yelled.

Seeing the detectives, Marino waved back as he tried to calm the irate woman.

"This way," said Ricco, leading MacTavish and Cavanaugh into the main detective bureau.

"Louie, I got something for you," one of the detectives called out, bringing papers over for him to sign.

The New York detectives followed Ricco into an office that accommodated two large desks, and several leatherback chairs.

As Mac reached for a cup and took a sip of the bottled water, he said, "What a surprise, I was sure it would be Scotch."

"Only when we have parties," smiled Ricco, as he walked over to the fax machine. "Cavanaugh, there's some paperwork for you from New York here." Handing him the faxes, he said, "We should be getting O'Hara's report soon."

Louie popped his head into the doorway and said, "Captain wants to see us."

"Now you'll get to meet the man in charge," said Ricco, escorting the New York detectives into Donatto's office.

In the captain's office, live plants accentuated the atmosphere and original artwork hung tastefully on the walls. MacTavish did a double take on what he knew was an original Picasso painting hanging on one of the walls. Behind the desk sat an extremely overweight, Godfather type of man. He was often referred to as D by his fellow detectives. The huge basket of sweets and baked goodies on his desk confirmed his love of sugar. Peering over glasses that hung low on his nose, Captain Johnny Donatto waved them in through the open door. Reaching out with his right hand he said, "Welcome. My boys been taking care of you?"

"They've been very accommodating," responded Billy.

"If the rest of your force is anything like Ricco and Louie," said Mac, "you have a hell of a great organization."

"Thank you, we try," Donatto smiled, as he reached for a cranberry muffin. "You guys hungry? This here's an open basket for everybody. We have it refilled five times a day."

After Louie grabbed a piece of Italian pastry out of the basket, Cavanaugh picked out a blueberry muffin. Smiling, he realized that food was important to the men in this Cleveland precinct—they were either talking about it or eating it. "You have a great set-up here captain," he said, while taking a bite of his muffin.

"Thank you, and its D or Donatto," he grinned. "We're very informal here."

"Except when he's pissed off," interjected Louie, "then it's Captain D."

"Or mother fucker behind my back," Donatto smiled. "Pull up some chairs and sit down, I'll only keep you a few minutes. Ricco and Louie are the best guys I've got here. I think the five of you can handle this Kingman case without any outside help...excluding the Agency of course."

"Five?" said Mac.

"You four and O'Hara. Now I know you've had the honor of meeting the Irish prick, but understand; he is the best in his field. Unfortunately, he also knows it. Once you get to understand his ways, you'll find him an invaluable asset. Now about this case...our information is that Kingman owned the house for about twenty-five years. He has no record, no minor violations, no wives, no kids and no friends. It also appears that he had no life. And if he had no life, why the fuck did somebody kill him? I've looked over everything on this guy and I've got to tell you, I've never seen such a perfect human being in my life. Got any ideas why somebody wanted him dead?"

"Well," Mac responded, "until today there's a possibility the shooter got the wrong guy, but with the house being swept and then blown up, we're pretty sure it was a hit. O'Hara seems to think—

"O'Hara doesn't seem to think about anything," Donatto interrupted, "he knows. He told me the house was rigged using state of the art equipment. Two men did the rigging and a team did the sweep—

leaving the window open to reinforce the blast. Whoever did this didn't count on a cat's curiosity. Gentlemen, this was not a cheap blow job." His terminology surprised the New York detectives and made them laugh. "It's what we call our bomb sites," Donatto chuckled. "O'Hara said you guys had a similar set-up at some warehouse in New York?"

"Yes, he did mention that," said Mac.

"He told me the two were somehow connected. If they were set-up the same way, then this is no coincidence. I want to know who's behind this, cause nobody fucks with my men," he said, placing his arms behind his head and rocking back in his chair. "I've talked to your captain and we're in agreement. One way or another, let's find out who's doing this, consider it a priority for all five of you."

All four men were in agreement when Ricco spoke out, "Anything else D?"

"No, that's it," Donatto replied, adjusting his glasses. "Oh yeah, there is one more unrelated thing. O'Hara said something about meeting MacTavish for High Tea at Mahoney's Pub."

"Did he happen to say what time that would be?" smiled Mac.

"Four o'clock," laughed Donatto.

On his way out, MacTavish stopped at the painting that originally caught his attention. "That *is* an original Picasso," he said appreciatively.

"I don't deal with imitations," said Donatto.

"Neither do I. I'm very impressed," Mac replied, as he followed the other detectives out of his office.

Leaving the precinct, Mac approached Ricco and said, "Exactly where is Mahoney's Pub?"

"It's about a twenty minute drive from here. Meanwhile, how about we get some lunch?"

"Sounds good to me," Louie replied heartily. "Where we gonna go?"

"Let Cavanaugh pick a place," said Ricco, "Cleveland's buying."

"Got any places that have great burgers?" Billy asked.

Louie placed his arm around Cavanaugh's shoulder and said smiling, "We got just the place...Bambi's Burgers." As they got into the car, the comical detective turned around and winked at MacTavish and Ricco.

Seated behind the steering wheel, Billy asked, "Bambi's Burgers...they serve venison there?"

"Yeah, in fact, they have the highest quality of meat in town," Louie answered, as they drove away talking about O'Hara and the case.

After a ten minute drive, Cavanaugh pulled into a very busy parking lot that resembled a '50s drive-in restaurant. A huge neon sign flashed *Bambi's Burgers 24 Hours.*

"Food must be good," said Billy, as he found a parking place and parked.

"I'll give you odds we won't care," mumbled Mac under his breath.

As the detectives got out of the car and walked towards the entrance, they could hear Huey Piano Smith's recording of *Don't You Just Know It* playing. The men let Cavanaugh enter first and watched as a well-endowed topless hostess, wearing only a g-string, approached him with a handful of menus. Surprised and a bit embarrassed, Cavanaugh laughed.

"Welcome to Bambi's. My name is Julie. Table for four?" she asked, while the young detective struggled to ignore the naked 38 DD's facing him.

Placing his hands on Cavanaugh's shoulders and shoving him forward, Mac said, "Four it is."

As she led them to a table, Louie snapped his fingers to the music and started dancing. Ricco joined Louie in a few dancing moves before the song ended. The '50s music, playing back to back without interruption, segued into Fats Domino's *Blueberry Hill*.

"How's this?" said Julie, seating them at a table close to the stage.

"Oh, it's great," Mac answered flirtatiously, focusing on her body as she bent over to light the candle on their table.

Handing them menus she said, "Your waitress will be here shortly."

"My dear Julie," Mac began, "could you do an old man a favor? When you walk away, could you do it very slowly?"

Walking away, she paused and looked back over her shoulder. "You're not an old man," she replied flirtingly. Taking a pencil off her menu list, she held it out in front of her. "Oops," she said slowly. "I seemed to have dropped my pencil."

Anticipating her next move, the four men watched as the pencil fell to the floor in what seemed to be a slow motion descent. Slowly and seductively, she picked up the pencil and continued to walk towards the entrance. The four men remained focused on the empty space where she had bent over until MacTavish spoke out. "I'm sure her pencil's not the only thing that got picked up."

Louie looked under the table and said jokingly, "Hey, we all got hard-ons."

Ricco grabbed him by the back of his jacket and yanked him up. "Just decide what you want for lunch," he said sarcastically.

Louie gave him an illicit smile and said, "I'd like a short brunette—"

"Food Louie, we're talking about food now."

"Right," smiled Louie.

Meanwhile, Cavanaugh had focused his eyes on the elevated dance floor where three semi-dressed girls in '50s outfits were dancing to Bill Doggett's *Honky Tonk (Part 2)*. Shaking his head, he looked at his fellow detectives and said, "I should have known...*Bambi's Burgers.*"

"My conclusion was confirmed when we pulled into the lot," smiled Mac. "No burger place could pack a parking lot like that."

"You get out much Kid?" asked Louie.

"Not that much," Mac interjected, "he's a little shy."

"That's okay," said Ricco, "Louie didn't get laid until he was twenty-two."

"Late bloomer?" smiled Mac.

"No," answered Ricco. "We couldn't find anyone who would have sex with him. We finally had to get him a prostitute."

Louie, surprisingly shocked at his partner's statement, said, "That girl was a hooker...you fixed me up with a hooker? Ricco, you told me she was a virgin!" As the three men laughed at the little Italian's antics, Louie said, "WHAT?" His expression only encouraged more laughter from the detectives. "You know," Louie said seriously, "I knew she was no virgin, cause no virgin would yell ride em' cowboy while I had my dick in her ass. Ricco, you should have told me she wasn't a

169

virgin; I would have got your money's worth. I held back thinking it was her first time. I can't believe you guys did that to me. Let's eat." Picking up a menu he said, "Oh-h, oh-h, I love this song," as Joe Turner's *Corrina Corrina* began playing. "You know, I once dated a girl named Corrina."

When the topless waitress appeared in front of them, the four men placed their orders very slowly. After she left, Ricco and Louie began discussing the family orientated precinct and the time Donatto picked up the tab for a fellow detective's wedding.

"That wedding set D back about fifty grand," said Ricco. "It went well except for one little setback."

"And that was?" Mac inquired.

"The wedding singer didn't show up and I had to fill in," Louie smiled gleefully.

"I could see where that could be setback," Mac mumbled.

"Louie's singing wasn't the problem," said Ricco. "He was quite good. The problem was, we couldn't get him off the damn stage. Everyone had gone and he was still singing to the clean-up crew."

"Yeah, I did," replied Louie sheepishly. "They really liked me."

"How could they not?" Mac laughed, as the men continued talking about their lives. Somewhat distracted by the nudity around him, Cavanaugh vaguely discussed the art of cow roping and bull riding.

After finishing their lunch, the detectives got up and made their way towards the exit. Cavanaugh took one last look at the girls on stage. Dancing their way to the car, Ricco and Louie harmonized together to the Drifters version of *Ruby Ruby* that was playing through the outside speakers. Listening to them sing, Cavanaugh realized that Louie did have a very good voice.

The ride back to the precinct was filled with the men singing of songs from the '50's. Louie did a great job singing *Please, Please, Please*—belting out the words as if he was on stage. One by one, they stopped singing and listened to Cavanaugh. Unaware they had stopped; he gave it a Delbert McClinton twist—singing very sexually *"please don't go..."* Smiling at each other, and impressed with the young detective's voice, they joined in and finished the song. Their musical lunch had temporarily distracted them from the seriousness of the Kingman case.

"You guys are really good. How long have you two been singing?" said Mac.

"We were kids together in New York," Louie answered. "We grew up singing on the corners in our neighborhood."

"Very good harmonization guys." said Billy, looking at him in the rearview mirror.

"You ain't so bad yourself," Ricco grinned.

Louie pulled out a small CD case out of his pocket. "Here Mac, throw this in. I have a sound studio at my place where I do my own mixing. I eliminate the voice tracks so I can sing without any competition. Push number eight, the song is *Once In A While* brought back by The Chimes in '61."

"Louie, you are not only talented, but also very informative," said Mac.

"Yeah, I get that a lot," he proudly replied.

The detectives laughed as they started singing again, with Louie taking the lead. As they drove towards the precinct, their voices carried through the air. *"Once in a while, would you try to give one little thought to me..."*

After they arrived back at the Cleveland precinct, the four detectives quickly re-directed their focus back on the Kingman case. In the homicide headquarters, MacTavish sat with Ricco at his computer—reviewing the data files on serial bombers.

Back at the One Nine, Keaton was answering her cell phone. Recognizing the caller, she said, "Billy, how's it going?"

"Okay so far. Do me a favor and get me whatever you can on that warehouse explosion Mac and I were involved in? We're pretty sure it's the same people. I need to know if there's any connection between Kingman and that photographer Austin."

"Sure," she said. "When are you guys coming back?"

"Christ, I don't know, he sighed. "We're all trying to put this thing together. The theory is that our two homicides, Kingman and Austin, are definitely related. This forensic profiler is positive that the same people are involved in both explosions. We have a meeting with him tonight to discuss it."

"Shawn O'Hara?" she questioned curiously.

"You know him?"

"You might say that. I met him when I was vacationing in Miami last year—haven't heard from him since."

Cavanaugh detected that something personal was going on. A sudden silence fell over the both of them until he said, "Vic...you okay?"

"Yeah," she answered. "I just hoped the fucker was dead."

Cavanaugh reacted with a startled expression. "What did you say?"

"Look, I didn't really mean that I wanted him dead."

"Vickie, if he's done anything to hurt you—"

"No Billy," she interrupted. "It's not about him. It's about me. My expectations of him were too high. He was very open with me and I guess I didn't believe him, or maybe I thought spending a week with me would change his mind. I fell in love and he didn't. The man walked away just like he told me he would. I'm sorry Billy; I didn't mean to unload all of this on you. I guess I'm not quite over him—something I need to work on. Life sure can throw you a curve when you least expect it."

Cavanaugh's brotherly protection kicked in, and since no one else knew about her affair, he wanted to reinforce her trust. Softly he said, "Vickie, I want you to know that this goes no further than right here."

"Thanks, I appreciate that. You're a good friend. I'll start researching that warehouse case and get back to you. And Billy..."

"Yeah?"

"Thanks for letting me vent," she said, disconnecting the call.

Cavanaugh looked at the phone before he put it down. He couldn't help being concerned with what happened to her—even if she left herself open to it. As he turned towards the computer, he saw his partner approaching.

"Grab your jacket Kid," said Mac. "We're going to High Tea.

"We're going to what?" Billy said, putting on his jacket.

"High Tea at Mahoney's Pub," replied Mac.

As they made their way to the exit, Ricco and Louie joined them. Leaving the precinct, Ricco filled his partner in on the High Tea meeting.

"What the fuck is High Tea?" said Louie.

While they all walked towards the car, Mac explained, "It's a British thing Louie. A place where you go and have tea served to you along with cucumber sandwiches and scones."

Louie leaned over to Ricco and said in a low voice, "Is he fucking kidding—cucumber sandwiches and ice cream cones?"

"Yeah, he's kidding," said Ricco nodding his head. "We're going to Mahoney's Pub."

"Well I hope he is," whispered Louie, as they reached the car. "Cause he ain't gonna find no fuckin' cucumbers and ice cream at Mahoney's."

"I need directions," said Billy, getting in and starting the car.

"When you leave the lot, take a right," replied Ricco from the backseat. "I'll update you as we go."

"Did I hear you say you wanted an ice cream cone Louie?" Mac inquired.

"No not me," said Louie. "I thought you wanted one."

"Me," said Mac, "whatever gave you that—"

Before he could finish, Ricco leaned forward and whispered, "This is one of those times Mac. You don't want to go there."

"Right," he agreed.

"Hang a left at the next block Kid," directed Ricco. "It's on the south side of the street."

Meanwhile, at Mahoney's Pub, O'Hara was throwing darts with one of the waiters. "Have time for another game?" asked the waiter, as O'Hara threw his final dart dead center.

"No," said Shawn, as he looked at his watch. "But thanks for the game mate."

"Anytime Shawn," he answered, putting the darts away.

O'Hara slowly moved to the bar and ordered a beer. Pulling out a wad of bills, he handed the bartender a five-dollar bill. "Keep it," he said to the bartender, who tried to give him change. Picking up his beer, he headed for a large red leather booth. Sliding into the booth, he saw the four detectives walking towards him.

"What, no tea?" smiled Mac.

"I didn't know what brand you liked," Shawn said, taking a swig of his beer.

"You're the profiler," Mac grinned, sliding into the booth as the dart playing waiter approached.

"What'll it be for your friends Shawn?"

"Scotch all around and five imported beers. And be sure to bring a couple of glasses with water and ice."

"I knew you were too good not to know what we drank," smiled Mac, watching the waiter leave. "So Shawn, what's your view on this explosion?"

"Well, it was an almost perfect job—beautifully constructed. They didn't count on early arrivals and anyone seeing the sweep. The things remaining in the house were left to give the evidence of normality after the explosion.

When the waiter returned with their drinks, Ricco said, "I got it," and paid the bill.

O'Hara remained quiet until the waiter walked away. "This was no ordinary hit and clean-up," he continued. "It was very well orchestrated. I've looked into that warehouse incident; I believe you're dealing with the same group of people."

Looking at the New York detectives, Ricco said, "You know, you guys never did tell us about the warehouse. Want to fill me and Louie in?"

Cavanaugh took the lead and explained the whole story—carefully leaving out the humorous details concerning Mac's *Monty Python* look and behavior.

"Is there any connection between Kingman and this Austin guy," said Ricco.

"I believe there is," Shawn answered, "and so does the Agency."

"This could be very big," said Louie.

"And very dangerous," declared Shawn. "You guys may have seen something in that house and that warehouse you weren't supposed to see." The men all looked at each other, wondering if there was something, anything that could give them a lead on who was responsible. "These people don't usually leave loose ends," Shawn continued. "You guys need to watch your backs. And don't be opening any more doors too fast. I don't believe they'll do anything that could endanger the lives of innocent people."

"You're sure about this," said Mac.

"As sure as I can be," Shawn replied. "It would happen in an isolated area like the warehouse or the Kingman house, and it would have to appear like an accident. I am sure of one thing; they don't want any type of notoriety."

MacTavish raised his eyebrows suspiciously. He was concerned about the life-threatening position he and Cavanaugh were in.

Observing MacTavish's demeanor, O'Hara tried to relieve his anxiety. Smiling he said, "If you like, I'll start your car up for you when we leave."

"We just might do that!" snapped Billy, as he thought about Vickie.

O'Hara could tell by Cavanaugh's attitude that something was bothering him. And whatever it was, it needed to be resolved. "You seem to have a problem with me Cavanaugh, would you care to discuss it?"

MacTavish immediately tried to defend his partner. "Look, the Kid is tired. We've had a rough week."

Cavanaugh's stare was filled with anger, as he thought about Vickie. "Yeah it's been a rough week Mac, but I'm not too tired to take on this asshole."

Stunned by his partner's statement, MacTavish immediately took control of the situation. Standing up abruptly, he grabbed Cavanaugh's arm and pulled him out of the booth. "Brooklyn, we need to talk. Let's take a walk. Excuse us," he said to the others, pulling his partner aside.

Cavanaugh shoved his partner away and reluctantly walked towards the Men's Room with MacTavish following closely behind. As they entered, Cavanaugh slammed the door against the wall.

"WHAT THE HELL WAS ALL THAT ABOUT," yelled Mac? "HAVE YOU LOST YOUR MIND?"

Unable to reveal what he knew about O'Hara and Vickie, Billy turned away and yelled, "HE'S A FUCKING ASSHOLE AND I'M NOT GONNA WORK WITH HIM."

MacTavish grabbed him by the neck and forced him to the sink. Pushing his head down into the sink and under the faucet, he held it there, running cold water over it.

"You're lucky I didn't shove your head in the fucking toilet," said Mac, releasing his hold. "What the hell has gotten into you?"

Cavanaugh, shocked by his partner's behavior, tried to justify his outburst. Standing up with a drenched face, he confronted his partner. "You don't understand Mac, that guy really is an asshole and if you knew—"

"Knew what...that the asshole is one of us," said Mac. "I'm not crazy about the bastard either, but I believe he can help us stay alive a little bit longer." Taking a deep breath, he softened his attitude and said, "You've got to admit that we almost heard the fat lady sing twice now. Look Kid, I don't know what's bothering you, but you just can't go off on someone. Everyone deserves the right to know what the problem is. You and I have been around plenty of assholes, but I've never seen you take one of them this seriously. There's something else going on here," he said, trying to rationalize Cavanaugh's outburst. "When you're ready to talk about it let me know. Or even better, let O'Hara know. Now dry your fucking head and get back out there. And Brooklyn," he added, holding the bathroom door open. "You do owe that Irish asshole an apology."

Drying his face, Billy said, "Okay Mac, I'll take care of it."

"Good. See you back at The Alamo?"

Nodding yes, Billy said, "Just give me a minute."

"Take all the time you need. Just come back as my partner."

Staring at himself in the mirror Billy thought, "Well that was really stupid. Here Vickie puts her trust in you, and you do everything to let both precincts know about her affair. Christ!" Taking a deep breath, he turned around and threw the paper towels in the trash. After walking out of the bathroom, he went back to the dining area. As he approached the booth another round of drinks was being served. He quickly directed his conversation to O'Hara. "Let me get that," he said, pulling two twenty-dollar bills out of his jeans. "It's the least I can do after what just happened. My apologies Shawn, a lot has been building up—professionally and personally. I guess I just lost it."

"No problem," Shawn replied, "We've all gone ballistic at times."

Seeing the coldness that covered Cavanaugh as he sat down, MacTavish gave him a reaffirming look of their bathroom discussion—watching as his partner grabbed a beer and chugged it down.

"Pray there are no more victims," said Shawn, re-opening their previous conversation. "This could get very complicated."

"It's not finished," interjected Billy.

"Beg your pardon?" Shawn asked quietly.

"The homicides," said Billy, as MacTavish breathed a sigh of relief. "These people aren't finished."

"And what makes you think that?" questioned Shawn

"Call it intuition," Billy responded nonchalantly.

"Well then, we all better be very careful in our movements," said Shawn, finishing his drink.

"You guys believe in that intuition stuff?" asked Louie.

"I do," replied Shawn. "It's saved my life many times."

"As it's done mine," Mac added, lifting his glass of scotch in tribute.

Billy lifted his beer and made a toast, "All for one and one for all." Smiling, the men lifted their glasses, honoring Cavanaugh's toast.

"Yeah," laughed Louie, "Like the Musketeers, all for one and one for all. Hey, we might as well eat while we're here, any objections?"

"Sounds good to me," responded Mac, as the other men nodded no.

"Then let's order," said Louie, Waving the waiter over and ordering five orders of fish and chips, mushy peas and more drinks.

MacTavish observed O'Hara's silence and took the opportunity to be more sociable. "So Shawn...you basically work out of Miami?"

"Right," Shawn answered, quickly diverting the conversation away from himself. "How is everything in New York?"

"If you're referring to 9-11," said Mac, "it's coming together."

"Were you there when it happened?" Louie inquired.

"No, I was in Boston," said Mac "I took some down time."

"And you Cavanaugh?" said Shawn.

"I was out west," Billy replied, fiddling with his beer bottle.

"The Kid follows rodeo competitions," interjected Mac.

"Actually, I spent some time on the road." Billy corrected. "Nevada had a drought and wild mustangs needed to be rounded up and relocated. The horses were dying from starvation and dehydration. I'm licensed by the Bureau of Land Management," he said modestly. "I go in whenever I'm needed."

"So, relocating these horses is that important?" inquired Louie enthusiastically.

"You gotta understand Louie, these wild horses date back to the 1700s—they're what's left of the old west. Without food and water, they would have been extinct within weeks. Facilities were needed in other states until they could be relocated back to Nevada, so I put a few of them on a ranch in Montana and took the rest to a reserve in Wyoming. Just trying to do my part to save what's left of our wildlife," he said modestly.

"You're a hell of a guy, you know that?" Louie said proposing a toast. "To Kid Cavanaugh," he grinned, as they all lifted their drinks—acknowledging the Montana cowboy turned detective.

"So Shawn," Mac began, "I understand you were born in Ireland."

"And you Mac were born in Scotland," smiled Shawn.

"Would you care to talk about your affiliation with the IRA?"

Challenging MacTavish, Shawn said, "You want to talk about your affiliation with British Intelligence?"

"I guess it's a stalemate," laughed Mac.

"So, Shawn," Louie interjected with a snicker, "What about you being a member of the Green Berets?"

"And Louie, would you like to discuss your Mob ties?"

Shocked and surprised, Louie leaned over and whispered to his partner, "I thought all that stuff was sealed."

"Nothing's sealed to other agents when you become part of the Agency," smiled Ricco. "You did read the fine print?"

"There was fine print?" Louie said seriously.

"Louie," said Ricco, "it's just a figure of speech."

Cavanaugh, taken aback about what he heard said, "You want to explain why our past becomes public knowledge?"

"Not public," Ricco answered, "only open to the WASP detectives. There's a feeling of security when you know everything about the guys you're working with. It puts us all on equal ground."

"So Shawn, I'm guessing what you don't want to talk about are all those innocent people you killed in Ireland?" said Billy, still carrying a bit of an attitude.

"I can see you're not very knowledgeable about terrorists," Shawn said softly.

"Oh I know what terrorists did to New York City."

"You're angry about that are ya?"

"Fuckin' right I am."

"You are of Irish heritage are you not?"

Billy gave him a slight nod and said, "Yeah, what's that got to do with anything?"

"Were you not angry when you found out about our forefathers—yours and mine?" Shawn said, in a low and quiet tone. "When the Irish and other immigrants came here, not only did they steal the land from its Native Americans, but went on to slaughter them. Those immigrants, our forefathers, nearly caused the buffalo to become extinct—the very animal that contributed the Indian's food, clothing and shelter. Those Indians who were left, were lied to, disrespected, treated like criminals...then relocated to land the government felt wouldn't be needed. And when that land was needed, they were herded again to another location. Are you angry with the government that gave them blankets contaminated with smallpox? Tell me Cavanaugh; was Custer a hero, or a fucking sadistic, racist, murdering prick?"

The detectives were captivated by O'Hara's rebuttal. Everyone remained silent as he continued his historic narration.

"Most of our ancestors came here from Ireland in the early 1900s," he continued. "This country was painted as Shangri-La. When my grandparents landed in New York City, they found it to be a haven of madness and violence. People were living like animals under the very dictatorships of other Irish people who were in control of the streets. My father was only eight when he saw his twenty-five year old mother raped and killed by her own people. My grandfather could take no more, so he packed up my father and his twin sister and sailed back to Ireland. Shangri-la turned out to be Devils Island. I'm talkin' about the island of Manhattan."

A deep silence hung over the men as the Irishman brought up issues that all the men could relate to.

Leaning into the table, O'Hara spoke directly to Cavanaugh. "If you believe in Karma, and I think you do, you must know that for every action there is a reaction. America is responsible for unmentionable crimes that only she will have to pay for. Lying to its people for decades has created a payback situation. If we as a people refuse to take responsibility for our actions, and I'm referring to all governments everywhere, we will all have to pay a horrible price. Does this country take care of its homeless or the veterans of the very wars they themselves have created? No...not like they should be taken care of. This country definitely falls short in that area. They spend billions of dollars supplying money to the very countries that are war orientated. Which brings me to the topic of gasless vehicles," he continued. "They've squashed those discoveries for years. Is anything made here anymore? The majority of products are made outside of this country. America has become very lazy, depending on other countries to produce what they need. When in fact, they're creating a future society of helpless humans. If some planetary aspect destroyed every country but this one, America and its people would become extinct for lack of self-sufficiency. It's just not your government that really doesn't give a fuck about the people as a whole, it's a global problem. Have you ever thought about how governments come clean when most people don't care anymore? Instead of being outraged, people have become desensitized.

Suddenly, Cavanaugh began to understand the man he thought he hated just twenty minutes ago. In so many ways, he felt the same way. He had always been sympathetic to the Native American's plight, and believed that all veterans—of all wars—who were drafted or joined any armed service, should have free lifetime medical, dental, and vision coverage from whomever wherever they chose to go to. He would also like to see that the Veterans Hospitals have the finest, if not the best, medical staff possible, so injured and sick service men and women could live out there lives with a well deserved dignity.

"And about my involvement with the IRA," Shawn continued, "I joined after my wife was murdered because of my political beliefs. She was four months pregnant when they put a fucking bullet through her head. I not only lost my wife that night, but also my unborn twins. I was beaten, tortured, and left for dead. So instead of just talking about my beliefs...I became physically involved."

"You have some very strong opinions about mankind," Mac responded.

"I have some serious issues with governments that not only use its people for their own agendas, but also turn around and abuse them," said Shawn. "This whole fucking planet is in trouble and the day of Armageddon is at hand."

Mac lifted his glass of scotch and said, "To a man who's not afraid to lay it on the line...to Shawn O'Hara."

"You ought to go into politics," Ricco said grinning, as they all raised their drinks for the toast.

"You must be kidding," smiled Shawn. "If I did, you men would probably be investigating my murder."

"I was getting to that part, but you beat me to it," laughed Ricco.

As the waiter brought their food, the men changed the topic of conversation. Cavanaugh, taking a bite of his fish, observed O'Hara conversing and laughing with MacTavish.

..."*Sounds like you got your tit caught in a ringer*—it's a very old Scottish joke," smiled Mac.

Ricco and Louie were in a deep conversation about the fish they were eating—Louie's was giving his point of view. "I'm telling you, this fish is from the Louisiana Gulf. I know my fish!" he argued.

As Cavanaugh looked around the table, he saw the connection they all had to each other. Their opinions seemed to coincide with the universal needs of humanity. "O'Hara's not so bad," he thought. "He wants what we all want, a world where people are not used as pawns in a corporate and political chess game. This man has strong and sincere views. Definitely not the man Vickie described—one who would lead a girl on and then dump her." He made a decision to talk to her about the Irish asshole he now identified with. An expression his mother always used came into his mind...*more shall be revealed.* As MacTavish told one of his war stories, Cavanaugh let go of his defensive thoughts and became more relaxed.

..."So here we are in the middle of this drug bust," said Mac. "It was two in the morning and I'm trying not to look at this really hot hooker in a very short mini-skirt. She was standing between me and two perps. My old partner had them covered from behind. I politely asked the woman to move. Now mind you, I was pointing my gun at her. Well...she became all hysterical and dropped her purse. She turned her back to me, bent over, and while picking it up, revealed a skimpy thong on a bare ass. Suddenly it broke, and out fell the biggest damn dick I'd ever seen."

"So what did you do?" smiled Ricco.

"I tackled the prick," laughed Mac. "He was part of the bust, only somebody forgot to tell us."

"So like Mac," asked Louie wiping tears from his eyes, "did you get hot when you tackled him?" His comment forced Cavanaugh to choke on his food.

Mac leaned into the table and said, "Even if I did swing both ways, I wouldn't have taken on that torpedo-carrying queen."

Everyone was roaring with laughter, when Louie cried out, "You're a scream Mac." Holding his chest he said, "Oh-h-h the pain."

O'Hara looked over to the window and observed a black SUV that was parked outside. He watched as an unrecognizable figure lit a cigarette and slowly drove out of the parking space. As another round of drinks were brought to the table, Louie told the guys about his elementary years in a Catholic school, and how his education ended abruptly when he told a Nun to go fuck herself.

As the evening went on, an Irish band had joined the festivities in the crowded Pub. The five detectives spent the rest of the evening drinking, enjoying the music, and playing darts. Needless to say, it was O'Hara who won all the dart challenges.

ಬಂಚ

REVELATIONS

AND

EXPLANATIONS

The next morning at the Ritz Carlton, Cavanaugh was awakened by his partner singing in the shower. Yawning, he stretched his arms above his head and climbed out of bed. "I guess this is my wake up call," said Billy.

"ORDER US BREAKFAST," Mac yelled out from his room.

"How the hell did he know I was up?" Billy said quietly. "OKAY," he yelled back, as he picked up the phone and called room service. After requesting bacon and eggs for two, he rushed back into his own bathroom and shouted, "IT'LL BE HERE IN TWENTY MINUTES."

"GREAT," Mac replied, as he grabbed a black terrycloth robe from the bathroom shelf and slipped it on. Tying it, he walked into the living room and turned on the TV.

A male newscaster was highlighting the events of a recent fire. ..."the fire occurred roughly around two in the morning in this shopping center. The fabric store was engulfed in flames, but luckily, it didn't spread to the surrounding stores. Faulty wiring is suspected and there were no injuries."

"Enough," said Mac as he sat down on the couch and changed the channel. "I need to find some breakfast entertainment." He surfed the channels until he found an old English sitcom.

Cavanaugh, still damp from his shower, walked into the living room with only a towel wrapped around his waist. "Oh, the dead parrot bit," he said, sitting down on the opposite end of the couch.

"Yes," Mac responded, "there's nothing like having a *Monty Python* performance start your day." Glancing over at his partner, he did a double take—eyeing the numerous tattoos that covered Cavanaugh's body.

"What can I say?" Billy responded, looking at his various inked areas. "I got really drunk one night."

"Must have been a hell of a long night," said Mac, as he continued watching TV.

A knock on the door interrupted their conversation. "Food's here," smiled Billy, jumping up and answering the door.

"Easy," said Mac, "we don't want that towel to fall off. I'd hate to see what else you have full of ink."

Cavanaugh smiled, as he refastened his towel tighter and opened the door.

"Good Morning Gentlemen, my name is Ricky," he said, as he pushed an elegant breakfast cart into the suite.

"Be right back," Billy muttered, rushing back to his room. Flipping off the towel, he slipped into the bottom half of his Led Zeppelin pajamas.

"Smells great," said Mac, as Ricky placed their breakfast on the dining room table. "I'll sign," he smiled, slipping Ricky a twenty-dollar tip. "I believe you've covered everything very nicely."

"Thank you, said Ricky leaving the suite, and if you need anything else, just give us a call. You gentlemen have a nice day."

"You too Ricky," Billy responded, as he rushed back into the room and sat down at the table.

"I'm starved," said Mac, joining him.

"It's all that vocalizing you did in the shower," Billy said sarcastically,

"So, how drunk did you get before you took the needle?" said Mac, pointing his fork across the table at Billy's tattoos.

Cavanaugh looked at the different designs covering his torso and arms and replied, "Very drunk."

"Was there a woman involved?"

"Yes. She had fifty-two tattoos and the only way she'd let me fuck her was if I had a substantial amount on my body too," he replied flippantly.

"I hope she was worth the ink," Mac smirked.

"I'd rather talk about your singing in the shower," Billy counteracted, while biting into a strip of bacon.

"Well I am rather good," bragged Mac.

"On a scale of one to ten...I'd give you a six...and your dog a ten."

"There's no need to be rude Brooklyn."

"Rude? Rude is singing louder than my damn alarm clock."

"Oh I'm sorry. Did I disturb your beauty sleep?" said Mac arrogantly, as he picked up a cup of coffee.

Pushing away his empty plate, Billy got up from the table and said, "Its okay, next time I'll bring my ear plugs."

Surprised by his partner's statement, Mac quizzed him. "You wear ear plugs at night?"

Cavanaugh moved around behind his partner and put his arms around his neck. "Only when I know I'm going to wake up to your singing dear."

As Cavanaugh removed his hands and headed for his room, Mac asked sweetly, "Is there anything I can do for you dear? Scrub your back, massage your feet...give you a BJ?"

The young detective didn't turn around until he reached his bedroom. "Not until you grow tits and lose your dick," he replied, closing the door behind him.

"He never ceases to amaze me," Mac mumbled. "A little crude at times, but he does get his point across."

Standing erect, MacTavish walked towards the large panoramic window and looked out at the city. "There's information out there somewhere," he thought. "After all, a man can't live in a city for over twenty-five years and not have a relationship with anyone—what the hell was he doing in New York?" As he deliberated about the case, his face suddenly brightened up. "Of course," he smiled, "this homicide has nothing to do with Cleveland, it's all about New York. Thank you Ms. Cleveland," he said, giving the city a military salute. Turning around, he rushed back to his room and started getting dressed.

"BROOKLYN," he yelled out. "The Kid must have found his fucking ear plugs," he mumbled, as he walked into his partner's room.

Wearing jeans and a Levi jacket that covered his black tee shirt, Cavanaugh was on the phone having a serious discussion. "Okay," he said, sounding a little upset while pulling on his black python western boots. "Look I don't mean to cut you off, but I gotta go. See you soon."

Disconnecting the call, Cavanaugh focused on MacTavish standing there completely dressed, except for his slacks. Staring at his designer silk boxer shorts, he smiled and said, "Is there a problem Mac?"

"No, not with me. But it sounds like you have one."

"Just a friend with some issues, nothing for you to get concerned about," said Billy, still puzzled by his partner's attire. Looking at his partner's hairy bare legs, he said, "Is this how we're supposed to dress for today...because if it is, I think I need to take off of my jeans."

MacTavish looked down at his silk underwear and then back to his partner. "Oh just...fuck off!" he said, walking back to his bedroom.

"Hey, I wasn't the one who walked in here in my shorts," laughed Billy.

"Listen, I've just figured something out," said Mac, as he slipped into his slacks.

"That I'm not attracted to you," smiled Billy, walking into the living room.

Ignoring his partner's whimsical statement, Mac continued getting dressed and said, "We need tickets."

"Tickets," Billy said playfully, "taking me to the theatre is not going to change my mind. I'm just not attracted to you."

Walking into the living room, MacTavish stopped suddenly and gave his partner an unreceptive look. "Tickets for the plane that will take us back to New York," he said firmly.

"I'm sorry," sighed Billy. "Was I playing to hard to get? Can't we spend a few more days together?"

Mac dropped his head in frustration. "Since you've decided to do your stand-up comedy routine, I see no reason to continue this discussion."

"Okay, okay," Billy said seriously. "So why are we leaving this investigation?"

"Because there's no investigation here," Mac said calmly.

"And you came to that conclusion because—"

"Listen Kid, whoever planned this has had five days to clean up his real home wherever the hell it is. I'll tell you where it's not; it's not in fucking Cleveland."

"Then all his identification...that was to jam us up," said Billy.

"Don't feel bad;" said Mac, "we were all misled—including two precincts and one intense Irish bloke.

"Should we notify the One Nine?" said Billy.

"No," Mac replied. "We're in WASP now. I think the best profile is a low one until we get back to New York. However, we do need to inform our wise guys. They're probably wondering what happened to us. Grabbing his jacket off the chair, he said, "We need to leave. Are you ready?"

"Yeah, let's go," Billy replied, following his partner out of the suite.

As they walked down the hall and headed for the elevators, MacTavish questioned his partner about his earlier phone call. Always one step ahead of him, he knew Cavanaugh occasionally skirted around the truth. "Was that Vickie you were talking to earlier?"

"Nothing slips by you, does it?" said Billy, as he tried to steer clear of any discussion about his personal call. "There's enough drama going on," he thought.

"I believe Vickie's interested in one of us and it must be you. After all, I am old enough to be her father," said Mac, as they got into the elevator.

"Don't you mean old enough to be her great grandfather?" smiled Billy. Reaching into his jacket, he pulled out his cigarettes just as the elevator doors closed.

They were still arguing when the elevator reached the lobby. "No," said Billy adamantly when the doors opened. "For the last time, I am not interested in her—we're just friends. Why do you assume some big affair is about to start?" As they walked towards the rental car, he threw Mac the car keys and said, "You drive. And why does the woman have to be interested in anyone?"

Getting into the driver's seat, MacTavish started the car and continued debating the issue. "I've studied women all my life, which is a hell of a lot longer than you've been around. That young lady has a deep interest in a man, and if it's not one of us, then you need to tell me who the hell he is?"

Looking out the window, Cavanaugh closed his eyes—realizing that his strong denial assured his partner that Vickie's interest was in

193

someone else. He also knew that because of his partner's stubborn Scottish attitude, he wouldn't quit prying until he found out who it was. "Fuck, I fell right into his hands," he thought.

As they drove through traffic, Mac glanced over to his partner and said, "Well Kid...who is it?"

"You know, I hate when you do this to me? Now I'm trapped into telling you something I promised not to tell."

"I'm a detective for Christ's sake; it's my nature to inquire. Besides...I'm a Scot."

"And you read minds, damn you're good," Billy smiled.

"I know," confirmed Mac proudly.

"Okay," said Billy hesitantly. But you have to promise that you won't mention it to anyone, including him."

"You've got my word. Who is him?"

"Shawn O'Hara."

Stunned by the answer, MacTavish slammed on the brakes. The sudden stop threw Cavanaugh slightly forward. "You're serious," said Mac.

"Yeah," replied Billy, readjusting himself in the seat. "Maybe we should discuss this when you're not driving."

"Christ, I would have never put those two together," he said, ignoring Cavanaugh's request.

As MacTavish continued driving, he listened with great curiosity while his partner described the two-week affair Vickie shared with O'Hara. "Evidently it all happened when she was in Miami."

"A good thing to remember," said Mac, as he pulled into the Cleveland precinct parking lot, "is that in life; there are two sides to every affair, one is hers, and the other is his. And until you hear both sides, you shouldn't form an opinion. So that phone call you had last night...it was from Vickie?"

"God, he never lets up," Billy thought as he paused for a moment and once again diverted the question. "Relationships...they're not easy are they?"

Mac, realizing his partner had taken the situation personally, said, "No they're not. You see mate, you already broke the golden rule by choosing to side with Vickie without hearing O'Hara's version. You're lucky he didn't retaliate like I did. Sorry about the head dunking, but I felt you needed cooling off."

"It's okay. You were right. I shouldn't have jammed Shawn up like that."

"You're a good person Brooklyn, and now you're learning how to be a really good detective. It's a twenty-four hour job, and sometimes you need to apply the principles of being a detective into your personal life too. Let it pass and start your day over," he said, parking the car.

Walking towards the precinct, MacTavish looked down at Cavanaugh's new snakeskin boots and said, "Nice footwear Kid. You're the only guy I know that travels with more boots than clothes."

"Yeah, like you got room to talk with your Dolce Gabbana designer shoes. Just how many pairs do you own?"

Meanwhile, inside the precinct, Ricco was standing at the front desk. "Toni," he said to the female officer behind the desk, "when our New York detectives come in, send them back to us."

"Sure Ricco," she replied, as he headed back to the WASP office—missing Cavanaugh and MacTavish by only a few minutes.

"Give me a break," said Billy, still discussing boots and shoes with his partner as they entered the precinct. "If you can put out a grand for your shoes, I can certainly put out a couple of hundred for my boots."

Officer Toni Morelli was on the phone at the front desk when the two men walked by her. "Hold on for a minute," she said, covering the phone with her hand. Seeing her, MacTavish dropped his head and kept walking. "Detectives," she called out, trying to get their attention and looking anxiously at MacTavish. As Cavanaugh stopped to see what she wanted, Toni said softly, "Ricco wants you in the back."

Staring at her curiously, Cavanaugh thanked her and quickly rushed down the hallway to catch up to his partner. "Is it me," said Billy, "or do all the cops in this precinct remind you of New York hoods and their families? I haven't seen one person working in this precinct that isn't an Italian offspring.

"Good perception Watson, took you long enough to realize that."

"And that Officer Morelli, she acted like she knew you."

"Probably a case of mistaken identity," Mac answered abruptly.

"Yeah...you're probably right," said Billy, as they stood in front of the WASP security doors. "Her with that jet black hair...she's definitely not your type, probably thought you were Sean Connery."

Seeing them on an overhead screen, Ricco buzzed them in and said, "Hey, how's it going?"

"Great," replied Mac.

Ricco opened a desk drawer and pulled out two airline tickets. "These are for you," he said, tossing them to MacTavish. "It's your tickets for home. You leave tonight on the ten-thirty flight. I had a small revelation while talking to O'Hara this morning."

"Really?" Mac smiled, pulling out a chair and sitting down.

"What's the revelation?" probed Billy, as he and MacTavish exchanged glances.

"I think we're missing the boat here," clarified Ricco. "I have a feeling that Kingman's home is somewhere else. It sure as hell ain't here."

Mac smiled at Cavanaugh and said, "Do you see what happens when exceptional detectives think alike and work together towards a common solution?"

"It's called Universal Consciousness," Billy substantiated.

Ricco, puzzled by their conversation, said, "Am I missing something here?"

"Holmes came up with your same theory this morning," said Billy "You said you spoke to O'Hara. So, where is he?"

"He had a fire call this morning," Ricco explained. "A fabric store across town got flamed."

"I saw it on the news this morning," interrupted Mac. "It had something to do with faulty wiring."

"That's what the media got," Ricco said, sitting down on his desk. "However, O'Hara penned it as arson."

"Any leads?" said Billy.

"No," Ricco answered, shaking his head. "We'll be talking to him shortly. He gave us permission to Catfish his work.

"Catfish..." Billy said curiously.

"That's our term for satellite tracking someone. Let's go to the big screen and I'll give you a crash course," said Ricco, leading them into their space command center.

"I'll bet the FBI would love to have this state of the art technology," Billy smiled.

"More like ASOTA technology," Louie answered, as he entered and joined them in the center of the room. "How you guys doin'?"

"We're good Louie. So what's this ASOTA?" Billy inquired.

"Alien State of the Art—a system that was confiscated from Hanger 51 in Nevada," said Louie.

"Are you saying that this system has something to do with Alien aircraft?" Billy smiled.

Louie looked at Ricco for his approval to answer. "It's true," acknowledged Ricco. "WASP has an underground division—a Special Forces unit that accomplishes things we can't get involved in."

"Like stealing alien aircraft from the government," said Mac.

"Yeah," Ricco answered deviously.

"I like that," said Billy. "After all, it's not stealing when the government says it doesn't exist."

Smiling at the humorous side of the situation, Cavanaugh looked around the room. In the center was a large circular desk with highly sophisticated electronic chairs that encircled the table. At the head of the table was a giant, one inch thick, flat screened television that descended down from the ceiling when the system was activated. Simultaneously, a round, computerized board rose up in front of each chair for individual viewing.

"This here is what we call The Round Table," said Ricco, sitting down in one of the high-back leather chairs.

"Knights Of The Round Table," Mac responded smiling, "very appropriate."

Cavanaugh noticed several hand scans throughout the room. "You use all these scanners?"

"All except the BT Scanner," said Louie. "That one's for un-welcomed intruders. Scanning it triggers Miami security and lock down begins immediately."

"And BT stands for—" inquired Billy.

"Bad Timing," Louie smiled.

"Louie, did you have anything to do with naming this equipment?" laughed Billy.

"Yeah, I also came up with Catfish," he grinned proudly.

Standing up, Ricco moved forward to the screen and opened up the main unit. "This system not only records your handprint but also matches it to your bone structure—only a living hand can be cleared. Over here," said Ricco, while entering his personal code and pointing to the digital EDB code box, "The eye detector box will open up when your code clears." As a high-tech silver container appeared before them, and an optic scanner popped up for visual identification of the retina and pupil. "Once completed, you're in. I'll show you how this works." As he placed his eyes into the EDB box, a rainbow of light passed in front of his eyes. The light quickly disappeared and emitted a chime. "When you hear the chime," he said, pulling back, "you're done."

"Tell me," said Mac, "what happens if they're eyes don't match up?"

"You don't want to know," Louie quickly interjected.

Turning to Ricco, Mac said, "Oh, but I do want to know."

"I'm telling you, you don't want to know," mumbled Louie.

"It'll send a laser beam into your optic nerve, destroying your vision," Ricco answered.

Bowled over by the remark, Mac staggered and said, "You can't be serious."

"I said you wouldn't want to know," Louie sighed. "Shouldn't have told him," he whispered to Cavanaugh.

Showing his unsettling concern about the EDB, Mac raised his left eyebrow and said, "And this is supposedly safe?"

"This highly classified system has been in operation over five years now with no casualties," said Ricco. "We're not out to blind anyone Mac, Miami can close down all WASP centers in a matter of seconds."

"Are we already programmed?" Billy inquired.

"No," responded Ricco, "that'll be done in Florida after your branch is launched."

"So how's this training work," said Billy. "Do we take turns going down there?"

"It depends on availability," said Ricco. "Two of your crew has already been programmed—one you know about."

Cavanaugh and MacTavish looked at each other. "Vickie," they said simultaneously.

"Her two week vacation," Billy confirmed with a nod. "Well that explains a lot," he thought.

"Getting back to the training process," said Ricco, "you'll get an authorized two week vacation in beautiful Miami."

"If you think this is something, wait 'till you get a load of what they have down there," said Louie.

"Hey Mac, how's Miami sound for a vacation?" Billy laughed.

"Perfect," replied Mac. "Do me a favor Kid. Go online and get me a Florida location of shark infested waters so I can throw you in when we get there."

"Here we go, said Louie, as he sat down at one of the keyboards and started to Rap while entering information into the system.

"Miami you know is very cool, except when it's hot, and then it's not. I go to the beach in the family car, but I really could have walked cause it ain't that far. Check it out. Check it out."

The three detectives stared at him—hoping he would stop. Mac shook his head and whispered to Ricco, "Are you sure it's safe to have him on this system?"

"Don't underestimate his talents," laughed Ricco. "He's extremely knowledgeable. Miami offered him a permanent position."

"Okay, here we go," said Louie, rapidly typing in the needed information and programming O'Hara's cell phone into the system.

Within seconds, the screen displayed the fabric store and O'Hara answering his cell phone. "Shawn here," he said, pulling off his latex gloves.

"You're on," informed Ricco, connecting the call to an overhead speaker.

Smiling, O'Hara waved at them and did a comical Irish jig.

"So now you're dancing in rubbish," said Mac.

"That I am mate," Shawn smiled. "So what do you think of the system?"

"Very impressive," responded Mac. "My only concern is the EDB. It doesn't give me a warm and fuzzy feeling."

"We all felt that way at first Mac, when you get to Miami you'll see how fool proof and safe it really is."

"Any idea who's responsible for the fire?" said Ricco.

"From what I have so far, I believe it to be a young male working alone. He left some debris in the air conditioning unit, plus we have a tennis shoe imprint."

"Disgruntled employee?" said Ricco.

"I believe it to be an outsider—a newcomer testing his arson abilities for something bigger."

"We're gonna scan your area," said Ricco, "Give these guys a chance to see how this system operates—we'll be off in five."

"You're on the clock," said Shawn, looking at his watch.

After Louie scanned the area using a highly sophisticated mouse, he pressed the parameter key and locked on to the selected arson sight.

"On this board you have different directional keys that enable us to see every inch of that dumpster," said Louie—showing the New York detectives all the little perks the system offered, including how the different angles made visual investigation a hundred percent complete. "It also tapes everything we're viewing—how fucking cool is that?"

"This set-up is awesome," said Billy.

Ricco looked at his watch and said, "We're almost at five minutes, we'd better sign off."

"What's with the clock watching?" asked Billy.

"This system," Ricco explained, "needs special clearance. Our agents have to give permission to view their crime scenes—everything is recorded and documented with precise accuracy and permission.

"So you're saying the crime scene can't be monitored without the investigator's clearance?"

"Yes," Ricco responded. "You'll learn a lot in Miami, this system will amaze you."

The men watched as Louie secured and closed the system in a matter of seconds. "It's fast; easy in, easy out," he said.

"We really do appreciate the heads up," said Mac, as they left WASP and walked towards the precinct's Detective Bureau.

"Getting back to this Kingman case," said Ricco, as he entered his office and sat down on the corner of his desk. "If there's anything we can do here, be sure and let us know."

"We appreciate that," Mac responded, "your department has been great. The hotel, the dinners—"

Ricco put his hand up as if to say, *enough already with the compliments.* "Oh, one more thing, because of the two explosions you both were involved in; the Agency has decided to send O'Hara to New York as an overseer."

"Great," responded Mac, "we look forward to seeing him there... don't we Brooklyn?"

"Yeah, that's great," he corroborated, as his thoughts immediately diverted to Vickie. Should he let her know O'Hara was coming? Leaning against the filing cabinets, he looked a little surprised and confused.

MacTavish, observing his partner's indecision, quickly put it all in perspective and walked over to him. Placing his hand on Cavanaugh's shoulder he said, "We'll be sure to let it be a surprise for everyone... won't we Brooklyn?"

As Cavanaugh nodded yes, Ricco acknowledged MacTavish's diplomacy with a smile; it was as if he too knew what was going on with the young detective.

"Why don't you guys go back to the hotel and checkout," said Ricco standing up. "Louie and I will pick you guys up for dinner and take you to the airport afterwards."

As they approached the front desk, Cavanaugh stared at Officer Morelli who was having a conversation with two police officers.

"Everyone asks about her when they come in," said Ricco. "I'm surprised you guys didn't."

"Great," Mac mumbled to himself, as they walked outside."

"What about her," said Billy curiously.

"She's a retired Cher impersonator. In three days she'll be a member of WASP," said Ricco, as he and Louie climbed into their car.

Driving away, Louie rolled his window down and cried out, "Hey Mac, while we're gone...enjoy fucking Cleveland!"

"Yeah Mac," laughed Billy, "maybe Connery and Cher could team up. You two could pick up some side work while we're here."

"Great. I'll make sure to call her and set that up," said Mac, as he climbed into the passenger seat. He was silent on the drive back to the hotel—his mind flashed back to another vacation he had with Red—Toni was performing as Cher in London at the same club where Red was singing. "She's probably wondering why I didn't speak to her," he thought. "Perhaps someday I'll be able to explain."

Observing his partner's solitude, Cavanaugh figured he'd let sleeping dogs lie and be quiet.

When they arrived back at the hotel, it was Cavanaugh who broke the silence. "So what do you think?" he asked, leaving the car with valet parking.

"It's a lot to comprehend," said Mac. "I feel like I'm in some fucking Hugh Grant futuristic *12 Monkeys* movie."

"It's Bruce Willis," Billy corrected, shaking his head.

"What," said Mac?

"You're talking about Bruce Willis...he's the one who did *12 Monkeys.*"

"Do I look like I give a damn which actor was in the movie," Mac retorted. "The point is; are we heading for a new world order here? Look, don't get me wrong. I admire WASP and what it represents—after all, we are here to stop crime. I just can't help but wonder about where this country is heading. We have organizations within organizations; we've got the CIA with so many off shoots that nobody knows who the hell they are...the FBI with all their hidden intelligence units—dealing with aliens, and who the hell knows what else? I'm not even going to get into the KGB.

"Let sleeping dogs lie, should have been left alone," Billy thought, as they walked through the lobby. "The big dog is on another roll."

"For all we know, we could be working for the Mafia," said Mac, as they walked towards the elevators.

Cavanaugh didn't respond to his partner's lecturing. He knew from past experiences that it was futile; for this wasn't the first time he had heard Mac's opinions. Shaking his head, he kept walking, knowing that when Mac was on his soapbox, there was no room for anyone else.

"I should know better than to get him going," Billy said under his breath, as they rushed into an open elevator that was about to close.

As the elevator doors opened on their floor, Mac was still going on. ..."they've been selling us out for years. O'Hara is right, this government has some serious debt to pay back to the universe.

When I was in British Intelligence," he said, walking down the hall to their suite, "this government knew all about *The Lusitania* carrying munitions. As did Germany—warning the U. S. not to let the boat sail or they would destroy it. But did anyone bother to tell the

205

people on board? No. It was another political maneuver to get this country involved in the war.

Reaching their suite, Billy unlocked the door and mumbled, "When am I ever going to learn?"

MacTavish was still going on and discussing the Vietnam War when he entered the suite and headed for his room. "What a fucking waste of time and lives that one was. The only good thing that came out of that war was the movie *Apocalypse Now.*"

"I need to take a shower," said Billy, going into his own room.

"YOU KNOW I'M RIGHT," Mac yelled out.

Closing his bathroom door, Cavanaugh stripped off his clothes—allowing his thoughts to overtake him. "Yes, Mac was right," he mumbled. "There were a lot of flaws among the leaders of the world." Vietnam was a particular subject that bothered him, for he empathized with the struggles of those surviving Vets; mentally, emotionally, and physically. Getting into the shower, he thought about those that ended up with severe psychological problems—and their problems of getting proper medical help. "The Veterans Hospital and health care systems in this country are in desperate need of rebuilding," he thought, as he slowly turned his focus on taking a shower.

In the living room, MacTavish had poured himself a drink. Sitting down on the couch, he turned on the television to the view the local news.

"The fabric store fire has now been declared as a wiring malfunction," said the reporter, playing down the report and moving on to another story.

As Cavanaugh walked in tying his robe, he grabbed a beer out of the fridge and walked towards his partner. "Anything on the news?" he asked.

"You don't even want to go there." said Mac with an uncaring expression, "I've had enough with the tainted news media." He walked into his bathroom humming another hit song by Engelbert, this time it was a verse from *The Last Waltz*.

Drinking his beer, Cavanaugh returned to his room. "It'll be good to get home," he thought, as he removed his clothes off the hangers and packed them up. He was looking forward to some privacy and solitude. It had been a very emotional week and he needed some space.

Mac opened his bathroom door and said, "I'll be finished and ready to go shortly."

"Take your time," Billy answered, walking back into the living room and sitting down on the couch. "They won't be here for another hour."

"Brooklyn," Mac called out, "could you call the house and tell Hildie we're coming back tonight? I don't need to surprise my house sitter by coming home in the middle of the night—the woman packs a Glock."

"Sure," said Billy, as he picked up Mac's cell phone and placed the call. "Hildie, its Billy Cavanaugh."

"Is everything okay, are you coming home?" she asked in a heavy German accent.

"That's why I called, we're coming back tonight. We should be there around midnight." He paused and listened as she explained a new situation that had taken place at MacTavish's home. "You're kidding," he said, pausing for a minute. "Oh, you're not kidding." Laughing and shaking his head, he said, "No, this is something you'd need to tell him, hang on.

Trying to regain his composure, Billy called out, "MAC, HILDIE NEEDS TO TALK TO YOU."

MacTavish walked out wearing brown Armani dress slacks with a matching brown silk shirt and tie. "What's going on?" he asked, as Cavanaugh handed him the phone.

"She'll explain everything," smiled Billy.

"Hildie, what's going on?" Mac inquired, putting the call on speaker phone. He paused and listened, as his housekeeper filled him in on the current events.

"Honey found this baby rabbit in the yard," she said, "She's treating him like it's her puppy."

"Well I'm not surprised," said Mac. "She always wanted to be a mother."

"She's ever so gentle with him," Hildie stated.

"Yes, I would think so," responded Mac. "She's a very gentle dog."

Cavanaugh gave his partner a look of disbelief as he crossed his eyes and listened in on his conversation.

"Yes," said Mac. "Let her keep him. It shouldn't be a problem."

"Mr. Mac, I'll be leaving for home soon...if you don't mind."

"Go on home Hildie. I'll see you during the week. And thanks again for keeping her company." Disconnecting the call, he saw the curious look on Cavanaugh's face. "Is there a problem Kid?"

"SHE'S A VERY GENTLE DOG...HAVE YOU BEEN SMOKING CRACK?"

"Most of the time she is very gentle," Mac responded indignantly, as he headed back to his room.

"Right," Billy answered sarcastically. "But not in this lifetime."

"I admit she's had her moments...it's the Rotweiller in her."

Cavanaugh took a swig of his beer and mumbled, "More like the Rotten-weiller in her."

"I HEARD THAT!" bellowed Mac from his bedroom.

"SO YOU GONNA LET HER KEEP THUMPER?" Billy yelled back.

"You have a reason why I shouldn't? She'll make a great mother," Mac replied, walking out with his luggage.

"Better make sure she's well fed," Billy muttered, as he headed for his room mumbling, "and not one of those mothers who would eat her young."

"I didn't get that," said Mac.

"I said...I hope we're not going to one of those mother pop Chinese places where everyone eats Egg Foo Yung," answered Billy, while getting dressed.

"The Kid's getting *really* good with his improvisations," Mac thought, as he fixed himself a drink with the remaining scotch and toasted his partner's bedroom door with his glass. Suddenly, his cell phone rang. Pulling it out of his jacket, he saw it was Ricco calling.

"We'll be right down," said Mac, and disconnected the call. "TIME TO GO BROOKLYN, THE BOYS ARE HERE," he yelled out— unaware that his partner was right behind him. "BRING YOUR LUGGAGE; WE'RE GOING STRAIGHT TO THE AIRPORT AFTER DINNER."

As he turned around, Billy said softly, "Why are you yelling?"

Startled and shaken, MacTavish jumped back holding his chest. "FOR CHRIST'S SAKE BROOKLYN, DON'T EVER DO THAT. I'M LIABLE TO

HAVE A DAMN STROKE!" Laughing, Cavanaugh picked up his bags and walked towards the door. "YOU THINK THAT'S FUNNY, DO YOU? SCARING A MAN THAT'S OLD ENOUGH TO BE YOUR FATHER?"

"You mean old enough to be my great grandfather, don't you?" said Billy, opening the door.

"Your sense of humor leaves a lot to be discussed Brooklyn."

"You mean a lot to be desired."

"Desired...NO! Discussed...only when I have six months of nothing to do with my life. Now let's go."

As they left the room, Cavanaugh smiled and closed the door to Suite 1812. Walking towards the elevator, both detectives found themselves looking forward to their farewell dinner.

ℰↄ℃ℜ

New York, New York

In the Ritz Carlton lobby, the two Cleveland detectives were standing at the front desk. "I'm gonna miss those guys," said Louie.

"We'll be in touch via satellite," Ricco responded. "And who knows; maybe we'll go to New York."

"Really?" Louie said happily.

"It's a possibility. We got some vacation time coming; let's see what we can work out with D."

"That would be fucking great. Maybe, we could catch a show. I sure would like to see that *Phantom of the Opera*. I'm not crazy about opera, but I'd like to see it anyway."

Ricco laughed as he signed the charge slip for Suite 1812. "Sure," he answered, patting Louie on the face. Together they turned away from the desk and walked towards the elevators to meet the New York detectives.

As the elevator doors opened, MacTavish and Cavanaugh were laughing about Honey adopting Thumper instead of eating him. ..."That's exactly why I keep her well fed," said Mac.

"You guys all set to go?" smiled Ricco.

Looking around, Mac responded, "I believe we have everything."

"Then what are we waiting for?" said Louie. "Let's go eat."

As the four men made their way out of the hotel and over to the car that the parking valet had waiting for them, Mac said, "Cavanaugh was hoping we wouldn't be eating Chinese food tonight."

"That's not what I meant," said Billy, putting his bags into Ricco's trunk.

Nodding for Louie to get into the front passenger seat, Ricco tipped the valet, and climbed into the driver's seat.

"I know exactly what you meant," said Mac, tossing his own bags into the trunk. Slamming it shut, he joined his partner in the backseat.

Glancing into the rearview mirror, Ricco began to drive away. "You guys hungry?"

"I could enjoy a nice relaxing dinner," Mac replied.

"Great," said Louie. "We know just the place."

"Honey is not the kind of mother who'll eat her young," Mac whispered to his partner, who was looking out the window.

"THIS IS ABOUT THE DOG?" said Billy.

"WHAT DOG, WHO'S DOG? DID WE JUST HIT A DOG?" said Louie, looking around apprehensively.

"It's Mac's dog," said Billy.

"WHAT? WE HIT MAC'S DOG? Louie shouted. "I didn't know he brought a dog. Ricco, did you know he brought his dog? We should stop.

Must be a little fuck; I didn't even see him in the lobby. Ricco, did you see him in the lobby? HOW BIG IS THIS DOG? Must be a neutral color, blends in with the traffic. HOW THE *HELL* ARE WE GONNA FIND HIM?" As the three detectives laughed, Louie gave them all a disgusted look and continued his rapid comedic dialogue. "WE HIT A LITTLE FUCKING DOG AND YOU GUYS THINK IT'S FUNNY?" No matter what anyone said or did, the men couldn't stop laughing. Cavanaugh tried to explain, but couldn't get the words out right.

"OH NO," Ricco cried out, as he wiped away his tears of laughter.

"That's better," said Louie, looking at his partner. "I'm sure the little fuck appreciates tears from *somebody!* The dog falls out of the car and no one notices! Then we run over the little fuck and his owner laughs about it!" Taking a deep breath, and looking out of the side window, he said, "I'll tell you one thing, you three guys are really fucking sick!"

The three detectives roared with contagious, tearful laughter. "Oh-h-h the pain...enough already," laughed Billy, holding his chest. After a few minutes of silence, they started to contain their emotions.

Suddenly, Louie yelled out, "DOES ANYONE HERE THINK WE SHOULD STOP AND PICK UP THE FUCKING DOG?" Once again, all three men laughed uproariously, while Louie shook his head and said, "No fucking compassion...I don't understand it."

"I think I'm having a heart attack," cried Billy, choking and laughing simultaneously.

"Don't you die on me," laughed Mac. "If I get paired up with Matthews I'll have to shoot the neurotic bastard."

Howling with laughter, Ricco said, "Fuck! I just passed the turnoff to the restaurant."

"Is that a problem," said Billy tearfully.

"Yeah," said Louie, laughing uncontrollably. "It's also the turnoff to his home." His statement made everyone laugh even more as Ricco drove off the next exit ramp.

"Well, this is it," said Ricco, as they finally reached their destination—a busy dinner house called The Sicilian Fisherman. As they all left the car, Louie walked over to MacTavish and looked up at him. "It's a fish place," he grinned excitedly.

Looking down at him, Mac placed his arm around Louie's shoulder and said, "I never would have guessed Louie, let's go eat." Together, they led the way to the entrance with Ricco and Cavanaugh following behind.

"You like fish?" Ricco asked.

"Love it," Billy replied as he looked out at Lake Erie. "Luckily, my neighborhood is filled with them."

"Expensive area to live in...I guess the rodeo circuit pays well."

"When you win they do—winning paid for my condo. I'm getting a little old to keep doing it; those bulls can wear you down."

"You don't talk too much about your trophies," Ricco said softly. You shouldn't be so modest. If you're good you need to be proud of it. I'm sure it wasn't easy to get to where you are. You must have had your share of broken bones and torn muscles. Those things aren't anything to be embarrassed about. If you pay your dues, you should acknowledge your talent."

Cavanaugh smiled in agreement, as they all walked into the restaurant. Looking around, they saw O'Hara seated in a back booth.

"Now there's a guy who knows how to tell other people how good he is," Ricco smiled.

"Are you always the first to arrive?" asked Mac, sliding in next to the Irishman.

"Astrologically speaking, I'm an Aries...I have to be first. I also had to make sure the booth was free of explosives."

"So did you find any?" Louie asked, as he pulled up a nearby chair.

"Only one under that chair your about to sit in Louie."

As everyone else sat down, Louie picked up the chair and looked under it. "What the fuck?" he responded curiously. Taped to the bottom of the chair was an envelope addressed to Detective Petticelli. Pulling the envelope off the chair, Louie looked cautiously at everyone before he sat down. "Is this a joke...an exploding envelope or something? What's going to happen when I open it?"

Ricco leaned over the table and said, "Just open the fucking envelope."

Looking around at everyone, Louie cautiously opened the envelope and pulled out two front row seat tickets to *The Phantom of the Opera*, compliments of Captain D. His reaction was like a kid given the key to a computer game store.

"This is so fucking great; I've wanted to see this show for the last eight years."

"So you guys are definitely coming to New York?" said Billy.

"Yeah," Ricco answered, "D's already taken care of our hotel accommodations. We'll be staying at The Plaza."

"And Louie," said Billy, "you'll get to meet Mac's little dog who *isn't* little, *didn't* come to Cleveland, *didn't* stay in the hotel, and *didn't* get hit by a car."

After filling O'Hara in on Louie's comedic performance and the history of Cavanaugh's relationship with his dog, Mac said, "You staying at The Plaza too Shawn?"

"No. I'm already set up with a friend."

"Oh-h-h—" Billy and Louie moaned simultaneously.

"A close friend?" pried Mac.

"You could say that," Shawn responded, with twinkling eyes.

"Do any of us know her?" hinted Billy.

O'Hara questioned the young detective's probing. He knew Cavanaugh's attitude was one of protection towards Vickie. He just wasn't sure if it was a romantic protection. "Should you know her?" he challenged with a smile. "If there's something you want to know, Cavanaugh, you need to come out with it. Why don't you and I go outside and clear this up?"

Cavanaugh was tempted to ask him about Vickie, but backed off because of his promise. Nervously, he pulled out a pack of cigarettes.

MacTavish, feeling the two men needed to resolve any ill feelings that were still in the air, quickly moved out of the booth and allowed the men to slip out. "You guys need a referee?"

"No," Shawn replied, as they headed for the patio

Once outside, O'Hara sat down on the brick wall surrounding the patio. Pulling out a pack of cigarettes, he said, "Are you a Protestant?"

Cavanaugh gave him a puzzling glance as he lit up a cigarette and replied, "Yeah, why do you ask?"

Shawn nodded an understanding yes and said, "Aye, that would explain our underlying hostility towards each other—me being a Catholic, and us both being Irish. If we were living in Northern Ireland we'd be arch enemies instead of co-workers."

"You're probably right," smiled Billy.

"So you're curious about my relationship with Vickie?" Shawn said, lighting his cigarette.

Apprehensively, Cavanaugh looked over at the cool and collected Irishman and said, "How did you know I—"

"It's obvious you've talked to her about me. Are you in love with her?"

"No," Billy swiftly responded.

"You're sure about that?"

"Yeah. And what the hell makes you think that?"

"You act like a knight mate, protecting the damsel in distress." A little stunned by O'Hara's insinuation, Cavanaugh turned away and continued smoking his cigarette. "Let me start with how we met," said Shawn. "Vickie came to Miami to train with WASP. We met while she was going through orientation—I was there in charge of arson technical assistance. I didn't really pay much attention to her. She was however, very attracted to me. I'll skip all the intimate details and move to the end of the two weeks with her."

"Thanks, I appreciate that," said Billy.

"I became attracted to her, but not in the way she wanted. Vickie wants the little house with the white picket fence and a man she can cook for and take care of. For some men, that can be a beautiful thing. But not for me, and I made that very clear to her. I told her I was not the man she was looking for, but she still wanted the affair. It started out wonderful, and then I began to feel smothered. She thought that the more love she gave, the more I'd need her and would want to marry her—when in fact, it pushed me further away." He paused for a moment as he put out his cigarette. "Don't get me wrong, she's a wonderful girl. With the right man, she'll be a magnificent wife. But I am definitely not the man she needs. When she realizes that, her disappointment in me will vanish and her broken heart will mend."

Recalling Mac's words, *there's always two sides to every story*, Billy said, "I'm beginning to get a clearer picture."

"And just for the record," added Shawn, "Vickie is not the friend I'm staying with in New York—that relationship is over."

Putting out his cigarette, Cavanaugh knew he had been acting inappropriately and decided to make amends. "I guess I really owe you an apology for the way I've been acting."

"Don't worry about it. You were just a knight who fell off his horse and got a little disorientated. Let's eat mate, I'm starved."

"Yeah, let's go," replied Billy, following O'Hara back inside.

Inside the restaurant, the other detectives were laughing and eating when the two men returned. Enormous ceramic bowls filled with pasta and meatballs, the sizes of baseballs, were on the table. Encircling the bowls of food, were several loaves of garlic bread and three large antipasto salads that added a colorful finishing touch to the table setting.

"What happened to the fish?" Billy inquired.

"No fish delivery today so we went with the pasta," responded Louie, with a mouth full of food. "Pull up a chair and dig in."

"I'm impressed," said Billy, as he sat down and helped himself to the enticing food.

"Everything okay?" Mac whispered.

"Couldn't be better," smiled Billy.

Grabbing a slice of garlic bread, Mac said, "Great."

As they began eating, the men talked about food, women, work and life. They each had a moment of silence as they reflected on their time spent together; MacTavish, feeling he had developed strong ties with all of the men, knew that this would not be their last meeting. In contrast, O'Hara didn't put expectations on seeing anyone again; most of his close friends were already dead. While Cavanaugh, reliving his experiences in Cleveland, realized there was a lot to learn from these men. And yet, in some bizarre way, he related to all of their issues. As far as the Cleveland detectives were concerned, Ricco had a satisfied opinion that the New York detectives would be beneficial enhancing the WASP organization. Louie, on the other hand, was thinking about where he and Ricco were going for breakfast tomorrow morning.

Outside and out of view of the restaurant, a dark van with its motor running was parked off the street—the driver's face hidden by the shadows of the night. Moving away slowly, the van left its parking space and merged into the traffic. The driver rolled the window halfway down and tossed his lit cigarette out.

The detectives evening dinner ended with a farewell to O'Hara as the men got into Ricco's car and headed for the Cleveland Hopkins International Airport.

At eleven o'clock, the plane bound for New York had made its way down one of Cleveland's airport runways.

"Well Kid, looks like we're in for one big adventure," said Mac, trying to get comfortable in his seat.

Cavanaugh, sitting next to the window responded casually, "Looks that way."

"You have something you want to discuss Brooklyn?"

"I was just wondering if you had a good time in fucking Cleveland."

"You know," responded Mac, "there are times when your behavior is a pain in my ass, and this is definitely one of those times." As the plane soared into the darkness and away from the bright lights of Cleveland, he adjusted his seat back and closed his eyes.

Cavanaugh smiled as he stared out the window, and after a few minutes, he too fell asleep.

It was after midnight when the two detectives arrived at New York's Kennedy Airport.

"So tomorrow we act like WASP doesn't exist right," said Billy, as they moved quickly through the airport parking lot to their cars.

"Right," Mac answered.

"And Vickie?" said Billy, lighting a cigarette. "We wait for her to approach us?"

MacTavish nodded yes, as they both unlocked their car doors and put their bags into the trunks of their cars. "You okay with all of this Kid?"

"Yeah, in fact I'm pretty excited about it all. Especially the two week vacation swimming with the sharks in fucking Miami," he said before driving away—his stereo blasting George Thorogood's *I Drink Alone.*

Climbing into his Lexus, MacTavish shook his head as he watched his partner disappear out of the garage. As he began his drive home, his thoughts ran back through all that happened. It had been a busy couple of days and he wondered if it had been a little overwhelming for his partner. "Then again...maybe it was a good distraction," he thought, as his mind drifted back to the lady in gray episode.

Listening to Engelbert's *A Man Without Love,* Mac said softly, "Some things are best forgotten. But why..." he mumbled, as he backed out of his parking space. Driving out of the airport and on to the Belt Parkway, he reviewed everything that happened since the homicide. The thirty-five minute drive gave him time to try to put it all in perspective. As he turned on to the Sothern State Parkway that led to his home in Islip, he thought about Honey and her new pet.

Pulling up in front of his home gave MacTavish a feeling of tranquility. Unloading his bags, he quickly walked to the front door and opened it. The house appeared calm and quiet, except for the living room television, which had been left on. Putting his bags down next to the staircase, he walked into the kitchen and read the note Hildie left for him.

The bunny is trained to the litter box.
Hildie

Looking around for his dog, he walked back into the living room towards the stairs. "You can come out now, the Kid's not here."

Honey appeared at the top of the stairs, carrying the bunny in her mouth like a mother cat carrying her offspring.

"Great," smiled Mac, walking up to see her. "Looks like you two have adapted well to each other."

221

Wagging her tail, she led her master into the spare bedroom, where Hildie had set up a large round pen with water, food, and baby blankets. In the corner of the pen was a litter box. Jumping into the pen, Honey dropped the bunny next to his little bed, and proceeded to cover him up with one of the blankets.

"I see Hildie has made a comfortable place for the two of you," said Mac, as the dog jumped back out and welcomed her master—standing on her back legs and placing her paws on his shoulders. "Yes I've missed you too," he said, petting and scratching her back. "Let's go unpack." Suddenly, Honey sat down with her head slightly cocked. "C'mon," Mac called to her. And as he turned and walked towards the door, she looked at the pen and wagged her tail. "Oh, that's how it is. Alright...go be with your baby." Happily, she jumped back into the pen and curled up with the bunny. As she washed him with long strokes of her tongue, each stroke moved the bunny a few inches away from her. "You're a good girl and a great mother," Mac smiled, dimming the light and walking slowly to his room.

As he started unpacking, his cell phone rang. He identified Cavanaugh as the caller. Shaking his head he thought, "Now what?" and grabbed his phone. "This better be good Brooklyn."

"Someone from an outside source hacked into my computer."

"Christ, are you okay?"

"Yeah I'm fine."

"You've lost me mate, care to explain?"

"Not tonight," Billy sighed. "However, the Cleveland download is gone."

"I don't like the sound of this; I think you need to get out of there now. What if they decide to pay you a visit?"

222

"You think," smiled Billy.

Cavanaugh's unruffled attitude bothered MacTavish. "Get over here now or I'll come and get you myself. Do you really want me driving all the way out there?"

"Mac, it's one-thirty in the morning and I do have a gun. They probably hacked into your computer too."

"Oh, so now I'm at risk?"

"You have more security at your home than San Quentin. And you have a dog."

"True. That's why I suggested that you come here."

"I'll be fine," said Billy. "I'm tired and I'm going to bed. I'll see you in the morning."

"Call me if there's a problem," Mac sighed.

"Before or after the coroner arrives?" laughed Billy.

"That's not funny. You just make the call!"

"Okay Sherlock," Billy responded, and disconnected the call.

MacTavish looked at his cell phone and smiled. He wasn't happy with his partner's decision, but learned long ago that you can't force someone to do what you want. "You can only suggest and threaten...and even that doesn't always work," he said softly.

Meanwhile, in Sheepshead Bay, Cavanaugh put his cell phone down on the couch and looked around the condo. His home had no resemblance to his ranch in Montana. There were no traces of rodeos or horses here. The condo had a modern, tropical island look, with classic rattan furniture. Subtle lighting gave off an amber hue throughout the home. The living room décor was done in various shades of brown. Centered in front of a gas fireplace was a large overstuffed couch with a subtle, palm tree designed linen fabric. Above the fireplace were several large antique candleholders that hung from the ceiling. Three rustic colored, East Indian trunks, were placed on the floor next to the couch. On top of one of the trunks, sat an antique metal lamp with an amber-colored linen shade. In the center of the living room, suspended from the ceiling by a large metal rod, was a replica of a 1940s three-blade revolving fan—turning slowly and silently through the air. A giant palm tree stood behind the couch against the wall. Next to the tree, was a beautiful scrolled rattan folding divider screen—angled perfectly. A large antique-brown rattan armoire with drawers on each side stood against the far wall. Its two large center doors had inserts of East Indian carvings. On top of the armoire, woven baskets and bottles were positioned next to a large fern, while plush beige and brown Persian rugs covered the hardwood floor.

"Well that was an interesting trip," said Billy, as he unpacked his bags in his bedroom.

His bedroom had a sultry, tropical, 1930s atmosphere. The plush sea green carpeting matched the color scheme of sea green blends and shades of brown throughout the room. Sheer gauze-like material draped a four-poster canopy bed that sat close to the floor, and six, dark brown down pillows and a matching comforter, covered the sea green colored sheets. An exceptionally large palm tree sat next to the fashionable bed, while a weathered looking ceiling fan revolved slowly overhead.

As Cavanaugh lit the three tall antique candle holders near his French doors, he said to himself, "I can't seem to shake the feeling that I just auditioned for some sci-fi fantasy flick." Turning on his elaborate sound system, he walked into the bathroom and lit the remaining candles that surrounded his tub and shower. One of his favorite CD's was playing. Paul Rogers, lead vocalist for Bad Company, was singing the live concert version of *Feel Like Making Love.*

After getting undressed, Cavanaugh stepped into his large glass enclosed shower. As the water washed away the stress of the week, his front door was unlocked silently, by someone wearing jeans, a leather jacket, and western boots. After locking the door, the figure walked cautiously towards the bathroom. The young detective was showering and singing along with the music, when his bathroom door was slowly pushed open. Feeling a presence behind him, he stopped singing and turned his head slowly towards the open door.

"Well it's about time you showed up...flight delayed?" The water from the shower continued to fall over his body, as he watched his Texas lover slowly strip down and join him in the shower.

As they embraced each other, Cavanaugh's lover returned caresses to every part of his body and whispered, "How much have you missed me?"

Grabbing his lover around the waist, Billy pulled the naked body tightly against him and said, "Give me five hours and I'll show you."

A foggy mist covered the shower glass, transforming their sexual activity into a very private affair.

ഌൠ

THESE BOOTS ARE MADE FOR WALKING

It was a usual Friday morning at the One Nine. The officers replacing the night shift were scurrying about when Detective Cavanaugh entered and climbed the stairs to the homicide bureau. As he walked in, he saw Detective Keaton working at her desk.

Looking up from her paperwork, she cheerfully said, "Hey...how was your trip?"

"Oh gosh...it was great," said Billy, "First class all the way. Remind me to tell you about the mob that runs the Cleveland precinct," he whispered.

Laughing, Vickie glanced around the office. With no one around, she removed her shield, flipped it over and showed him her magnetic WASP pin. "So...were you impressed?" she said, quickly clipping her shield back to her waist.

Knowing that she was inquiring about the WASP set-up, Billy replied, "Yeah, they have a hell of a system."

"We'll talk later," she replied, sorting out her paperwork. "Mac... welcome back," she said enthusiastically, as he walked into the bureau.

"Thanks," he responded, taking off his jacket and placing it on the back of his chair.

Observing MacTavish's agitated state, Vickie pried, "Is everything okay? You look upset."

"Everything's great! Just great," said Mac, leaning over his chair. "And you Brooklyn are *you* okay?"

Playfully imitating Antonio Banderas, Billy said, "Did you miss me?"

"You know you could have called me this morning."

"Okay boys settle down," Vickie intervened. "You sound like newlyweds when the honeymoon is over."

"Mac, I'm fine," sighed Billy.

"You could have called," said Mac, pulling out his chair and sitting down. Looking around the office, he said, "Where's our receptionist?"

"He called in sick," Vickie answered.

"Great! You have anything new on Kingman?"

"Pathologists report came in," she said, getting up and handing him the report.

"It's in our system," she said to Cavanaugh, who immediately logged into their network to find it. "You two guys have any plans for later? I thought maybe we' could get together for dinner."

"Sounds good to me," Mac responded quickly. "What about you Kid?"

"I already made plans."

MacTavish stared at him curiously, waiting for an explanation. Feeling his partner's eyes on him, Billy quickly looked up and said, "I do have a life away from here."

"Do we know who she is?" Mac joshed.

"Angelina Jolie," Billy sighed, as he stood up and grabbed his jacket.

"When she dumps you Brooklyn, be sure and give her my number. I have a red wig she'd look great in."

Heading downstairs, Cavanaugh gave him the finger over his shoulder.

"I think he's pissed," said Vickie.

"He'll get over it."

"So who's the new girlfriend Mac?"

"Your guess is as good as mine. He never mentioned anyone to me," he replied, shrugging his shoulders. "Well my dear, looks like you have a date with an older man tonight. Any objections?"

"I'm thinkin' it'll be great," she responded with a Scottish brogue that sounded like a little Leprechaun. "Do I get to wear that red wig," she laughed. Having second thoughts she quickly said, "Never mind. I don't think I want to know anything about the red wigs."

Smiling, Mac looked through the report folder on Kingman and said, "I'll take care of the reservations Lassie."

Outside, Detective Matthews was on his way in when he saw Cavanaugh coming out. "Welcome back Kid."

"Thanks, it's good to be home," said Billy, as he lit a cigarette.

"Thought you were going to give those up," he said, hurrying inside the entrance. "I'm running a little late, glad you're back."

Looking around, Cavanaugh walked behind the building to the new addition site. Knowing its true purpose, he studied it and wondered how it would work out with everybody involved—the mysterious lady in gray was temporarily stored away in his memory bank. WASP and their current homicide, was his central focus. Putting his cigarette out, he went back into the precinct.

Inside the bureau, MacTavish and Matthews were rehashing the Kingman homicide as Cavanaugh entered. ..."and, we lost a lot of evidence because of the rain," said Marc. "The autopsy report showed it was a single shot into the heart that did him in. The shooter really new his business. One of our witnesses thought the guy was having a heart attack. I have to admit, we're at a standstill here. You get any leads in Cleveland?"

MacTavish explained what happened at the Kingman house, conveniently leaving out their personal encounters with O'Hara. He didn't want to exploit Vickie and Shawn's relationship in front of Matthews.

"Unbelievable," said Marc, "I'm gonna get some coffee. Anybody want a cup?"

Everyone, except Cavanaugh, nodded no. "One of these would be good," said Billy, holding up an empty water bottle.

"I'll get you one Kid," said Marc, as he walked towards the break room.

Taking advantage of Matthews being out of the room, Mac said "We got a small briefing on the Agency while we were there."

"So I heard," replied Vickie, showing him her WASP shield. Looking around the office to make sure no one could overhear, she said, "Just remember, they keep all agents up to date on everything."

"You knew we were going to be recruited," said Mac.

"Yes. So Billy, tell me what you thought about O'Hara."

Cavanaugh got up and walked over to her desk. Leaning over her shoulder, he whispered in her ear, "I think you could have done better."

"You're probably right," she laughed.

As Matthews walked back into the room with his coffee and Cavanaugh's bottled water, Billy said, "Do me a favor Marc and see what you can pull up on a Howard Austin."

"The photographer involved in the warehouse explosion last year...isn't that where Mac almost lost his shirt?" he said, wearing a quirky smile.

MacTavish dropped his papers down on the desk, sat back in his chair, and gave Matthews a very disgruntled look.

"Yeah, that one," confirmed Billy loudly.

MacTavish quickly gave his partner that same disgruntled look.

"Anything you guys want me to keep an eye out for?" said Marc.

"Yes," said Billy, walking back to his desk, "the gun and how it was used. Run it through the system and see if anything comes up—look for similarities. I need to check with the M. E. about Austin's autopsy report and compare it to Kingman's."

"And your reasoning for all this is?" Mac inquired.

"Just a hunch," said Billy, as he sat down and focused in on his monitor.

All of the detectives spent most of the morning researching other crime scenes and investigating similar cold cases. When lunch was brought in, Cavanaugh and MacTavish re-focused on the Kingman case. It was an unsuccessful attempt towards any conclusions.

Later that afternoon, MacTavish's cell phone rang. Recognizing Ricco's voice, he spoke quietly into the phone. "And how's everything in fucking Cleveland?"

"I need to talk to the captain," said Vickie, getting up from her desk. "He wants this report I just finished. Cover the phones for me?"

"Sure," Billy responded. Glancing across the desk to his partner, he questioned, "Ricco?"

MacTavish nodded yes and grabbed a notepad. Cavanaugh leaned over the desk to read what he was writing. "Monday morning, Flight 210. We'll meet you at the passenger exit." Disconnecting the call he said, "They'll be here next week."

"And O'Hara?" asked Billy.

"He's already here," Mac said softly.

Looking at his watch, Cavanaugh grabbed his cigarettes and jacket. "I'm gonna cut out a little early...take some down time."

"Did you let Rollins know?" said Mac, as Vickie returned to her desk.

"Would you let him know I left? Tell him something came up, something personal."

"Do everything I would do, and you'll make that lady very happy tonight," smiled Mac.

"Does it always have to be about sex with you? I'll see you guys tomorrow," Billy declared, rushing out and racing down the stairs. Leaving the precinct, Cavanaugh anticipated returning to his Texas lover who was waiting for him in his condo. Getting into his car, he recalled the immediate attraction they had for each other when they met on the rodeo circuit. However, over the past few years, his lover had become extremely jealous and possessive. This last year had been especially difficult for him. Turning on his radio to 104.3, he listened to one of his favorite classic rock stations, WAXQ. As he headed for Brooklyn, he thought more about his lover's confining, smothering, and emotionally draining nature. He wondered if they were heading for another break-up.

Pulling into his garage, Cavanaugh quickly parked his car and rushed upstairs. Unlocking the door, he entered and walked over to the couch, where Boots—wearing a very tight tee shirt and a pair of form fitting jeans—was sitting on the couch watching the CMTV channel.

"Shall we pick up where we left off this morning?" Billy asked, reaching out with his hand.

Boots immediately grabbed it and followed him to the bedroom—laughing as he stripped off their clothes. After climbing into bed, Boots slid down under the covers, giving the young detective a pleasurable experience.

Later that evening, Cavanaugh was dressed for an evening out when he yelled from his bedroom, "I'LL BE RIGHT OUT." Boots, sitting on the couch and being unresponsive, continued watching TV. Walking up and kissing back of his lover's neck, he said softly, "Let's get out of here." After leaving the condo, they headed silently down the hall and entered the elevator. Once inside, he tried to give his lover another kiss, but was coldly rejected. As the elevator doors opened, they rushed towards his Mustang convertible. "I'm glad you're here," he said, getting into the car. "I've really missed you; this separation was a lot longer than I anticipated." Adjusting the rearview mirror, he started up the car. "Can we drop the silent treatment? Like I told you, I was in Cleveland on business," he said, pulling out of the garage. "How many times do I need to explain about doing my job? I thought we resolved this last time we were together." As he drove through the city traffic, he stroked his lover's leg in a very sexual way. Boots removed his hand by pushing it away. Feeling the cold anger emanating from his lover, he thought, "It always ends up like this."

As Cavanaugh pulled his car into the parking lot of Navajo Joe's, he could hear the live country band performing Delbert McClinton's version of *Victim Of Life's Circumstances*. After finding a parking place, he quickly got out of the car and escorted Boots inside. The band recognized Cavanaugh when he walked in, and several customers waved with their drinks in hand—making it obvious that the young detective had frequented the club before.

"CAVANAUGH," a hot looking young bartender, wearing a black western hat yelled out. "C'MON DOWN HERE. THESE SEATS ARE YOURS." Removing a few empty beer bottles, he replaced them with two fresh ones.

Cavanaugh and Boots quickly made their way to the end of the bar and grabbed the seats. "Thanks Zachary," said Billy, as he reached in his jeans and tossed him a twenty dollar bill. "Let's dance," Billy

233

whispered to Boots. Walking out on the dance floor together, they began to do the two-step to Alan Jackson's *Who's Cheating Who*. As they danced around the floor, Cavanaugh continued whispering in his partner's ear while Boots remained unresponsive to everything he tried to do or say.

Meanwhile, across town, Detectives MacTavish and Keaton were having dinner at one of New York's premier dining establishments—The Water Club. Manhattan's first waterfront restaurant was located on the East River at 30th Street and FDR Drive—cozy fireplaces and piano music made for a romantic setting.

Seated at a river-view table, Vickie said, "This is awfully nice. I've never been here before."

"Well I'm glad you're enjoying it," smiled Mac. "It's a shame the Kid couldn't join us."

"Do you think he's seeing someone?"

"I'm not sure," said Mac. "He's a very private person. He hasn't opened up to me about what he does in his off time." Looking at her he stopped eating. "Are you asking because—"

"Oh no," she interrupted, taking a sip of her wine. "He's like a brother to me. There could never be anything between us." Sensing MacTavish's disappointment she said, "Were you hoping there could be?"

"He needs someone like you."

"Mac, my feelings..." she paused for a moment before continuing, "It's just not there. I'm sorry."

"It's okay Vickie, it wasn't meant to be. He'll find someone when the time is right."

Picking up her fork she said, "The food is wonderful. And I am having a great time."

Meanwhile, back at Navajo Joe's, Zachary was having a private conversation with Cavanaugh. "So what's going on between you and Boots?" he said, as he served the young detective another beer.

"You don't wanna know," said Billy, giving a disgusted sigh. "It's so fuckin' hard to explain your every move to someone. I don't know how much more I can take."

"How long you two been together?"

"Five years, off and on," Billy sighed, as they looked out at the dance floor where Boots was dancing with two cowboys.

"Long time," said Zachary, glancing out at the dance floor. "Some sexy moves going on out there Kid. Your lover looks hot and happy now."

"That's a perfect example of what I mean. If that was me out there, I'd never hear the end of it," said Billy, turning back towards the bar.

"Maybe it's just a game to get you jealous."

"Please," said Billy, as he picked up his beer, "At this point I could go home alone and be very happy about it. Except for the great sex, this last day has been pure hell. I've had to explain every mother fucking breath I've taken since the last time we were together. Before we have sex *it's great*. Once we have it, I'm living with The Ice Queen and getting accused of sleeping with everybody in the fuckin' country."

"When was the last time you were together?" Zachary asked, reaching under the bar for his cup of coffee.

"Three weeks ago and of course I'm to blame—even though the queen hates New York and refuses to move out of state of Texas."

"Christ, I couldn't take it," said Zachary. "I'd have to walk."

"Well I'm just about to do just that."

"Was it always like this?" Zachary questioned.

"Are you fucking kidding? I wouldn't have stayed five years if it was always like this. This all started about a year ago." Leaning over the bar, he looked in both directions before speaking. "Even our sex is scrutinized. If I dare do something different, I'm accused of being with somebody else, but what's never mentioned are the two affairs *that one* had this year," he said, pointing to Boots.

"It doesn't seem too healthy Kid. Sure sounds like some misrepresented loyalty issues are going on here."

"I'm at a standstill Zach; I don't know what to do."

"You're gonna have to do something before it gets out of control," said Zachary, in a concerned tone. "You've been around here long enough to see what happens when someone crosses the line. Remember that couple from last year? One ended up in jail, the other in the hospital with multiple stab wounds. You really need to evaluate where the hell this is going."

Cavanaugh looked out at the dance floor and made a decision. Turning back to Zachary, he stood up and said, "You're right. I do need to do something about it, and the time is now. What do I owe you?"

"Nothing, it's on me," Zachary smiled, "Get your bull riding ass out of here before you change your mind."

Leaving thirty dollars on the bar, Cavanaugh walked out without turning back. Once outside, he took a deep breath and looked up into the star filled night. "Finally, it's over," he said loudly, while lighting a cigarette and walking towards his car. After getting in and putting down his convertible top, he drove home with his car radio playing *Don't Think Twice*—recorded by blues player Gatemouth Brown. "That's exactly what I need to do. *Don't think.*" Stopped by a red light and glancing once again at the sky, he acknowledged God. "Thanks. I've been wondering if you were still up there. I guess I owe you one," he smiled, as if some silent voice was speaking to him. "Okay...one Sunday Mass. No. No confessions. Don't push it."

Back at The Water Club, MacTavish and Keaton were almost through with their dinner. "Tell me more about your art work," said Mac.

"Well," she responded, "it's something I've always done since I was a child. It came naturally to me. My grandmother used to put my drawings up on her refrigerator. She told me someday they would be worth a fortune." Remembering the fun times she and her grandmother had spent together, she smiled, and said, "I used to carry pens and paper around with me all the time. I would just sit and draw things around me. I actually won some adult contests as a child."

"I'd like to see your work," said Mac with great interest.

"They're hanging all over my apartment. Would you like to come up and see my *etchings?*"

"That's supposed to be my line," laughed Mac. "You know if you're open to it, and your work is saleable, I could help you promote it. I *do know* a lot of people in Europe," he said, taking a swallow of his scotch.

"Oh that would be wonderful," she responded.

MacTavish remembered how his wife Catherine had gotten him started. He thought fondly of her and their times together.

Seeing him begin to drift off in his thoughts, Vickie paused for a few moments—allowing him to complete those memories. "You seem to have left me and gone somewhere else," she said softly.

"I was just thinking about the woman who helped me when I was starting out."

"Oh," smiled Vickie. "Do you keep in touch with her?"

"She was my wife."

"I'm sorry. I had no idea it was her who—"

"It's okay Vickie; she's been gone a long time."

"Now," Mac began, brightening up and changing the conversation, "tell me about your style of painting." As Vickie began talking about what she liked to paint and why, MacTavish showed a great interest in what she was saying. It had been years since he was able to discuss art with another artist.

Meanwhile, back in Brooklyn, Cavanaugh had entered his condo and was closing the door behind him. He stared at it for a few seconds before he reached for the deadbolt and secured it—closing another chapter of his life. After turning on his stereo, he walked into the bedroom and started to undress. Barefoot and wearing only his jeans, he lit a cigarette and picked up everything that wasn't his. Listening to Bon Jovi singing *You Give Love A Bad Name*, he put everything in his lover's bag, zipped it up and dropped it by the front door. Sitting down on the couch and listening to the words, *promised me heaven and put me through hell,* he continued smoking and waited for the inevitable.

Thirty-five minutes later, Whitesnake's CD of *Here I Go Again* was playing when the lock on Cavanaugh's condo door was jarred. As the doorbell rang, he lit another cigarette. It rang several times before he responded. Walking to the door, he picked up his lover's luggage and unlocked the dead bolt. As his cigarette dangled from his mouth, he opened the door and dropped the bag in the hall. "It's over," he said coldly. As Boots reached out to touch his face, he said, "Don't," and backed away. "I think you've humiliated yourself enough for one night.

238

Do you really want more from me?" He saw the tears welling up in his ex-lover's eyes, but was too detached to care. "It's a little late for those too," he said firmly. "I would have done just about anything for you, but over this last year you've become an obsessive, controlling, manipulating jealous bitch. The little bit of hope and love I had for you is gone. You're going down a road I don't wanna go, and *frankly my dear,* I don't give a damn anymore."

"Billy, please—"

"No!" he said, backing away and putting his arms out to stop the continuing advances. "It's over darlin'. I want you to listen to me very carefully. There's nothing left," he added icily. "You need to go!" Backing up, he closed the door and locked the deadbolt. With his back against the door, he stood perfectly still as tears welled up in his eyes. "Long time," he thought. "Five years is a fucking long time." Walking over to his balcony window, he looked out. Parked below, was a blue SUV Ford with its motor running. Staring at it, he knew it was waiting for his ex-lover. He watched as Boots climbed into the SUV and kissed the driver. "Looks like I don't have to call you a cab," he said, watching his five-year relationship drive off with another lover.

A wave of relief washed over him as his stereo played Barry White's *Let The Music Play.* "Pain is mandatory, suffering is optional," he mumbled, as he danced his way into the kitchen and grabbed a beer. Dancing back into his living room, he smiled as he performed some intricate ballroom Samba steps that his mother had taught him. As he continued dancing, all his sorrow seemed to be lifted from him. He sang along with Barry until the Disco song ended. "...*let it play on and on and on and on.*" Dancing into his bedroom, he turned on the TV. After putting out his cigarette, he slipped off his jeans and climbed into bed.

Surfing the channels, he found a *Law and Order Special Victims Unit* show. Watching it, he repeated drowsily, "Detective Benson..." over and over until he fell asleep.

Across town, Detectives MacTavish and Keaton had left the restaurant and walked outside. "We'll have to do this again," smiled Mac, as they waited for the parking valet to bring his car. "It was quite enjoyable. And I meant what I said about helping you with your art. You'll have to come to my home and see my studio."

"I would like that," she smiled.

"Now, let's go to your place and look at your etchings," he said, escorting her into his Lexus.

It was quiet outside Cavanaugh's condominium complex until a dark van with its motor running interrupted the midnight silence. The driver was looking up at the young detective's condo. After a few moments, it moved stealthily away from the complex.

Meanwhile, in Vickie's apartment, MacTavish was surrounded by framed and unframed artwork that represented outdoor activities accomplished by various women. He was critiquing one named *Ageless Garden*—a painting of a young woman working in her floral garden. In the upper right corner, an elderly woman was looking down at her herself, remembering her youthfulness and the love she had for her flowers.

"I'm impressed," said Mac. "My God woman, I wasn't half this talented when I started out. There are a few rough edges, but I can help you with that."

For a brief, romantic moment, their eyes connected. Vickie took the initiative and kissed Mac softly on the lips. For a few seconds, he

240

reciprocated, and then gently pushed her away. Still holding her arms he said, "You're a very beautiful young lady and I'm very flattered. However, I must be honest with you...."

"There's someone else," she sighed. "Is she important to you?"

Removing his hands from her arms, he replied, "Yes. I've been with her for a very long time."

"And there's never been anyone else Mac?"

"There have been romantic encounters. But Vickie; you're not the type for something that ends when I walk out the door. Knowing that, I cannot take advantage of you."

"And what is it that I really want Mac?"

"What you *need* and *want* is the ring, kids, a home, and someone who'll be there only for you. I could never offer you that."

"Wow," she smiled. "I hope someday, someone will love me the way you love this woman."

"Someone will, even if I have to find him myself." Looking at his watch, he got up and moved towards the door. "We best call it a night and get some sleep. I am looking forward to helping you. Let's arrange it for Sunday morning at my home. Say, seven-thirty?"

"Sure. I'm looking forward to it," she confirmed. "See you tomorrow." Closing and locking the door, Vickie was brightened by MacTavish's appraisal. Looking around at her paintings, she was pleased with the thought of improving and selling her work.

As MacTavish entered the lobby, he looked at his reflection in the glare of a window and sighed, "What can I say? They *all* want you." Humming one of his favorite Engelbert recordings, *Les Bicyclettes De Belsize*, he left the building.

๛ఌ

THANKS FOR THE MEMORY

It was Saturday; all the detectives were putting in an extra work day to solve the Kingman case. MacTavish and Matthews were already at their desks when Cavanaugh arrived. Sitting down at his desk, he glanced at Keaton's empty chair and smiled at his partner.

"You keep her out too late?"

Ignoring Cavanaugh's personal question, Mac said, "I checked my computer. Like you said, there's nothing."

"We should have figured that this information would go nowhere...just like the damn house," said Billy, as he continued reviewing his download. "There's nothing here either."

"Well," said Mac, "sometimes long shots pay off, other times they don't."

"Sorry I'm late," said Vickie, as she rushed into the bureau and quickly sat down at her desk. "I had an early breakfast with a very close friend. I guess I lost track of time," she smiled, putting her purse in her desk drawer.

"Someone we know?" hinted Mac. "A colleague perhaps?"

Cavanaugh shrugged his shoulders questionably when Vickie looked at him, and began to take a sip of his coffee.

"Well if you must know...I was with Shawn O'Hara," she replied happily.

Cavanaugh choked and spat out his coffee—spraying it across his desk. MacTavish quickly backed his chair away to avoid the shower of coffee coming towards him from across his desk.

"Am I missing something here?" she questioned.

"No, but I think the Kid is," replied Mac, as he watched his partner wipe his mouth and try to clean up the mess left by the splattered coffee.

"I need some coffee," she said, walking away happily.

"More has just been revealed," said Mac. "Evidently they're on better terms than you thought."

"Women," said Billy, as he threw the coffee stained napkins into his wastebasket. He was still cleaning his desk, when Vickie came back with her coffee. "So you're not upset with O'Hara?" he said.

"No," she answered. "Whatever gave you that idea?"

MacTavish gave his partner a wide-eyed expression as he listened to her explanation.

"No, we're fine. Shawn and me...we're just friends, nothing more. *"It was just one of those things,"* she sang, *"just one of those crazy flings."*

MacTavish, observing and hearing the other side of the story, leaned over and whispered to his partner, "This is definitely a different interpretation than the one you gave me in Cleveland."

Cavanaugh ignored his partner's response and changed the subject—focusing in on Matthews. "Hey Marc, you sure are quiet over there. What's going on?"

"I've been looking at Kingman's autopsy report," he answered, getting up from his desk. "Take a look at this," he said, walking over to Cavanaugh and handing him the report.

As Cavanaugh quickly reviewed it, something in the report caught his eye. "Does this mean what I think it does?"

"Yeah Kid, that caught my attention too," Marc replied. "This *could be* our big break."

"C'mon," said Billy, tossing the paperwork to MacTavish. "We need to talk to Sarina about this report," he continued, as they quickly rushed down to the basement.

"What's that all about Mac?" said Vickie. "What's in the report?"

"Christ! Here take a look," he said, as she walked over and stood next to him.

"This could explain a lot," she responded, reading the report.

Meanwhile, Cavanaugh and Matthews were downstairs walking through the doors of the morgue. The odor from the lab almost knocked Matthews off his feet as he staggered in. "Oh-h-h..." he moaned.

Widely respected for her analysis reports of unsolved cases, Sarina Montez was an exotically attractive woman in her late-forties. A former homicide detective and having previous medical training in Spain, she decided to transfer into forensics. She greeted the detectives while dissecting the stomach of an exposed male body.

"How can I help you guys?" she said, cutting and removing the organs of her most recent body.

As the two detectives moved closer, Matthews got a very graphic look at the internal organs of the fresh corpse. Lightheaded, and holding his left hand across his forehead, he said, "Oh my...that's more information than I need to see today."

"I just reviewed your report on Larry Kingman," said Billy.

"What about him? Oh damn!" she said, as blood squirted on her clear plastic facemask. "Better back off a bit cowboy. I wouldn't want to ruin those expensive designer boots."

Looking down at his crocodile boots, Cavanaugh backed away from the examining table. "No...we wouldn't want that," he smiled.

"You guys don't mind if I stand back by the door?" said Marc. "I think I need some air."

"Yeah, go ahead," Billy snickered.

"Thanks," replied Marc, covering his mouth as he walked back towards the entrance.

"Getting back to the Kingman report," said Billy. "Other than the 58 grain hollow point slug you found, your secondary report stated that there were also traces of two different tranquilizers. This re-evaluation gives us the possibility that his death was caused by lethal injection."

"Actually, it's more than an accurate possibility," she said, removing more organs as they talked. "I was wondering when one of you would be down here to ask me about that."

"We didn't think too much about the first report," replied Billy, "figured the guy was a mark. Why look for anything else when he was shot through the heart?"

"So why the new interest?" she said curiously.

"We seem to have a similar cold case homicide."

"Wait a minute, similar rings a bell," she said, putting down her tools and covering the cadaver. "You're talking about the warehouse explosion last year?" Taking off her protective clothing, she bagged them up and walked towards the sink. "That photographer...I did his autopsy. I remember him having a similar bruise." After washing her hands, she turned to Cavanaugh and said, "Let's take a look at his files. I believe that was done through the One Five. I remember them writing it off as a hit."

Cavanaugh followed Sarina back to her office and watched as she sat down at her computer—pulling up Howard Austin's report. Together, they watched as it flashed on the monitor in front of them.

"There it is," she said. "Light traces of Valium, several bruises, and a small puncture wound in the right arm."

Leaning on the back of her chair, Cavanaugh got a strong whiff of her Jasmine scented body. The aroma excited him into replying, "WOW!"

Sarina turned around and looked up at him. "I think I would have given this information a little more than a *wow.* Want my opinion?" she said, standing up.

"Sure," he replied faintly, while backing away from her.

"Both reports showed identical puncture wounds and similar amounts of sedatives. Same bullet wounds, different guns. You gotta admit, it's pretty brilliant if it's what I think it is."

"Sarina, you have my undivided attention."

"Try this scenario," she said, "Your victims were probably dead before they were shot. Not long either, perhaps a second or too. The timing was so precise and perfect. I believe they never even felt the bullet."

Seeing the crime scene through her eyes, Billy sat down on the edge of her desk and said, "So you're telling me that both victims died from lethal injections."

"You wanted my opinion."

"The shot in the heart...why bother?"

"Possibly some significant meaning or making a statement," she responded. "Looks like my psychological profiling studies are paying off."

"You are an incredible woman Sarina."

"Oh detective," she said, "I remember you saying that to me one night when you were fucking me in your car."

Cavanaugh, slightly embarrassed by her provocative statement, laughed. "I guess you're just an incredible woman in every way— personally and professionally."

Their conversation was interrupted by her ringing cell phone. "I'll be right back," she said, walking away to answer the call.

Cavanaugh remembered the night Sarina was talking about. He and Boots had broken up for the second time that year—that night took place five months ago during the *Thanksgiving Day* Weekend. Several precinct cops and detectives were celebrating the holiday at a neighborhood bar. Somehow, he and Sarina ended up together.

...They drink to the Pilgrims. They drink to the Indians. And they drink to all the turkeys working in the precinct—laughing and enjoying each other's company as if they've known each other for years. When it came time to call it a night, and because of her inebriated condition, MacTavish suggests someone drive her home.

"She lives near me," says Billy innocently. "I'll take her home."

"Good," Mac replies, turning around and addressing his fellow workers. "It was great being with all of you. Now I must bid you all a Happy Thanksgiving and a good night."

As MacTavish leaves the pub, Cavanaugh helps Sarina get to her feet. "Hey, I'm okay," she says. "A bit of fresh air and I'll be able to drive."

"Not tonight Esmerelda. Tonight you're riding with me," he says firmly, while placing her jacket over her shoulders.

Leaning on him for support, she lays her head on his chest and laughs. "That sounds like a wonderful opportunity."

Giving her a boyish smile, he asks, "And what kind of opportunity are we talking about here?"

Putting her finger to her lips she replies, "Sh-hh."

"Okay, here we go," he says, walking her to the door as she holds on to him tightly. Once outside, she takes a deep breath and appears to be a little better balanced as he assists her into the car. Closing the door, Cavanaugh can't help but notice her sexy legs in the tight mini skirt she's wearing. Taking a deep breath, he walks around his car and slides into the driver's seat.

As he begins the drive to Brooklyn, Sarina, feeling frisky, tosses her hair back off her face in a teasing way. "It's a little warm in here, don't you think?" Glancing at her body, Cavanaugh reaches over to turn off the heater. As she leans forward to turn on the radio, her jacket falls off her shoulders and reveals her open, orange satin blouse. After giving

Cavanaugh a few tantalizing peeks at her bare breasts, she begins to move her body provocatively to an upbeat Latin song playing on the car radio—*I Need To Know* by Marc Anthony.

"It's definitely getting warm in here," he realizes; as the words of the song *wondering if you're ever gonna take me there* begin to have an effect on him. "Are you trying to seduce me Mrs. Robinson?"

"Sh-hh," she said, helping him off with his jacket. Leisurely, she begins to fondle his ear and lick the side of his neck. Leaning over in front of the steering wheel, she reveals everything that was hidden in her blouse.

"Hm-m, no bra," he sighs, glancing down at her breasts.

"I don't believe in them," she softly replies, reclining back in her seat. Making sure he has a good view, she begins to caress her right breast—and very slowly, angles her legs to face the young detective. As she separates them slightly, he sees a black lace thong.

Watching her body move with the music, and listening to the words *it's getting harder not to think of you*, he couldn't help but be turned on. "Boy he's got that part right," he smiles, as his jeans get uncomfortably tight and the car windows begin to steam up. Leaning forward, she strokes his leg up and down, with an occasional slow stroke across the front of his jeans. Hot and excitable, he looks at his watch. "This is the longest ride home I've ever had to make. Just fifteen more minutes, Sarina," he envisions, as she sits up and moves closer. Slowly, she caresses and fondles his face while kissing his neck. Sliding her mouth up to his ear and while unbuttoning his shirt, slipped her hands inside.

Trying not to look at her, he says, "You do realize that if you keep this up you may not make it home."

"You can pull over anytime," she brazenly replies.

"If I did that we'd never get home," he laughs, as she reaches over to where he has an obvious hard on and unbuttons his jeans. When she slides her hand inside, lust overtakes him. "Okay, that's it," he says, and pulls off the next exit. Taking advantage of her open blouse, he moves his hands and mouth over her body while removing her thong as she unzips his jeans. Lifting her up by the waist, he pulls her down on top of him. As he moves inside her, she lets out a pleasurable moan—lusting and enjoying the feel of their bodies locking together. Cavanaugh is very vocal about his orgasm; he could actually feel the earth move under him. Suddenly, he realizes that it's the car that's moving and not the earth. The car has slipped out of park and is rolling down the roadway.

"FUCK!" he yells out. "QUICK MOVE OVER. THE BRAKE—" Reaching behind her, he lunges for the emergency brake and stops the car.

As Cavanaugh sits back in his seat, Sarina begins to laugh hysterically. Looking at her, his moment of fearful frustration quickly turns into loud laughter. "Shall we continue this at my place?" he asks, while zipping up his pants.

Twirling her thong in-between her fingers she replies, "Home Sir William."

"You're a wild woman Sarina," he says, driving back onto the Bell Parkway.

"And you can't seem to get enough cowboy," she smiles.

Thirty minutes later, the tires on Cavanaugh's Ford Mustang's squeal loudly as he pulls into his underground parking garage. The two lustful lovers could barely get out of the car with of all the playful intimacy that's going on between them. Sarina laughs gleefully as she opens the passenger door and teasingly, climbs out backwards. As Cavanaugh tries to reach for her, she says "Uh-uh." He quickly jumps out of the driver's side, slams the door shut, and begins to approach her in a stalking manner. "Detective? You need to restrain yourself," she says, as he shakes his head no and continues stalking her. Holding her coat in front of her open blouse, she backs up slowly. Glancing at the elevator, she decides to make a run for it. He takes off after her and grabs her around the waist. Squealing with laughter, she pushes the button that opens the elevator doors. Cavanaugh pushes her into the elevator—kissing her neck and bracing her up against the wall while pushing the number four button. Halfway up, he pulls out the silent emergency stop button. As he slides down the front of her body to his knees, he lifts up her skirt and begins kissing her legs. After moving his tongue up and down her inner thighs, he gives her oral sex. Holding on to the side railings and experiencing total ecstasy, she realizes that his timing and knowledge of a woman's body is incredible. As he brings her to orgasm, the lights from the fourth floor buttons begin to flash erratically.

Sliding back up to her face, he wipes his mouth with the edge of his shirt. "We'd better go up," he says, releasing the stop button.

As the doors of the elevator open on the fourth floor, his neighbor, a flaming queen with plenty of attitude, is waiting impatiently. "Cavanaugh, I should have known!" he says, scrutinizing the two, half-dressed and very satisfied lovers. Rushing past them, he storms into the elevator. Pushing the down button with a vengeance, he says, "Take it inside Thelma and Louise. Other people have agendas too!"

Laughing and running down the hall, the two lovers can hear him yelling from the descending elevator.

"NEXT TIME BRING AIR FRESHENER. SMELLS LIKE A DAMN WHORE HOUSE IN HERE!"

As Cavanaugh unlocks his door, he turns on the light switch, which turns on his stereo, ignites the fireplace and dims the lights. Kissing passionately, they both move inside. Pulling away from him, she looks around and says, "Wow...it's like a movie set. So romantic. I'm very impressed."

Grabbing her wrist, he pulls her to the bedroom. As she begins to take off her blouse, he removes his shirt and kicks off his boots. "Wanna get wet?" he says, pulling her into the bedroom and slipping out of his jeans.

Looking at his naked body, she says, "I think I already am."

"C'mon," he says in a sexy tone. Leading her into his bathroom shower, he turns the water on.

Sarina takes charge and turns him around. As his palms lay flat against the back of the wall, she begins to kiss the back of his body. Her lathered hands move up and down the front of him, caressing every part of him as the water rushes over them. As he turns around to face her, she slides her body down the front of his. Her hands reach behind his back and settle on his hips. As she pulls him to her mouth, he stretches his arms out to the shower walls and watches her rhythmic motion. As the eroticism sweeps over him, he looks up at the ceiling and closes his eyes. After a few moments of pure ecstasy, the showers stall door opens and Sarina steps out. Grabbing two towels, she throws one inside to Cavanaugh.

The ringing of his cell phone brought the young detective out of his shower flashback and back into the morgue. "Cavanaugh here," he answered.

"I hope I haven't interrupted anything," Mac said suspiciously. "Rollins was inquiring about your whereabouts."

Ignoring his partner's innuendo, Billy said, "Sarina is pulling together reports on the warehouse victim. We have corresponding data on both homicides. I'll fill you in when I get upstairs. This shouldn't take much longer."

"Okay, I'll let Rollins know."

Disconnecting the call, Cavanaugh's mind immediately returned to that time in his condo and shower when his hot lover threw him a towel.

..."HEY," Billy hollers, "I haven't rinsed off yet."

"Sorry. I'll be in your kitchen," Sarina sighs. "I'm hungry."

"DO YOU COOK?" he yells out while drying off.

"HEY GRINGO, I'M SPANISH. ALL SPANISH WOMEN COOK," she replies, walking into the kitchen. Opening the refrigerator and looking in, she can feel Cavanaugh's hands exploring her body under her towel. "Does this mean I'm spending the night?"

"We'll start with tonight," he whispers in her ear. "I hope you don't have plans for the week-end."

Turning around she says, "Nothing I can't cancel." Wrapping one of her legs around his left leg and placing her arms tightly around his neck, she kisses him passionately.

"Time out for food," he declares, pulling away from her. "We're getting distracted again."

Draping herself across the front of his body she says, "Who needs food when we have love."

Cavanaugh pulls her up and faces her toward the open refrigerator. "Okay Esmeralda...start cooking," he says, handing her a jar of salsa out of his cupboard, while she reaches inside the fridge grabbing eggs, red peppers, spinach, and jack cheese. Her mixtures in the frying pan give the kitchen an aroma of being in a Spanish restaurant.

Cavanaugh's flashback was once again interrupted as he sat in the morgue—this time by Sarina. "Sorry about that," she said, walking back into her office. "I'm going to pull up all the report data I have and print it out for you. Do you want to wait, or do you have to get back upstairs?"

"I'll wait," he said softly.

The tone of his voice sounded more personal and less professional. She gave him a double take as she sat down and researched the computer files.

Capturing another whiff of her body oil, Cavanaugh smiled. "God that brings back memories," he thought. Once again his mind drifted back to that night in his condo when he was sitting on his couch.

...Sarina is lying on the floor in front of the young detective's fireplace wearing one of his oversized Miami Dolphins football jerseys. Hearing about her childhood in Spain, he can't believe how mesmerizing she is. Moving off the couch and extending his hand to her, he pulls her up and holds her close before slowly lifting her up and carrying her to the bedroom. As he gently releases her, she raises her arms—allowing him to pull off the *Dolphins* jersey. Throwing herself backwards on the bed, and batting her long eyelashes, she says softly, "Alright Zorro, I am yours to do with as you wish. I will no longer fight your advances. Just be gentle…it's my first time."

Laughing, Cavanaugh slips out of his flannel bottoms and says, "I will be very gentle." With his arms on either side of her, he holds himself up over her inviting body and begins to imitate Antonio Banderas. "I have removed my mask, cape and boots, but not my sword—never my sword." Rising to the occasion, he kisses her passionately. Pulling his mouth away from hers he says, "You're an incredible woman!"

"Billy," she says lovingly.

"BILLY!" Sarina's voice jolted him back to the reality. "Detective Cavanaugh," she grinned, getting up from her computer. "You left the scene. Having memories of last Thanksgiving?"

Slightly embarrassed, he said, "Oh gosh, I guess you got me."

She walked over to him and put her hand on the side of his face. "You're a great lover. And I don't regret that weekend, not one single part of it. Though I must admit," she continued, removing her hand, "that following week was pretty rough—telling me you were going back to your roller coaster lover."

"Sarina," he said, grabbing her hand. "I never meant to hurt you."

"No, I believe you" she said, pulling her hand away from his. "But what really amazes me is why you keep hurting yourself by going back to that cow-riding bitch." Realizing that her words startled him and that it wasn't her best approach to the situation; she took a breath and lost her attitude. "Hey, I'm sorry. But what hurts you, well, it affects me too," she said, turning away. "So how is the on again lover?"

"Off. We broke up."

"And when did this breakup take place?"

"Yesterday."

"So this makes what...three times this year?"

He moved closer to her and held her face in his hands. "Meet me tonight at Pershing Square."

Sarina gently removed his hands and placed them on the front of his jeans zipper. "You have great hands. Use them on yourself. I'm not going to be there every time you're on the rebound. I won't go through that again."

"I wouldn't use you like that. That was never my intention. Look Sarina, I can't change what happened. I guess I just had to go through it one more time. If I've lost any chance of ever being with you again, well I can't change that either. I'm sorry I hurt you, but the pain and misery I went through these past few months have finally convinced me that I was in a very unhealthy relationship. Believe me, it is over and I won't be going back."

"These were done while you were dreaming about the past and what could have been," she said, handing him the copied files. As he turned away and walked towards the door, she suddenly called out, "Cavanaugh? I'm willing to talk."

"Okay," he smiled without turning around. Leaving the morgue, he bumped into Matthews coming down the stairs.

"Sorry Kid, I had to get rid of my breakfast," said Marc. "It was like the fucking Exorcist movie. Once I started, I couldn't quit—had to change my shirt and all."

As they walked up the stairs, Cavanaugh handed him Sarina's files. "We need copies for everyone. Can you bring them up to date?"

"Sure. I'll get right on it."

As they walked back into the bureau, MacTavish was talking on his cell phone. "Tonight would be great. We'll see you then." Disconnecting the call, he said, "How'd it go downstairs?"

"Really good," Billy answered, sitting down at his desk. "It's all in the report that Matthews is copying. Who was on the phone?"

"O'Hara. He wants to meet with us tonight after we get off."

"Oh Christ, I can't, not tonight."

"You got plans again?" Mac asked with raised eyebrows. "You didn't get enough while you were downstairs?"

Ignoring his partners' sexual innuendos, he became a little unsettled in his thoughts. "There's this situation I need to clear up. Can we postpone this meeting until tomorrow?"

"You need any help with that situation?"

"No," sighed Billy. "But thanks for offering."

"Do what you need to do," Mac replied softly, "I'll handle the meeting and fill you in. Besides, this will give me a chance to beat the Irish bloke at another game of darts."

Matthews walked into the bureau looking a little green. He was carrying copies of the reports in one hand, and a bottle of antacids in the other.

"You okay Marc?" Mac inquired.

"I'm really not doing well," he answered, holding his stomach. "I'm telling you, it's a good thing Sarina's on our side. She could make Hannibal Lechter look like a Gay dancer on Broadway."

"She's just passionate about her work," laughed Billy.

MacTavish caught the sentimental tone in his partner's voice and gave him an inquisitive stare. As their eyes met, Cavanaugh quickly refocused on his computer and thought, "He knows...somehow he knows."

MacTavish's focus was quickly redirected by Matthews's comical adlibbing.

"I'm telling you," said Marc, "that woman is faster than those slice and dice machines on TV. You know where she would be great? Deer hunting. Think about it, she could have that thing cleaned, gutted, filleted, and packed in ten minutes."

Cavanaugh dropped his head on the desk laughing.

"There's one in every precinct," Mac said amusingly. "There must be some kind of prerequisite code. *Attention all precincts—one comedian detective is a requirement,*" he said, imitating Groucho Marx.

Vickie rejoined them in the midst of their laughter. "Okay, what'd I miss?"

"We were talking about Sarina's expertise with her tools of trade," said Mac.

"Oh," she said, sitting down at her desk, "you mean *the queen of slice and dice?*"

"Yep, *that's her,*" Marc agreed.

"C'mon you guys," said Billy defensively. "You make her sound like Jack the Ripper."

It was the words MacTavish was waiting for. "Jacquelyn," he interjected softly, giving Cavanaugh the, *I know you've been fucking her* smile. "It would be...Jacquelyn the Ripper."

"I need a smoke," said Billy, grabbing his cigarettes and jacket.

"Wait," Matthews called out, "I need some fresh air too. All this conversation about carving flesh is getting to me again."

"GOOD IDEA. YOU DON'T LOOK SO GOOD," Vickie yelled out, as they walked towards the stairs. Looking over at MacTavish, she said, "What's with Cavanaugh's attitude?"

"Growing pains."

"Oh," she said, reviewing Sarina's medical reports.

They both worked silently for a several minutes before MacTavish got up and walked over to her desk. "Vickie, the night before we left Cleveland...you and the Kid were on the phone—"

"It wasn't me," she interrupted. "That was my Pilates night."

"Oh," he responded indifferently.

"So he's got an interest in somebody and you thought it was me?"

"No. He was talking to someone who appeared to be troubled. I thought it might have been you—it wasn't a romantic call. Look Vickie," he said, getting up and walking over to her, "what happened last night? Nothing needs to be said about it, if you get my drift." Leaning towards her he whispered, "I mean the kiss and all."

"Mac," she responded softly," we're friends who went out for friendly dinner and then went to see my artwork. That's all."

"Thanks," he said, returning to his desk.

Pulling out her cell phone, she called his extension. "I have just one thing to say before we erase last night. When I kissed you, it was very special and romantic. I'll never forget the moment, but I can and will put it behind me."

Disconnecting the call, MacTavish smiled affectionately at her— appreciating her gentleness and understanding.

Cavanaugh arrived back just in time to catch their magic moment. Tossing his cigarettes on his desk, he pulled out his chair and sat down, facing them. His head bobbed up and down with a *know-it-all-look*. "You two never did tell me how it went last night. You know...dinner and all?"

"You should have been there," Vickie responded. "We had a great time at The Water Garden. Mac with his war stories and me with my art history...it was a lot of fun."

"And very romantic I'm sure," he teased, hoping for more intimate information.

"Batting her eyes at him, she flirtatiously said, "I'm sure it would be with the right person. Are you offering me a romantic dinner cowboy?"

MacTavish snickered at her brilliant performance. "You go girl," he said under his breath.

"Me?" Billy questioned. "I don't think so."

Suddenly, Captain Rollins walked in and said, "Sorry to break up the party. I need a squad to go to Greenwich Village. Some good old boys desecrated a Baptist Church. Matthews and MacTavish, it's all yours. This could be related to an old homicide case you two worked on a few years ago. Words out that these guys are wanted for lot more than trashing a church so be careful."

"We'll see you guys later," said Marc, grabbing his jacket and antacids. Putting on their jackets, he and MacTavish rushed down the stairs.

"TAKE BACKUP," yelled Rollins, as he approached Cavanaugh. "Any new leads on your case?"

"Just what you have on your desk," said Billy.

Rollins looked at him intensively and paused—as if he expected more information. "You and Mac wouldn't be holding anything back from me?"

"No. As we get it you get it."

"Make sure you follow through on that. And that goes for your partner too. I don't want any more buildings blown up."

"Hey captain, that building...we weren't—"

Rollins held up his hand in front of Cavanaugh's face to stop him from explaining. "No more re-playing the *Butch Cassidy and the Sundance Kid* movie. Are we clear?"

"Yeah," Billy answered, as he watched Rollins walk back to his office. Biting his lower lip, he quickly reviewed something in his mind. Turning to Vickie he said, "What do you think Vickie?"

"About what?"

"What the captain just said."

"You and Mac really have to be more careful. Somebody out there tried to blow you guys up."

Looking at her strangely, he replied, "*Not that*. Which one does the captain think I am, Butch or Sundance?"

"Neither," she responded flatly. "I'm thinking more like you doing stupid human tricks on David Letterman.

"Yeah right," he said, while answering the ringing bureau phone. "19th Precinct, Detective Cavanaugh." He paused and rolled his eyes at Vickie—making her laugh at his facial impression. "No sir. You need to call the 21st Precinct. Yeah, you live in the 21st Precinct." Hanging up, his cell phone rang. Looking at the calling number, he abruptly said, "I don't think so."

"Bill collector or spurned lover?" smiled Vickie.

"Cute Vickie...you are so damn cute," he said, getting up from his desk. As he walked past her on his way to the bathroom, he reached over and squeezed her nose.

The two detectives had always had a brother/sister affiliation. Sometimes sibling rivalry prevailed, other times it was sympathetic and protective.

ಏಡಿ

FRANCOISE JOUBERT

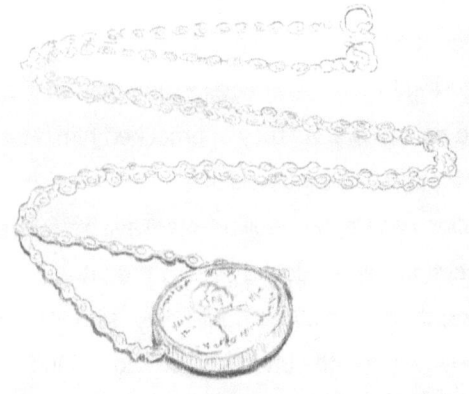

As MacTavish and Matthews pulled up in front of the Baptist Church, they saw Nazi emblems spray painted Red everywhere. In front of the church, a group of uniformed officers were gathering evidence and inserting them into protective bags.

"Christ," said Marc, as he looked around at all the graffiti. "Some sick fucking people. It's a church for Christ's sake. I can't believe this."

"Believe it," Mac answered. "In some parts of the South, this is still considered recreational activity."

"Has CSU been here yet?" said Mac, approaching one of the officers.

"Just left," he answered. "They gave us clearance to bag this stuff."

"Any leads?" asked Marc.

"We lucked out. Two witnesses were making out in the alley across the street."

"You have their names?" Mac inquired.

"Yeah," the officer replied, giving up his notepad and pointing to a young Black couple seated in the back seat of a police car. "They're in the car."

"Thanks," said Mac, as he and Matthews walked towards the witnesses—focusing in on an average looking man that was standing near one of the police cars. As they approached him, MacTavish's cell phone rang. "Mac here," he responded.

The caller was Captain Rollins. MacTavish's face exhibited a variety of expressions as he looked over at the unfamiliar stranger who was approaching them. "Yes, he's right here," said Mac, as he and Matthews move towarded the oncoming stranger. "In fact, he's looking at us as we speak. Now he's waving to us. Okay captain. We're on it," he said, disconnecting the call.

"What's going on?" Marc inquired.

"Let's go meet Inspector Clousseau; he's joining our unit," smiled Mac.

There was a silent vigilance about the Canadian detective with a five o'clock shadow. His long European raincoat covered a frame that revealed someone un-athletic.

After introducing themselves, MacTavish tried to explain their awkwardness. "If we appear a bit confused it's because we didn't know you were on board until just two minutes ago. Captain Rollins said you've joined our squad."

"I hope you aren't too inconvenienced," replied Joubert with a French accent. "I realize that surprises are sometimes uncomfortable."

264

"Welcome aboard," smiled Marc. "Due to all the transfers, we have been a little short on detectives."

"Shall we go see what our witnesses have to say?" suggested Joubert.

"After you," Mac said politely—following the captain's request to let Joubert take charge. As they all walked towards the witnesses, he said, "You're to be the primary Joubert."

"Thank you," he replied, approaching the open car door. Leaning in, he began to speak softly to the two witnesses. "I'm Detective Françoise Joubert. These other gentlemen are Detectives MacTavish and Matthews," he said, glancing back and acknowledging them. Turning back to the witnesses he said, "We need to ask you some questions."

"Oh God! I can't believe this happened," the girl said hysterically, as she hung on to her boyfriend.

"It's alright, you and Tyrone are both safe. That man out there," said Joubert, pointing to one of the uniformed police officers that stood near the front of the car. "He told me your name is Sherawn. It's a beautiful name. Sherawn, I would like you to look at me as I speak. I'm going to explain something and it's very important that you do not look away," he continued with a slight smile. "In fact, you really don't want to look away, do you?"

Sherawn shook her head no, as he continued speaking slowly and softly. His voice had a calming effect on her.

"Good," he continued. "I want you to know that I understand your fear, but you are safe now. In fact, you feel safe don't you?" Sherawn nodded in agreement as Joubert continued explaining the procedures that would take place. "We need to take you both to our precinct to talk about this incident. So, here's what's going to happen.

You and Tyrone will stay right here. Officer Daniel and his partner," he said, pointing to the same officers he spoke of earlier, "are going to drive you there. I will be following you in that car over there," he added, pointing to his dark green Mercedes SUV. "And these detectives," acknowledging MacTavish and Matthews, "will be driving in front of the car you are in. Now Sherawn, I need you to do something for me. Whenever you feel you're doing okay, I want you to turn and wave to me through the back window. Are you willing to do that?" The young girl was very tranquil as she nodded another yes.

"And you Tyrone...are you comfortable with all this?"

"Yeah," he said, holding Sherawn's hand. "Hey, we'll do whatever needs to be done."

"Good. Now just relax," said Joubert, acknowledging the two teenagers. "We'll leave in just a moment."

Stepping out of the car, Joubert, with MacTavish and Matthews by his side, walked over to the two police officers. Standing in front of their vehicle, he explained to the officers to act as if they were alone in the car and discuss any humorous situations that they themselves had personally experienced.

"Sure, we can do that," Officer Daniel added, looking at his partner Officer Tully.

"How about we talk about that camping trip when a bear chased you up a tree?" asked Tully.

"I'd rather discuss you falling off the ferry on the way to the Statue of Liberty," said Daniel, as they got back into their car.

"Comedians, they're everywhere," said Mac, as he and Matthews walked back to their car and got in. "What do you think about our new addition?"

"He's got something going," answered Marc. "The way he calmed that girl down...it was almost like hypnotism. Just like the Pied Piper of Hamlin."

"We're not dealing with an abundance of rodents here," said Mac. "I'm talking about his intellectual approach. He does have a certain psychological persuasion about him. Whatever you want to call it, it does seem to work. However, I wouldn't tag him as the vengeful Pied Piper."

Matthews, leading the caravan of three cars, kept his eyes on the rear-view mirror. Looking at the police car behind him, he saw that the two officers were having a humorous conversation. "Falling off the ferry or climbing with a bear up a tree," Marc pondered. "I would go with the falling off a ferry story."

Driving behind the witnesses, Joubert watched the police car in front of him. Every now and then, Sherawn turned and waved to him. He smiled as he trailed the two cars to the stationhouse.

Back at the precinct, Rollins was walking into the squad room. "Okay, heads up everybody. We got a new detective joining our precinct. He's out on a case with MacTavish and Matthews as we speak. They'll be here shortly, so be kind," he grinned. "He's from the Toronto force."

"Canadian?" Vickie asked.

"Born in France and moved to Canada as a child. "Are we okay with this?" asked Rollins, looking around the room.

Billy thought about WASP and their replacements when someone needed to be transferred out and said, "Is this a replacement or an addition?"

"An addition. Nobody's getting transferred out. Any other questions," Rollins asked?" No one responded. "Good. Now let's get back to work," he said, turning around and walking back to his office.

"Introduce yourselves when he comes in. I have a conference call in three minutes."

The voices filtering up the stairs let everyone know that the detectives had arrived. MacTavish and Matthews were the first to enter, followed by Joubert and the two witnesses.

"I'll take them back," Marc offered, leading the teenagers away from the bureau.

"Thank you. I'll be there shortly," said Joubert.

"Do you guys want a couple of sodas?" Marc asked, escorting them to an interrogation room.

"Yeah, that would be cool," answered Tyrone.

Cavanaugh was the first to introduce himself to Joubert. "I'm Billy Cavanaugh, and this is Vickie Keaton," he said, extending his right hand. Joubert acknowledged by shaking his hand.

Turning to Vickie, Joubert said, "May I call you Vickie...or do you prefer Victoria?"

"Vickie's fine," she smiled. "I haven't been called Victoria since I was a little girl."

"Vickie is acceptable for a detective," said Joubert. "But the renowned artist...she shall be known as Victoria."

Detective Keaton was momentarily puzzled, but quickly realized her personal information came through WASP. The fact that Joubert knew about her art, and considered it high-quality work, pleased her. As she reached out to shake hands, he turned her hand over and gently kissed it European style. She was startled by the elegant gesture, but found it quite delightful. As he released her hand, she looked over at MacTavish—signaling to him that Joubert was WASP by tapping on her shield.

268

"The Agency...of course," Mac thought, as he stared at her.

Cavanaugh, also impressed by the Canadian's finesse, sat down smiling. Observing MacTavish's intense look at Vickie, he assumed it was personal and mumbled softly to his partner, "I think there's a new knight on the floor."

"Cavanaugh, I want you to sit in on this interview," said Rollins coming out of his office.

The young detective got up to follow Joubert, but not before leaning over his desk and whispering to his partner, "I think there's trouble in Camelot King Arthur. Lancelot has arrived and Guenivere seems interested."

MacTavish stopped typing and gave him an annoyed look. "I believe you're expected in interrogation," he said coolly.

"I was just leaving," Billy smiled, as he hurriedly left his desk and headed for the interrogation room.

"What did he say to you?" asked Vickie.

"He told me *Camelot* is on television tonight," Mac responded. "He knows I like Richard Harris...met him on a cruise once."

"Oh," she responded, answering an incoming call. "Detective Keaton here."

MacTavish took a moment and tried to rationalize his partner assumptions. "The Kid's incorrect hypothesis could do him in one day," he thought.

Meanwhile, in the interview room, Joubert had introduced Cavanaugh to the witnesses. "Thanks for helping us on this," said Billy, as he sat down on the corner of a desk that was placed against the wall.

"I see Detective Matthews got you something to drink," Joubert said calmly, as he casually moved to a chair that faced the teenagers.

"Yes, thank you. You've all been so nice," Sherawn answered peacefully.

"How was the ride in?" Joubert asked.

"Oh, it was cool," she said. "We've never ridden in a police car before."

"Tyrone, I'm going to direct these particular questions to Sherawn. We'll get a statement from you later," he said, speaking in a low and soft tone.

"Sherawn, he said, looking directly into the girl's eyes. "I want you to tell me exactly what happened."

"Okay," she replied.

"If it's alright, I'd like to use hypnosis on you. It will help release more information. Tyrone is here, so you can feel safe. I will not ask you about anything that doesn't pertain to the crime. Do I have your permission to do this?"

"Yes," she answered.

Cavanaugh observed that the Canadian's calm and assertive energy made the teenagers very relaxed. Intrigued by his technique, he welcomed the new learning experience.

"Sherawn, I want you to take a deep breath and close your eyes. Now...take another deep breath," he instructed calmly. "Know that you're safe and nothing or anyone here can harm you. I want you to keep your eyes closed until I ask you to open them. Nod yes if you're okay with that." She responded by nodding yes, and continued following his instructions. "Then let's begin," he said, putting her under by using *The Crossing of a Bridge Hypnosis Technique.* "I want you to picture yourself on the way towards the church. Tell me where you are?"

"We are walking towards the alley across the street from the church. Tyrone and I are laughing as we go into the alley. He wants to kiss me."

"As you walk into the alley, exactly what do you see around you?"

"An old man with an umbrella," she smiled. "As he walks past us he winks at me."

"What else do you see?"

"A van, an old white van. It's moving down the street real slow. It's going towards the church."

"Are you looking at the back of the van?"

"Yes," she responded confidently.

"Can you see the license plate from where you are?"

"Yes."

"Read it to me, please."

"West Virginia—" she answered, having the ability to remember the license plate number.

"Whoa," Billy thought, as he quickly pulled out a notepad and wrote down the information as she recalled it.

"Good," Joubert said to her. "Now tell me what is going on with you and your boyfriend? Where are you?"

"Tyrone is pulling me into the alley, and we're laughing. Looking over his shoulder, I see the van stop. It parks in front of the church."

"Tell me everything you see," Joubert said softly.

"Three men are getting out of the van, "she continued. "They are wearing dark plastic coats. The driver isn't getting out. His head is bald, and on the side of his neck is a large tattoo."

Sherawn gave major details about the men involved; height, weight, clothes and all the details that could break a case, including which man did what and how. When she finished, Joubert finalized his debriefing.

"Sherawn, I want you to take a very deep breath. As you exhale, you are to open your eyes you will remember everything you told me."

Opening her eyes she exclaimed, "Oh my God! I didn't realize I saw all that."

Cavanaugh was in awe of what happened. "It was like watching a movie. Or better yet, a video of the crime." he thought.

"Thank you Sherawn. You have helped us tremendously. The mind is similar to a computer," Joubert explained. "It records everything around us. In a conscious state, we tend to remember only what we want. In a subconscious state we remember everything. Now that you've expressed it, you won't forget it. I don't believe you'll even have to testify. Tyrone, do you have anything to add?

"No. I had my back to the church. It all came down so fast. When I turned around all I saw were some guys getting in a van and driving away."

"Well it's a good thing you were with her," said Joubert, standing up. "Just one more thing, are you willing to meet with an artist who is able to draw pictures of the men based on your descriptions.

"Gladly," she replied. "They need to pay for what they did."

"And they will. I assure you these guys will be out of circulation very soon thanks to both of you. The artist will be right with you," he said, as he and Cavanaugh left the room.

Walking down the hallway, he said, "I need to talk to your sketch artist before he meets with our witnesses."

"I'll take you downstairs and introduce you," replied Billy. "He's on the force." As they headed down the stairs, he saw the sketch artist approaching them. "K. C. Landers, meet our new detective—"

"Francois Luc Joubert," the Canadian interjected politely. As they turned around to go back upstairs, Joubert explained the crime scene to Landers. "What I need from you is a storyboard. Have you ever done one before?"

"I'm familiar with them."

"Good. Cavanaugh will give you his notes and our witnesses will fill you in on the details. Can you take care of this for me?"

"Sure can," Landers confirmed, walking towards the interview room.

"Thank you," replied Joubert, as he turned around and walked back into the detective bureau with Cavanaugh.

"Can you get an APB out on the van?" said Joubert.

"I'm on it," Billy responded.

"I need to see Rollins," said Joubert, heading for the captain's office.

As Cavanaugh sat down at his desk, he glanced over at his partner. "You are not gonna believe what just happened in that interview," he said, picking up the phone.

"Is everything alright?" asked Mac.

"Yea," Billy replied, calling dispatch to put out a call for the West Virginia van. Reading them the license number, he continued having both conversations. "Mac, this guy is amazing, he—" Interrupted by the dispatcher, he said, "Yeah, and have them picked up. We don't care who's driving—you need to bring them all in," he said, giving descriptions of the suspects. Hanging up, Cavanaugh had everybody's undivided attention.

"Our new detective...he conducted the most incredible interview I've ever seen. He got everything out of the girl, including the damn vehicle tags. She described those perps as if she saw seem them on a daily basis."

"Did she appear to be hypnotized?" inquired Mac.

"Actually, she was."

"I knew it!" Marc responded. "Instead of rats, he does it with people."

"What the hell are you talking about?" said Billy, staring at Matthews.

"Ignore him," Mac interrupted. "I'll explain later."

"That meeting," continued Billy, "it was awesome. Joubert's got Landers in there working on a storyboard. That girl gave us everything except their names. Look, I got to go. He wants me back in there," he said, getting up and rushing back to the interview room.

"What the hell is a storyboard?" Mac asked.

Matthews, eager to respond, said, "They use it when they make movies. It's a drawing of each scene—scene by scene. I actually saw it on an old episode of *Columbo* last week."

Looking over at Vickie, Mac scratched the back of his neck and mumbled, "First an explosive Irishman, and now a hypnotizing Canadian."

"It'll all work out," Vickie said calmly. "It always does."

"God I need a drink," Mac sighed.

"Want a soda?" Marc asked.

Mac looked at him like he was crazy and asked, "How long have you known me?"

Matthews looked around the office and answered, "Three years."

"Have you ever seen me drink a soda?"

"No, I can't say I have."

"Then why would you ask me that?"

"Because you were thirsty," he responded lightly.

MacTavish got up and slowly and walked over to Marc's desk. Standing behind him, he placed his hands on Marc's shoulders. "I appreciate the thoughtfulness of your gesture." Glancing over at Vickie, he said, "You know, I just may have to start smoking again."

Innocently, Marc asked, "Why is that...I mean, why would you wanna do that to your body?"

"I believe it to be a better alternative than homicide," Mac smiled.

Marc cracked a smile and replied, "Oh I get it...you're kidding."

"Vickie," said Mac, with a frustrated look on his face—gripping Marc's shoulders tightly.

"Marc, can you take these papers to the captain for me?" she quickly intervened.

"Sure," he answered, breaking away from MacTavish's tight shoulder hold. Taking the papers from her, he headed for Rollin's office.

"He means well," said Vickie.

"I know," Mac agreed. "It's just that this whole week I've had to deal with so many different personalities?"

"Were most of them yours?" she laughed.

"Very funny. How about joining me for dinner tonight?"

"I thought you were having dinner with O'Hara?"

"Christ, Vickie, I forgot about that. I'm sorry, but I'll see you in the morning?"

"Looking forward to it."

"Great. I'll acquaint you with my studio and then we can get started. Victoria Keaton is going to be introduced into the European Art World. He wrote down his address on a piece of paper and handed it to her. "Call me if you get lost."

"Okay," she said, folding the paper and putting it in her purse.

As Cavanaugh and Joubert came back into the bureau, Rollins came rushing out of his office and quickly alerted everyone about a pressing situation that was taking place.

"Okay, heads up everybody," he said loudly, walking up to MacTavish's desk. "They found the van and our four racists. They're in a local bar in the 15th Precinct. Joubert, Matthews, and MacTavish, go bring them in. Take reinforcement from downstairs. You'll be hooking up with One Five."

As Matthews and Joubert quickly headed for the stairs, Rollins yelled, "MACTAVISH WILL BE RIGHT BEHIND YOU." Holding him back, he said, "You're meeting with O'Hara tonight right?"

"Yes," Mac responded, "tonight after work."

"I want an update first thing Monday morning." Turning to Vickie, he asked, "Anything else to report, other than what Cavanaugh found out in forensics?"

"No," she responded, "I just finished reviewing it."

"Well let's put our heads together and see what we all get," Rollins added. "Mac, get over to the One Five. I got a bad feeling about these four guys."

Putting on his coat, MacTavish rushed out of the bureau. As he walked down the stairwell, he passed Landers going up. They acknowledged each other briefly, as he hurried outside to catch up with Matthews and Joubert.

"Jump in. We got two squad cars on their way," said Marc, turning the emergency light on. After MacTavish climbed in behind Joubert, Matthews drove away—heading to the One Five terrain.

At a sleazy downtown bar, two 15th squad detectives and four police cars were already on the scene. As Matthews pulled up, the three detectives saw a high security police wagon on the scene. Four suspects wearing waist chains and leg irons were already handcuffed. As they got out of their car, one of the detectives from the One Five yelled out to them.

"Hey Scotty...slumming?" he asked approaching MacTavish.

"I was in the neighborhood. Had a date with your mother Bobo," said Mac, putting his arm around the Black detective's shoulder. "Meet Detectives Matthews and Joubert. Joubert has just joined our precinct.

"Welcome to *Escape From New York*. It takes all kinds to live down here," Bobo laughed.

"How the hell have you been?" Mac asked, looking him over. "Looks like Luwanda's been feeding you a lot of down home cooking."

"She's been doing that alright," he answered. "That woman sure can cook."

"Does she cook as well as she sings?" smiled Mac.

"It's a toss up," he laughed.

Looking at the prisoners, Mac said, "Your guys seem to have everything under control."

"We picked these guys up inside the bar. They got a little racist with some of the customers, but nothing to cause an arrest." As the two detectives talked, the uniformed officers began moving the suspects into the police wagon and chaining them down.

"Then why the heavy gear?" Mac inquired.

"I guess you didn't get the update. These good old boys...seems like they're wanted in five states for three murders and five rapes," he explained, handing MacTavish the report.

"Great work Bobo," smiled Mac.

"Anytime Scotty, Bobo replied, watching as the impound truck towed the van away. "That's why we're here. I just hope someone doesn't hire these assholes some expensive lawyer to get them off."

"Well, let's see if we can get them to cooperate before they lawyer up," Joubert responded calmly. "We need to get them back to the precinct quickly. No press releases until we talk to them." Reaching out to shake hands with Bobo, he said, "It was good meeting you. This was very nice work. Good job."

"Thanks Scotty," said Bobo. "I'll have Luwanda set up a barbeque for us. Now I got to get back to the One Five, Kurt Russell is planning another escape. Take care," he laughed.

As the three detectives watched the officers from the One Five clear the area, Marc asked, "What's with the new nickname Scotty?"

"The name is only for a privileged few," said Mac. "A very few if you get my drift."

"Absolutely. Not to be mentioned again. I'll pull the car up," Marc replied, as he quickly walked away.

"Thank you," said Mac.

"Bobo's a good man," Joubert whispered. "The Agency would be smart to pick him up."

Matthews drove the car up to the waiting detectives. As they got in, MacTavish quickly refocused their discussion. Heading back to the precinct, he briefly explained his trip to Cleveland. And then it happened, Matthews said the words MacTavish thought he would never hear again.

"Sounds like Cleveland would be a great place for a vacation."

"Oh God," Mac mumbled.

ಏಐ

THE GAME'S AFOOT
IN CENTRAL PARK

With everyone gone to pick up the white supremacy boys, Cavanaugh decided to take a break. "C'mon," he said to Vickie, grabbing a set of precinct car keys. "Let's get some lunch...my treat. I'll tell Rollins we're leaving," he added, as he walked towards the captain's office. "Is it okay if Keaton and I grab some lunch?" he asked, leaning inside the open door.

"Sure, that's fine," Rollins replied. "Our detectives are still in the One Five area. They'll be bringing back the convicts within the hour."

"Convicts?" said Billy surprisingly.

"The suspects turned out to be escaped convicts wanted in five states. The U. S. Marshals are on their way in to pick them up."

"Do our guys need any help?"

"No," smiled Rollins. "They've got it under control. You and Keaton go ahead and leave."

Cavanaugh closed the captains' door and joined Vickie who was waiting at the top of the stairs.

"Ready?" she asked.

"Yeah, let's go," he said, putting an unlit cigarette in his mouth and looking at the empty receptionist desk. "What's going on with our receptionist?"

"He's still out sick," she answered, as they walked down the stairs.

"I sure to hell hope he gets back soon," expressed Billy. "Answering the phones is getting old. A receptionist I'm not." As they walked outside, he stopped to light his cigarette. Getting into the car and driving away, he filled Vickie in on what Rollins said about the convicts.

Arriving at Central Park, Billy parked the car and said, "I thought we'd eat outdoors." Leaving the car, they walked to a nearby hotdog stand. "This okay with you?"

"Sure," she laughed. "It beats Mickey D.'s."

Cavanaugh ordered and paid for two hot dogs and a couple of sodas. They began eating as they walked into the park. Unexpectedly, his cell phone rang. "Great," he said, a little dissatisfied with the disruption. "Cavanaugh," he replied into the phone. "Yeah, we're at the park. Okay boss, we're on it," Disconnecting the call, he tossed the rest of his soda and half-eaten hotdog into a nearby trashcan and said, "We got another homicide."

"Where is it?" she asked, tossing her lunch away and wiping her mouth with a napkin.

"Right here...a half a block away," he said, as they hurried through the park.

Arriving at the crime scene, they saw four uniformed officers already there. Two officers were busy roping off the area at Fifth Avenue with yellow crime tape, while the other two officers, Jim Gleason and William Best, were standing near the body. As Cavanaugh and Keaton showed them their identification and ducked under the crime tape, Officer Gleason explained the circumstances of the homicide. "Male...shot through the heart at close range."

"How long ago did this happen?" Billy asked with a concerned look—observing the surrounding area.

"Five minutes, eight tops," answered Officer Best. "We were a half a block away when we got the call."

Cavanaugh's eyes kept re-focusing on the bordering crowd.

"See something?" Vickie asked.

"Just a lot of people who probably didn't see anything. Try to make a note of anything unusual and keep looking."

Putting on the latex gloves that Officer Gleason handed him, Cavanaugh leaned down over the body and removed his wallet. Checking the identification, he was able to identify the victim as Carson James—having a home address in Westwood, California. "Now that's a stretch," he thought to himself, after examining the wound. He slowly stood up and stared at the victim's body and face. Looking at Vickie, he said, "Would you say that this guy is about the same age as Kingman?"

"He's definitely in the same ballpark," she responded, looking down at him. "What are you thinking?" she asked softly.

"I have a feeling that this homicide is somehow connected to our Kingman case," said Billy, as he turned around and looked into the crowd. Moving Vickie away from the officers, he whispered, "What if these guys knew each other and there had some sort of connection? Somebody wants us to go to LA and I'll place a bet that the home in Westwood has been cleaned and rigged just like the house in Cleveland," he said, pulling off his gloves.

"Should we notify them?"

"Call it in to Matthews," said Billy. "Have him call LAPD and be sure they notify their bomb squad." Looking out at the street, he saw the crime unit driving in. Taking out his cell phone, he called his precinct, while Keaton placed a call to Matthews. "Cavanaugh here, let me talk to Rollins."

"Hold on while I transfer you," said the front desk officer.

"Tell me you're heading for Central Park," Rollins quickly answered.

"We're already here...covering it as we speak," he verified. "We need clearance to get this body back to Sarina."

"You want to explain why?"

"I think Kingman and this new victim have some sort of connection. It's the same kind of hit."

"Okay," said Rollins, "We'll take care of the body. You two try and get some answers. And stay put until the Two O gets there. This is their call. I'll get everything straightened out on my end."

"Will do," Billy replied, as he disconnected the call and slipped the phone into his jacket. Approaching Vickie, he said, "Captain's getting this body to our precinct. He wants us to stay put until the detectives from Two O show up. Vic, can you cover this? I want to check the surrounding area."

"Sure," she responded, disconnecting her call to Matthews. "Go ahead, Marc's taking care of the Westwood situation."

Cavanaugh moved out from under the crime tape and headed for the curb. While looking up and down Fifth Avenue, he reached for his cigarettes and lit one. The city's inhabitants seemed oblivious to the homicide scene as honking cabs made their way through the heavy traffic. Taking a puff off his cigarette, he was suddenly overcome with that familiar feeling he had as a child. He began to perspire as he looked up and down the street—trying to steady himself as his eyes drifted toward the oncoming traffic. Sitting in an approaching horse drawn carriage was his lady in gray. Only now, the lady in gray was the lady in black. He flung his cigarette into the street and focused on the driver as he memorized the license plate. Repeating the numbers, he watched as the carriage moved down Fifth Avenue. Pulling out a pen and pad, he wrote down the remembered number and rushed back to the crime scene where Vickie was talking to the two homicide detectives that had just arrived from the Two O Precinct.

"Is everything taken care of?" she asked one of the officers.

"Yeah," replied Detective Kyle Kantrell—a Gay Black man in his mid-thirties. "Carson is all yours," he said, as Cavanaugh approached.

"This is my partner—" Vickie began, but was quickly interrupted by Kantrell.

"Cavanaugh, hey guy...you in on this?"

"Yeah," Billy said aloofly. "We got two similar cases and I'm pretty sure they're related. Are we all clear here?" he asked anxiously.

Slightly confused by Cavanaugh's attitude, Kyle looked at him and said, "Yeah, you guys are good. You can go."

"Thanks for finishing up for us," Billy said hurriedly. "We have to leave. Something else has come up."

"C'mon, let's wrap this up," Kyle said to his partner.

"It was good to see you again Kantrell," said Billy, as he grabbed Vickie's arm and hurried her away.

"Sure Kid, see you around," Kyle yelled out.

Keaton was a little confused by Cavanaugh's abrupt behavior. "You know that cop?" she asked as they rushed away.

"Yes, I met him at this country western bar I go to."

"Oh-h-h" she said.

"What is it Vickie? Why did you want to know?"

"No reason, except—

"Except what?" he interrupted impatiently.

"Well he's—

"He's what Vickie? Black, Gay?" he inquired impatiently.

"Gay and he seemed—

Cavanaugh stopped abruptly and said, "I didn't think you had a problem with Gays and I really don't have time for this right now."

"I don't!" she declared. "And where are we going? What did you mean when you said something else came up?"

"Let's go. We need to take a ride," said Billy, leading the way towards Fifth Avenue. Rushing toward the traffic, he hailed a taxi. As it pulled over, he opened the door for her and said anxiously, "Get in."

"Does Rollins know about this?" she whispered.

"Later," he answered, pushing her into the cab.

"Where to?" the taxi driver asked.

"Straight ahead down Fifth Avenue, I'll let you know where to stop," said Billy, as he sat back and looked out the window.

Leaning close to him, Vickie said, "Billy, I'm confused."

"Nothing to be confused about," he responded intensely.

Keaton closed her eyes for a minute to overcome her anxiety. Opening them, she took a deep breath and said, "You do realize our car is in the other direction?"

"Yes," he said sarcastically, "I know that. Now please be quiet and enjoy the ride. I'm looking for some witnesses. I'm just not sure where they are. They can't be too far ahead, they're in a carriage."

As Vickie reflected on Cavanaugh's behavior, she pondered, "This is so unlike him. He is a good detective...maybe he does have a good lead." She decided to travel along on this journey.

Suddenly, Cavanaugh spotted the horse carriage he had seen earlier. "This is it. Stop here," he said to the taxi driver, who quickly pulled over to the curb. "Let's go...out," he said to Vickie, pulling a wad of bills out of his jeans.

"Well that was fun," she said, getting out of the cab.

After paying the taxi driver, Cavanaugh joined her on the sidewalk and led her to the parked horse carriage. Pulling out his notepad, he matched the number to what he had written earlier.

"So we were chasing a carriage," she said. "Are you going to explain all of this to me?"

Ignoring her question, Cavanaugh walked up to the horse and stroked her back—feeling her head and then her nose. "First stop for you?" he asked the horse affectionately. "Yeah...this is definitely your first stop."

Vickie placed her hands on her hips and said, "Oh, the horse you can talk to. Okay Cavanaugh, talk to me. What the hell are we doing here?"

"Not now Vickie, it's a very long story," he said softly as he looked around to see where the disappearing lady and her escort may have gone. Grabbing her arm, he looked at her and said, "I'll explain everything, just give me ten minutes."

"Okay," she said reluctantly. "But we better have a hell of a story when we get back to the precinct."

Spotting the carriage driver coming out of a nearby restaurant, Cavanaugh released his hold on her. "Let's go," he said, rushing her down the street. "Excuse me," said Billy, approaching the carriage driver, "the blonde lady that was riding in your carriage...can you tell me where she is?"

"In there," the driver answered, pointing to the nearby restaurant. "I was told to wait for them."

Cavanaugh looked at his name badge. It read Wm. Kidd. "Thanks William," said Billy, as he turned around and ran towards the restaurant.

"WAIT UP," Vickie yelled out, rushing after him. She watched as he entered the restaurant and quickly followed in behind him.

A hostess, observing Cavanaugh checking out her customers, said, "Can I help you two? You seem to be looking for someone."

"I don't see her," Billy said apprehensively.

"What does she look like?" whispered Vickie.

"It doesn't matter, she's not here. Look," he said, addressing the hostess. "A blonde woman came in here with a guy. He's probably in his fifties. They were wearing black leather coats."

"Oh them," she responded, pointing to the bar where they were sitting. "They're over there waiting for some food to go."

As Cavanaugh looked over at the couple, a young blonde flirtingly looked back at him and smiled. "No. That's not her," he said, turning back to the hostess. "She's too young."

"Sir, I assure you...those are the only carriage riders who came in here today."

Cavanaugh looked at the nametag she was wearing—it read B. Parker. "Look, Miss Parker," he said impatiently, while showing her his badge. "I'm a detective and that is *not* the woman I saw in the carriage."

"I'll start again *detective*," said the hostess, giving a disgusted sigh as she once again pointed to the same couple. "*That* is the woman who walked through the door with *that man*."

Cavanaugh gave her a dark and defiant stare. His anger about the situation became clearly visible to everyone. One of the managers, sensing the tension, interrupted their conversation.

"Is there a problem Bonnie?"

"Not yet Sonny, but this guy's working on creating one," she unalterably replied.

"Excuse me," interrupted Vickie, as she squeezed in between them. "Detective? Outside," she said with determination.

Backing up, Cavanaugh turned around and walked slowly to the entrance—eyeing everyone in the restaurant. His slow departure gave him a chance to make sure that the lady in black was not lingering around somewhere.

"Look Ms. Parker, it's been a long day," said Vickie. "We're trying to get some leads on a homicide. I apologize for my partner; he's trying desperately to find a killer."

The hostess pointed to the entrance where Cavanaugh was standing and replied, "Well he's very confused. We're not so damn busy that I can't remember who the hell walked through that door."

"That's it," Billy said to himself and called out, "Vickie?"

"Gotta go," she said. "I'm sorry for any misunderstandings. Thanks for your help."

As she joined Cavanaugh at the door, she verbally laid into him as they walked outside. "Have you lost your mind? We're not even supposed to be here. You may want an early retirement, but I need this job. Christ, what were you thinking? Who the hell is this blonde and what does this have to do with our homicide?"

"Nothing," he answered, lighting a cigarette.

"Nothing?" she questioned sarcastically.

"She's my mother."

Startled by his response, she said, "*Your mother*?"

"Yes, my mother," he answered, turning to her with his cigarette dangling in his mouth. "Only here's the rub, my mother died when I was fourteen."

"Okay," she said. "Let's start over. That girl didn't look old enough to be your mother. And if she is, I want the name of her plastic surgeon."

Cavanaugh's attitude softened as he looked over at the carriage driver, who was standing next to his horse and carriage. "Look, she's not my mother. And she's not the person *I thought* was my mother. Don't you see? There had to be a switch. The woman I saw got out of the carriage and this other girl got in."

Keaton looked at him in utter frustration. "Why do I feel like I'm in the middle of an Alfred Hitchcock movie? Take your choice... *The Lady Vanishes* or *Foreign Correspondent*?"

"C'mon," he said, grabbing her hand, and walking up to the cabbie. "I can prove it."

"Remember me?" Billy asked, as he let go of Vickie's hand.

"*Oh yes*. How could I forget?" the man replied sardonically. "Did you find your lady?"

"Actually, I did," said Billy, with his own vocal retaliation. "There's just one small detail I can't figure out. Where did the first lady go?"

"The first lady?" the carriage driver asked.

"Yes," Billy answered with a quiet strength.

"I've never given the first lady a carriage ride. I don't believe the president or the Secret Service would allow it."

Keaton started laughing at the driver's comical feedback. Turning around, Cavanaugh gave her a very displeased look.

"Sorry," she smiled.

Turning back to the carriage driver, Billy said, "Let's you and I start over." Frustrated, he pointed in the direction of the homicide and said, "Back there a few miles, you drove past a homicide scene with a different lady in your carriage—an older lady. Where is *that lady*?"

"It's always been the same lady and she's in there," he said, pointing to the restaurant.

Frustrated, Cavanaugh closed his eyes and dropped his head.

"And here she comes," the carriage driver smiled.

Cavanaugh turned around to see the young blonde and her escort walking towards him. His angry stare forced Keaton to quickly move in front of him—blocking his view. "Listen to me before you get us both arrested for harassment," she said. "I don't want to be in front of the review board. I am going to be the primary here and I will call the precinct if you try to intervene," Pulling out her cell phone she said, "Which way do you want to play this?"

Surprised by her manipulation of the situation, he knew that she would make the call if she had to. "You're the primary," he said softly.

"Try to keep your mouth shut," she replied, as she turned to the couple standing with the carriage driver.

"Is there a problem?" the man asked, as he helped the young blonde climb into the carriage.

"No sir. I'm Detective Keaton and this is my partner Detective Cavanaugh. We had a homicide down the street. A police officer saw you two riding past the scene. We're just doing a follow up."

"We really weren't aware of too much," the man said, looking at the young blonde. "I guess we were so deep in conversation that we weren't conscious of anything else. I'm sorry," he concluded.

"It's okay," Vickie answered. "One more question if you don't mind? Where exactly did you get into the carriage?"

"I believe it was four miles from here?" the man quickly answered.

"Well, that should do it." Turning to the carriage driver she asked, "Can you verify that it was four miles?"

"Yes. That's quite accurate...four miles," the carriage driver said adamantly.

"Thank you all for your cooperation," she said, finishing her interview. As they walked away together, she grabbed Cavanaugh's arm and said sternly, "Don't look back!"

Tossing his cigarette away, Cavanaugh was a little confused by her abrupt secretiveness, but quickly realized that she controlled their situation. As they reached the corner, they flagged down a cab. Getting in she said, "Straight ahead, we'll tell you where to stop."

"Vickie?" said Billy, as he climbed in next to her.

"Sh-h-h," she said, nodding and glancing at the cab driver. The two detectives sat quietly as the cab drove past the now desolated crime scene.

Arriving at their destination, Cavanaugh paid the driver and followed Keaton out of the taxi. Watching it pull away, he said, "Okay, why the silence?"

"There could be agents all around us," she said, as they got into the department car they had left behind. "Oh my God...your paranoia is contagious."

"So you think I'm paranoid," he replied, lighting another cigarette.

"Of course not. It's just that...something's not right about that carriage driver and his customers. I just need to rethink this. Something's off."

"So you do believe me," said Billy.

Keaton looked at him and raised her eyebrows questioningly. "I don't know yet," she replied, turning away and staring out the passenger window.

"You were right," he said, as she glanced at him with a questioning look. "To take over as the primary...you were right. I was out of control. It was the right thing to do."

"And," she said.

"And I'm sorry for my behavior. I was way out of line," he added. "I pulled you into this when I shouldn't have. It could have cost you your shield and your job. I did the same thing to Mac. I apologize."

"Wait a minute; you went through an episode like this with Mac?"

"Yeah, it was during the Kingman homicide."

"The day he told us you were sick."

"Same situation, I saw my mother in the crowd and we went to look for her."

Cavanaugh briefly explained about the search for the lady in gray. By the time they reached the precinct, he had finished the story with her disappearing into thin air.

"Oh my God," Vickie responded, "Did you ever think of talking to someone about this?"

"Please," Billy said sharply, "I don't have a problem. There's no psychotic episode going on here. And I'm not having a mental breakdown for Christ's sake," he answered, as they got out of the car.

"It seems as though you are the only one who has seen her—at two different locations with hundreds of people around. How can you explain that? Maybe you are hallucinating."

"Is that what you think?" he said angrily, as they walked toward the precinct. "First you think I'm paranoid and now I'm supposedly hallucinating. What if all those other people are lying?"

"*Conspiracy Theory* I suppose," said Vickie sarcastically. "Are you having a Mel Gibson meltdown?"

Tossing away his cigarette, Billy defensively said, "I am not crazy."

As they approached the front steps of the precinct, scenes of the movie flashed through Keaton's mind. "What if someone was re-creating the movie?" she thought. "You know what," she said softly, as they entered the building, "Mel wasn't crazy either. Maybe someone wants to make us all believe you're having a breakdown. We'll figure it out. We should talk to Mac. You're not crazy Cavanaugh, a little bizarre at times, but definitely not crazy." Walking up the stairs, she tried to put the pieces together—it was a weird experience that didn't make any sense.

As they walked into the bureau and approached their desks, Rollins walked over to them and said, "Anything I should know about?"

"Following up on some witnesses at the scene," Vickie immediately responded. "Cavanaugh had a lead on three people that might have seen something. We tracked them down and spoke to them. I was the primary."

"Come up with anything?"

"No," she responded. "You know captain; there were a lot of people around. It's really odd that no one saw anything."

Rollins, observing her concern and frustration said, "Its okay. It'll all fall into place. Listen, our convicts are here and so are the Marshals."

"Need our help?" she asked.

"No. They've got it under control. Work on this Central Park case," he said, as he turned and walked back to his office.

"God...that was good Vic," Billy whispered, pulling out his chair and sitting down.

"You better let me write this up," she said anxiously while turning on her computer. "You can read it when I'm through."

"I'm gonna see if I can track down Mac," Billy said, getting up.

"That's a good idea," she smiled, looking up at him. "You can fill him in on what happened today."

"I'll do that...the disappearing woman and all."

"Yeah, that's what I meant," she sighed.

Walking toward the interrogation room, Cavanaugh saw Matthews, Joubert, and MacTavish heading his way. "Anything I can do?" he offered.

"No, we're just about done here," said Joubert.

"The Marshals are here," said Marc, making his way through the oncoming entourage. "I'll be with the captain if you guys need me."

Four U. S. Marshals joined the remaining men in the hallway, followed by two detectives from San Francisco—fifty-six year old Jack Reilly and thirty-eight year old Andy Chan. Their appearance revealed them to be highly qualified in the martial arts. "Jack Reilly," he said, identifying himself and reaching his hand out to the New York detectives. "This is my partner Andy Chan.

"We're here to transport the prisoners," said Chan, pulling out his Con Air Special Unit Forces identification. "We understand they've already confessed."

"Signed, sealed and delivered," Joubert said with satisfaction.

"You guys have any trouble rounding these boys up?" asked Chan.

Cavanaugh was quick to respond. "Credit goes to Joubert here; he got the ball rolling in interrogation. If it wasn't for him I don't think we would have gotten any leads or descriptions."

"You're Joubert...Francoise Joubert?" said Chan, extending his hand out. "You have quite a reputation for solving cases. It's an honor to meet you sir."

"We need to get these guys to the airport rather quickly," interrupted Reilly. "They're holding a Pelican Bay flight for us."

"Can we get the area cleared so we can take these guys out?" asked Chan. "They have friends and we sure as hell don't need any complications."

"We'll take care of it. Give us five minutes," Mac replied. "I'll be at my desk if you need me for anything else. Nice meeting you gentlemen," he added, nodding for Cavanaugh to follow him.

"They're in the cage...this way," said Joubert, escorting the Marshals down the hall.

Cavanaugh started filling MacTavish in on what happened at the park, but was suddenly interrupted by Mac whispering, "We'll talk later..." making him aware with an eye signal that Rollins was approaching. Sitting down at their desks, MacTavish placed the call downstairs about the high priority safety alert, while Cavanaugh cleared the upper levels.

"Where are the guys from Con Air?" Rollins asked.

"They're in lock-up with Joubert," replied Billy.

"We just cleared the area so they could get those guys out of here," added Mac.

"Looks like Butch and Sundance have just scored some points with the sheriff," smiled Rollins. "I better get down there to sign the release and transport paperwork." Walking by the empty reception desk, he yelled out. "DOES ANYBODY KNOW WHEN OUR RECEPTIONIST IS COMING BACK?"

"Tomorrow," confirmed Vickie—passing him in the hallway.

"THANK GOD!" he replied loudly and walked away.

"Damn it," said Billy frustrated.

"What," said Mac, puzzled by his partner's subtle outburst.

"I still don't know which one I am, Cassidy or Sundance?"

"Not too hard to figure out Kid, think about it," Mac smiled. "If it doesn't come to you in the next five seconds I'm going to request a new partner. It's either that or start calling you Louie."

"Sundance! I'm Sundance," Billy laughed happily.

"Thank God," smiled Mac. "There are times that you remind me of Satchel in the *Get Fuzzy* cartoons and this is definitely one of those times."

Major activity started to take place in the precinct. Officers and detectives rushed to clear and protect the building while the Marshals prepared their departure with the prisoners.

Returning to her desk, Keaton pulled out her chair as she sat down. "I'll be so glad when this day is over," she sighed.

"You got special plans for your day off?" Billy asked.

She immediately looked over to MacTavish.

"I didn't say a word," said Mac, shaking his head.

Cavanaugh looked at them both suspiciously and asked, "Dinner again?"

"No," she responded caustically. "We thought a carriage ride through the park would be more appropriate."

"Ouch," whispered Mac, looking at his partner.

Cavanaugh closed his eyes and gave a disgusted sigh. He grabbed his cigarettes and left the bureau.

"I need to talk to him," Mac said, slipping into his jacket.

"Mac, I didn't mean to—"

"Vickie," he interrupted, "sometimes the Kid pushes people too far with his little innuendoes. Personally, I think it was a very appropriate answer. I would have told him to fuck off."

Rushing down the stairs, MacTavish quickly headed outside and walked behind the precinct where he knew his partner would be smoking.

Cavanaugh was focused on the new renovation for WASP. Glancing over his shoulder, he saw his partner walking up behind him. Turning back to the construction site, he continued watching the workers. As a large crane placed a steel beam on the new building, he said softly, "Always wanted to drive one of those."

"At the rodeo or up my ass," stated Mac, trying to cheer him up.

Cavanaugh laughed, as he puffed on his cigarette. "Occasionally, you do come up with some good ideas."

"You know Kid, sometimes you push people to the point where they just go off on you."

"It's my chart."

Mac gave him a perplexed look and said, "*You're chart*?"

Billy sighed heavily and said, "Sun in Sagittarius, Moon in Aries with a Taurus Rising makes me stubbornly charge ahead without looking at the outcome of what I say or do. I have a tendency to speak before I think."

"No shit!" Mac responded. "I can attest to that. Remember the warehouse disaster?"

"Are you ever gonna let me forget that?"

"You must be kidding. Let you forget one of the highlights of my career, hell no."

"Vickie okay?"

298

"Oh yes. I believe she's starting to understand your quiet and subdued nature."

"I remember how my mother used to get really pissed at me when I used to tease and pry for answers."

"You miss your mother don't you?"

"Yeah...at times."

"Tell me what happened today," said Mac, as he sat down on some loose cement blocks. "Start at the beginning."

Cavanaugh began his story at the hotdog stand in Central Park and continued from there. Watching the crane driver operate his equipment, he told Mac everything. When he finished, both men stared silently at the crane. Putting out his cigarette and tossing it away, he said, "Well, have I created my own Hitchcock movie?"

Mac stared at the moving crane and replied, "Let's go with this thought. Everything you believed...really happened. I've done enough work for British Intelligence to know that it can be done. Everything you've gone through could be a massive cover-up. Let's say you've seen things that somebody doesn't want you to see. Or on the other hand, maybe someone does. I'm not quite sure yet."

"But why, I don't get it. Why would anyone—"

"More shall be revealed Watson," interrupted Mac. "I think we should discuss all this with O'Hara and Joubert tonight. Are you sure you can't make this meeting?"

"I'll try to get away. I need at least an hour for myself and then I'll be clear."

"Okay, we'll all talk later," he responded, putting his hand on Cavanaugh's shoulder. "Kid, I do believe you. I don't want you to doubt that. Just remember, I'm on your side. I'll figure out a way to handle all this."

"Mac, you have no idea how much that means to me," Billy sighed.

MacTavish's words gave Cavanaugh hope and a bit of emotional liberation. Someone finally believed his story about the lady in gray.

ഇന്ദ

Fantasy, Fun, And Funerals

Matthews and Keaton were busy at their desks when Cavanaugh and MacTavish rejoined them in the detective bureau. Walking over to Vickie's desk, Mac leaned over her shoulder and whispered, "Can we talk?"

"Sure," she answered, getting up and following him into the locker room. Closing the door behind her she asked, "What is it?"

"I need a favor," he replied. "What happened today at the crime scene, I want you to treat it as if the Kid's theory is accurate."

"You two talked about it?"

"Yes," Mac replied. "He told me everything and I believe him. There's been something off kilter about these crimes from the very beginning. What I'm going to tell you must remain in this room—it can go no further."

"I understand," she said, relieved that Mac also believed his partner.

"This woman he's been seeing," Mac began, "his mother...I believe she exists. Think about it, what if it was you and no one here believed you. What would you be thinking, how would you feel?"

"We've already talked about it," she replied. "Could someone be setting him up?"

"You're a good detective Vickie, why would anyone set him up? He's a cowboy for Christ's sake. There's something else going on here and I plan to get to the bottom of it." His thoughts overtook him and his mind wandered. "Why the hell is she showing herself after being officially dead for twenty-two years?" he thought.

"Maybe she just looks like his mother," said Vickie sympathetically. "They say we all have a double out there somewhere."

Laughing, MacTavish recalled saying the same thing to his partner. "I already tried that one Vickie, he didn't buy it."

"Well, what do you think is going on?"

"Vickie, if I could answer your questions I would. Unfortunately, I can't."

"Mac, I've wanted to talk to you about something else that happened today. Something involving our witnesses didn't sit right with me."

As she told him about the four-mile incident remarks with the carriage driver and the male passenger, Mac said, "Where are you going with this?"

"Well how many people would know exactly how far a horse and buggy would go to make four miles?"

"Evidently, the driver had to be involved," confirmed Mac. "His instructions were to stop the carriage four miles up Fifth Avenue. Is all this in your report?"

"All except the version I just told you."

"Write it up just like you told me. We need to start filling in the gaps."

"And the new favor?" she asked.

Pulling out two, single hundred dollar bills, he handed them to her. "Take Matthews to dinner and fill him in on everything. I want everyone on our team filled in before I take this to the captain.

"Okay," she smiled. Looking down, and reaching into her red satin jersey blouse, she slipped the bills inside her red bra. As she looked back at Mac, she saw that his eyes were locked on to her chest. Smiling, she cleared her throat to get his attention.

"I was just trying to imagine where you keep your change," he grinned.

Turning towards the door, and with her hand on the doorknob, she said, "You know Mac, you sure give a woman mixed messages." Smiling, she left him alone with his fantasies.

"Oh, to be twenty years younger," Mac said, looking into the mirror. As he began to leave, he backed up and glared into the mirror. "Okay, thirty years younger," he replied before leaving.

Rollins had finished his conversation with another detective in the unit when he saw MacTavish following Keaton out of the locker room. "Anything I should know about?" he asked them.

"No," they responded simultaneously.

"Okay then," said Rollins, before going back to his office.

Off in a corner, Cavanaugh was having a quiet discussion with Matthews, explaining the lady in gray episode. ..."So after all that running around in the rain, I spent the night at his place," said Billy, as they walked back to their desks.

"Okay, enough," Mac interjected quietly. "Vickie will fill Marc in tonight; Rollins has his eye on us."

Glancing into the captain's office, Cavanaugh quickly sat down at his desk. "Thanks for the heads up," he whispered, as he began to work on his computer.

Matthews quickly arranged some new paperwork, placed them in a folder, and carried them over to MacTavish. "Any plans for tonight?" he asked, acknowledging the three detectives.

"Dinner with me," said Vickie, as she reached into her shirt and pulled out the money. "It's on Mac."

"Oh that's terrific! Where are we going?" smiled Marc.

"I thought Martoni's would be nice," she said. "We could even—"

"Could the two of you discuss your plans to spend my money when I'm not around?" Mac interrupted.

"We could do that," Vickie said, smiling at Matthews.

"It's a Scottish thing," replied Billy, looking up from his computer.

"It's a Scottish thing?" Mac repeated.

"Now don't let the air blow up your kilt," said Billy.

"Don't let the air blow up my kilt?" repeated Mac, in an agitated tone.

"Is there a fucking echo in here?" Billy laughed.

Vickie started laughing and said, "Here we go again, it's *Comedy Central* at the One Nine."

"Hey MacTavish," Marc said, winking at Vickie, "is it true what they say about kilts...that you guys don't wear anything underneath?"

"Yeah," interjected Billy, "it's true. Only Mac has to wear something underneath."

"And why is that?" Marc asked, goading him on.

Cavanaugh leaned over his desk and quietly said, "His dick is so long and huge, he'd get arrested for indecent exposure. Paramedics would have to be called because the banging of his dick against his legs would probably dislocate his knees."

MacTavish couldn't help but laugh at his partner's improvisation. "Well, it is true," he boasted. "I have had a few ladies turn me down because it was too much to handle."

"Oh-h-h," Marc and Billy moaned simultaneously.

"You just haven't met the right woman yet," said Vickie.

"Does that sound like an offer to you Kid?" Marc asked.

Billy gave her a seductive look and said, "I don't believe it was directed to me." His statement caused her to blush and look down at her desk. Lowering his head, he tried to make eye contact with her. "Vickie?" he called out softly, in a teasing way.

"Okay," Mac intervened, "we should all get back to work."

Vickie quickly grabbed her purse and said, "I'll be in the can if anyone needs to know."

Looking up at her, Billy said softly, "Are you okay?"

"I'm fine," she answered sarcastically.

"You're right about that," smiled Billy. "You are fine."

Ignoring him and his comment, she abruptly walked away.

Rollins came out of his office shaking his head. "Somebody please tell me this day will go smoothly from here on."

"Why, what's up?" Mac inquired.

"Our receptionist was picked up for lewd behavior in the men's bathroom at the park. I thought he was home sick." Shaking his head, he turned around and walked out of the bureau.

Turning to his fellow detectives, Marc said, "What kind of lewd behavior do you think was going on?"

They stared back at him for a few seconds before MacTavish broke the silence. "What the hell kind do you think he was doing?"

"He's Gay," said Billy.

"Oh-h-h," Marc replied.

"He may be our Gay receptionist, but they need to lock him up and throw away the key," Mac alleged.

"Don't you think that statement is a little prejudicial?" said Billy.

"I have nothing against Gays or Lesbians," Mac defended. "What I am against, are the nut cases who expose themselves in public places. It's a park for Christ's sake, a place where children are supposed to be safe. If a kid walked into something like that, he'd end up needing therapy for the rest of his life."

Rollins, overhearing the comment as he walked back into the bureau, said firmly, "MacTavish, in my office now."

"Great...now what?" Mac mumbled, as he followed the captain.

Rollins entered his office and immediately sat down on the corner of his desk. As he nodded for MacTavish to close the door, he said, "You want to tell me what's going on?"

"Look I don't have a problem with Gays," said Mac, closing the door behind him.

"I'm not talking about the park or what you said, I want to know what's going on in this bureau. I realize everyone knows that I made captain by sleeping with my superiors."

Startled by his remark, Mac said, "You made captain by sleeping with your superiors?"

"No. That was a joke," Rollins smiled. "Look, do you think I haven't noticed all the whispering and cover-ups going on around here. First you and Cavanaugh disappear from a crime scene. Then Keaton disappears with him at another crime scene. Now I've come up with only two possibilities. Would you like to hear them?"

Nodding yes Mac thought, "This could be quite entertaining."

"The first one is; Cavanaugh is bisexual and you and Vickie are having quickies with him on company time. The second one is; there's more to these crimes than you're telling me and the three of you are trying put this all together without consulting me. Now I would prefer to believe the second possibility. I'd hate to have to write up the first one, especially after what's happened today with our receptionist."

"This could take a while," Mac said, as he pulled up a chair and sat down.

"I'm in no hurry," smiled Rollins.

MacTavish made a decision to set things right—telling Rollins all the events that involved his partner and the disappearing lady in gray.

"It was raining when we pulled up at the Kingman homicide scene," he began.

Rollins listened closely to every detail, as MacTavish brought him up to date on the Central Park incident.

..."so that's how it all came down," said Mac. "Personally, I believe the Kid."

"So do I," Rollins answered.

Startled by his statement, Mac said, "You believe him?"

"Yes, I do. Remember back when you two were involved with that warehouse explosion?"

"How could I forget jumping out of a three-story building?" smiled Mac.

"Do you know who the detectives were on that case?"

"No, we never met them. I believe they were from the One Five." He looked at the captain curiously and remembered him mentioning being on the One Five. "You were the detective on that case. Christ, why didn't you tell us?"

"I didn't see you guys rushing into my office to keep me in the loop," responded Rollins. "I know I'm fairly new to this precinct, but that's no reason to withhold information from me. In case no one noticed, I am the one in charge here. Did it ever occur to any of you that I might have information that could help?"

Mac realized that he had made a mistake and apologized, "You're right, I guess we're all just a little self-protective. We all owe you an apology."

"It's not necessary. Just pass the word along about our little talk and make sure it doesn't happen again."

"I'll take care of it," replied Mac.

"Good. Now let's move on. I believe your partner because I also saw this disappearing woman."

"Where did you see her?" questioned Mac.

"It was during that warehouse episode," said Rollins. "That building was in a rough part of town. We got a 911 call from one of the victim's models who showed up unexpectedly. We were there within ten minutes. It wasn't a good day. I was just getting over the flu, and nothing I ate was staying down. With CSU's ongoing investigation, all facilities were off limits. So I went for an emergency stroll and came upon this isolated bar. I'm rushing through the front door, when this beautiful blonde comes hurrying out and just about knocks me over. Her purse hits the ground and everything went flying...like to know what fell out of her jacket?"

"Enlighten me," said Mac.

"Her CIA identification," answered Rollins. "As I go to pick it up, she grabs it out of my hand. But not before I got to see her name, C. Alegna. I figured I'd reassure her by showing my badge. I tell her its okay, no problem. She rushed off and I hurried into the bar to find the john. I basically wrote the whole incident off. I certainly didn't want to blow her cover. Why the hell would I think there was any connection? Until—"

"Until what," Mac interrupted.

"Until, I pulled her up on a confidential CIA list."

"You can do that...access their files?"

"I can access and retrieve anything that's in any computer system."

MacTavish was intrigued by his captain's background and wanted to know more. "So, you were a professional hacker?"

"Head of the class in high school and college," Rollins answered proudly, as he continued his warehouse story. "When I punched in C. Alegna, guess what came up?"

"Oh I can't imagine," said Mac.

"Deceased in 1981. Now this lady was as alive, and I didn't see a trace of decomposition. I got into every existing file trying to track her down. There was nothing. Now here's where you can probably relate. After I shared all this with my partner, we decided to go back to that bar. The bartender denied she was ever there, said I was confused. He went on to say, that he would have noticed if a hot blonde came into his bar, but one didn't. He remembered me all right, but not her. Now what do you think my partner thought?"

"That you were losing it?" smiled Mac, nodding his head.

"Right."

Mac looked at him for a few moments and said, "When you talked to the bartender, repeat what you asked him, your exact words?"

Rollins took a moment to quickly review the incident in his mind. "I introduced myself and my partner. The bartender said, *yeah, I remember you from the other day.* I told him I was trying to get some information on the blonde who left before I came in. Then he said, *you're crazy, I would have noticed if a hot blonde came into my bar, but one didn't.* That was it."

"How did he know she was attractive...hot?"

"Christ," responded Rollins, "How the hell did I miss that? You're right, I never once said that she was attractive."

"So the bar was a setup, as were our buggy riders today," said Mac.

310

Confused about MacTavish's statement, Rollins said, "You lost me. Please explain about the buggy riders." MacTavish quickly filled him in on what happened when Vickie questioned the couple in the carriage. After hearing Keaton's and Cavanaugh's last encounter, Rollins was somewhat relieved. "It looks like everything is starting to fall into place."

"I'm meeting with Joubert and O'Hara tonight," said Mac. "I'll run all this by them and get their position on this whole thing."

"Good," said Rollins. "I believe this was a very productive day. Thank goodness we're off tomorrow. We all need a break to regroup our thoughts. Just pray we don't need to come in on another homicide. Our Cleveland detectives will be here Monday, and if we all pull together, we should be able to crack both cases."

"You think this lady...C. Alegna is the Kid's mother?"

"I don't know," Rollins replied. "But there is someone out there who he and I can both identify. And somehow, she is connected to both these crimes. I hate to think his mother is our shooter."

"His mother—" MacTavish paused as if he changed his mind about what he was going to say. "The Kid said he was fourteen when she died and told me all about her funeral."

"Was she cremated?"

"No," Mac responded. "It was a ground burial."

"Well, there's one way to find out if it's her."

"Dig her bones up?" Mac asked indignantly. "I don't think that's a good idea."

"We need to find out if she's in that coffin," Rollins sighed.

"But digging up his mother's corpse...Christ!"

"You should talk to him about it," said Rollins. "Considering all the doubt he has about his mother's death, he might even want it. It's one way he could be sure."

"It's a bit morbid, but I'll bring it up to him," Mac said reluctantly.

"Look," Rollins said seriously, "I don't want any more secrets around here. You do see how everything could have moved faster if I had been informed?"

"I was wrong. It won't happen again."

"One more thing, when you talk to your partner, leave out the part about digging up his mother's bones. See if you can rephrase the statement?" smiled Rollins, as he followed him out of his office. "And good luck with the meeting tonight."

"CAVANAUGH," Rollins yelled out. "I WANT YOU IN ON THAT MEETING TONIGHT."

"Yeah, I'll be there captain," Billy answered, glancing at his partner.

"I'll be in my office if anyone needs me," said Rollins, walking back to his office.

"What the hell was that all about?" Vickie asked, keeping her eyes down on the desk.

"Our captain," Mac explained, "is a professional hacker."

Stunned by the statement, the three detectives looked up and focused their attention on MacTavish.

"You're kidding right?" said Marc.

"No," said Mac. "I'm quite serious."

"What's he been hacking into?" Vickie asked.

"People involved in these homicides. Before I get into all that, let me tell you that he knows everything."

"Everything?" asked Billy.

"Everything," Mac answered.

"Mother fucker," Billy responded, leaning back in his chair. "I am so screwed!"

"Actually, you're not," said Mac. "At least not by him. He believes you're telling the truth about everything you saw."

"Did he give you a reason why?"

"Because he's seen her too," Mac said softly.

"Oh my God," responded Vickie.

"So there really is a woman out there," Matthews interjected.

"Not only did he see her, he spoke to her," said Mac.

Cavanaugh wasn't sure how to react to this new information. A part of him wanted to believe that his mother was alive. And yet, he didn't want her to be a cold-blooded killer either. "Where...when?" he sighed.

MacTavish repeated everything Rollins told him, the expressions of disbelief on the faces of the three detectives became solemn. "So, no more secrets," he said. "The captain needs to be informed and involved in everything we do. I made him a promise and I intend to keep it."

"So her name is C. Alegna?" Billy asked out of curiosity.

"That seems to be the name she's using," said Mac.

"And she supposedly died in '81," Billy questioned.

Observing a physical and attitude change overtaking his partner, Mac questioned him. "Where are you going with this?"

Cavanaugh seemed to be lost in time as he stayed focused on his computer. "My mother died in '81," he said solemnly. "She always said if anything ever happened to her she didn't want me to ever visit her grave. She made me promise so I never went back."

"Billy," Vickie said sympathetically, "I don't know what to say."

"It's okay," Billy responded. "Like Mac said; we'll figure it all out. I'm going online. Let's see what I can dig up?"

Everyone was quiet except for MacTavish. Startled, he rolled his eyes and picked up his phone and dialed Rollins' extension. "Yeah, captain it's me. Cavanaugh just informed us that his mother died in '81."

"Are you following up with the cemetery?" Rollins inquired.

"Haven't got that far," answered Mac.

"Take it easy on him," said Rollins. "I'm concerned how he's gonna handle all of this."

"Yes, I feel the same," Mac responded, looking around the bureau. "I'll take care of it," he said softly, before disconnecting the call.

Cavanaugh went online and pulled up the information he needed. Finding Forest Lawn Cemetery, he picked up the phone and dialed their number in Glendale, California.

The three detectives watched and listened, as their fellow detective appeared to be in his own little world.

"Yes, I'm calling from the New York Police Department," said Billy. "My name is Detective Archie MacTavish. We're investigating a homicide and we need the information on a burial back in '81. Her name was Kelly Cavanaugh, plot 23, Section E." Pausing he said, "Yeah, I'll hold."

"So you're a MacTavish now?" Mac smiled.

Billy confusingly shook his head and spoke into the phone, "Yeah sure, that'll be fine." Hanging up he said, "Their manager is calling us back to make sure our call is legit." The seconds seemed like hours as he and the other detectives waited silently until the phone rang. "Vickie, you answer it," he said anxiously.

Picking up the phone she responded, "19th Precinct, Detective Keaton speaking." After listening to their request, she said, "Sure, let me get him for you." Transferring the call to Cavanaugh, she whispered, "It's them."

"Detective MacTavish here," responded Billy. "Sure, I'll hold." Covering the phone receiver he said, "The manager is going to look it up, everything got updated last year." Minutes passed, as everyone waited with great anticipation for a response. When the manager returned to the phone, Cavanaugh listened intently. Slowly, his expression became unsettling. "You're sure?" he asked shakily," and there's no mistake? I understand and thanks."

Hanging up the phone, Cavanaugh appeared to be frozen in time as his mother's funeral flashed across his mind.

MacTavish quickly broke the silence. "You want to tell us—"

"There's no body," Billy interrupted. "I was there. I remember it as if it were yesterday. There was a funeral and a dugout grave that they put her into, only she's not there."

"What do you mean when you say she's not there?" asked Marc, breaking Cavanaugh's trance.

"Evidently my mother had a final request that nobody knew about. After everyone left the cemetery, she was to be removed from the grave and cremated, which is what they did."

"Oh Billy, I'm so sorry," Vickie said sympathetically.

"You never knew about that request?" asked Mac.

"No, but it does explain her never wanting me to visit her grave."

"Gee Kid, I don't know what to say," replied Marc. "Losing your mother twice—that must be really tough."

They all looked at each other and began to laugh. Their laughter made Cavanaugh feel better as he joined in.

"Thanks, I needed something to break the tension," he smiled, as his cell phone rang. "Christ, I forgot. Don't leave, I'll be right down." Grabbing his jacket and cigarettes, he looked at MacTavish and said, "I'll meet you at Pershing Square. Give me an hour," he added, rushing out the door.

"Whoever she is, she must be a hell of a lay," Mac mumbled, as he picked up his phone and placed a call to Rollins. "Captain, about those bones we were gonna dig up..."

Outside the precinct, Sarina was waiting for Cavanaugh. Rushing through the exit, he apologized as he lit up a cigarette. "C'mon, I'll drive," he said, as they walked into the parking lot.

Sarina stopped walking and said, "No, I'll drive. I'm not repeating last Thanksgiving."

Cavanaugh thought her attitude appeared to be slightly hostile and cold. He shrugged off her behavior, believing it was because he forgot to meet her. Putting away his keys, he said, "Where are you parked?"

"Over there," she responded, pointing to a dark green Sebring JX black top convertible with black leather interior.

"Nice," he said getting into the car. "Had it long?"

"A couple of months," she replied, closing her door and starting up the engine.

"How about we go to my place for that drink?" he said, giving her a fiery look. Seeing that she was unresponsive to his suggestion, he said jokingly, "Okay, it was worth a shot."

As she drove down the street, she gave him an intimidating glare and said coldly, "You're turning into Fields from *Night Court.*"

"John Larroquette?" he smiled.

"Not the actor," she said sarcastically, "the sleaze ball attorney that would do just about anything to get laid."

Suddenly, her behavior reminded him of Boots, and for no other reason, he had to get away from her. "Okay that's it. Stop the fucking car," he said adamantly. Hitting her brakes, she quickly pulled over to the curb. After getting out, Billy leaned back inside the open car door and said, "I just ended a five-year relationship that was pure hell. If you think I'm going to get involved with someone identical to what I just walked out on you're crazy. Evidently you're not the woman I thought you were."

A stranger, hoping for a parking place, pulled up behind them and began honking his car horn multiple times.

Cavanaugh, taking out his frustration on the honking driver, stood up, he pulled out his badge and flashed it at the driver. "GO AROUND," he yelled out, "THIS IS POLICE BUSINESS. AND LIGHTEN UP ON THE GOD DAMN HORN; YOU AIN'T IN FUCKING TIJUANA MOTHER FUCKER!"

Leaning back down into the car, he said, "I can't believe you're still angry about me going back to Boots. That's something you're gonna have to work on Chiquita, 'cause I sure as hell don't deserve what you're dishing out. I'm done here."

Her hostility emanated from her body, while her cold eyes remained focused on the front window.

"I never realized how much I had hurt you until now," he continued. His anger began to diminish as he remembered how he had dumped her without any explanation. "You must have gone through hell," he said firmly. "Look, I can't change what happened, but if you're going to carry that resentment into this relationship, we can't even be friends. Its way too much rage for me to deal with right now. I'll give you a call in a couple of months. Maybe after some time apart we can work through all this. Right now for me, there's no going back to what I had with—"

Cavanaugh paused as he remembered his obsession with Boots and the co-dependant relationship it had turned into—recalling all the affairs his lover was having on the side, how he tolerated them and took Boots back when the affairs were over.

"There's no going back to that relationship, Sarina. It's over— has been for a long time. I was just too dumb to realize it. I hope you understand that I really did want to try this again with you. In a way, I wished I had asked you to marry me that holiday weekend—God knows I thought about it. I'm sorry Sarina...I really am. Looks like we both have some relationship homework to do. I'll see you around."

After closing her car door, he started walking towards the precinct. As he pulled out his cigarettes, he looked at them and said, "You're next." His thoughts quickly jumped back to Sarina. "Maybe it's her Spanish nature. God, that woman's coldness could freeze the island of Tahiti." He remembered the soft and gentle side of her, her passion, those beautiful eyes, her intelligence, and most of all, her humor.

"Christ, I do love her. I guess I'll just have to marry her someday," he decided, as she drove up alongside him.

Rolling down the passenger window, Sarina said seductively, "Hey cowboy, need a ride? I'd like to start over."

Looking down at his feet, he stopped and smiled. Slowly, he lifted his head and looked over at her. Her warm eyes and smile seemed to be very inviting. "Now that's the Sarina I know and love," he thought, as he walked towards the car and leaned through the window.

"It all depends," smiled Billy.

"On what?" she inquired tenderly.

"What's it worth to you?" he asked playfully.

Sarina studied him for a moment and began to understand what he was doing. He was role playing by pretending she was looking for some action with a male hooker—she decided to play along. "Oh, I could make it very worthwhile for you. How much do you charge?" she asked, while undoing the buttons on her blouse.

"It's strictly about the money," said Billy. "Show me the money."

"How much?" she asked, licking her lips.

"Tell me what you want me to do and I'll give you a price," he replied, smoking his cigarette.

Sarina found the challenge very erotic. "What's your price for oral sex?"

"It depends."

"On what?" she asked seductively.

Giving her a big smile he said, "On whether I'm giving or receiving." Sliding his hand into his jacket, he began to unbutton his shirt.

After shutting off her car's engine, she slowly turned towards him. Sliding her right hand inside her blouse, she began caressing her partially exposed breast. "Let's start with a hundred," she said softly—lifting one leg up to reveal that she wasn't wearing underwear and sliding her other hand up and down the inside of her thighs. "Tell me... what would you be willing to do for a hundred?"

Cavanaugh realized this was a game of sexual poker and thought about, "Who would fold first." Leaning further into the window, he continued speaking in a slow and sexy voice, "I'd start by kissing and sucking on your toes."

Leaning back against her car door, Sarina kicked off her shoes—putting one bare foot on his arm. Billy leaned further into the car and said, "I'd move my mouth up to your ankles...then I'd rub my face, head, hair, and hands, up and down every part of your legs. And before I begin to use my mouth on you, I would use my hands to get you highly aroused." Reaching up under her skirt, he gave her an example of what he could do. As he touched her, she gave out an erotic moan. As their conversation escalated, they both became extremely excited. "I'd keep doing this until you couldn't take anymore," he sighed. "I wouldn't stop until you pulled my head to you." With a smile on his face, Cavanaugh removed his hand—leaving Sarina to play the next hand or fold.

"A hundred?" she asked playfully.

Cavanaugh got very hot and excited, as he watched Sarina slowly move one of her hands under her skirt to finish what he had started. As she moaned and moved her body erotically and got close to having an orgasm, he quickly opened the door and climbed in. Moving her over, he closed the window, unzipped his pants and put his hand inside. "Oh yes," he said, as he watched her every move. Their voyeurism escalated their orgasms with loud, vocal responses. "Oh my God," he yelled, grabbing and holding onto her. "I fold! I fold!"

Smiling she said, "What did you say?"

"It's just a poker expression," he laughed, holding her tighter.

"You Americans have the strangest way of expressing things," she replied.

Outside, car horns were honking as they passed by them. One guy drove by and yelled out, "GET A ROOM OR TAKE IT IN THE ALLEY."

Cavanaugh pulled away from her and quickly zipped up his pants. "Damn, Sarina, we need to get outta here before we're arrested for lewd behavior. I don't think my captain could take two in one week."

"You've lost me," she said, as she started her car.

"It's another story for another time," he interrupted. Smiling and checking his watch, he said, "I need to get back to my car, I told Mac I'd meet him in an hour."

"So the plan for tonight was just to talk?" she said, driving towards the One Nine.

"Yeah, until you propositioned me lady," he laughed, giving her a seductive wink. "Look, this shouldn't take long. If you still want to talk, I can swing by your place."

"It would be better if we went to your place. Call me on my cell."

"Okay," he responded softly, as she pulled her car into the precinct lot and stopped. After giving her a passionate kiss, he opened the car door and got out.

"Billy, maybe tomorrow would be better?"

"I'll call you later," he replied softly. "Drive safely."

Walking towards his car, he watched as she drove away. Sarina," he sighed, as he got into his car and looked in the mirror.

"Christ," he expressed, observing his disheveled appearance. He quickly jumped out of his car and ran back into the precinct—heading for the nearest bathroom. Taking off his jacket, he washed up and splashed some water through his hair. Looking in the mirror he said, "That's better." Moving towards the bathroom door, he opened it while putting on his jacket.

Simultaneously, MacTavish had come down the stairs. Seeing his partner he said, "Great. You're still here. We can ride together." Scrutinizing his partner, he proposed, "You okay? You look a little flustered...and wet."

"I'm fine. Can we just go?" Billy said defensively, leading the way through the front doors.

MacTavish glanced back to the bathroom, as if he expected someone else to walk out.

Meanwhile, at the Pershing Square Pub, O'Hara had already ordered drinks for the expected detectives. Sitting down at a table, he pulled out his cell phone, dialed a number and waited for someone to answer.

"Hello beautiful lady, I just wanted to let you know this shouldn't take too long, maybe an hour or so." He paused and listened to the voice on the other end. "Me too," he continued, as the waiter brought the drinks to the table and quickly left. "I can just picture you in that tub with all those bubbles." He chuckled at something she said. "Will you be in bed when I get there?" Laughing again, he saw MacTavish and Cavanaugh walking through the front door. "Got to go, the teams here, see you soon."

As the two detectives approached the table, Shawn disconnected the call and said, "How's it going?"

"Great," responded Mac, as he and Cavanaugh sat down.

"Yeah, thanks," said Billy, downing his shot of J & B Scotch and quickly following it with a swallow of his beer. "I really needed that. It's been one hell of a day." He waved to the waiter to bring another round, while MacTavish filled O'Hara in on the homicides—starting with the lady in gray episode and ending with the Central Park incident.

"So," replied Shawn, "Looks like we have an invisible suspect."

"What do you mean by invisible?" said Billy. "I fucking saw her."

"Hold on, I didn't mean the woman doesn't exist," said Shawn. "I'm just wondering why you're the only bloke who sees her."

Meanwhile, Joubert had entered and was walking up to the table when he overheard O'Hara's statement. "If I may interrupt, I believe you have it backwards," he said, pulling up a chair.

"Shawn O'Hara, meet Detective Françoise Luc Joubert from Toronto," said Mac.

The Irishman acknowledged him with a smile and handshake. "You were saying mate?"

"Captain Rollins filled me in," Joubert began. "I believe no one was supposed to see her. Think about it, why would any organization take that kind of a chance? It would mean risking their whole operation. I don't think these people are aware she's being seen. We all agree it's an organization and not some random shooter," he said, looking around the table.

They all nodded yes, as Mac said, "I don't see it being any other way."

Joubert flipped his shield out and turned it over to reveal the WASP emblem. As he put it back in his pocket he continued explaining his theory. "This is a very sophisticated organization. They would not

323

endanger their operatives in such a careless way, and in no way would they expose them just to discredit one detective. Believe me, they don't work like that."

"You think this woman is involved in all three homicides?" asked Billy.

Because Joubert knew Cavanaugh couldn't comprehend his mother being an assassin, he replied softly, "Perhaps not all of them, perhaps not any of them."

"Well if this woman is involved then she can't be my mother," Billy said defensively. "My mother could never be a cold blooded killer."

A veil of cold silence fell over the three men. They didn't quite know what their next move should be. No one wanted to hurt the young detective. Joubert, feeling Mac and Shawn's dilemma, was the first to speak. "No one here is saying she is."

"Then what the hell are you saying?" said Billy.

Joubert stared into Cavanaugh's eyes and saw the pain, anger and denial welling up in him. "Billy, please work with me here and let's try to get to the truth. Answers and solutions, isn't that what we are all looking for? That's how we all find peace within ourselves. None of us wish to be lost souls. We have a chance here to find the truth. We cannot let fear stop us from moving forward. You do want to know the truth so you yourself can move forward?"

Joubert's hypnotic tone had a calming effect on Cavanaugh. Looking into the Canadian's eyes, he nodded and responded, "Yeah, that's what I want."

Good," said Joubert, "Let's begin. One, I believe the woman has some psychic connection with you. Whether she is your mother has yet to be established. Two, this woman is involved somehow; otherwise her existence would not be denied by everyone. Three, if she is your mother, we need to quietly establish that she is not dead."

"Well there's no body in my mother's grave. She was supposedly cremated," interjected Billy.

"Then it's possible that your mother is alive," paused Joubert, realizing that Cavanaugh had just absorbed a tremendous amount of emotional information. He was careful not to push too hard lest he broke under the stress. "If she is your mother, it would explain why she feels the need to see you—you are her son. However, you must realize that she could be in grave danger by what she's doing. These people could consider her a threat to their operations if you try to make contact with her."

Although Cavanaugh's eyes expressed some sort of hope in his glare, he was still filled with fear and confusion.

MacTavish knew his partner's limits and quietly intervened. "Why don't you spend the night at my place? It'll give us both a chance to absorb all of this and I'd feel better if you weren't alone right now. There could also be somebody out there looking to cause you some more problems. Besides, I'm not ready to train a new partner."

MacTavish's statement about a new partner brought a smile to Cavanaugh's face.

"Excellent idea," said Joubert, "this is not a time for you to be alone. Take the time tomorrow to relax. You have received a volume of disturbing information and your mind and body needs time process it."

"You okay with all this Cavanaugh?" Shawn asked. "If you need any help—"

"I can handle it," Billy interrupted, as he pushed back his chair and stood up. "Are we done here Mac, we should go. Joubert's right, I need some quiet time and some air."

"Until Monday then," Joubert said quietly, as he watched Cavanaugh walk slowly away and pull out his cell phone.

Mac finished his drink and stood up saying, "Gentlemen, it's been very enlightening. We'll see you on Monday."

Walking outside, Cavanaugh dialed Sarina's number. It rang consistently until he finally heard her voice mail and responded, "Sarina, it's me, I'll be at Mac's overnight. Call me when you get a break." Seeing MacTavish approach, he disconnected the call and said, "Swing by the precinct so I can pick up my car, that way you don't have to drive me back in tomorrow."

"Sounds good to me," said Mac, as they got into his Lexus and drove towards the One Nine.

Meanwhile, back in the Pub, Joubert and O'Hara were discussing Cavanaugh. "I'm concerned for him," said Joubert, "a few more shocks like this could push him over the edge."

"He's tough," Shawn replied.

"On the outside perhaps," explained Joubert. "On the inside, he's a tortured soul, filled with rage, disappointments, rejections, and loneliness. He fixates through some other form of addiction.

"You're very perceptive," said Shawn, "I had a similar feeling about him. However, I believe he'll get through it."

"Did you get a chance to review the evidence," Joubert asked.

"I got filled in this morning."

"And you agree with the findings?"

"I do," Shawn replied, pausing for a moment. "You believe his mother's alive don't you?"

"Do I have any proof? No...but everything leads me to believe it to be true," Joubert said firmly. "She is however, a pebble amongst the many rocks and boulders in the river."

Back in Brooklyn, candles were burning throughout Sarina's apartment. She was wearing red, silk pajamas. Her cell phone was on the nightstand next to her. Yawning, she picked it up and listened to Billy's message. As she climbed into bed, she decided not to return the call. Turning off her phone, she laid it back down on the nightstand and dozed off watching TV.

A re-run episode of *NYPD BLUE* woke her up several hours later. Yawning, she heard her front door open.

Turning to face the open bedroom door, she said, "Great timing, I just woke up."

Her lover leaned into the open doorway and said, "Good, because I wouldn't want anything to distract us tonight." Undressing, as he closed the bedroom door behind him, he said softly, "How was your bubble bath?"

Looking at his naked body, she said seductively, "Oh Shawn, you are ready for me."

Meanwhile, at the MacTavish's home, Mac, Honey and Thumper had already retired for the night. Cavanaugh was sitting on the couch watching a *Law and Order SVU* sitcom. "Wow, that Mariska is one beautiful woman," he said to himself. "Wonder if she'd be interested in joining the One Nine? Now let's see if I can get a hold of another beautiful woman," he added, as he as he picked up his cell phone and dialed Sarina's number. Once again he got her voice mail. This time he didn't leave a message. Finishing his beer and turning off the TV, he headed quietly up the stairs. Entering the spare bedroom, he looked out of the window for a few minutes—his mind and body were drained from the experiences of the day. Getting into bed and lying there, he quickly fell asleep.

The aroma of Sunday breakfast awakened Cavanaugh out of a restless sleep. He looked at the clock, it read 10:35. Sitting up, he ran his hands through his hair and said, "Sarina," as he picked up his phone and dialed her number—there was no answer. "Later," he said, as he tossed his phone down on a pillow. Grabbing some clean sweats out of the closet, he dropped them on the bed, stripped off his shorts and walked naked to Mac's room and the shower. As he pushed the half open bathroom door, he saw Vickie standing there drying her hands. Shocked and embarrassed, he yelled out, "VICKIE, WHAT THE HELL ARE YOU DOING HERE?"

As he fumbled for a towel to cover his exposed body parts, she said, "Good morning," and gave him the once over—getting a full view of his naked body.

Confused and frustrated he asked her again, "Why are you here?"

"I've been painting up in Mac's attic. I didn't want to wake you, so I had to use his bathroom to clean up because you were in the guest room."

Looking at her with his mouth slightly open, he was speechless.

Leaning towards him, she reached for his face and closed his jaw. Pinching him on the cheek, she said, "Don't worry, I'm not a virgin."

328

As she turned to leave, she grabbed him through the towel and said, "And I've seen lots of these before."

"DAMN, VICKIE," he exclaimed, as she walked out of the bathroom. Leaning around the open door, he yelled out to her. "I THINK OF YOU AS A SISTER! WHAT YOU DID BORDERS ON INCEST," and slammed the door shut.

Downstairs in the kitchen, Honey greeted Vickie with a welcoming woof. "Smells great," she said, while petting the dog.

"Did I hear the Kid making his usual appearance?" Mac asked, as he carried trays of sausages, bacon and ham into the dining room.

"Oh yes, he made quite an appearance," she said, washing her hands again in the kitchen sink.

"My partner is very predictable." smiled Mac.

"You know him so well," she laughed, while drying her hands. Picking up the platters of scrambled eggs and toast, she walked into the dining area. Impressed by Mac's wonderful place setting, she smiled, "The table is beautiful."

MacTavish's dining room had a Renaissance feel to it. The beautifully styled high back chairs were very comfortable. A royal purple tablecloth with matching napkins adorned the table. MacTavish had cut some of his fresh garden roses, and placed them in an enormous, beautifully carved crystal vase that sat the center of the table. The scent of the lilac branches, that surrounded the vase of roses, permeated the room.

"Let's eat," Mac said, pulling out a chair for Vickie.

As they sat down and began to eat, they heard Cavanaugh rushing down the stairs. Still embarrassed, he tried to distract himself from what happened upstairs. "You locking Vickie up in the attic now?" he asked, pulling out a chair and sitting down next to her.

"It's voluntary," interrupted Vickie playfully. "He lets me out when he wants to be serviced and then its back to the attic."

Cavanaugh, stunned by her statement, choked on a piece of toast.

"There, there," she added, patting him on the back, "are you okay?"

"I suppose Mac put you up to all of this, him knowing I'd be heading naked for the shower—I should know better, he's even got the damn dog working with him," Billy said sarcastically, while eating his breakfast."

"The dog?" she asked.

After Mac explained Honey's game with his partner, she looked at Cavanaugh and said, "You're right, you should know better."

"I have a better one," began Mac. "We go to the Blue Magnolia—"

"Don't even go there!" Billy challenged, while reaching for the crystal pitcher that held the orange juice.

"Another time," whispered Mac.

Vickie quickly changed the subject and said, "You have a very beautiful home, Mac."

MacTavish began to tell her what it was like before it was built, and explained about the imported wood that was used in some of the interior design. The morning discussion for the three of them was very entertaining—discussions about work were avoided. They talked about various things, including music, films, and theme parks.

Feeling relaxed and comfortable, and after a lot of coaxing from Vickie, Cavanaugh revealed a secret desire—when and if he got married, he wanted to spend his honeymoon in Disney World.

"Okay," said Billy humorously, "where in the park would you like to spend your honeymoon night?"

Vickie thought for a moment, then said, "Pirates of the Caribbean...always had a fantasy about being ravaged by a pirate. And you Mac?"

"Well," he smiled, "I believe it would be on the Liberty Square Riverboat. I would love to play the Mississippi gambler role."

"How romantic," Vickie said. "Okay Billy, your turn."

Smiling he replied, "First, I'd propose on Peter Pan's Flight, and as far as the honeymoon night, I guess that would be spent at the Animal Kingdom Villas."

"Great choice," she said, "It's nice to know there are still romantic men out there."

"Well Vickie," said Mac, "are you ready for those lessons?"

Billy gave him a questioning look and said, "Lessons?"

"Art classes," Mac clarified.

"I'll get the dishes and take the dog out for a run," said Billy, as he finished eating.

"Great," replied Mac, "Thumper is in the backyard keeping my grass trimmed. "Are you ready my lady?" he asked, giving Vickie his hand. "Oh, and one more thing—"

"Yes," Billy questioned, looking up at them.

"Ignore the moans and screams from the attic," said Mac, imitating a sinister Boris Karloff.

"Very funny," replied Billy, picking up his tray and heading for the kitchen. As he put the dishes into the dishwasher, he gave Honey the leftovers and headed upstairs for his phone. Running back down the steps he and Honey left the house.

Once outside, he tried to reach Sarina again, this time he left a message. "Hey it's me again. I'm at Mac's. Call me when you have a minute." Disconnecting the call, he and Honey began their run to the park.

In Brooklyn at Sarina's apartment, the candles had burned out long ago. She and O'Hara lay naked and entwined in each other's arms—her cell phone flashing that she had unanswered messages.

In the Rollins home, Al and his wife were getting their twins ready for church. Smiling and laughing, they discussed their planned trip to the Museum of Natural History after lunch.

Francois Luc Joubert was in his hotel room speaking on the phone in French. His discussion was of a serious nature—his voice conveyed pure love and sympathetic understanding.

In another part of the city, Marc Matthews was unlocking the door to his apartment. He looked rough as he put his keys on the coffee table and emptied his pockets. Lying down on the couch he turned on the TV and fell asleep watching one of his *Columbo* DVD's starring Jack Cassidy—1971's Murder By The Book.

Back in Cleveland, Ricco Gambino was at his mother's home finishing breakfast. The table was filled with other family members; grandparents, nieces, nephews, cousins and their families. Louie was also there. There was laughter, happiness, and talk of their trip tomorrow to New York. Most of their conversations were spoken in Italian. "Arrividerci," his great grandmother kept saying.

Sunday had passed quickly for everyone; after cooking dinner for Keaton and Cavanaugh, MacTavish had retired for the evening with his pets.

At Sarina's apartment, she and Shawn had spent most of their day and evening in bed.

At the Rollins home, everyone was asleep. Tucked under the twins' arms, were toy dinosaurs that the boys received on their visit to the history museum.

Matthews, after sleeping most of the day, was watching another 1971 *Colombo* DVD—The Most Crucial Game starring Robert Culp. Owning every episode, his favorite shows were in the first season.

Back in Cleveland, Louie was spending the night at Ricco's home—along with Ricco's two uncles and a deaf and farting great grandmother.

80CR

PHOENIX RISING
FROM THE ASHES

It was a busy Monday morning at the One Nine. Upstairs in the detective bureau, Matthews was on the phone at his desk and Keaton was working at her computer. Joubert was talking with Rollins in his office when MacTavish made his entrance.

"Good morning Vickie...where's our bull rider?" said Mac.

"I don't know," she smiled, while looking up at him. "He hasn't come in yet."

Outside in the parking lot, Cavanaugh was getting out of his car. Walking towards the One Nine, he lit a cigarette and glanced at the improved construction site. "Damn, those guys work fast," he mumbled. "The only guy I've seen get anything up faster, is Mac when he sees a redhead." Tossing his unfinished cigarette into the street, he rushed into the precinct and darted up the stairs. Walking into the bureau, he took off his jacket and said "Hey," acknowledging MacTavish and Keaton. As he slipped his jacket over the back of his chair and sat down at his desk, he glanced at his partner. "You going to the airport to pick up the Mob?"

"That's the plan Jeff Foxworthy. Are you going with me?" Mac retorted.

"Nah...I thought I'd work on the case with Larry the Cable Guy. Why don't you take Vickie with you? Maybe we all could do dinner tonight."

"I'll go with you Mac," she quickly volunteered.

"Okay, we'll leave in about an hour," he responded, giving her a fleeting look. "We'll discuss dinner arrangements later."

Cavanaugh glanced into Rollins office and said, "What's going on in there?"

"Don't know," Vickie responded, "they were in there when I got here."

MacTavish observed his partner looking anxiously at his watch and questioned his anxiety. "You expecting somebody Brooklyn?"

"No," Billy answered, in an indistinct way.

Vickie stood up and walked over to Cavanaugh's desk. "Here," she said, handing him a list of names. "This is everybody we documented at the crime scenes." Picking up more paperwork, she said, "I need to give the rest of these to Rollins."

MacTavish stared at her as she walked away. His mind however, was on someone else. The way Vickie's hair was piled up on her head reminded him of Red.

Cavanaugh was quick to notice his partner's interest in Vickie. "Is there something personal going on between you two?"

"No, nothing like what you're thinking," Mac responded softly.

"Mac..." he said teasingly.

"There's nothing going on. I'm helping her promote her art," he said defensively.

"She's a good kid," smiled Billy.

Nodding yes, Mac said firmly, "Good point. She's younger than you."

"Oh-h-h-h," said Billy playfully.

"She's forty years younger than me," Mac snapped back. "And why would you—"

Cutting him off, Billy replied, "At eighty-six, Cary Grant married a woman forty years younger."

"I'm not that old. Maybe I'll consider it when I'm eighty-six."

Cavanaugh decided to have some fun with his partner. "You're right. Vickie is definitely different than what you usually pick up, her being blonde and all. Of course, you do have those wigs. You know, I'd feel so much better if I knew there would be someone taking care of you when you're old. And I'm sorry; I thought you were eighty six."

MacTavish picked up an eraser and threw it at his partner, who quickly avoided the flying eraser. Spinning around, Cavanaugh watched as it hit Matthews in the back of the head.

"What the fuck?" said Marc, turning around suspiciously.

MacTavish and Cavanaugh quickly re-focused on their computers, pretending not to have seen what happened.

Matthews looked around the room suspiciously, and then bent over to pick up the eraser. Cavanaugh smiled as MacTavish picked up another eraser and aimed it once again at Matthews. This time, it hit him square in the ass.

"Okay," Marc said turning around, "If I find out who threw these..." Pausing, he slowly looked around at everyone who was within throwing distance. Unable to decide on the guilty party, he returned to his desk.

Cavanaugh and MacTavish looked at each other and tried to contain their impending laughter.

"You know," Billy continued, "if you're really interested in Vickie, don't let the age difference get in the way. If it doesn't matter to her, then go for it."

"It matters to me," replied Mac, as he thought about Red.

"What if she died next year?"

Mac gave him an inquiring look and asked, "Who?"

"Vickie," said Billy. "What makes you think she'll outlive you? What if you knew for a fact that she only had a year to live, what would you do? Look, society puts such an importance on age that it stops a lot of us from achieving, loving, being healthy and a lot more. It undermines our attitude toward life itself. You can't start school until you're six, can't graduate until you're eighteen, can't vote until you're twenty-one, can't retire until you're sixty-two, the list goes on and on. Sometimes the can'ts turn into shouldn'ts; you shouldn't do this, shouldn't do that. The government and society does its best to tell us how to live every year of our life. My mother had the right idea. I don't know how many times I heard her say that it's one day at a time and we only have today. Yesterday is gone, tomorrow may never come, so make the most of today—it's a gift, and all we really have is this moment in time. I try to live my life like that. If I met a woman that was old enough to be my mother and I was really attracted to her mentally and emotionally, I'd have that woman in my bed so fast I really wouldn't give a damn what anybody thought or said. Hell, I'd probably even marry her if she'd have me. So be careful Mac, you could lose the best thing that ever happened to you."

"I already have," Mac replied softly.

Cavanaugh looked at him and remembered their conversation at Neptune's Grotto. He suddenly realized that his partner would never settle down with anyone except Red—his one great love. "You're talking about Red," he said, sympathizing with his partner's feelings.

"I wanted to marry that woman so many times. Being married early on...well, it wasn't an option. And after Catherine died it became complicated. Red kept saying no, so I quit asking."

Seeing his partner's sensitivity surfacing, he said softly, "You're still in love with her."

"I'll always love her. With Red it's like you said, one day at a time."

Cavanaugh now had a deeper understanding of the red wigs in the armoire and the incredible love his partner felt for the red haired woman.

The two men were silent when Detective Keaton walked back to her desk. Sensing that something of a serious nature was going on, she said, "Am I interrupting some deep, dark discussion here?"

"No," Mac quickly responded with a smile.

"I figured you might want to leave a little early for the airport, in case there's heavy traffic," she smiled.

"Sure," he responded. "Good idea." Putting on his jacket, he looked at his partner. There was so much more he wanted to discuss with him, but this was not the time or place. "Thanks for the talk Brooklyn. You gave me a lot to think about."

"No problem. Isn't that what life's all about? Thanking, and thinking," he said, as his partner left to join Vickie on the stairs. Watching them leave, thoughts of Sarina suddenly came into his mind. "Oh God," he thought. Picking up the phone, he dialed the morgue, only to get an unavailable message on Sarina's recorder.

"Great," he said, as Matthews walked by. "Marc, can you cover the phones for me? I need a cigarette break."

"Sure Kid. I'll work on Vickie's list," he responded, walking back to his desk.

Cavanaugh grabbed his jacket and cigarettes and headed outside. Lighting up a cigarette, he saw Sarina's car in the parking lot. Tossing his cigarette aside, he rushed back into the precinct and hurried downstairs to the morgue. As he walked through the double doors, it was extremely quiet and empty. Moving quietly toward her office, he heard her speaking to someone on the phone.

"It's for the best, I just can't do this anymore," she said softly. "No, we're fine. Of course I do—always." Trying to get her attention, Cavanaugh cleared his throat. She turned around and saw him standing in the doorway. With a startled look, she spoke quietly into the phone. "I have to go," she said, and disconnected the call.

"Who was that?" he asked seriously.

"A friend," she sighed.

"Were you with that friend when I tried to call you last night?"

"I got your messages," she replied, "I just needed some time to think.

"So, is everything in order?" he asked.

339

"Almost," she smiled.

Walking over to her, he grasped her hands and said, "Maybe I can help." He led her into one of the empty examining rooms and locked the door.

"You know this is crazy, don't you?" she said.

"Take your clothes off," he smiled. "I locked the front door when I came in."

"You've got to be kidding," she responded. "What if—"

"Sh-h-h, start with your skirt, he said softly. As she slowly slipped off her skirt, he whispered in her ear, "Don't stop now." Sarina stood there wearing a tight, low cut lime green jersey top that hung snugly above her naval and a matching green thong. As she slipped off her top, he said, "Is this what you want?" Kissing her and turning her around, he bent her over the table as he unzipped his pants. The sensation of him moving inside of her began to excite her. As she stretched her arms above her head, he bent over and kissed her back passionately.

"Billy..." she began, then paused for a moment. Moving her hips in a welcoming manner, she said, "Oh yes...yes. Oh God! It feels so good."

Her mounting emotions made him aware that she was about to have an orgasm and it escalated his own eroticism. "Oh God Sarina," he sighed.

"C'mon baby," she said to him. "Now, now...yes, yes, yes!" she said—both of them letting out moans of ecstasy and reaching an erotic climax together.

"It just keeps getting better and better," he said with great pleasure, as he slid off her back and pulled her up off the table. Turning her around, and while holding her face in his hands, he kissed her passionately.

Looking down at his exposed body parts, she laughed, "You better put that back in your pants before you get mistaken for an autopsy subject."

"Ouch!" he responded, as he zipped up his pants.

Sarina quickly grabbed her top and slipped it over her head, while Cavanaugh picked up her skirt, and handed it to her. "Thanks," she said with a sexy smile as she slipped it on.

"For the skirt or my services?" he asked flirtatiously.

"Thank you for fulfilling another one of my fantasies," she said, kissing him on his neck.

"Except for one thing...you forgot to put me on the table," she sighed.

"You shared that fucking fantasy with me last November. How the hell could I remember everything?"

"It's okay," she said smiling, "everything else was perfect."

"You do have some interesting fantasies," smiled Billy. "Fucking in a morgue, now that is really weird. I guess there's a first time for everything."

"It wasn't the first weird time with you," she replied. Looking at her curiously, Cavanaugh had no idea what she was referring to. "On the way to your condo?" she questioned. He still couldn't comprehend what was so unusual about where they had sex. "That secluded area off the Interstate where we pulled off?" Staring at him she said, "You really didn't know where we were?"

"Some out-of-the-way random spot?" he guessed.

"It was where the Son of Sam killer took one of his victims."

"Oh my God," said Billy stunned. "Why the hell didn't you say something? I had no idea that's where we were. Now that's really fucking creepy."

"Well, I'm glad we cleared that up," she laughed. "I was beginning to think you were kinky with borderline psychotic tendencies."

"And your role playing scenarios aren't? Come here," he said, pulling her close and kissing her passionately, "When I'm with you everything else seems to disappear."

Meanwhile, upstairs in the Bureau, Rollins and Matthews were talking about the homicides.

..."So this is our completed list," said Rollins. "Let's get the dry erase board out and put these names up. Maybe one of us will get lucky and figure it all out."

"I'll go get the board," Marc said, walking toward the locker room. Rollins, while waiting patiently, reviewed the list of victims and witnesses. "Be sure and put up every name," he said, as Matthews returned with the board. "Start with the victims."

"Sounds good captain," said Marc, as started to transfer the list of names to the board.

Victims

Howard Austin   San Francisco 64
Larry Kingman   Cleveland 63
Jim Carson   Westwood 62
Bob Jefferson   Sherman Oaks 65

Witnesses

Franklin James - Security Guard
Crimescene PO's Wm. Kidd - Robt Ford
Cabbie Barrow ≈ Hostess B. Parker
Vinnie Price - Bob Steele - Elle Parker
Kay Francis - Zach Scott - Mr. Power
E. D. Robinson - Bob Ryan - Lee Tracy

Officers

Will Best - Jim Gleason

"Okay, that's it, said Marc after adding the last name. "This one," he added, pointing to the name Bob Jefferson. "Vickie discovered this two year cold case homicide. Same MO—identical hit. He was a truck driver for the film studios in LA."

"So now we have four identical hits," said Rollins, reviewing the board. Glancing down the hallway, he saw MacTavish and Keaton arriving with the Cleveland detectives—they were laughing when they walked into the bureau. After welcoming them on board, Rollins introduced them to Detective Matthews and took them on a quick tour of the precinct. "Let's start downstairs," he said, leading them out of the bureau. "I'll introduce you to everyone along the way."

Keaton walked over to the board and reviewed what Matthews had written on it. "Good move Marc, did you see this on Columbo?" she whispered.

"Actually it was the captain's idea," explained Marc. "He figures if we all look at it we might trigger a lead." Looking around, he said, "Well I guess we better get back to work."

"I need to get some coffee first," said Vickie, as she headed for the break room. "You want a cup?"

"No, thanks, I'm good," he said, sitting down at his desk.

Twenty minutes later, while discussing the flight to New York, Rollins walked back in with the Cleveland detectives.

..."I'm sure the flight attendants were glad when Louie got off the plane," said Ricco.

"You always give women a hard time Louie?" Rollins laughed.

Grinning from ear to ear, he replied, "Only when they got really big bazooms."

"Keaton?" said Rollins, "can you give these guys the downstairs tour including the new morgue?"

"Sure," she replied, "Let's go."

"Looks like you guys will be up and running soon," Louie whispered to her, as they headed for the stairs.

"Yes, and I'm really looking forward to it."

Louie and Ricco glanced around the precinct as they made their way towards the basement.

Downstairs, Sarina was re-applying her lipstick when she heard the bell alarm for the front doors. "Christ," she said, straightening her clothes and hair as she walked towards the entrance. Unlocking the doors, she saw the three detectives standing there. "Sorry," she said flustered. "Security...I had to take care of something in my office. I'm Sarina Montez."

Vickie, introduced the Cleveland detectives and said, "I'm giving them the grand tour."

"You can call me Louie," he said flirtatiously. "Actually...you can call me anytime."

"I heard you guys were coming," she smiled. "Welcome to New York."

Vickie wondered how Sarina knew they were coming. It wasn't common knowledge in the precinct.

"This is it, our new morgue. Or I should say our Criminal Investigative Emergency Unit," Sarina smiled, escorting them back to her office.

Suddenly, the bathroom door flew open in front of them, and Cavanaugh rushed out—his expression was one of surprise and embarrassment. "Hey, you made it," he said, giving them each a hug. "God it's good to see you guys."

"Its good to see you too," Ricco said with a familiar grin, as he looked at Cavanaugh's freshly washed face and wet hair. "Sarina's got some high-end equipment here," he said, giving her a quick, once over look. "I'm sure there's some very interesting work going on down here."

Cavanaugh knew exactly what Ricco was talking about. He was sure the Cleveland Detective had figured out something sexual was going on before they arrived. "Some of the best I've ever seen or had the pleasure to work on," smiled Billy.

Sarina, standing there a bit embarrassed, realized that Ricco was aware of her sexual activity with the young detective. Seeing her embarrassment, Ricco subtly reserved any further discussion on the subject.

Examining the new and highly advanced technology, Louie and Vickie ignored the sexual innuendos that were being passed back and forth.

"Hey guys," said Billy. As they all came together, he stood behind Sarina with his arms around her waist. Dropping his chin on her shoulder, he said, "I want you all to know that this is the woman I'm going to marry."

Surprised by Cavanaugh's statement, Sarina struggled to keep her composure while they congratulated her and Cavanaugh.

"She hasn't said yes yet," said Billy. "I've been waiting a long time for her answer."

"When did you ask her?" Louie inquired.

As Cavanaugh gently turned her face around and looked into her eyes, he said, "Last Thanksgiving."

"Well, I guess I'm long overdue for an answer," she replied, staring back at him. And with an exuberant amount of excitement she said, "Yes!"

Cavanaugh lifted her up in the air and said, "Yes?"

"Yes," she repeated.

"Oh my God," exclaimed Vickie, with tears of joy in her eyes. Rushing forward, she hugged them and said, "I'm so happy for both of you."

"This is great!" yelled Louie. "Oh, I just love weddings. When's the wedding...you guys need a wedding singer?"

"I just hope she doesn't make me wait as long as she did to give me an answer," Billy replied hugging her and kissing her forehead.

"Look," said Vickie, "let's go upstairs and tell everyone."

Sarina hesitated, as Cavanaugh took her hand and began to lead her to the door. "Yeah, let's go," he said.

"Wait, I need to use the bathroom," said Vickie. "Don't leave without me, I'll be right back." Rushing into the bathroom she flushed the toilet. Pulling out her cell phone, she called upstairs and said, "Mac, listen..." quickly filled him in on Cavanaugh's engagement.

"Okay, I'll let everyone know," Mac answered. "The Kid sure is full of surprises." Disconnecting the call he immediately informed Rollins, who had Matthews remove the eraser board from sight before everyone showed up.

Keaton flushed the toilet and left the bathroom. "Okay I'm ready," she said, leisurely leading everyone out of the morgue and up the stairs. Walking in front of them and blocking everyone's way, she climbed the stairs very slowly. Her odd behavior was especially noticed by the men—they were looking at each other and wondering about their slow departure.

"Vickie, can you pick it up a little?" said Billy, "Louie's getting cobwebs on his feet."

Louie frantically jumped all over the steps and said, "Cobwebs, spiders...where the fuck are they? Ricco, you know how I hate spiders," he said, swatting the air around his feet. Flailing his arms around, he tried to brush off his clothes and back. "You didn't tell me we were gonna have to deal with fuckin' spiders."

"Louie its okay," said Billy. "It's just a figure of speech, there's no spiders up here."

Without Louie's knowledge, Cavanaugh winked at Ricco and fabricated, "Except for the big one we got from South America, he must have been asleep when we were down there."

As they continued walking up the stairs, Louie whispered to Ricco, "He's kidding...ain't he?"

"I don't know," replied Ricco, leading him on seriously. "There was a moment down there when I thought I did see a long hairy leg in the corner."

"Just how long was that fuckin' furry leg?" Louie asked seriously.

"Three, maybe four feet," Ricco said casually.

"THREE OR FOUR FUCKING FEET," Louie yelled out, as they approached the top of the stairs.

"Discussing my sexual appendage again?" said Mac subtly, as he walked out to greet everyone.

Cavanaugh shook his head and turned to Sarina. "This is what I have to put up with on a daily basis," he said, as MacTavish stepped aside—allowing the future bride and groom to enter first.

As they walked through the door, Cavanaugh and Sarina saw that everyone in the precinct had gathered to pass on their best wishes.

"CONGRATULATIONS!" they all yelled out.

"Oh my," said a surprised Sarina.

Cavanaugh was speechless, as he looked at all the people surrounding them. Realizing that Vickie had set it up, he smiled at her with a look of gratitude and brotherly love.

"Heads up everyone. Tonight," Rollins began, "we'll be celebrating at Kellaway's Pub. Now, we all have work to do. Let's get it done so we can go celebrate this future wedding."

"I'll see you later," Billy said to Sarina.

Everyone else quickly returned to work, while the Cleveland detectives continued their tour with Vickie. As Sarina left to go downstairs, Cavanaugh saw his partner approaching.

"I'm happy for you Kid," Mac smiled, "when's the big day?"

"We haven't set a date. Mac...would you be my best man?"

"Of course I will. It would be an honor. That is..." he paused, as Cavanaugh waited for his unfinished response. "Only if I can wear my kilt," he said eloquently.

Heading back to his desk, Billy replied. "Mac, you can wear anything you want as long as you're there next to me."

"Then it will be a memorable event," Mac replied, sitting down at his desk.

"Just make sure you pack in the family jewels, I don't want it to be that memorable," smiled Billy. "I'll keep the duct tape handy just in case."

MacTavish gave his partner a look of agreement as he walked back to his desk. He was happy that his partner had found someone— but wasn't quite sure that their Forensic Director was the woman he really needed—those doubts made him uncomfortable about the upcoming marriage.

Cavanaugh walked over to where Matthews was pulling away the eraser board from the wall behind his desk.

"Looking forward to tonight," said Marc. "Getting back to our homicides, I put this data board together," he said, turning it around so it could be viewed once more.

"This is interesting," said Billy, studying the board. "Good job Columbo."

"Joubert had Vickie research all homicides for the last ten years—searching for similarities," said Rollins. "She came up with this guy Robert Jefferson—a two-year cold case file with the same MO."

"Three out of California and one from Ohio...I don't see any connection," declared Marc.

"That's because it's not really where they lived," said Billy, as he went back to his desk.

"Have we excluded that they lived here?" Mac inquired from his desk.

"I have," said Joubert, walking into the bureau. "I can guarantee these are undercover names and not who they really are. Can you add just the initials of these men?"

Responding to what Joubert asked, Matthews grabbed a marker and completed the task.

L K   H A   R C   B J

"You think there's a connection?" asked Mac.

"Perhaps," Joubert replied. "Marc, would you write out only the last names of the victims."

"Sure," said Marc, as he quickly wrote them on the board.

Kingman

Austin

Carson

Jefferson

Silence filled the room as the detectives stared and studied the data board. "Anything stand out to you guys?" Marc asked.

Standing there silently, they were interrupted by Vickie's voice, as she returned with the Cleveland detectives.

...."So that's about it," she said, standing in the doorway after ending the precinct tour. "You saw the renovation that's taking place outside when you came in," she added, as they walked into the bureau.

Louie, seeing the information board, got excited and quickly went towards it. "Hey, what are you guys doin'?" he smiled.

"We're looking for a connection," said Marc.

"Wow, looks like a game of anagrams," Louie replied, moving closer to the board. "Ah-h, its cities."

Aroused by Louie's statement, Cavanaugh and MacTavish got up from their desks and joined the other detectives as they all walked over to the board behind Louie.

"What did you say?" said Mac.

"Cities, these four guys all have the last names of cities, Louie repeated—writing and pointing to each name. "It could be where they lived. Kind of cool, huh?" he smiled, leaving the detectives stunned by his discovery.

Kingman - Arizona

Austin - Texas

Carson - Carson City, Nevada

Jefferson =

Jefferson City, Tennessee OR MissourI

"And you questioned his intelligence Mac," smiled Ricco.

"I stand corrected," Mac replied, as he walked over and patted him on the back. "Louie, you're astonishing. You always pull the cat out of the hat."

"Mac," said Louie seriously, "I think you're wrong. There's no cat involved here." Leaning closer he whispered, "The cat was in Cleveland, and...it was in a bag...not a hat."

"Mac," said Ricco, as Cavanaugh headed back to his desk smiling.

"Yes, I know," Mac interrupted, "Try not to be the straight man."

Joubert, standing next to Matthews and Keaton, stared at the board for a few minutes before speaking. "I think Louie's on the right track here."

"You believe the government is somehow connected to all of this?" asked Marc.

"Yes," Joubert said, pausing for another minute before he spoke. "These men," he continued, while staring at the board, "have their age as a common denominator. Being connected to some sort of conspiracy would make sense."

"I guess I owe Mel Gibson an apology," replied Vickie, focusing in on Cavanaugh. Walking up behind him, she placed her hands affectionately on his shoulders.

"Watch the hands Vickie," said Mac, sitting down at his desk. "He's practically a married man."

"I'm not married yet," Billy responded, leaning backwards and looking up at her.

"You'd better watch that flirtatious side of your being, Cavanaugh," she said, shoving him and his chair into the desk. "You're getting married to a woman who could easily remove your sexual parts."

"Ouch," Billy laughed, as he watched her go back to her desk.

"Maybe you better try out those parts before they're removed, said Mac.

"Knock it off, the both of you," she said.

Looking at her, Joubert smiled. He believed that Vickie was extremely attracted to MacTavish, who represented a missing link in her life—probably a fatherly figure that was taken away from her at an early age. "Cavanaugh was the other male figure she longed for," he thought. "Most likely, she was an only child, and he represented the missing sibling brother in her life."

Ricco and Louie were still looking at the board when Louie yelled out, "YOU GUYS NEED HELP WITH THESE WITNESSES, BYSTANDERS, SLASH SHOW BIZ NAMES?"

Hearing his boisterous statement, everyone stopped what they were doing. MacTavish, Cavanaugh and Keaton got up slowly and walked back to the eraser board where Louie was busy focusing on the names. Joubert, Matthews, and the other detectives, followed in a silent procession until everyone in the bureau was standing behind the little guy. Rollins, seeing everyone crowding around the board from his office, quickly joined the entourage.

Louie was intensely focused on the board names and didn't realize that everyone had crowded behind him. Turning around, he said, "If you...WHAT THE FUCK?!" he exclaimed loudly, as he jumped back against the board. "YOU GUYS NEARLY GAVE ME A FUCKING HEART ATTACK. DON'T EVER SNEAK UP ON A LITTLE GUY LIKE THAT!"

"Sorry Louie," said Ricco. "What about the show biz names?"

"This witness list over here," Louie said, pointing to the names. "They're all old actors. I mean some are really old, even dead. These others...are outlaws."

"Outlaws," Billy inquired?

"Yeah, these guys here," answered Louie, pointing to the names as he read them out loud;

...1. "Franklin James, the security guard...he's the outlaw Frank James—that was the guy in the building where you went lookin' for the lady in gray," he said assertively. "Got news for you Kid, he ain't no security guard.

...2. "B. Parker, the hostess at that restaurant on Fifth Avenue? Well, that's Miss Bonnie Parker," smiled Louie.

...3. "Her partner in crime, the buggy driver who also gave you a hard time, William Kidd? He's Billy the Kid.

"Hey, lookout...we got two Billy the Kids'. One good, two bad." Louie laughed. "Hey Cavanaugh, did you know that cowboy Billy the Kid was a Sagittarius? Now that's irony for you—both of you with the same name and birth sign. And lets not forget Scotland's hard-hearted pirate William Kidd; born in 1655, arrested in Boston, and hung in May of 1701 at Execution Dock in London. They coated his body in tar and hung it in an iron frame to remind other pirates of their fate." Looking around, he realized he was the only one enjoying his travelogue. Turning his back to the detectives he quickly became serious, which was a stretch for the little buffoon. "No interest in history trivia," said Louie, "Okay...back to the list."

...4. "Here's another guy that gave you fuckin' hard time...Robert Ford, the wisecracking cop under the umbrella at your homicide in the rain? As history recalls, By the way, Bob Ford was the guy who shot Jesse James."

As Louie clarified each name, Cavanaugh had flashbacks of each situation.

...the stuttering security guard, "No, laa-dy. I hav-ent seen no...one since...the r-ain, st-started." The hostess at the Fifth Avenue restaurant..."Sir, I assure you, those are the two who came in here," the horse drawn buggy driver..."Did you find your lady?" The cop holding the umbrella..."Would one of you tell me what the hell is going on, because this body's about to float down Fifth Avenue."

"So much for becoming a great detective," Billy said to himself, as Louie continued his analysis.

...5. "And let's not forget C. L. Barrow otherwise known as Clyde Barrow," continued Louie, as he turned back to look at the non-responding detectives. "You know...Bonnie and Clyde?"

The other detectives were so involved with the board that they didn't interconnect with what Louie was saying. The little guy continued to explain how it all fit together.

"They made a movie about them...Warren Beatty and Faye Dunaway...someone needs to pay attention here," he mumbled, as he imitated shooting a machine gun.

The detectives gave Louie a quick glance of bewilderment, and then silently refocused their attention to the information on the board.

Louie took a deep breath and turned back to the board mumbling, "The whole fucking precinct just went into an Alzheimer's time warp."

"Tell us about the show biz people." said Ricco.

"Thank God one of you has re-entered this dimension. Showtime," he said dramatically, while pointing to the names.

...6. "These are the two witnesses from the first homicide. You got Bob Steele—actor from the old black and white early days that made a lot of westerns.

...7. "And here's Kay Francis, from the '30s." Turning around, Louie faced the detectives and began discussing her career. "An attractive woman for her time, she was Cary Grant' wife *In Name Only*. She played a hell of a bitch."

Louie looked around at the serious faces staring back at him and quickly turned back to the board imitating Rodney Dangerfield. *"Tough group, tough group.* Okay...moving on."

...8. "Bob Ryan, professionally known as actor Robert Ryan, was one of my favorites—good character actor, especially good at playing the bad guy.

...9. Lee Tracy usually played a detective or a reporter in the old back and whites.

...10. Vinnie Price is Vincent Price—*Laura, Dragonwyck, And His Kind Of Woman*, were just a few of his many dramatic roles before he went into making the horror classics. All of these people," Louie pointed out, "were actors."

...11. "Elle Ξ Eleanor Parker."

...12. "Ed Ξ Edward G. Robinson."

...13. "Zach Ξ Zachary Scott, he did the classic *Mildred Pierce*. You guys remember *Mildred Pierce?*"

A solemn silence filled the room. No one responded to Louie's question.

"Okay...evidently, nobody remembers seeing any of the classics," said Louie, turning back to the board. "I would definitely recommend a psychiatric evaluation for this precinct." He continued to explain his theory and actor analogy. "In the report I read, there were two police officers that also fell into this anagram."

...14 and 15. "Will Best and Jim Gleason, the two officers at the Central Park homicide—they were also actors. Willie Best; tall, skinny Black guy, played petrified character roles in the old comedy, horror, and detective films. James Gleason was a great character actor from the 30's up through the 50's—usually played a detective. He also appeared in *Arsenic and Old Lace* with Cary Grant. Now that was a great movie. NOT THAT ANY OF YOU GUYS WOULD REMEMBER, CAUSE IF YOU DON'T REMEMBER *MILDRED PIERCE*—"

"We remember, we remember," Ricco quickly interjected. "Get back to the damn list."

"Yeah, we remember," smiled Marc sympathetically.

"Great job," Vickie said, giving him a wink.

"Thank God," said Louie wiping his brow. "I thought I was alone here. Which brings us to the common denominator," he continued. "All these stars have played a detective; helped solve a crime, or been the bad guy. Whoever put this together was definitely a fan of old movies. I can appreciate this work...very creative," he said, reviewing his summation.

Cavanaugh stared at the board. He was, as were the other detectives, in awe of what Louie had uncovered. "Unbelievable," he said, "who would have thought...if it wasn't for Louie, I don't think we could have got this far."

"Amazing," Mac replied to Ricco, "he's absolutely amazing!"

Breaking everyone's concentration, Rollins said, "We need to find out what the hell is going on here with our victims. Let's start with the cities; Keaton, I want you to take Austin. Mac, you check out Carson City. Matthews, research Kingman and Cavanaugh, you take Jefferson. Look up every Jefferson city on the map. Everybody else...take an early dinner break. Let them know downstairs that you guys are on call if anything comes up."

Rollins and his five detectives watched as the other detectives in the bureau quickly left. "Okay," he said to his team, "let's see if we can find out who our guys really were."

The four detectives went to their computers and searched for the missing information by uploading photos of the victims.

Joubert watched as Louie, backed up slowly from the board, and looked at it sideways and then straight up. After a slight hesitation, he once again turned sideways to review it again. "What's he doing Ricco?" Joubert inquired.

"It's a Louie thing," Ricco replied, as they quietly watched him.

"Okay," Louie said with a sinister laugh, "try to fuck with me? Well you have met your match Mr. Movie Trivia."

Louie removed the first initials of the victim's names from the line, leaving only their last initials K, A, C, and J—then he rearranged them.

Everyone stopped what they were doing and focused once again on Louie and the board.

$$K \; A \; C \; J \; = \; J \; A \; C \; K$$

"Jack?" Rollins inquired.

"That appears to be their connection," interjected Joubert as he turned to Ricco. "Your partner is very gifted."

"Got it," Vickie yelled out, as her computer screen pulled up the requested information. "Our photographer's real name is Cal Simmons, and he really is a photographer."

"Got mine too," said Marc. "Kingman is Gary Lynch. He has no personal data."

"Mac," Rollins inquired?

"He's coming up...Carson James is Terry Collins in Carson City Nevada. He has no history."

"Cavanaugh, how about you, you got anything on Jefferson?" said Rollins.

"Yeah, in Missouri, he came up as Alvin Jeffries."

"Any history on him?"

Billy, looking up with a solemn look replied, "He's a cop."

"Active?" said Rollins.

"Retired," said Billy, upset with what had been revealed. Conspiracies never set well with him, especially when they involved fellow police officers.

"Pull up the precincts where he's worked," Rollins directed, "and let's see what we find?"

Cavanaugh entered the information and waited. As the screen came up, he stared at the information intensely. "Christ," he said solemnly.

"Well?" asked Rollins.

"Only one location until he moved to Missouri." Looking directly at the captain he replied, "Dallas Texas from '61 to '65."

"Heads up, I want everyone to check and see where the other guys were from '61 to '65," Rollins said unwaveringly. "If anybody can't get in, let me know. I'll give you a crash course in hacking."

"I'm having a problem boss," said Marc, pulling away from his desk.

Rollins quickly walked over to Matthews and sat down next to him. As he began to work on the computer, the other detectives stood behind him and watched as their captain displayed his computer skills— breaking security rules and restrictions. "Marc," said Rollins, "I need you to time me. I only have a certain amount of time to get in and out of this system. After three minutes, they can trace us and we don't want that. Start when I say go, and give me a countdown and keep it accurate." He started typing so rapidly that his fingers were a blur on the keyboard— while the screen flashed all sorts of confidential accesses. "Go!" he said, and quickly moved through classified sections belonging to the CIA. Scrolling down the list, he entered a section named Confidential Security Forces.

"Two minutes left," replied Marc, watching the time.

As Rollins typed in Gary Lynch, the computer screen through a number of CSF search pages, it rolled to Special Undercover Forces. "Somebody take notes, we won't have time to scan it all," he said.

"I wouldn't worry about that," said Ricco. "Louie has a photographic memory and he's on it."

"One minute to go," said Matthews.

"C'mon, c'mon," Rollins said impatiently. "Finally," he smiled, as Lynch's history was displayed on the screen under Special Undercover Forces, revealing that Gary Lynch was a former Green Beret and Navy Seal.

Matthews counted down the time Rollins had left. "29, 28, 27—"

While the detectives were mesmerized by what they saw, Louie was acutely focused on the monitor—memorizing everything that came up.

```
>>Data request granted. . .
>>>
++ SPECOPS - Outstanding abilities in
undercover work.
++Classification Sniper - Excellent
marksman with all types of weapons.
++Termination assignments >> Classified.
++New identity >> Classified.
++Relocation >> Classified. >>>
```

Rollins quickly found that Kingman, alias Gary Lynch, was also in Dallas, at the same time as Jefferson, alias Alvin Jeffries.

"Five, four—" Marc continued. Rollins closed the files just as Marc said, "Two—"

We're out!" Rollins said, exhaling deeply.

The detectives, astonished by what their captain had achieved, were absorbing the new data they had.

"Great job, you give private lessons?" smiled Billy.

"Yeah, by appointment only," Rollins laughed, wiping his damp forehead.

"That was some pretty fancy finger work," said Ricco patting him on the back.

"Are we going after the other three?" asked Marc.

"Not a good idea," Rollins replied. "We have two out of four and I can live with that. We don't want to arouse suspicion. This network will show that someone tried to access information, and with no other searches, they'll think it was a CIA error and disregard the try."

"So are we all in agreement here?" said Billy, looking at the other detectives, and acknowledging the huge undercover operation that had taken place.

Rollins looked around at his crew and said, "Our job now is to find out who's behind the vigilante hit on our four victims. We now know who these guys are and we know why they had their identities changed. I want all the documentation on this case in my office before anybody leaves."

"So the victims were the shooters in Dallas," said Louie, as his mind did some calculating.

Ricco looked at MacTavish and pointed at his watch. Nodding yes, he remembered the four and a half minute mind delay that Louie occasionally experienced.

"Personally, I always believed there was more than one shooter that took out JFK," said Marc.

"May I?" asked Joubert, standing up. "If we could tap into each confidential file, I'm sure we'd find that they all were assassins. I would surmise that a photographer, a cop, detective and a secret serviceman, could come and go without question or suspicion, especially if they had the proper identification. Now the next question is, would the same people that relocated them, want them dead? I believe they wouldn't. They could have disposed of them long ago. They went through a lot of trouble to protect them."

"Then who?" asked Marc.

362

"Perhaps another agency," Joubert responded. "Some highly advanced vigilante group that believes in retribution I suppose."

"How could they work without getting exposed?" said Vickie.

"More than likely, they are a secret group that's branched off from its original operations. Their leaders may be unaware of their activities. It is not uncommon," replied Joubert.

"And the woman," Billy inquired.

"Ah yes, the woman, she may be what my father used to refer to as The Arranger. Many of these undercover groups have someone who arranges the hit. They became friends—building a relationship of trust. That relationship could continue for several years before the hit is scheduled."

"In Sarina's forensic report," said Billy, "she believed in a two drug theory before the final shot was fired. In fact, she mentioned something similar to what you're saying."

"After examining her report I agree with her findings." responded Joubert.

"How do you think it went down?" asked Rollins.

Having everyone's attention and curiosity, Joubert said, "Let's say The Arranger is a woman. She calls the victim, who by now is a close friend, and sets up a casual meeting. Perhaps their meeting takes place in a bar or restaurant. That would be where she slips the first medication into his drink. They would then leave and go for a walk down a busy street where she could accidentally trip. As the target helps her up, another accomplice passing by injects the victim with the second medication or drug. By now the victim is very close to death. The Arranger would quickly disappear into the moving crowd allowing the next assassin to finish the job. The shot through the heart was meant to make a statement. You must understand that timing is very essential in this line of work—these assassinations were professionally done and well choreographed with precise timing.

"Why would she let herself be seen?" asked Billy.

"Perhaps it was a mistake," Joubert continued. "If she's been doing this a long time she could be tired and unconsciously wish to be stopped. Another possibility is the timing could have been off. Her route to leave the scene could have been blocked or delayed. It could be one of many reasons. The only reason you saw her, was because of your intuitive cold sweat. Otherwise, you probably would have paid her no attention.

"So you think this woman is my mother?"

Joubert looked at him and replied delicately, "I do, and it's only based on your intuitive powers. You understand, this is only my opinion."

"One question," said Billy, looking down at his desk.

"Yes?"

"How could anyone bring a dead woman back to life?"

"I've seen it done before in Europe," Joubert began. "It's performed with illusions. Did you ever touch your mother when she was dead?"

"No," Billy replied softly.

"You believed what you were told and focused on the illusion of her death. Is that correct?"

"Yes."

"Then this is how I believe it went down," said Joubert. "One of many common ailments could have been used to explain her death. The people involved would make sure the coffin was open at the grave sight. Usually, it would be just the top half. She would have been heavily sedated to decrease her heartbeat—there would be no sign of life. Grieving people are not going to look for life because they have already accepted her death.

"At the grave site, they closed the casket in front of me," said Billy. "I saw them lower her into the ground and toss a shovel of dirt on top of the coffin before we left."

Joubert understood Cavanaugh's denial. There was a side of the young detective that needed to believe she was dead. "Let's start over," he said. "If you wanted to make someone believe this woman was dead, how would you go about it?"

Cavanaugh thought about what he said, and began to get some clarity. Remembering the grave sight in his mind, and the distance that he and the others kept from the casket, he flashed back to his childhood and the old Christopher Lee's Dracula movies—the vampires only appeared to be dead.

"You must remember that this is an illusion," Joubert continued. "Magicians do this sort of thing all the time. It's a performance which has been thoroughly rehearsed and acted out, just as the performances at the crime scenes were rehearsed and acted out." Pointing to the board with the names of the witnesses, he said, "Nothing was real...nothing, except the murders."

Cavanaugh somberly reviewed the board again. He saw and heard the evidence confronting him and still didn't know how to react. One more time, his emotional state was on the brink of collapse.

Joubert, realizing Cavanaugh's state of mind quickly interacted and said softly, "Let's assume the funeral was staged. In the coffin, a large oxygen tank was placed underneath her body, perhaps the kind used in scuba diving. A hidden light fixture would have been installed above her head. After the lid was closed, a light would have immediately turned on and dropped a breathing apparatus on her face. The oxygen tank would release itself at the approximate time she began to wake up. It would have also triggered an injection needle to bring her around. I believe she was wired to communicate with her people."

Remembering his mother's acting ability, Cavanaugh began to accept the theory of how her death could have been faked. "We all left after the first shovel of dirt was thrown on the coffin," he replied uneasily.

"And that's what they were counting on," said Joubert, "all of you leaving quickly. I'm sure she was brought up swiftly, probably after that first few shovels of dirt. If you look at this as a staged performance, you would realize there were many rehearsals to pull this off."

"Staged performance," thought Billy, recalling the few weeks before his mother's death and remembering all the late evening rehearsals she had to attend—telling him that she was working on some new stage play. However, she didn't talk about it like she usually did when she got a part—taking him out of school two weeks before she died and using a long overdue vacation as her excuse. Those last few weeks of her secretiveness and her so called death now seemed to fall into place. "All those trips she took me on," he recalled, "Disneyland, Knott's Berry Farm, Sea World, The San Diego Zoo—it all made sense now, as did her spending more time with him. She knew she wouldn't to be around and wanted me to remember good times." He scrutinized the possibility of her being alive. "Assuming my mother is alive," he sighed, "why would she fake her death and go to work for these people?"

"You've got to understand how these people work," said Joubert. "They are very powerful. I've seen priests, teen-agers, loving fathers,

366

and professionally trained agents, who end up working for these people as informants or assassins."

Cavanaugh realized Joubert's knowledge came from a personal source and said sympathetically, "And your father, which was he?"

"You are very perceptive," Joubert smiled. "My father was a freelance contractor, as they prefer to be called; he worked for whoever needed him—I am alive today because he chose that path."

"They threatened his family," said Billy.

"These people do not threaten," said Joubert, "they deal in fact—explaining and giving examples of what will happen accidentally. My father made the choice to keep us alive as perhaps your mother did."

"To be taken down," said Ricco, joining in on the discussion, "the same way as the president...this organization is making a statement to the original assassins and those who contracted them."

The Karma theory," Billy said wisely. "What goes around comes around. Only they're not waiting for *The Universe* to take care of it."

Rollins knew he had to secure all the information about this woman being Cavanaugh's mother. "Heads up," he said softly, as he gathered them around him. "There's to be no connection to Cavanaugh. I don't want anyone referring to this woman as his mother—she is a suspect. What was heard here stays here, are we clear?"

The detectives were all in agreement of their captain's request.

"Okay," Rollins continued, "then let's go with Joubert's theory and find this woman. If I have to break security in the CIA files I will. Let's do what we can before we leave tonight—we have a party to attend later."

Cavanaugh got up and singled out Joubert. Their conversation between them became a private affair.

367

"Can you tell me who was cremated?" asked Billy.

"That I don't know," Joubert responded. "It wasn't your mother that I'm sure of."

Cavanaugh began to see the complexity of everything around him. He never dreamed his choices as a teenager would have led to this. He wondered what would have happened if he had listened to his friend that night and never walked into that convenience store—how different his life would be today. He quickly realized that he would never know the answer to that question.

Joubert, observing Cavanaugh's dilemma, could only imagine what he was thinking. He thought of a way to give him some hope for the future. "If she's found and arrested," he began, "I can tell you for a fact, that she won't go to jail and there will be no trial. These companies and agencies protect their people. All data concerning her, including the homicides, will vanish, and she too will disappear."

"So you feel this case is closed?" said Billy.

"I do, but your captain needs to follow procedure and the chances of finding her are minimal. Unfortunately, she has left a few loose ends."

"Are those loose ends because of me?"

"I'd like to believe there is a side of her life that she wants to explain to you," he answered. "That would be good, for the both of you."

Cavanaugh felt Joubert was talking about himself. Softly he said, "Your father...are you two close?"

Pausing for a moment before answering, Joubert carefully considered his reply. "There are no happy endings to these types of stories," he sighed. "My father is alive, but we seldom see each other—

haven't seen him for years. He stays on the move, never in one place too long. It's safer that way, for all of us."

"Are you telling me I could put my mother's life in danger if I tried to see her?"

"Yes, most definitely," said Joubert. "Hopefully, you will learn to live with certain boundaries. Eventually, it becomes a way of life. As long as the people she works for don't know that you are aware of her true identity, she has a strong chance of survival. I expect they will go to great lengths to relocate her." Pausing, Joubert thought about the situation he had with his father, then continued, "Perhaps one day, two strangers will cross each other's path, look into each other's eyes, and without speaking a word or acknowledging each other, will know the truth." Putting his arm around Cavanaugh's shoulder, he said comfortingly, "And when that day comes, everything you both have given up will temporarily disappear from your minds, and joy will replace despair. Remember, if you see her, you must never acknowledge her as your mother."

"Matthews was right," Billy replied. "Losing my mother twice is hard. He has no idea just how hard. I believe it's the hardest thing I'll ever have to do."

"Maybe not the hardest," said Joubert. "You should put more focus on your relationship with Sarina."

"Yeah, you're right...thanks Joubert, I'll see you at Kellaway's," replied Billy, as he grabbed his keys and cigarettes. Taking his jacket off the back of the chair, he rushed out the door and headed downstairs to meet Sarina.

Joubert looked down at his hands and thought about his own father. His intuition told him that their times together were coming close to an end. "Endings can be very painful," he thought, and wondered if he should have said anything to Cavanaugh about his intuition concerning Sarina. "Perhaps not...it would be too much for him to handle right now."

In a far corner of the bureau, MacTavish and Ricco were discussing the development of WASP, while Detectives Keaton and Matthews were finishing their work for Rollins. Louie on the other hand, was standing at the entrance of the bureau, flirting with a Black woman who was filling in for the bureau's absentee receptionist. "So you've never been with an Italian Stallion," he grinned.

"Let's call it a wrap," Rollins yelled out, locking his office and moving toward the stairs.

"Hey, I like that!" Louie interjected, "it seems appropriate for today's work. "It's a wrap!" he repeated whimsically. "Catch you later doll face," he said to the receptionist, as he joined Ricco, Rollins, and Matthews at the top of the stairs.

In the bureau, Mac turned to Joubert and asked, "Do you need a ride over to the Pub?"

"No, but thank you for the offer."

Putting on his jacket, MacTavish pulled out his cell phone and dialed Shawn's number. "Vickie, you want to ride with me?" he asked, waiting for a response from O'Hara.

"Sure," she replied, getting her things and rushing after him.

O'Hara was sitting in the backseat of a taxicab when his cell phone rang. Pulling it out of his jacket, he saw the call was from MacTavish. "Aye," he said.

"There's been a change in plans," said Mac, as he and Vickie walked out of the precinct and into the parking lot. We're meeting at Kellaway's Pub,"

"Sounds good," Shawn responded.

"Actually, the precinct is throwing a little party for Cavanaugh. He's getting married."

O'Hara became silent and controlled as he looked out at the passing traffic.

"Did you hear me mate?"

"Yes, that's great," Shawn replied. "So who's the lucky woman?"

"It's our Forensics Director, Sarina Montez. The Kid shocked the hell out of all of us. We never even knew they were seeing each other." O'Hara sat quietly in the taxicab—realizing that Sarina would no longer be a part of his life. "O'Hara," said Mac, "are you there mate?"

"I guess we have a bad connection," said Shawn.

"Hey I forgot to mention," added Mac. "Rollins, Louie, and Joubert, broke the case. We'll fill you in at the Pub."

"That's great. I'll be talkin' to you then. I have to make one quick stop before I get there." Disconnecting the call, he spoke to the cab driver. "We need to go to Sheepshead Bay." Shaking his head, he smiled, as he lit a cigarette and said softly, "Sarina, Sarina, what am I going to do with you. You are so full of surprises."

Meanwhile, back at the One Nine, Cavanaugh was in the morgue with Sarina—telling her about what went on upstairs and conveniently leaving out the information about his mother. "You know, you were the one who got the ball rolling in the right direction," said Billy, putting his arms around her waist. "You sure you don't want to come back upstairs?"

"I got out of detective work because I was tired of cold cases and unsolved mysteries," Sarina smiled. "This is where I belong. Besides, you guys pulled it all together."

"Listen," he said, as he looked into her eyes, "There's a rodeo going on in Vegas. We could go there and—"

"So in-between marriage and sex you're planning to ride wild bulls," she interrupted.

"The only riding I do in Vegas will be on you babe," he said seductively, as he lifted her up and sat her down on her desk.

"You love the rodeos, don't you?" she asked.

"Yeah, I do," he answered, while trying to figure out where she was going with her questions. "Why do you ask?"

Putting her arms around his neck, she gave a big sigh and said, "No reason, just curious," she smiled, pulling him closer until they kissed.

Pulling away from her, he said, "We have plenty of time for this later. We have the rest of our lives. Let's get going, everyone will be waiting for us."

"Sure," she answered. As they left the morgue, Sarina thought about what Cavanaugh said. "The rest of our lives," she kept repeating in her thoughts.

Meanwhile, in Sheepshead Bay, O'Hara had just finished packing up his things in Sarina's apartment—turning off the light and locking the door as he left. Looking at her unusual door key, with the initials SM engraved on it, he sighed softly to himself. "It's been wonderful Miss Montez, I will miss you." Putting the key in his pocket, he left the building and got into the waiting taxicab. His next destination was Kellaway's Pub.

More Shall
Be Revealed

The celebration was well underway at Kellaway's Pub. Everyone, except for O'Hara, was there when Cavanaugh and Sarina arrived. The couple were welcomed and congratulated by the police officers and detectives of the 19th Precinct. After spending a few minutes with their fellow workers, Cavanaugh escorted Sarina to a small, empty table at the back of the room.

"Oh my God," said Sarina, looking around the room apprehensively. "Looks like everyone showed up."

"Hey," smiled Billy, as he grabbed her chin and turned her to face him. "It's okay, there's nothing to be nervous about—we're not getting married tonight.

"I'm sorry," she said tensely. "It's been a very long day."

Glancing at the bar, Cavanaugh saw his partner walking towards them.

"I don't know where O'Hara is," said Mac, looking at his watch, "I called him before I left the precinct."

"You spoke to Shawn?" said a stunned Sarina.

"Yes," he replied, looking back at the entrance. "And here he is," smiled Mac.

Sarina was sure everyone could hear her heart pounding loudly.

Standing in the doorway, O'Hara made eye contact with her long enough to let her know it was okay. He walked over to where Ricco and Louie were sitting at the bar and immediately started discussing the details of the solved cases.

As their laughter pervaded the room, MacTavish looked at the men and said, "I'll be back; Louie's stories are longer than mine." His drink in hand, he left the two lovers behind and joined his fellow detectives at the bar.

Louie had already informed O'Hara about the recently hired actors and was getting into his comedic mode. "Hey...hey," he said, "check this out! Picture the classified ads...*Wanted: Unknown Actors to give Oscar generated performances while real murders are taking place. Various character types wanted—victims need not apply.*"

"Louie, you are one sick mother fucker, but I love you," Shawn smiled.

Meanwhile, Billy, observing Sarina's stressful nature said, "Honey, I think you need a drink."

"You're right," she responded. "Make it a double anything straight up."

"You got it," he replied, as he turned and walked towards the bar.

Sarina's emotions were torn. Looking down at the table her mind drifted off to the relationship she and Shawn had; their bubble baths surrounded by candles made her smile. Suddenly, she wished she was home in one.

"Sarina," Mac called out, trying to get her attention.

Hearing MacTavish's voice, Sarina's memories were interrupted. Standing next to him was O'Hara with a familiar smile on his face. It appeared as though Shawn had tuned in on Sarina's thoughts and was acknowledging the pleasantry of her silent moment. His look and demeanor seemed to make her even more uncomfortable.

"Sorry," she said. "I guess I'm a little stressed out and tired."

"Nothing that a nice bubble bath wouldn't cure," smiled Shawn.

"You're right," she said curtly, as MacTavish introduced him. As he sat down next to her, she tried to avoid looking at her Irish lover. "How does he do it?" she thought. "He always knows what I'm thinking." As her eyes searched the crowd for Cavanaugh, she spotted him returning with their drinks.

"Hey Shawn" smiled Billy, "I'm glad you made it. Have you met Sarina?"

"Sort of," he answered.

As O'Hara and Cavanaugh began getting re-acquainted, MacTavish focused in on Keaton who was sitting alone at the bar. "I need a refill, please excuse me," he said, and quickly walked towards the bar.

Putting their drinks on the table, Cavanaugh sat down and put his arm around Sarina. "She's beautiful isn't she?"

"Very beautiful," Shawn replied, giving her a look that she quickly recalled. It was the same happy expression he had on his face right before they were about to have sex. His words made her very uncomfortable.

Looking at her, Billy said, "I'm a very lucky guy."

"Very lucky," Shawn answered. Raising his beer he said, "A toast to you both; May you Billy, have a happy life with a lovely wife."

"Oh for Christ's sake," she said under her breath, as Cavanaugh thanked him for the toast.

"Did you say something sweetheart?" asked Billy.

"Yes. I said I was craving some cake."

Standing up he said, "Let me get you some sweetheart." Turning to O'Hara he said, "Can you keep my girl entertained for a while?"

Staring into her eyes, Shawn replied, "I'm sure I could," only to receive a kick from her under the table.

"Don't do anything I wouldn't do," said Billy, as he walked away.

Looking at her, Shawn whispered, "Problem is, we've already done everything that he's now doing with you."

"You are not making this easy for me."

"I didn't know I was supposed to," he said, showing very little concern. "Smile Sarina, people are watching us. You know how fast rumors fly in a precinct."

"Why didn't you let him know we knew each other?" she whispered.

"Then what?" he questioned, looking straight ahead at the bar. "Surely his next question would be; and how do you know each other? Looking back at her he said, "Were you ready to tell him I was fucking you all weekend? And don't forget to throw in the shower scenario we shared this morning." Mimicking Sarina's voice, he said, *"Yes Billy, I was on my knees sucking Shawn's dick this morning. That's how I know him."* I told you how he went off on me when he found out about Vickie and me and he wasn't even involved with her. So unless you wish to create a department explosion, I suggest you forget everything about us." He placed her apartment key on the table and slid it under her napkin.

"I never meant to hurt you," she said, as she looked into his eyes.

"Don't look at me," he said quietly, staring down at the table. "And smile lady, you're getting married. You're supposed to be happy for Christ's sake."

"I tried to call you. I didn't want you to find out this way."

"Do you love him?"

"Now I'm not sure," she sighed. "Ever since I said yes I feel like I can't breathe...like I'm some trapped animal. These feelings have nothing to do with him. It's the marriage thing; I don't think I can go through with this."

"You know Sarina; you're a woman who knows her limitations. Yet you allow yourself to go beyond those limits. For the record," he said, touching her leg under the table, "I do love you very much and that feeling you're now having is exactly why I never asked you to marry me. You're a free spirited soul who cannot be tied down and tamed. I'll miss you." Squeezing her hand before he let it go, he said, "I'm leaving for Miami tomorrow. Thought I'd take some time off and do some deep-sea fishing. I heard a song today," he laughed, "it's called *The Fishing Song*. It reminded me of our situation. Staring at her for a few moments, he suddenly realized how much he cared for her. "Sarina, I really do love you."

Reaching for him she said, "Shawn—"

"Not a good idea," he interrupted, as he stood up. "Although... you have had some good ones—every sexual idea you ever had was excellent. I'm leaving with some very good memories and fantasies. You take care of yourself." Turning away from her, he headed for the bar. Sarina dropped her head to hide the tears welling up in her eyes.

Cavanaugh, delayed by officers from the precinct, glanced over and saw Sarina sitting alone. He made his apologies for leaving abruptly and rushed back to be by her side.

"Sarina?" said Billy, sitting down next to her. Reaching over with his left hand, he lifted up her head and saw the tears. He immediately looked over to O'Hara. "Did he say something to upset you?" he asked standing up.

Grabbing his hand, she pulled him back down into his chair, and said, "No. He was telling me about his wife and child and how they were killed. I suppose we remind him of what he had with her. He just wants us to be happy."

"That must have been rough for him. I would have probably snapped."

"Billy...I do love you."

"I know you do," he replied, kissing her lightly on the lips. "Do you wanna leave?"

"Would you mind? I really am tired."

"No, I don't mind," he said, brushing the hair away from her face with his hand. "Let's go, I'll take you home and pick you up in the morning. I think we both need a good night's sleep."

Looking forward to some time alone, Sarina agreed for the quick departure. "So much has happened so quickly," she thought, waving to everyone as they left.

Once Cavanaugh and Sarina had left, the Pub quickly emptied out, except for Matthews and Joubert, who were off by themselves at a corner table. MacTavish and Keaton were among the few customers who were still sitting at the bar.

"Do you think it will last?" asked Mac.

"Mac...they just got engaged!"

"Hey, the one thing I can spot is sexual obsession. I guarantee their relationship is 99% sex, and that can only last so long. Sooner or later, conversation will determine whether they stay together or not. The big shocker for me is Sarina. The woman never impressed me as being the marrying kind. She and the Kid are from two different worlds."

"They say love is blind," Vickie responded tenderly.

"True," he replied. "But in this case, I believe it's also deaf and dumb."

"I have to confess," said Vickie, "I do have a slightly uncomfortable feeling about her. This afternoon when I was taking Ricco and Louie on a tour through the morgue, she mentioned to Ricco that she knew they were coming to New York to help work the case. Didn't you tell me that information was classified and only our department knew about it?"

Finishing his drink, Mac said, "Maybe the Kid told her about it."

"I don't think so," she replied, taking a sip of her wine. "That's so unlike him."

"Something's not right," Mac added, while ordering another drink. Suddenly, he realized what that something was. "Christ," he said, looking back at her. "When I walked over to the table and told them I called O'Hara, she asked me if I spoke to Shawn."

"So?" asked Vickie.

"I never mentioned his first name."

"Well, maybe Billy—"

"When we were in Cleveland," Mac interrupted, "I asked O'Hara to stay at my place. He said he'd made plans with a friend, but the way he said it let us to believe it was a female friend. Then tonight he tells me he checked into a hotel. And the way Sarina said his name, she didn't just know him...she knew him. I'll bet you anything she knew him very well.

"Excuse me," a waiter interrupted, "the couple that was sitting over there," he said, pointing to the table where Cavanaugh and Sarina had been.

"Yes," questioned Mac, looking at the empty table, then back at the waiter.

"The lady, she left her key under the napkin," he said, as he handed it to MacTavish.

"Are you sure it was hers?"

"Yes," replied the waiter. "The gentleman that she was sitting with...I saw him put it under her napkin."

"You mean the groom to be?"

"No," said the waiter, "it was the guy with black hair; I believe his name is Shane."

"Shawn," Vickie corrected, as she placed her hand across her eyes and shook her head in disbelief. "Oh no," she whispered.

"Thank you," said Mac, taking the key. "We'll make sure she gets it." Holding it up, he said, "If this was only a video."

"Do you think Billy has any clue about what's been going on?"

"You must be joking. I told you how the Kid went off on O'Hara while trying to defend you. Do you have any idea what he would be like if he knew about this? Trust me...he doesn't know."

"But he gave her the key back and moved out. It must be over between them."

"That would be the positive way to look at it. Somehow I don't believe this is a positive situation," said Mac, staring at the key. "Tomorrow I'll give her the key discretely and let her know how I feel about all this." Turning the key over, he saw the initials SM engraved on it. "I just hope this O'Hara affair is over. However, something inside of me is sending up a big red flag about this upcoming marriage."

Meanwhile, back in Sheepshead Bay, Cavanaugh was unlocking Sarina's door. He looked at the unusual key with her initials on it. Handing it back to her, he followed her into the apartment—it was his first visit. Their short relationship of four days last year, took place at his condo.

"Give me a heads up to your bathroom," he said, hugging her around the waist, as she pointed him in the right direction. As he walked down the hall to the bathroom, she looked around at her dimly lit apartment. Looking at the couch, she recalled her relationship with Shawn; how they laughed and talked about being home in Spain and Ireland and remembered the safe feeling she had when he held her in his arms.

Meanwhile, in her bathroom, Cavanaugh was looking into the mirror over the sink. He ran his hands through his hair and pulled out his cigarettes. "Damn!" he said softly, feeling around in his jacket for his lighter—it appeared to be missing. Grabbing a book of matches that were lying next to the candles on her tub, he turned around and walked back into the living room. After lighting his cigarette, he placed the matches in his jacket while admiring her Spanish-Mediterranean décor.

"Nice place," he said, walking up behind her. Kissing the back of her neck, he whispered in her ear. "Now show me your bedroom."

"Not tonight, my room is a mess. I haven't had time to straighten up."

Ignoring her request, he led her down the hall. "It's this way isn't it?" he said softly, pulling her towards the bedroom.

"Please Billy...no."

"What are you afraid of? Is there a man hiding in your closet?"

"That's not funny," she said, remembering having sex with O'Hara that morning and how her bedroom was left in disarray; her lingerie strewn all over the bed.

Peeking around the corner and into her room he sighed, "Oh-h-h."

"No," she thought to herself, as he released his hold on her and walked into her bedroom. Leaning back against the hall wall, she waited for his confrontation.

"Sarina?" he called out.

Turning around, she rushed into the bedroom, ready to explain everything. "Billy I need to tell you—"

"It's very romantic," he interrupted.

With a surprised look, she saw that O'Hara not only had cleaned up the room, he also changed the sheets and made the bed.

"You must be a perfectionist. I don't consider this messy. What is it you wanted to tell me?" he asked, putting out his cigarette in the ashtray near the bed.

"I wanted to tell you how much I love you. And no matter what happens along the way to either of us, I will always love you."

"So serious...come here," he said softly, pulling her close and kissing her.

"Once more," she whispered in his ear.

Taking off his jacket and shirt, he undressed her. But before he could slip off his jeans, Sarina pulled him down on the bed and wrapped her legs around his waist. She moved her body rhythmically with his and raised her hips until he moved inside of her. After reaching their sexual gratification, Cavanaugh held her close and whispered in her ear. "Did you know that you're an incredible woman?" Sarina remained silent as she held him tightly against her body.

The evening had come to a close for the detectives of the 19th Precinct. Cavanaugh had left Sarina in her apartment and was asleep in his condo. Back in Islip, MacTavish was also asleep. Stretched out on a pillow next to him, Honey had snuggled up with Thumper. In Detective Keaton's apartment, Vickie sat on the floor in her living room. Surrounded by her paintings, she smiled happily—studying each piece of her many creations. Meanwhile, Joubert sat alone in a dark hotel room. As he waited for the phone to ring, his thoughts dwelled on his father and the personal contact they lacked because of his father's way of life. Across town, Matthews's apartment was vacant. Lonely and empty, a dark aura fell over it. Back at the Rollins home, Al was in bed speaking softly to his wife. As he told her what he could about his day, she told him how much she appreciated him being in her life.

Outside the Plaza Hotel, Ricco and Louie were returning from a very late dinner. As they walked through the entrance, Louie was talking about Sarina and Cavanaugh. "So he fucked her in the morgue?"

"Looked that way," Ricco grinned.

"Don't you think that's kind of creepy?"

"You know I remember a lab tech—"

"You didn't," Louie interjected.

"Yeah, I did," said Ricco, as they walked towards the elevator. "I even looked like him when I walked out of the bathroom."

"So how was it?"

"Some of the best sex I ever had."

As the elevator doors closed, Louie replied, "Hm-m-m, I'll have to try that sometime."

Darkness covered the city of New York. Another day was nearly over, and a new one was about to begin. It was a day that would affect everyone's lives and one no one would ever forget.

Morning came quickly over the city of New York, revealing a clear sunny day. Cavanaugh, rushing out of his condo, practically trampled over his friend Randall. The hairdresser had been cutting the young detective's hair ever since he moved into the building.

"Good God Cavanaugh," said the Gay man in his late fifties. "It took me two hours to put this face and hair together and you're trying to destroy it in two seconds." Randall's dyed dark black hair surrounded a masculine face which he tried, ineffectively, to make look feminine. About forty pounds overweight, he would rather sit home eating chocolate and watching the soaps, than go to the gym. His favorite saying was, "If we were meant to run, God would have put wheels on our heels."

"Sorry Randall," said Billy, as they got into the elevator together.

"Looks like you're due for a trim," Randall replied, eyeing all sides of Cavanaugh's hair.

"Yeah...I just haven't had time."

"That bitch is taking up too much of your time. You need to cut that cow loose!"

"I already did," said Billy, as they entered the garage.

"Oh, and are we on the available list again?" Randall inquired flirtatiously.

"No," Billy smiled, as he opened his car door. "I'm getting married."

"Do we know the lucky guy?"

"Very funny," responded Billy. "I'll call you for that trim," he said, as he climbed into his car and started the engine.

"You do that. And don't you let anyone else touch that head of yours. Oops...sorry," Randall said, as he put both his hands over his mouth. "I meant the head on top of your neck."

Cavanaugh shook his head no as he backed out of his parking space—smiling and waving to Randall as he drove away. He reached for his cell phone and listened to the message from Sarina. *"It's me,"* her recording said, *"I'm already at the One Nine. So there's no need to pick me up. Take care."* Calling her back he got her voicemail. "Yeah, it's me. I'm on my way in. Love you." Disconnecting the call, he smiled and continued driving towards Manhattan.

Simultaneously, Sarina had pulled out her cell phone and listened to his message. Without responding, she put the cell phone into her purse. She was seated at La Guardia Airport holding a ticket in her hand. A voice came over the speakers and announced her outgoing flight. As she stood up with her carry on bags, she got into the boarding line. Suddenly, a hand reached over her shoulder.

"I see we're ready to go," said Shawn.

"Yes," she replied with a half smile. "He just called. I didn't answer. It's better that he reads the letter I left for him at the precinct."

"Where did you tell him you were going?"

"Home to Spain."

"Did you ever tell him you're working undercover for WASP?"

"No," she answered, looking straight ahead.

"You know that would explain our relationship. He would eventually understand."

"No Shawn, he would never understand. He could never forgive my relationship with you. I don't know what it is between you two, but there's a deep-seated resentment inside of him and it's directed toward you. It's like a love-hate relationship. Even if I didn't go to Miami with you, I couldn't marry him. This is for the best."

Booked in first class, they walked down the corridor to the entrance of the plane. After entering and putting their bags up, they walked to their seats.

"Are you sure about all this?" said Shawn.

Looking at him with tears in her eyes she sighed, "I found out that there could never be anyone for me but you. You're the one who accepts me for who I am. Because of your love for me, you were willing to let me go. He doesn't understand what I need to be happy. To you, I'm more than a sex object. What I had with you was more than I could ever have with him. I am so sorry. I don't know if you can ever forgive me for my foolishness. You were right when you said I'm not the marrying kind. I guess I was hearing that you didn't care enough to have me for your wife. I realize now is it's not about some damn contract."

O'Hara looked at her with a love he thought he would never experience again in this lifetime. "It's never too late," he said, pulling her across the seat and into his arms.

"Oh Shawn, I would have given anything not to have hurt you like this."

"It's in the past and we need to begin again. I can show you how, since I've done it so many times." Unexpectedly, his cell phone rang. "O'Hara," he answered, and paused as he listened to the caller. "I understand. I'm going now." Disconnecting the call, he said, "It's WASP, they're holding the flight. They want me on a land phone."

"Go," she said lovingly.

"I'll be right back."

As O'Hara left the plane, one of the attendants pointed towards the hanger. He hurried across the field. Once inside the hanger, he went to the phone and dialed WASP in Miami. "Yes, I'm out. Hello," he said, as the line went dead. "For Christ's sake," he said, redialing. "It's O'Hara, we got cut off."

"Can you hold for the director?" a male voice asked.

"Sure I'll wait," he said giving a big sigh, as he checked his watch. After a few minutes, Miami headquarters came back on the line.

"The director will be right with you, please remain on the line."

Looking at his watch again he said, "I'm here." Several minutes had passed when he heard it. The sound he was so familiar with in Ireland and other parts of Europe—a ground-shattering explosion that rocked the terminal. He dropped the phone and rushed out. As he turned the corner, he saw the result s of the explosion. There wasn't much left of the plane, and what was left, was being consumed by fire and smoke. "NO!" he screamed out. "MOTHER OF GOD!" Looking up at the sky he yelled out again. "NO. THIS WAS NOT SUPPOSED TO HAPPEN HERE, NOT HERE!" When his cell phone rang, he answered angrily. "What the fuck just happened?"

"You are to leave the area immediately," responded the Director of WASP. "You're on our surveillance screen and we need you to move now. Turn around and go behind the hanger and out the rear gate. There will be a white SUV there with Maryland plates. Get in and do not look back."

O'Hara immediately followed the directions. He had been trained by the IRA to put his emotions on the shelf and follow orders. Wiping away the tears, he put Sarina and everyone aboard the plane out of his mind. As he turned the corner of the building he saw the waiting SUV. He approached it with an expression carved from granite. Getting into the vehicle he said, "Drive."

The Irish driver was a very attractive young man. Sandy brown hair complimented his flawless features. He was in excellent physical condition, and like O'Hara, he too possessed sapphire blue eyes. He tossed O'Hara his new identification and a new cell phone that began ringing.

"Code Red responding," answered Shawn.

"Go ahead and use your new name," the Director of WASP told him. "We will continue to watch over you until you reach your destination."

Disconnecting the call, he looked at his new identification. "Who am I today? Interesting, but not very original," he replied to the driver.

"They do have a sense of humor at times," said the driver, in a heavy Irish brogue. "Eavan Connelly," he said to O'Hara.

"You IRA?"

"Aye. We're close to the private airport. It shouldn't be long now."

"Ireland?" asked Shawn, as he looked out of the windshield.

"It be lookin' that way. We'll know more when we're on board."

The two men were silent as they headed for the private terminal located on the outskirts of the city. Behind them, the sky was filled with black smoke, reminding them of other terrorist aftermaths. It was a very familiar scene for both men.

෨෬

ANGEL
RETURNED

Cavanaugh was in his car listening to a news flash about another possible terrorist bombing in the city. "It was a commercial jet at La Guardia Airport bound for Miami," the newscaster said, as Cavanaugh pulled into the One Nine parking lot. Parking his Mustang, he quickly left his vehicle and ran across the lot. Darting up the steps and rushing into the building, he walked into a bedlam of activity. The phones were extremely busy with calls from concerned residents and tourists. Panic, fear and shock increased once more in the city, as it did during 9-11.

Upstairs in the bureau, MacTavish leaned over to Keaton and asked, "Didn't Shawn tell us he was leaving for Miami this morning?"

"Oh God, you don't think he was on board?" she cried out.

"Who was on board?" asked Billy, as he rushed into the bureau.

"Shawn," Vickie answered, grabbing her purse and searching for her cell phone. "He was leaving for Miami this morning."

Cavanaugh pulled out his cell and dialed O'Hara's number. "It's disconnected," he sighed.

"I'm calling the WASP emergency line," Vickie replied anxiously, as the two detectives watched her make the call. "Victoria Keaton here," she said, "New York City, Code MIA333 concerning Shawn O'Hara. His communication line is disconnected." She paused and waited for a response, while addressing her fellow detectives. "You'll learn all about this when you go for training. Whenever an agent breaks any form of communication, we have to report it immediately." She was quickly interrupted by an agent's voice in Miami. "They're locking in on us as we speak," she whispered. "Yes," she acknowledged with a nod, while getting an explanation. "Right, I understand. Yes, I'll let them know." Disconnecting the call, she looked at the two anxious detectives and sighed, "He's fine. He wasn't on board."

"Thank God!" said Mac. "Do we have another number on him?"

"Not yet," she sighed. "The Agency has relocated him with a new identity. He'll resurface as soon as he completes this job."

Relieved by the news, Cavanaugh removed his jacket and sat down at his desk. "So what's going down with this plane explosion, are they pulling us in on this?"

"It's a nightmare," replied Vickie. "We just begin to recover from 9-11 and now this."

"They're pulling forces in from the Bronx, so we're out of the picture," Mac responded, as the seriousness of the situation laid heavily on his mind.

"Anybody claiming responsibility?" asked Billy, conversing with his partner.

"Not yet," Mac responded.

"How many on board?"

"A hundred and nine."

"Christ!" said Billy, as the vision of more than a hundred victims meeting their death at the hands of terrorists infuriated him.

"Heads up everybody," Rollins said, rushing out of his office. "Let's pull ourselves together. We have local business to take care of. MacTavish, Cavanaugh, Matthews and Keaton, grab your coats and head over to the Ritz Carlton at Central Park South on West 3rd. They found your disappearing lady. She's registered under the name of Angela Cain."

"C'mon Vickie, you can ride with me," said Marc.

"Great," she responded, quickly picking up her things and joining him at the top of the stairs. Together, they rushed down the stairs and into the parking lot.

For a brief moment, Cavanaugh allowed his anger towards his mother to surface. Feelings of love and hate were unbalanced, and his confused mind wondered how the mother he loved so much could have put him through all this. "My whole life has been a lie," he thought.

"The lady travels first class," said Mac, as he stood up and slipped on his coat.

"Yeah," Billy responded, grabbing his cigarettes and jacket. "Very appropriate for a first class killer," he said sarcastically—following his partner out of the precinct and into one of the bureau's cars.

MacTavish ignored his partner's comment. He understood the pressure Cavanaugh was under. "More shall be revealed," he thought,

392

waving from the passenger seat to Joubert who had pulled into the parking lot.

After parking his car, Joubert entered the precinct and walked slowly up the stairs to the Detective Bureau. As he headed for the captain's office, Rollins could see the despair in Joubert's eyes as he approached. "Something serious and personal has happened," he thought. The two men sat quietly and talked—it appeared to be a very disturbing situation for both of them.

Meanwhile, at the Plaza Hotel, the two Cleveland detectives were waiting for the valet to bring their car. Ricco was on his cell phone talking to MacTavish. "Yeah, Vickie just called and filled me in on O'Hara," he answered. "It's all over the news. Sometimes I wonder what it's gonna take before the government tightens our security and really gives us the resources to make a difference instead of just talking about it."

MacTavish quickly changed the subject and began filling him in on the lady in gray and where they were headed. "Rollins requests you and Louie meet us back at the precinct."

"Okay, we'll see you there," said Ricco, disconnecting the call and putting his phone into his jacket. "That was Mac," he said to Louie. "We need to go to the One Nine. They're bringing in the lady in gray."

"We have time to grab a bite?" asked Louie.

"With everything that's going on, you're thinking about food?" Having a moment of clarity, Ricco recalled that Louie's first thoughts were always about food. Putting his hand on the little guy's shoulder he said, "Sorry, we'll get something after we go to the One Nine."

"Hey, it's okay. We can eat at that Italian place near the precinct," said Louie, as they climbed into their rental car.

Ricco decided not to respond as he drove away.

"WE'RE SUPPOSED TO MAKE IT LOOK LIKE A VACATION!" Louie yelled out.

As Cavanaugh and MacTavish pulled up in front of the Ritz Carlton Hotel, they saw Keaton and Matthews rushing into the lobby— followed by two police officers from the One Nine.

Cavanaugh started perspiring. "Mac, I don't think I can do this. Please call it in." His trembling hands on the steering wheel revealed his emotional state—the fear of seeing his mother overtook his confidence in working the case. "No, I can't do this," he said, as Joubert's words absorbed his every thought. *Acknowledging who she really is could mean her death.*

"Sure Kid," Mac sympathized. "It's probably better we're not involved. I'll let the team know what's going on." As Cavanaugh drove away from the hotel and headed back to the One Nine, MacTavish called Keaton and filled her in.

Meanwhile, back at the precinct, Joubert was shaking hands with Rollins. "You will tell them all good-bye for me," smiled Joubert. "Perhaps I will be back when this is all resolved."

"I'm looking forward to it," Rollins said seriously. "And good luck to you and your family." He walked with him to the stairwell, where they both said their final farewells.

Shortly after Joubert's departure, MacTavish and Cavanaugh arrived back at the precinct. After parking the car, they made their way back into the busy building and went upstairs. As they approached their desks, Rollin's got their attention with a waving gesture from his office— signaling for them to come into his office where he stood with Ricco and

Louie. "Sorry boss, I just couldn't come in contact with her," said Billy, as he walked through the open door.

"That's okay, I understand. Actually, I called you two in here to discuss Joubert."

"What's up with him?" Mac asked.

Rollins took off his shield and said, "First, I need to show you this." Flipping his shield over, he revealed the WASP emblem. "Joubert had to take a leave of absence and return to Europe—there was a fire on a train in France."

"His family, are they okay," asked Billy.

Pausing for a moment, Rollins took a deep breath and said, "His father is dead."

"Mother fucker!" Billy responded, as he turned towards the wall and hit it violently with his fist.

"It happened on the way to Munich from Paris," continued Rollins, "he was in a sleeping compartment that had an electrical short-circuit. The compartment filled with smoke so quickly that he never knew what happened—his death was declared as an accidental asphyxiation. Sadly, the train wasn't equipped with any fire or smoke detectors, and witnesses that observed the passing train, said black smoke poured out of the train as it raced by. He wasn't the only one who died; altogether there were ten charred bodies."

"Are they sure it was his father?" asked Ricco.

"Yes," said Rollins, "that's why he's going back. It's all under close investigation."

As Cavanaugh turned around and looked at Ricco, he said, "You knew about his father?"

"Yeah," said Ricco. "We had a long talk about him last night at the party."

"He told me he'd be back as soon as he clears everything up," said Rollins. "He wants to bury his father in Europe. I told him our prayers would be with him."

After a moment of spiritual silence filled the room, Cavanaugh made the first move by rushing out of the captain's office. He went to his work station and kicked his chair into the desk. Grabbing his cigarettes, he stormed into the locker room.

"Look," Rollins continued delicately, "some pretty heavy things have come down today, the plane explosion, four related homicides, Joubert's father, and now the arrival of our mystery lady—Keaton and Matthews brought in Angela Cain. Let's try to keep our emotions under wrap. With all this renovation going on we'll need to stay on top of everything around here."

"I believe Louie and I can get clearance from Cleveland and Miami to stay and help out," said Ricco. "It's important you guys get up and running and we can help in that area."

"That would be great if you guys could swing it," Rollins agreed. "We would really benefit by having the two of you here."

As they walked out of his office, Ricco pulled out his cell phone and dialed Captain Donatto in Cleveland.

"How fucking great is this? We're going to be working with you guys," smiled Louie.

Cavanaugh, walking out of the locker room, overheard Louie's statement and gave him a thumbs up. "Yeah Louie, that's great. We sure can use the help."

"Donatto gave us clearance," Ricco shared, as he disconnected his call.

Extending his hand out to the Cleveland detectives, Rollins smiled. "Glad to have you aboard."

"This is, as Louie would put it, fucking great," said Mac, giving the little guy a hug.

"What did we miss?" asked Vickie, as she and Matthews walked in.

Rollins filled them in on Joubert's departure and Ricco and Louie's commitment to the precinct.

"Welcome to the One Nine," she said happily.

Louie walked over to her, bent her over backwards and laid a passionate kiss on her.

Surprised by Louie's demonstrative behavior, and being the overly protective brother, Billy said, "Louie, what the hell are you doing?"

"Oh, sorry," he smiled. "I thought she was the welcoming committee."

"It's alright," said Vickie, "he's quite a kisser."

Cavanaugh snickered and smiled, as the other detectives laughed and showed their gratitude to the two detectives that were now helping the One Nine.

Louie had a satisfied look on his face. He had accomplished what he had set out to do, releasing everyone's tension. He was very sensitive to pain and despair, but he knew that his fellow detectives needed to move through everything that had happened. For him, the way through anguish and stress was always done with humor.

"I guess it's unanimous," Rollins said. "We're all glad you're now part of the One Nine."

"Hey, if you guys need anything, just let me know," said Billy, shaking their hands.

"Yeah, ditto," Marc added.

The other detectives looked at him in a humorous way. "Ditto?" Mac and Vickie questioned simultaneously.

"What," Marc asked, wearing a confused expression.

Louie moved close to Vickie and said softly, "So, since I'm staying in town, what's your opinion of short men—you can reach me at The Plaza," smiling, and twitching his eyebrows as he winked at her. Moving away from her, he smacked MacTavish on the back, knocking him slightly forward. "I know, I know," Louie laughed. "I won't try to steal your lady."

"Speaking of ladies," Rollins interrupted, "I believe we have one downstairs that needs interrogating. Mac, why don't you get the interview?"

A startled Mac replied, "Alone?"

"Yes alone. Why...you feel you need some back up? Think this woman might overpower you?"

MacTavish walked over to his desk and picked up his keys. "You have no idea," he mumbled, as he turned and opened his desk drawer. Pulling out an envelope, he tossed it over to Cavanaugh. "That was left for you earlier," he said, turning around and heading down the stairs.

Cavanaugh sat down at his desk and opened the letter. Taking it out of the envelope, he read:

Billy,
I love you so much. I'd do just about anything not to have to write this letter, but I must. It's all happening way too fast. We both

398

need so much healing. You just got out of a painful relationship and I just ended a very loving relationship. Billy, I think I owe it to you to explain all of this. I've been in this relationship since we stopped seeing each other last year. He's a good man. He didn't abuse or neglect me. All he did was love me unconditionally. Then you reappeared, and there I was, back in your arms—loving you like he never existed. But he does exist and he doesn't deserve this. You see, my problem is this, I love you both. When I'm with him I feel loved and safe, and when I'm with you I feel alive and vibrant. So this is where I am my Zorro, torn between two lovers—two wonderful men that any woman would be proud to be with and love. Perhaps I really don't know what I want. All I do know is I cannot hurt one of you without hurting the other. So I'm choosing to leave you both. I'm going somewhere to find peace of mind and happiness—home to Spain. I hope you can understand this decision. Please do not try to find or contact me. Allow me to do what I need to do, and give yourself time to heal. I will always remember the romantic cowboy in my life. God go with you.
Sarina

Cavanaugh began to perspire; his hands trembled as he put the letter down. Grabbing his cigarettes, he realized that he had again lost another lighter. Desperate for a cigarette, he remembered that MacTavish always kept a spare lighter in his drawer. Walking over to his partner's desk, he opened the top drawer. As he looked around for the lighter, his eyes locked on to an unusual key. His hand began to shake as he reached for it, recalling opening Sarina's door with an identical key. Picking it up, he turned it over—the initials SM were like an arrow that pierced his heart. Putting it back, he closed the drawer.

"Did you find what you were looking for?" asked Vickie, returning to her desk. Cavanaugh didn't hear a word she said. His thoughts raged at the idea of Sarina being with Mac. "Billy," she repeated, "Did you find what you were looking for?"

"Yeah, I sure did," he said, as he visualized his partner being Sarina's lover. His numbness quickly turned to anger. "Mother fucker!" he mumbled.

Overhearing him, Vickie walked over and said, "What's wrong?" Not getting an answer, she pleaded, "Billy, please talk to me,"

Cavanaugh held the letter up and put it in his jacket. "There's not going to be a wedding," he replied quietly, while grabbing his things. "It seems my lover is also in love with someone else. She's decided to dump both of us and is off to Spain. Me...I'm out of here too."

"Wait until—"

"Don't try to talk me out of this Vickie," he interrupted. "Oh, and be sure to tell Mac evidently he is the best man."

"BILLY," she called out, as he stormed down the stairs. Knowing that something devastating had happened, she rushed over to Ricco and quickly explained what had taken place.

Rushing down the stairs after him, he approached the front Desk Sergeant. "Seen Cavanaugh?"

"Faster than Superman," the sergeant replied, pointing to the front door.

Cavanaugh was already in his car and pulling out of his parking space. "FUCK," he yelled out.

Rushing outside, and running in front of the Mustang, Ricco yelled out. "CAVANAUGH!" Dodging the car, he watched as the young detective swerved the car around to avoid hitting him. "Son of a bitch," said Ricco, as Cavanaugh disappeared into the oncoming traffic. Turning around, he quickly walked back into the One Nine.

Upstairs, Vickie had gathered the remaining detectives and told them about Cavanaugh's letter.

"Hold on," said Rollins, "she called me this morning and asked for some time off. I thought he knew about it."

"Evidently not," Vickie replied. "He was furious when he left. I just can't believe this," she said, sitting down.

Meanwhile, MacTavish had approached the downstairs interrogation room where the beautiful, blonde haired Angela Cain was sitting. Looking through the glass window, he stared at her. She was wearing a short black skirt and a blue sweater. He stared at the black high-heels that enhanced her beautifully crossed legs. "Christ," he said, leaning back against the wall. After giving a big sigh, he turned around and walked into the room. Silently, and without acknowledging her, he went to the observation window and closed the blinds. Reaching up, he disconnected the cameras and audio equipment in the room.

Angela Cain sat there calmly, watching MacTavish's every move before speaking. "Are you planning an intimate moment detective?"

MacTavish turned around and glared at her. "What the hell were you thinking," he said firmly. "What made you believe you could get away with this? Of all the ignorant, brainless, senseless, imbecilic, unintelligent, mindless, pointless, inane—"

"Mac, you're repeating yourself," she interrupted. "One of those words would have described it all."

Frustrated and shaking his head in a comical way, he said, "You know I can't get you out of this."

"Calm down, you don't have to do anything. I'm already out."

"I don't want to know," he said. "Don't tell me what they're going to do," he continued, waving his arms around.

"They're not sending me to Langley," she smiled.

"I TOLD YOU NOT TO TELL ME THAT!" he answered in a comical way. "WHY DO YOU DO THAT? YOU ALWAYS DO THAT? I know we agreed never to discuss your occupational hazards, but good God, Red—"

"Mac," she interrupted, "we agreed that our intimate time together was to be kept sacred. And under no circumstances were we ever to discuss my undercover work—it was a way to keep our Paris romance alive and ongoing."

"And I kept that bargain," he said. "Even when we were together on Saturday...I never said a word. Now you're sitting in my precinct and we will discuss this case. You've not only involved me, you've involved your son. Allowing us to see you at our homicide scene...now that was original. And who the hell thought up your wardrobe scenario? Gray suit, blonde hair up in a twist—a scene straight out of Alfred Hitchcock's *Vertigo*. Your son and yours truly, looking for the disappearing Kim Novak. And that lobby? I recall seeing that exact set in two movies from the 40's. Your set decorators are getting a little lax—time to hit some yard sales."

Standing up, she placed her hand on Mac's chest. "It's okay," she smiled. "I knew by the wardrobe and hairstyle that you'd make the connection. After all, it is one of your favorite films."

"Well you're lucky your son didn't make the fucking connection," he lectured. "When I saw you across the street I almost had a stroke. Do you have any idea how long I had to stall in the pouring rain to keep him from running after you? That was the longest twenty minutes of my life."

"How is he?" she sighed.

"How the hell do you think he is? He can't figure out whether he buried you or cremated you. For a while there, he thought he was seeing your ghost. Then we go and tell him that you're alive and your new occupation is a hit woman for the CIA. Oh-h-h, I think you've done wonders for his mental stability. In about two days he should be weaving baskets at the local loony bin."

"Mac," she said softly, "I have no control over where they send me. Do you really think I wanted this to happen in your precinct?"

Looking lovingly at her, he sighed, "You know you're putting your own life on the line here?"

"I know," she replied. "Does he want to see me?"

"He did at first."

"And now?"

"No," he said softly. "He knows he can't. He's come to understand how this all works."

Tears filled her eyes as she thought of her son. "Twenty-two years ago I did what I had to Mac."

"I know," he said, as he took her in his arms. "I know." His eyes also filled with tears, as he kissed her passionately. As he slid his hands gently through her hair, he sighed, "I still like it better red. Perhaps someday you'll change it back?"

"Perhaps," she answered, with a twinkle in her eyes. "They should be here soon to pick me up."

"Red, I need to know...is he my son?"

She looked at him tenderly and said, "You really want him to be yours, don't you?"

"More than anything in the world."

403

"No Mac, he's not."

"Would you tell me if he really was?"

"No."

"I didn't think so."

"Have you told him about us yet?" she inquired.

"I tried to the other day. I told him about a woman named Red. Where we met, how I searched you out, the Celebrity Cruise, and how I still see you. He just doesn't know that Red is his mother. He only knows you by your alias, Angela Cain."

"It'll all fall into place the way it's supposed to. Evidently, it's not time for us to meet."

"Do you want me to give him a message?"

Red sighed as she stood up. "No, there's too much at stake here for both of you."

Suddenly, there was a quiet tap on the door. Rollins opened it slowly. "You two need more time?"

Mac looked into Red's eyes and responded, "No, we're done." Pulling her close, he whispered in her ear. "For now, but not for long."

"Her escort is here. I'll send them back," said Rollins, as he quietly closed the door.

MacTavish quickly realized that Rollins was aware of their relationship. "Red...was this a special request?"

"Yes," she whispered, as she walked towards the door.

"Be careful," said Mac, "I can wait, I always have. Just don't take any more unnecessary chances. I don't think your son could handle burying you again." Pulling her to him, he kissed her again.

Rollins tapped on the door and opened it. Two CIA agents quietly entered the room and escorted her outside to their vehicle.

MacTavish and Rollins followed them out and watched as they drove her away. Standing outside, he approached Rollins about what he knew. "About my relationship with that woman—"

"I don't know what you're referring to," interrupted Rollins. "You took a twenty minute break; I took a twenty minute break. According to the men who left...they were never here. By the way, Miami knows all about the two of you and they have no problem with it—your personal life will remain private and personal. However, we do have a new situation upstairs."

"What kind of situation?" Mac inquired.

"Sarina broke off the wedding and went back to Spain. She left the groom-to-be a *Dear John* letter. And apparently, you were the one who gave it to him."

"Good God! How's he taking it?" said Mac, as they walked back into the precinct.

"Well the way he stormed out of here, we're not too sure. Ricco tried to stop him and nearly got run down in the parking lot."

Mac shook his head and said, "The woman is probably one of the best Medical Examiners around, but when it comes to relationships, well...she's never been too stable. I had a bad feeling about her and the Kid being involved. What was in the letter?"

"According to Cavanaugh, she was in love with someone else."

"Oh that was real intelligent. Did she tell him who?"

"All I got from Vickie was that there was someone else."

"Wonderful!" said Mac sarcastically.

"You know who we're talking about here?" asked Rollins, as they walked up the stairs.

"O'Hara."

"And, is that good?"

"Maybe it is. Perhaps being pulled out and relocated will provide a cooling off period for everybody."

"I agree with you there," said Rollins, as they walked into the bureau.

"Any word from the Kid," Mac asked Vickie.

"He's not answering his cell," she replied solemnly. "I called his home and left a message."

"Doesn't sound good," said Ricco.

Aware that everyone was concerned about Cavanaugh's state of mind; Mac, while putting on his jacket said "I'm going to swing by his condo."

"I'm going with you," said Vickie, grabbing her things and rushing out after MacTavish as he headed towards the stairs.

"Captain," said Marc, "if you need me give a yell, I thought I'd go ahead and finish this up. Save Vickie some time...her having to leave and all."

"Yeah, that's good," smiled Rollins. "I appreciate that. Meanwhile, I need to call Miami for a new Forensics Director. Listen," he said quietly, "according to the Langley agents, they were never here and neither was Angela Cain. Which means—"

"We never picked her up," interjected Marc. "So we lose the paper trail."

"Yes," Rollins stated.

"You got it captain," said Marc, sitting down at his computer. "I'll take care of it right now."

Rollins re-directed his attention to the Cleveland detectives and said, "Ricco, Louie? Come with me."

"We could have a problem here with the Kid," expressed Ricco, as they walked into the captain's office.

"I know," replied Rollins. "I want MacTavish to have a chance to talk to him first."

"I don't think Cavanaugh would deliberately blow the operation," Ricco interjected. "It all depends on what kind of drunk he is when he's wasted. And believe me, after what he's been through today, he's going to be on one hell of a bender."

"Maybe not," replied Rollins. "He could go in another direction—burying his feelings and denying the pain."

"I agree with both of you," Louie said seriously. "But I also think he'll take off someplace and hole up for awhile. I got the impression he works his problems out by being alone." Turning to Rollins, he said, "Maybe you could give him some time off to do that?"

"Louie's got a good point," Rollins replied.

"It'll be okay," said Louie. "I know this guy—he can be trusted. We're all he's got left and he can't afford to lose us."

Rollins decided to go along with Louie's assumption—giving Cavanaugh a leave of absence. Smiling, he said, "I think you're right Louie. I'll clear an undetermined amount of time off for him. He needs some distraction away from here...a new environment to help him focus until he sorts things out."

"Louie, you're quite the negotiator," said Ricco smiling.

"Hey, are you forgetting what I used to do for a living?"

Placing his arm around Louie's shoulder, Ricco recalled a time when Louie was called in to negotiate with a thief who was holding eleven people hostage in a bank. It took thirteen hours, but Louie got them all out unharmed. "You're a true friend, Louie," he expressed kindly. Suddenly, he had an idea. "Captain, I have a suggestion."

"Go ahead," Rollins replied with anticipation.

"Before I left Cleveland, I got a call from a friend of mine, his name is Captain Brannigan. He has some unsolved homicides popping up in New Orleans. There could be a serial killer on the loose. This could be the perfect hook-up for the Kid."

"Oh-oh-oh...that would be perfect," whispered Louie. "Brannigan's a great guy and he would really look out for the Kid. He's one of us."

"Italian," smiled Rollins.

Louie gave Ricco a questioning stare. Then looking back at the captain, replied very slowly "No-o-o-o...he's WASP."

"I'll give this Brannigan a call," laughed Rollins, "and then ask Cavanaugh to look him up. I actually feel good about this. I think this is exactly what the Kid needs. God knows with everything this team has been through, plus throwing in his personal issues, let's just say he needs a break. Thanks."

Wearing a big grin, Louie looked over at Ricco and poked him in the ribs with his elbow. "Chalk up another point for the two Italians from WASP." Suddenly, as though a light bulb went off in his brain, he yelled out, "OH OH OH, I GET IT." Laughing, he walked over to Rollins and slapped him on the back. "You're a riot captain that was good. Italian, WASP...I love it."

Ricco looked at his watch and said, "Exactly four and a half minutes...right on schedule Louie."

Meanwhile, back in Brooklyn, Cavanaugh's Sheepshead Bay condominium was dark and silent. Exiting the elevator and heading for his condo were Detectives MacTavish and Keaton.

"You think he's home?" Vickie said softly.

"We'll soon find out," replied Mac, as he rang his partner's doorbell and placed his ear against the door.

"Anything," Vickie asked?

"Nothing," he replied," as he began to bang on the door. "Brooklyn, answer the Goddamn door!"

Silence filled the hall, as the two detectives stood there waiting for a response.

"Why don't you try calling him on his home phone?" suggested Vickie.

MacTavish pulled out his cell phone and dialed Cavanaugh's home number. Both Detectives could hear it ringing in the condo until the answering machine picked up the call. After listening to the message, Mac responded, "It's me. There appears to be a communication problem and I sure as hell don't know what the fuck it's about. So please have the courtesy to at least call me and explain." Disconnecting the call, he said, "C'mon Vickie, let's go. This could go on all night, and I have a dog waiting for me at home. He'll call when he's ready to talk." Before leaving, he leaned into the door and said, "I know you're in there. I just want you to know that I know." As they walked away and headed for the elevator, MacTavish vented out. "I knew that woman was trouble!"

Inside the elevator, Vickie's cell phone rang. "Detective Keaton," she responded.

Simultaneously, MacTavish's cell phone rang. "Christ," he said, answering the call. "Mac here."

"Oh, hello." replied Vickie softly into her phone. "No, Mac and I are at Billy's condo. We didn't see him, but I'm sure he's in a really bad way about being dumped by Sarina." The two detectives exited the elevator while talking concurrently on their cell phones. "It's Shawn," she declared to Mac, as she moved to the other side of the lobby to enhance the reception of her connection. Turning her back to him and blocking out his conversation with Ricco.

O'Hara was sitting in a private Lear jet next to Eavan Connelly. He hurriedly explained what had taken place. "Listen carefully, I don't have much time. The plane that exploded? Sarina was on it."

"What," she said shocked, "No, that can't be true. She told Billy she was going to Spain. That plane was headed for Miami."

"Believe it Vickie; she was on the plane with me. We were going to Miami together." O'Hara quickly filled her in on their sudden plans to get back together.

Nearby, MacTavish was talking to Ricco about Cavanaugh. "Look," said Mac, "he doesn't do benders, it's not his style. We were just upstairs and I'd bet a year's salary that he's sitting in that fucking condo, smoking a Marlboro cigarette, and drinking his J & B Scotch right out of the bottle. That's his style, he isolates."

Neither one of the detectives could stop to explain their individual conversations.

"Vickie," continued Shawn, "there was no way she could tell him she was going away with me. She didn't want to hurt him any more than she already had. At the airport, the Agency called me to a land phone. They didn't know she was on board. Leaving with me was a last minute decision. I had no idea what was coming down or I would have taken her off with me."

"Oh my God," she moaned.

"Listen to me," said Shawn, "this is important. The Agency is eliminating her from the passenger manifest. Our undercover DHS agents have removed all traces of her being on board. Miami is setting it up as a car accident near her home in Spain. Inform only those you feel need to know.

"I'll take care of it," she said, disconnecting the call. Tears rolled down her cheeks, as she turned around and faced MacTavish.

Mac, observing her distress said, "Ricco, I'll call you back." Disconnecting the call, he quickly rushed over to her. "What is it...is it about the Kid?"

"No," said Vickie shaking her head. "It's Sarina...she's dead."

Stunned, he stared at her in disbelief. "What the hell happened?"

Distraught, Keaton began to relate the story O'Hara told her. MacTavish remained still as she explained what happened. After she finished, he held and consoled her. "I'll call Ricco back and fill him in...that's who I was talking to."

As she pulled away from him, she wiped her eyes and looked out of the lobby window while he placed his call. "Dear God," she said tearfully, walking to the front of the lobby.

"Ricco, its Mac. You might want to sit down," he said, as he began to explain O'Hara's phone call. Slowly, he repeated every detail as he walked over to Vickie and put his hand on her shoulder. Standing behind her, he continued his conversation. "Yes, he called Vickie while I was talking to you. This information on Sarina, maybe we shouldn't share it with the Kid right now."

"I think that's a good idea," said Ricco. "He's been through way too much already. I'll let everybody here at the precinct know, just in case he tries to contact someone. He's had a hell of a day. I wouldn't wish his day on anyone."

Reflecting on his encounter with Red, Mac thought, "Somehow I can relate." Focusing on Keaton he said, "Vickie and I are heading back to the precinct. Would you let Rollins know we're on our way in?"

"You got it," Ricco replied, disconnecting the call.

"C'mon Vickie, we need to get back," said Mac, as he slid his hand down to her arm and escorted her through the lobby door. Walking to the car, he told her about the precinct's decision to keep Cavanaugh from learning about Sarina's untimely death.

As they climbed into their car, a shadowy figure looked out of Cavanaugh's patio window. The figure struck a match and lit a cigarette. The flame shed light on the young detective's face. An empty scotch bottle was in his hand as he watched his partner drive away with Keaton. Turning away from the window, he headed for the kitchen— tossing the empty bottle on his couch as he walked by. Grabbing a new bottle from the kitchen cabinet, he opened it as he removed his cigarette from his mouth. After drinking almost half of it, he turned around and walked into the bedroom carrying the bottle. He started pulling out clothes and luggage with his free hand. Suddenly, he stopped to use the phone. After dialing the number, he waited for someone to answer.

"It's me," said Billy. "Get your ass over here right now. I need a favor." He paused as he listened to the response. "Okay, your beautiful ass. Just get the fuck over here."

412

Hanging up, he put the cigarette back in his mouth and went into the bathroom, where he began tossing items into a carrying bag. Walking back into his bedroom, his heard his doorbell ring. "This better be the right person," he mumbled. Removing the cigarette from his mouth, he walked to the door and looked through its security eyehole.

On the other side of his door was his hairdresser Randall Rochard. "Oh for God's sake Cavanaugh, open the door before I freeze the family jewels." His face covered in moisturizers, Randall was wearing a red silk kimono with a giant embossed water dragon on the back— furry red slippers adorned his size thirteen feet.

"What's the favor?" he asked as Cavanaugh let him in.

"I'm leaving town and I need you to take care of the place while I'm gone."

"I take it the wedding's off. How long will you be gone this time?"

"Maybe a year or two," answered Billy, as he went into his room and finished packing.

"Are you serious?" Randall asked, following him from room to room.

"Very," he responded, as he brought his bags to the front door.

Randall was very dramatic with his response. Putting his hands on his hips, he said, "And just what am I supposed to do here?"

Looking directly at him, Billy said, "Any fucking thing you want Randall, except redecorate."

"Oh you would take the fun out of it," he answered sarcastically.

"I mean it," Billy said with determination.

"Okay, okay," he replied, flipping his hand in the air.

"Here's my spare keys," said Billy, handing them to Randall as he moved towards the door. "You have my cell number.

"How about if I rent your place to my older brother? He's looking for a place and you can make a few bucks."

"Yeah, that's fine," said Billy. "Just don't let him redecorate."

"Oh sugar, he's as straight as they come. He just transferred here from Chicago. He's one of those big corporate lawyers. I bet he'd pay eight grand a month for this place. He's also a neat freak," whispered the flamboyant Randall.

"Sure, that would be great. Tell you what, I'll split the fee with you for taking care of the place. If you want, give it to him for four grand...him being family and all."

"Jennifer Love Hewitt, are you crazy? That little fuck traumatized me when I was a child."

Cavanaugh was slightly startled by Randall's statement. "I didn't know," he responded, trying not to smile.

"All I wanted to do was use my mother's make-up and dress up in her clothes, wigs, and shoes. That fucker would make me go out and play basketball, football, baseball and soccer. I never have gotten over that childhood torture."

"Yeah, I could see how that turned your life around," Billy snickered.

"So we have a deal?" asked Randall.

"Yeah, we have a deal. You know where I keep my deposit slips."

"I'll pack up your personal stuff and put it in your spare bedroom under lock and key."

"Thanks Randall, you're a good friend. Take care of the place."

"Don't I always?"

Billy smiled and replied, "Yes you do, except when you redecorate...the last time you cost me a fucking fortune."

"You must admit, it did turn out extremely well," he said, looking around. The plastic beads and that talking dead fish you had on the wall just had to go!" With tears in his eyes, Randall looked at him sadly.

"Oh come on, we'll be in touch," Billy answered, giving him a hug.

"You take care of yourself, and make sure you take that head of yours to an established hairstylist. Don't you be going to some chop shop." Fussing with Cavanaugh's hair he said, "I'll put my brother on a month to month, just in case you change your mind."

"Thanks," Billy said softly, as he patted him on the cheek.

"Now go! Get out of here before I fall on the floor, grab your ankles, and beg you to stay while you drag me to the door. This could get very messy. The last thing you need is to be dragging this queen to the elevator screaming, "No, don't leave me!"

Cavanaugh smiled as he picked up his bags. "Thanks Randall...take care," he said, closing the door behind him.

"Don't forget to call," Randall yelled out, as tears rolled down his cheeks. Placing his hand over his mouth he said, "God, you take care of that guy and keep him safe." After patting his face dry with a tissue, he turned around. "Now let me see," he said. "Where do I begin? We definitely need to update a few things. He's just going to love my changes." Walking over to Cavanaugh's sound system, he picked out one of his favorite Gloria Gaynor's CD's and selected the song *I Will Survive.* Being very theatrical, he sang and danced his way into the kitchen. *"First I was afraid, I was petrified, kept thinking I could never live without you by my side.*" Grabbing a notepad, he began making notes on his new restoration ideas.

Downstairs in the garage, Cavanaugh walked out of the elevator carrying his bags. Dropping them behind his car, he lit up another cigarette. After opening the trunk, he tossed his bags in with a vengeance—pausing for a moment before slamming the trunk shut. Opening his car door, he pulled out his cell phone and made a call.

"Get me Rollins," he said. "Tell him it's Cavanaugh."

The call was quickly transferred to the captain. "You okay?" asked Rollins.

"I've had better days, I just can't remember when. I'm calling because I really need some down time."

"You got it Kid."

"Thanks, I really appreciate that," said Billy, sitting down in his car.

"Everyone agreed that you're entitled to some down time. However, I do have one favor to ask."

"Name it captain, it's the least I can do," said Billy, lighting a cigarette.

"I don't know where you're going, but the New Orleans Police Department is under renovation for WASP. They could use your input. Miami is willing to cover your expenses as long as you're there."

"There's no mistake in the universe," Billy thought—smiling about the coincidental request he had received. "Sure, I can work it in."

Rollins nodded yes to the Cleveland detectives who were hoping for this outcome. "You'll be looking up Captain Brannigan. His precinct covers the French Quarter."

"I'll find him."

"Hold on Kid, Ricco wants to talk to you."

"Sure, put him on."

Taking the phone from Rollins, Ricco tried to encourage the young detective.

"I'm not going to ask how you're doin', it's got to be tough. I just want you to know that Louie and I will be working here until you get back. So don't feel guilty about leaving the precinct shorthanded, we got it covered. Take as much time as you need."

"Thanks I appreciate that," replied Billy. "I know there's a bigger concern here than what I've gone through. I want you to know that I wouldn't jeopardize you guys or the Agency. I just need to get out of this city for a while. And Ricco...sorry about the near hit and run in the parking lot."

"Don't worry about it. It made me realize I need to start working out again. I almost became an Italian hood ornament on your car."

"A FAT ITALIAN HOOD ORNAMENT," Louie yelled out in the background.

Being careful not to bring up Sarina's death, Ricco said, "Listen, about Sarina, are you okay with her leaving?"

"Christ," answered Billy, "it's not the first breakup I've ever had, and it probably won't be the last. I'll do a few rodeos, wrestle a couple of bulls...it'll all come together. Be back to my old self in no time."

"You sound like you're on the way already."

"Hey, I learned as a kid that it's all about change. If there's no change, a person can't grow. Sometimes the change is painful, other times joyful. This change just happens to be a painful change, but it'll pass...always has."

"You sound good. Stay in touch," said Ricco. "Oh yes, there's something I thought you might want to know. That lady we picked up... Angela Cain?"

"Yeah?" Billy asked curiously.

"Well it seems she never got to Langley and neither did the agents. It was another set-up. They all disappeared, as did everything about her in the system."

Cavanaugh smiled as he finished smoking his cigarette. "Fucking miracle...that's my mom," he mumbled under his smile.

"You still there Kid?"

"Yeah, I'm still here. You just made my day," he laughed, as he started his car.

"I thought it would," Ricco replied, joining in on the laughter.

"You take care," said Billy, hanging up.

As he pulled out of his garage, an identical red Mustang convertible with Massachusetts license plates, cut in front of him and quickly pulled into the next parking garage. "And I thought New York drivers were bad," he said, as he drove away and headed for the Brooklyn Queens Expressway—anxious to get away from the city and over to the New Jersey Turnpike.

Back at the One Nine, Ricco looked at the other detectives and said, "The Kid's okay. He's already getting his feet back on the ground." Smiling, he handed the phone back to Rollins.

"See, why doesn't anybody listen to me?" Louie bragged. "I hate to say I told you so, but I fucking told you so,"

"You were right Louie," Rollins said smiling.

"I know I was right," laughed Louie. "Look, I know when I'm right. Problem is, nobody else knows when I'm right."

"Okay Louie, I'll make a mental note of that." laughed Rollins.

"You don't want to encourage him captain," whispered Ricco. "Trust me on that one."

"I had to learn that one the hard way," Mac interjected, as he entered the bureau.

"Where's Keaton?" Rollins asked.

"Downstairs bathroom, she's correcting her runny mascara," replied Mac. "Anybody hear from the Kid?"

"He just called," interjected Ricco. "You were right. He was in his condo when you were there."

"I need to call him," said Mac, reaching for his cell phone.

Rollins reached over and put his hand on top of Mac's hand to stop him. "I don't think that's a good idea. Give him some time. Why don't you wait until he calls you," he said, removing his hand. "It's important for him to make the first move. He knows we're here for him— try not to take this personally. His issues are with himself and regardless of what he believes right now, he will call you."

"Does this have anything to do with his mother?"

"I don't think so," answered Ricco. "When I told him what happened to her he laughed and said I made his day."

"Exactly what did happen to her?" Mac asked.

"Oh, that's right, you don't know," said Rollins. "She disappeared again. This time her disappearance involved the so-called agents that picked her up. Langley knew nothing about the pick-up and they're denying any involvement. Either way, she's gone and so is everything about her in the system. The woman has disappeared again," he said with a sheepish grin and a wink of the eye. One by one the detectives began to laugh. Their laughter carried over to roaring hysteria as they realized how all of this had ended.

The only one not laughing was Louie, who just stood there shaking his head. "Okay, okay," he said. "You guys find this humorous? Cavanaugh's mother keeps disappearing on him, and you guys think it's funny? You know, this is almost as bad as running over the dog in Cleveland."

Remembering Louie's monologue in Cleveland, Ricco and Mac's laughter became contagious and quickly escalated.

Vickie walked back into the bureau in the midst of their laughter. She was as confused as Rollins, and only caught the last part of the story about the canine. "Dog in Cleveland?" she asked.

"That's another story for another time," said Mac, wiping his eyes. "I'm going home to my own dog."

"Now that really amazes me," Louie added.

"Why's that?" asked Rollins.

MacTavish and Ricco looked at each other and shook their heads. Leaning close, Ricco whispered in MacTavish's ear, "Some people have to learn the hard way."

"I remember," said Mac, recalling what happened when he encouraged Louie.

Having an opening from Rollins, Louie took center stage and once again began his comedic routine. "That a dog that small, being run over by a couple of irresponsible cops, would want to make his way back home to a negligent owner." Looking at his watch he said, "He made really good time for a little fuck...must have picked up a ride here and there."

"I'm going home," Mac laughed. "See you all tomorrow. Louie...I love you!"

Louie leaned over to Ricco and whispered, "Why does he keep saying that? You told me he wasn't Gay." Heading for the door, he stopped suddenly and said, "Wait a minute." Walking back to the chalkboard, he grabbed a marker and made some changes that he was quite happy about. Smiling from ear to ear, he joined Ricco at the top of the stairs and continued their conversation. "Ricco, you told me the guy wasn't Gay. You were telling me the truth right?"

"Louie, he's not Gay!"

"Why don't I believe you?" Louie bickered. "You know I'm a very attractive guy. I can feel this chemistry between him and me. There's definitely a connection."

"Louie, are you Gay?" asked Ricco.

"NO!"

"Then shut the fuck up," said Ricco as they walked down the stairs.

Back in the detective bureau, Keaton and Matthews were getting ready to leave. Rollins had finished locking up his office and was on his way out. "You guys calling it a night?"

"Yeah, it's been a long day," yawned Vickie.

"It's pretty amazing how it all turned out," smiled Marc. "That Louie...he really is something."

On their way out, the three detectives stopped and stared at what Louie had changed on the board. They were mesmerized by what the little guy had written.

C. Alegna___backwards is___ Angela C.

Angela C. is really____Angela Cain

Drop the a off Angela.

Voilá • • • Angel Cain!

Looking at each other, they all began to smile. Their smiles quickly turned into loud laughter.

"I'll see you guys tomorrow," said Marc, leaving the bureau. "I have a meeting tonight with *Columbo.*"

Rollins picked up an eraser and removed all the information on the board. Leaving the bureau with Keaton, they walked together through the parking lot towards their personal vehicles. Suddenly, his cell phone rang. Answering it, he motioned for Keaton to come back. "Yes," he said, as he listened to the caller. "Hold on while I turn the speaker phone on. I want Detective Keaton to hear this. As she came closer, Rollins said, "It's the WASP director in Miami. They've uncovered the person responsible for the plane explosion at La Guardia."

"This wasn't a terrorist attack," the director began, "Calvin Myers is responsible. He planned his own suicide by putting explosives into an unchecked container which went into the cargo hold. Myers was released from a mental facility four weeks ago. His wife found a suicide letter that he left for her. Unfortunately, it was too late for anyone to do anything about it. Please let the other WASP members know that Sarina was working undercover for us—trying to help clean up your precinct. Her mistake of not checking in with us caused her demise. We pulled O'Hara out because of an emergency situation overseas—he got lucky. I hope all our agents learn from this unfortunate loss. Any sudden changes must be reported to us. We'll be in touch."

"I'll be sure to reinforce those rules," replied Rollins, as he disconnected the call. He looked solemnly at Keaton. He could tell by the look on her face that this is one rule she would never forget or disregard. "Well, I have a wife waiting for me," said Rollins, walking towards his car. "Keaton," he called out, as he unlocked his car doors. "Pass the word, excellent work on everyone's part. I'm proud to be working with all of you," he smiled."

"Thanks captain," she said, getting into her car.

Rollins placed a call to MacTavish, filling him in on Sarina and WASP. After telling him about Louie's final statement on the eraser board, MacTavish smiled. He was relieved for some closure to the bizarre events that had taken place involving the conspiracy homicides and the lady in gray—his lady in gray.

$$\wp\partial\mho$$

MOVIN' ON

Cavanaugh had been driving south for over six hours. Leaving the city of Richmond, Virginia behind him, he was heading south on Interstate 95. As the evening moved forward, he occasionally stopped for hot coffee to keep him awake. Lighting another cigarette, he briefly thought about where the direction of his life was going. The oncoming traffic lights were taking their toll on him. After rubbing his eyes, he took a sip of the coffee he had stopped for earlier. It wasn't long before he was falling asleep at the wheel. Snapping out of a doze, he decided to pull into the next rest stop. Parking his car, his mind drifted back to Sarina. "What is it that you're really angry about?" he pondered. "Is it because Sarina and Mac were lovers...why would you be mad about that? She said she broke it off. After all, I was with Mac that Sunday, maybe that's why she couldn't call. She said she wanted to tell me...maybe he did too." Catching a glimpse of himself in the rearview mirror he said, "And who are you to judge Billy Cavanaugh? You, who dumped a woman after a glorious four day weekend then hooked back up with your old lover. You really don't have much to complain about. Sarina did to you, exactly what you did to Boots...only she did it in a kinder way." He dropped his head for a moment and as he looked back up and realized he had learned another one of life's old lessons—what goes around comes around. "After all, relationships are not always till death do us part," he said, and quickly fell asleep.

...His dreams involve Sarina. He sees her in Mac's arms wearing one of the red wigs from the infamous armoire.

Cavanaugh awoke to the sound of a semi truck pulling up next to him. Looking at his watch, he realized he had been asleep for four hours. Getting out of his car, he did some stretching and smoked a cigarette before continuing his journey. Creating his own drama in his mind, he began talking to himself as he drove away. He continued driving through the night—recalling something he had learned from Jennifer...how relationship should be resolved; amicably, without anger or rage, and by both parties communicating, listening, and letting go. He remembered how incredibly healthy his relationship with Jennifer had been. Remembering one of his mother's favorite quotes, he repeated it to himself out loud, "Pain is mandatory, suffering is optional." He looked at himself again in his rearview mirror. "So just how long do you plan to suffer this time Kid Cavanaugh?"

Pulling out another cigarette and reaching for the car lighter, he saw it was missing. "Fuck!" he said, as he felt around on the floor for it. Giving up, he reached in his jacket for the book of matches he found in Sarina's bathroom. Lighting the cigarette, he noticed the labeled matchbook cover. It read: *Welcome to Cleveland*. "I guess nobody was trying to hide it," he mumbled.

The darkness of the sky seemed to fade away, as the light of dawn surfaced on the horizon. Cavanaugh enjoyed driving in the early morning hours. There was something about it that gave him peace of mind. A spiritual tranquility fell over him, as he drove through The Jefferson National Forest. Observing the wonderful woods around him, he thought about the ranch in Montana and its beautiful surroundings.

"Maybe, I need to go back," he said to himself, as he continued thinking about his life at the ranch—recalling one winter when he was teaching Jennifer how to ski in Montana.

...They are on the ski slopes and Jennifer is very wobbly on her skis. "Okay," says Billy, facing her and holding her hands. "I'm going to back up a few feet," he says, letting go of her hands. "I want you...very slowly...to come to me."

"You've got to be kidding," she smiles.

"You can do this. Just stay focused on me."

"Okay," she laughs, and takes off fast. She comes soaring into his body, pushing him backwards several feet. As he grabs her around the waist, they fall backwards into the snow laughing and hanging on to each other. Each time they would try to get up, they would fall back down laughing.

The young detective smiled, as he recalled Jennifer's ten unsuccessful attempts to ski, and how she kept knocking both of them down in the snow. He laughed, remembering how stable she was when the hour lesson was over. Her confession about deliberately falling into his arms was revealed when they ended up in bed together.

As Cavanaugh continued driving toward Knoxville, Tennessee, he listened to one of Journey's CD's. Journey was one of Jennifer's favorite bands. Listening to *Faithfully*, he wondered about her. Where she was...if she was married? He thought about getting in touch with her. Making several pit stops and taking some time out to eat at a country diner, he continued on Interstate 40 into Nashville.

Three hours later Cavanaugh had checked into a small motel in Nashville. Entering the room, he tossed his bags on the floor and sat down on the bed. Reaching into his jacket, he pulled out his cell phone and called Vickie.

"19th Precinct, this is Detective Keaton."

"Hey, it's me."

"Billy, how are you? Where are you?"

"I'm good, I'm in Nashville. I just checked into a motel. Look Vickie, I'm sorry for the way I took off."

"Hey, don't worry about it. I'm just glad that you called and you're okay. Have you called Mac?"

"No, not yet...but I will. I need to get some sleep first."

"You made great time if you just got there."

"You can make great time when your car can do a hundred and twenty."

427

"Billy!"

"Relax, I got here didn't I?"

She felt the need to talk about Sarina and Shawn. "I take it you know about Sarina's affair with—"

"Vickie, its okay," he interrupted, "I don't want to get into it. It happened, and I need to get on with my life."

"We wanted to tell you."

"We?"

"Mac and me...just how did you find out?

"Some Cleveland matches I picked up in Sarina's bathroom and then...her apartment key—"

Vickie quickly interrupted. "Mac assured me it was over between—"

Cavanaugh interrupted her again. "Enough already, I know all about Mac, my mother and Sarina. Tell him I'll call him later. I'll keep in touch."

"Oh God," she said excitedly. "I need to tell you about Shawn."

"What about him?"

"He's been pulled out by the Agency and relocated to Ireland."

"Do we know why?"

"I'm not sure yet. He's working undercover."

"You sound a little worried."

"Oh you know me, the mother hen. I worry about everyone including you. Billy, please be careful and slow down for Christ's sake."

"Okay little sister, I'll talk to you soon." Disconnecting the call, he collapsed on the bed. Closing his eyes, he was asleep within seconds.

At the 19th Precinct, Vickie was analyzing her conversation with Cavanaugh. "God, he sure is handling this well," she thought. "He wasn't at all angry with Shawn."

Glancing up, she saw MacTavish coming in to work. He smiled at her and said, "Good morning. Please tell me we're having a somewhat calmer day."

"Billy called from Nashville. He's fine. He said to tell you he's going to call you after he gets some sleep."

"Nashville...well I'm glad he's okay. Did he say anything about the affair?"

"Well, it was a strange conversation," said Vickie. "He knew everything about Shawn and Sarina, but what he said was—"

"Vickie, what did he say?" Mac inquired.

"He said he knew all about Mac, my mother and Sarina. Those were his exact words."

"He said it exactly like that?"

"Yes."

"You're sure?"

"Mac, I'm a cop for Christ's sake. Those were his exact words— Mac, his mother and Sarina."

Nervously, Mac took his hand and rubbed it across his mouth. "I'm sorry Vickie."

"Mac, what is it?"

"Nothing I can talk about right now. I need some coffee." MacTavish believed that his partner had somehow figured out the relationship between himself and his mother—wondering if he would understand why he never discussed who Red really was.

Back in Nashville, Cavanaugh slept most of the day away. He woke up in the early evening—hungry and needing a shower. Pulling himself together, he headed for the bathroom.

Meanwhile, back at the 19th Precinct, the construction of WASP was close to being finished and everyone was winding down from the daily activities. MacTavish looked at his watch as he put on his jacket and left the bureau. Louie and Ricco had left earlier to visit friends from their old neighborhood in Queens. Everyone else, except for the captain, had already left. Rollins was alone in his office, talking on the phone to his wife.

"Yeah, it's pretty quiet. The night shift is coming on. How about if we do a night out, dinner and a movie?" he said, listening for her response. "Do I need a reason to take my wife out? Honey, I consider myself a very lucky guy to have you and the kids in my life. This job keeps me so busy that sometimes I forget what I have at home. Tonight I want to have a special time with you." He paused and then responded, "I love you too and I'll be home shortly. You get yourself ready for a wonderful evening." Hanging up, he felt very grateful as he got up and left his office. Walking out, he stopped in the center of his quiet and empty Detective Bureau. He slowly looked at each detective's desk. First to where MacTavish and Cavanaugh sat, and then to where Keaton and Matthews sat. He glanced at the two desks now assigned to Petticelli and Gambino. "This is a good crew," he thought, as he looked up to the ceiling and spoke to the God of his understanding. "I need your help," he prayed. "Watch over each and every one of them and keep them safe. I'd really appreciate that." As he turned to leave, he stopped abruptly. "Oh yeah, and be sure to add Joubert and O'Hara to that list, thanks." Slipping his coat on, he headed for the stairs.

Back in Nashville, Cavanaugh was downtown at The Catfish Cove finishing his dinner. After paying the check, he went for a walk in the fresh country air. On a side street he saw a blues/jazz club. As he walked inside, he reminisced about being at The Blue Magnolia with Mac. Sitting down at the bar, he ordered a beer and watched a guitar player, wearing overalls, sing Blues music. He sat there for an hour before he decided to call it a night. After listening to the song *Feels Like Rain* he left and looked at the marquee. "I'll have to remember that guy," he thought, while walking down the street and getting into his car. "He's definitely one of the best damn guitar players I've ever heard. Funny...he reminds me of the guy that was singing with Luwanda at The Blue Magnolia. What was it that Mac said...*everybody has a twin somewhere*?"

Across the street, a black van had its engine idling. It waited until Cavanaugh had driven out of sight before it pulled out and followed him.

Meanwhile, in Islip New York, MacTavish was sitting on the couch with Honey, listening to a CD that Red gave him. It was one of his favorite songs, *The Man I Love*. "God, the woman can sing," he said, with a scotch and water in his hand, reminiscing about the last time he brought Red home. It was a Saturday afternoon—the day after the Kingman homicide.

...Cavanaugh is asleep on the couch, when he and Red tiptoe in and quietly walk up the stairs. Entering Mac's bedroom they close the door behind them. "Don't worry about your son waking up. I slipped a Valium into his orange juice this morning."

"You care a lot about him," she said sentimentally.

431

"Of course I do," he replies, pulling off his sweatshirt and reaching out for her. "After all, he is your son, which makes him very special."

Leaning into him, Red moves her left hand down the side of his face and across his slightly hairy chest. Slowly, she pushes her hand down into his sweatpants.

"You do have the magic touch, my dear," Mac responds happily, as he pulls off her black sweatshirt to expose a gorgeous, full-busted woman. Turning her around gently, he begins caressing her breasts as he kisses and licks the nape of her neck. As she lifts up her long red hair, he brushes his mouth across the back of her shoulders and down along her spine. As he removes her sweatpants, black lace panties are all that remain on her naked body. She smiles as he picks her up in his arms and carries her to his bed.

Woven, cream colored sheer drapes hang from the four-poster of MacTavish's Renaissance framed bed. A rich tapestry comforter of royal colors including navy blue, burgundy, gold and hunter green cover his king-size bed.

As he lays her down on the matching cream-colored sheets, he slides his naked body down next to hers. Stroking her hair and kissing her face, his fingers move gently down the side of her neck and across her throat. Reaching over to his stereo, he turns it on and begins to sing along with Engelbert. *"Unforgettable, though near or far"*—he stops suddenly. "How much longer are you going to be around before you move on?"

"Mac, does it really matter when I have to leave?"

"It does to me," he answers, fiddling with her earlobe.

"Mac," she says softly.

"I know, I know. One day at a time is all we really have," he says. "Seems like we've been saying that for how many years now?"

Looking into his eyes, she reaches for his face—remembering the Celebrity Cruise and the love they both felt for each other when they met again. Pulling his face to hers, she begins to kiss him fervently. "Oh Mac," she sighs.

As their lips part, he says, "Red, what am I going to do with you?"

"Just what you've been doing all these years," she smiles.

"Your incorrigible." he laughs, nuzzling his way down the front of her body and easing off her black lace panties. Erotic emotions consume her, as he slides his moist mouth up and down her inner thighs. She reaches down and pulls his face up to hers—kissing him passionately as he embraces her in his arms. She slides underneath him, kissing his chest and working her way down to his stomach. His eyes express both joy and ecstasy as she reaches her destination. Their lovemaking is hot and sensual—each knowing exactly what the other one needs. As they reach their climaxes together, Red is very vocal. Her cries and moans end in joyful laughter. As he lies on top of her, Mac smiles, "There's never a doubt when you've been completely satisfied, my Parisian mistress."

As he holds her in his arms, Honey begins to scratch at the door. "Your dog has great timing, I'll let her in," she smiles, picking up one of the pillows off the bed and placing it in front of her naked body.

"You notice she waited until we were through," he laughs. "What's with the pillow?"

"Just in case my kid wakes up," she responds shyly. "How would this look?" she asks, dropping the pillow.

"You better get dressed fast," he says, staring at her naked body. "I think I'm getting another hard on." Looking down at the sheet that covers his private parts, and with his hand underneath, Mac raises the sheet to an exaggerated height.

"Unbelievable, that's what you are," she sings out as she grabs her panties from the bed and slips them on. Pushing down the inflated symbol that lies underneath the sheet, she says, "Don't let Honey see that. She might think she's found an old bone." As he tries to grab her, she quickly pulls away. "You behave now," she says, while slowly grabbing her sweats.

"You know you're the only woman that can get me horny putting her clothes on." Giving him a flirtatious wink, she opens the bedroom door and sees Honey sitting there. "She wants outside," says Mac, slipping into his jogging clothes. As he follows his dog downstairs, Red closes the bedroom door behind them.

Downstairs, MacTavish glances at his partner sleeping on the couch. He walks Honey silently through the kitchen and opens the back door. As he steps outside and onto the back porch, he lights up a cigar and watches his dog romp through the yard.

Fifteen minutes later, Red walks outside to join them. She has showered and discarded the red wig for her own blonde hair. "Where's the wig?" Mac asks, getting up from one of the chairs on his back porch.

"In the armoire with the others."

"I guess I'm just sentimental. Your hair was red when I met you in Paris...it brings back lots of wonderful memories." Putting out his cigar he asks, "Are you ready to go?"

Red leans over and kisses him passionately. "Now I am," she whispers.

"You know Red, after all these years you'd think this would get easier, but it just gets harder. As time goes by, I worry about you more."

Red begins to sing one of Mac's romantic old favorites, *Someone To Watch Over Me*. Suddenly, she stops and looks into his eyes. She can feel the magnificent love this man has for her. "I love you, Mac. Please don't ever forget that."

"Never. There's nothing in this world that could ever make me stop loving you," he says, as they kiss again.

Pulling away slowly, she whispers, "We have to go."

"Honey…inside," Mac says, commanding the dog into the kitchen. "Good girl," he adds, as he closes the kitchen door behind her.

Honey saunters into the living room and curls up on the floor. She glances up at the young detective on the couch who is still asleep. She gives a sigh and drops her head on her paws. It isn't long before she too is asleep.

Outside, Mac reaches his hand out to Red and says, "We'll go out through the backyard."

"You know, you are my biggest fan," she smiles.

"Just one of many my lady," he answers, as he kisses the top of her hand. "The very moment I saw your face in Paris, I fell in love with you." he says, guiding her down the steps. Holding her hand as they walk to the car, he kisses it again and opens the passenger door—watching as she climbs in. Before closing the car door, he looks down at her and says, "You still are the most beautiful woman in the world."

Looking up at him she replies, "And you are the most charming man in the world. Now get in the fucking car before my kid wakes up."

MacTavish closes her door and rushes to get into the car. As he turns the key in the ignition, the radio is playing *Night And Day*—a Cole Porter song. "For my Angel," he says, as he drives away and sings, *"Only you beneath the moon and under the sun."*

"You missed your calling Mac," she smiles.

"You're the great singer in this car. God, I love hearing you sing," he says intensely, as he reminisces about their time together in France. "I remember that wee dog of yours...how he would stick his head up in the air and howl whenever we reached a climax together. He brought me to my knees and I've been down there ever since—loving every minute of it. Sing to me Red, for old time's sake?"

She begins to sing along with the radio. The words express their relationship and her love for him. *"Till you let me spend my life making love to you—"*

With tears in his eyes, Mac pulls over to the curb and parks. Holding on to the steering wheel, he looks straight ahead. "What's happening to us Red? All these years...how the hell did we end up like this?" As he brushes his tears away with his hand, she grabs his damp hand and kisses it.

"Remember our agreement, it's for the best. We knew that from the very beginning," she says. "It was a wonderful two-week affair with a married man that ended when we left Paris."

"Correction my lady, it did not end in Paris. It's still going on thirty-six years later. And in case you haven't noticed, I'm not married anymore."

"Mac, the problem was never your wife. The problem was you and all women. I couldn't handle that wandering side of you."

"And now?"

"Now is complicated."

"I was young then. What I thought was important were my own insecurities looking for a quick fix. I had to learn the hard way. I know now that there are no quick fixes. The only woman I live for is you. I don't want anyone else."

"Mac, I put my wig in the armoire. Are you going to tell me all those other wigs are for Honey?"

"If I thought you'd buy it I'd say yes."

Red laughs and nods her head. "Let me love you for who you are Mac, and not who you promise to be. All I ask is that you love me the same way."

He brushes his hand through her long blonde hair. "Paris," he sighs.

"We can't go back in time Mac; we can only take time out of today, and pretend...like we did this afternoon." Smiling, she turns away from him and looks out the front windshield. "And by the way, I find it very complimentary that the women you choose to sleep with need to look like me."

He reaches out and turns her face to his. "Every time I'm with you, I'm in Paris again."

"My handsome kilt-wearing tiger," she sighs, kissing him passionately.

As they pull apart, he asks, "Any idea when we'll be meeting again?"

"I don't know. Every time we're together, it gets more difficult to leave you," she says softly. "And that could become very complicated for all of us."

"How hard is it getting?" he asks with a boyish grin.

"Very hard."

"This hard?" he asks, as he places her hand below his stomach. As she pulls her hand away he says, "Sometimes I wish we would have met before I was married."

"Catherine was a wonderful woman. You needed her and she needed you."

Becoming overly sentimental, he grabs Red' shoulders and pleads, "And now it's you I need, my little red fox. Not just some of the time, I want you with me always."

"Mac, you crave the faithfulness you can't return. You're a wonderful, loving, warm, romantic man, and I wouldn't want you any other way," she replies tearfully.

Pulling her into his arms, he dries her eyes with the tissue she is holding. "It's time to go," he says softly, and begins to drive away from the curb.

"Mac...this past week with you has been wonderful."

"Yes it was," he answers with a glimmer in his eye.

As the memory of his longtime lover faded, once again he was sitting in his living room with his scotch in hand—her voice still singing the song *At Last*. Lifting his glass in the air, he said, "To you Red, wherever you are." Finishing his drink, he and his dog headed for the stairs. As they passed the armoire, Honey glanced at it, and then quickly followed her master and Thumper up the stairs.

Back in Nashville, Cavanaugh was getting on the Interstate heading back to his motel. Pulling out his cell phone, he made a call.

In Mac's bedroom, the phone rang. Picking it up, he looked at the caller ID and hurriedly answered it. "Brooklyn, how the hell are you?"

"I'm fine," said Billy.

"I believe I owe you an explanation Kid."

"You don't owe me any explanations Mac. When I found out you two were having an affair I just couldn't handle it. And I certainly wasn't ready to talk to you about it."

"Listen to me. I need to explain."

"You don't have to—"

"Goddamn it Brooklyn, listen to me!"

"Okay. But please, no sordid details."

"What kind of man do you take me for? First of all, there is nothing sordid about our relationship. I should have told you that day at the Grotto that Red was your mother."

Startled by the confession, Cavanaugh hit his brakes so hard that his car swerved and nearly collided with another car.

"What's happening?" Mac asked, as he heard the squealing of brakes and horns honking. "Are you alright?"

"Yeah...I'm good," said Billy, pulling off the highway and turning off the car's engine. His mind flashed to France, the cruise, and the red wigs in the armoire. "Go on, you were saying?" he said, staring out of the window.

"We both felt you shouldn't know what she was doing. Your mother always wanted the best for you. Joubert was right, she was coerced into working for the CIA. They threatened to jam you up for that convenience store case you were involved in as a boy—locking you up in juve until you were eighteen and then to prison. Your mother couldn't live with you being incarcerated.

Cavanaugh listened, as his partner filled in the gaps of his childhood—beginning with the time that he was in the hospital after the convenience store episode. "All those noble claims of deduction by a

439

great detective," Billy thought to himself—realizing that his partner knew everything about him and his past. All the comments MacTavish made flashed across his mind; *his mother's maiden name, Walker being dead*—it all made sense. He sat back in his parked car and listened to his partner's explanations; from seeing her as the lady in gray and stalling so she could get away, then revealing her visit to the house on Saturday when he was drugged and asleep on the couch.

"You fucking drugged me?" Billy interrupted.

"Just a couple of Valium, it wasn't my fault you poured two glasses of orange juice. I couldn't take a chance on you drinking the wrong glass. I didn't know which glass you'd pick up so I jacked them both. I never expected you to drink both glasses."

Meanwhile, Kelly Cavanaugh was on an Amtrack train headed away from Virginia. As she leaned back in her seat, she remembered another train ride to San Francisco with her young son Billy. "That was so long ago," she said to herself, as she reached into her purse and pulled out her wallet. "Let's see who we are now." She opened her new falsified identifications. "Now that's what I'd call irony," she said softly, as she stared at her new ID photo. "I guess it's time to be a redhead again." Laying her head back against the seat, she thought about MacTavish and the Saturday she spent at his home.

...Coming down from Mac's bedroom, she pauses in the living room and moves slowly to the couch. Her son is tossing in his sleep—his face covered with perspiration. She pulls up the quilt he threw off and gently covers him. Pulling a tissue out of her pocket, she pats his face dry. She touches his forehead and moves her hand softly across his face. Kissing him softly on his cheek, she turns away with tears in her eyes—wishing she could have held him in her arms just one more time. Turning around, she walks into the dining room and stands in front of the armoire. Looking into the mirror, she removes her red wig, shaking loose her long blonde hair. Opening the doors, she places her hairpiece on the shelf next to the other wigs. After closing the armoire, she quietly joins MacTavish on the back porch.

A passing train quickly brought her back to reality. She realized she acted foolishly, putting everybody in harms way, especially Mac and her son. She loved them very much, and didn't want to risk losing either one. "It's time to focus on a new life," she thought, staring at her new passport. It read:

Name in Full: Ember Harrigan

Sex: F

Occupation: Entertainer

Marital Status: Single

Date of Birth: 6 20 53

Place of Birth: Dublin, Ireland

Meanwhile back in Nashville, Cavanaugh was still listening to MacTavish's explanations.

..."That day you went to MacArthur Park with Walker, Granger had set up a hit on the both of you. Unfortunately, the bastard was a dirty cop. After Walker died, your mother knew they meant business and with him out of the way you were vulnerable. So she had to find a way to disappear and relocate you. I wanted to tell you, but I made a promise to her years ago. Even when we pulled her in last night—"

"Angela Cain," said Billy.

"Yes. I had a chance to speak to her privately. She's aware that you know who she is and what she's doing. I don't know any woman who would have done what she has just to keep you alive."

"And the affair with Sarina?" he said, as tears rolled down Billy's face.

"Kid, I can't tell you how glad I am that you know. How did you find out?"

"Her key...I saw it in your desk," he said, wiping away the tears.

"You didn't think I was her lover?" said Mac, pausing, as he quickly realized what his partner thought. "Brooklyn, it was never me. It was O'Hara."

Once again, Cavanaugh was taken by surprise. Flashbacks of Cleveland came into his mind. He thought about when he and Shawn were on the patio smoking and remembered him having the book of matches that were now in his pocket. He even admitted that he was staying with a close friend in New York.

"Kid, are you there?"

"Yeah, I'm here."

"I hope you understand how I feel about your mother. There can never be anyone else for me. I don't have affairs, occasionally a one-night-stand. And about Sarina's key—" Mac continued, explaining how the key got into his possession and his plans to give it to her the following day.

Cavanaugh laid his head back on the seat—realizing how easily he had misread everything, and once again assumed things that didn't happen. "Mac, I'm so sorry for the distance I've put between us. I realize you couldn't expose my mother. I'll tell you one thing; you are a master at juggling events. If I were you, I don't think I could have pulled it off."

"I've had years of practice. Consider it water under the bridge."

Cavanaugh's life suddenly burst before him. He tried to reduce it all in his mind, but it didn't work. He had a deep need to verbalize it. "So let me put this in perspective," he smiled, as he lit another cigarette. "I have a hit put on me at the age of thirteen. My mother dies, but isn't really dead. Her double life includes working for the CIA and having a thirty-six year affair with a New York detective, who just happens to be my partner. She pops back into my life as some hired assassin, and after she's brought back into my precinct for an interrogation of three homicides...disappears. Now she has a new identity and is off somewhere looking for the next victim, while I end up working all the cases she leaves behind. Not only am I put in the middle of various movie sets with contriving actors, but even the detectives around me look like famous fucking actors. Christ, do I need a vacation! Mac, I'm going to hang up now. I will call you when I get to wherever I'm going. Because, like my mother, I don't know where the hell I'm going—it must be hereditary." As Cavanaugh disconnected the call, he threatened to throw the phone out the window. Frustrated, he stared at it before putting it back into his jacket pocket. After starting his car, he drove it back onto the highway, and yelled out loudly, "JERRY BRUCKHEIMER, DO I HAVE A MOTHER FUCKIN' MOVIE SCRIPT FOR YOU!" Flooring the gas pedal, he sped away down the highway.

Back in Islip, MacTavish's thoughts were centered on Cavanaugh; he knew his partner would come around after he had time to rethink everything that happened. "At least he knows. Come on girl," he said to his dog. Knowing her master longed for the woman who wore the red wig; Honey looked at him and licked his arm comfortingly. "I know girl," said Mac, as he sat down on the bed next to Thumper. "He'll be missed by both of us."

Returning to his motel in Nashville, Cavanaugh quickly got out of the car and made his way towards the door—the dangling cigarette from his mouth was tossed aside as he unlocked the door. Once inside, he secured the lock and threw himself down on the bed. Staring at the ceiling; visions of Sarina, Mac, Shawn, and his mother, swirled through his mind. He turned over, grabbed a bottle of scotch off the nightstand, and guzzled some of it down. As the empty bottle dropped from his hand, he fell into a deep sleep.

In Dublin, Ireland, O'Hara and Connelly had already landed and left the private jet. Walking across the field, they were met outside by a young raven-haired woman. "This is my sister Katelyn Connelly," said Eavan, "she works with us."

"Pleased to meet you," she said, staring into O'Hara's blue eyes.

"Katelyn, we should go," smiled Eavan.

"Aye," she responded, leading them to her parked car. "We won't be here long. Tomorrow we drive to Belfast."

As Katelyn started to drive away, a somber silence fell over the three of them. It was difficult for all three to unknowingly be prepared for the worst. But prepared they would be, for they had done this work so many times before.

The next morning, as Cavanaugh raced along Interstate 59, a bright sun shined down on him in his convertible. Wearing a black tee shirt, jeans, and designer sunglasses, he smiled while listening to an upbeat Delbert McClinton rock/blues tune—*Going Back To Louisiana*. The song reminded him of something his mother once said to him. *New Orleans would be a great place to get lost if someone wanted to get away from the world.* A part of him hoped she would be there with a new identity. "New Orleans is my destination," he thought. "Whatever the reason, *The Universe* seems to be directing me there." Still unaware of Sarina's death, he thought about her. "I'm gonna miss that lady. Maybe she'll find some peace in Spain," he said softly. Glancing into the rearview mirror, he noticed a black SUV that had been steadily traveling along with him since he left Nashville. "Maybe he's going to New Orleans too," Billy mumbled, as he floored the gas pedal and sped down the highway.

Inside the black SUV, two men were discussing their objective. "Turn down the music," said the driver.

"Hey...this is the best part of Walsh's Funk #49. Go Joe...go Joe...go Joe."

"TURN THE MUSIC OFF!"

"Okay, Okay."

As the driver placed a call to Boston, his partner whispered, "Sorry Joe."

"Talk to me," the voice in Massachusetts said.

"Our information was right," said the driver. "He switched the Massachuesetts plates to New York plates before he left. In Nashville, we changed vehicles and picked him up leaving and heading south toward Birmingham."

"You're sure it's him?" the Bostonian asked.

Pulling down a photograph from the visor, the driver looked at it and said, "It's him alright. We just stopped at a gas station and both of us identified him from the photo. It's definitely him."

"You sure he's not on to you?"

"No. And from what I've observed, he seems pre-occupied with something else. There's been a couple of times when I thought he was gonna do himself in."

"Explain."

"He's been taking un-necessary chances. Hitting curves too fast, driving way over the speed limit—"

"That's odd," the man in Boston interrupted. "This behavior is so unlike him. Take care of this quietly, I don't want any publicity and make sure you lose the body and the car."

"We'll take care of it," he said, disconnecting the call.

The SUV's window slowly rolled down on the passenger side, revealing a high-powered rifle that was cautiously raised out the window and aimed at Cavanaugh's convertible's tires.

"NO, NOT YET," the driver yelled, as he hung up on his Boston call. "WHAT ARE YOU DOING? YOU KNOW THE OLD MAN WANTS IT DONE QUIETLY WITHOUT ANY NOTORIETY. SHOOTING A RIFLE OUT OF A MOVING VEHICLE IS NOT CONSIDERED DOING SOMETHING QUIETLY WITHOUT NOTORIETY."

Pulling the rifle back into the car, the second man gave him a confusing look and said, "Can I ask a question?"

"Yeah, what is it?" said the driver.

"What does notoriety mean?"

Glancing over at his partner, the driver said, "Maybe I should just SHOOT YOU and go back to Boston."

"If you shoot me...would you do it with notoriety?"

"Why me?" muttered the driver under his breath.

As Cavanaugh's stereo blasted Paul Rogers singing *Movin' On*, the two vehicles moved swiftly along the highway. Destination for both drivers was The Big Easy.

ഇറ

ROAA

ASTROLOGICAL

CHARACTER

CHARTS

CONTENTS

♐ Billy Cavanaugh • December 3, 1965

Ascendant in Taurus · Sun in Sagittarius · Moon in Aries
Mercury in Sagittarius · Venus and Mars in Capricorn
Jupiter in Gemini · Saturn in Aquarius · Uranus in Cancer
Neptune in Scorpio · Pluto in Virgo
Solar Eclipse in Sagittarius · Lunar Eclipse in Sagittarius
Mode: Mutable · Element: Fire · Key Idea: Freedom

ASCENDANT IN TAURUS ♉

Because Billy Cavanaugh's primary motivation is security, he becomes very good at accumulating money. He doesn't work for money alone, but more for what it can do for him. Desiring one with whom he can share a mutual respect and someone who will stand up to him, he will be loyal and true.

SUN IN SAGITTARIUS ♐

Billy is adventurous, blunt, clumsy, humorous, metaphysical, open, optimistic, and philosophical. He is the seeker of truth and has an unbeatable sense of intuition—his curiosity is never-ending. This man appreciates the wisdom and experience of older people. High-spirited and yet refined, he resents coarseness in others and sudden attractions often turn into lasting friendships. It is very important for him to become personally involved with a lover. Physical sex to him is an expression of closeness and communication. Happiness comes when he can share his intellectual interests with his partner—enjoying a partner who spends time working and having fun with him. In turn, he will make her realize she's a woman to the fullest degree. He doesn't often take the time to explain his actions, but you can count on him to keep his promises. His love for freedom is uncompromising—granting everyone around him that same freedom. Attracted to the outdoors, he enjoys being physically active. Under prolonged emotional strains, he is unfortunately subject to having nervous breakdowns.

SUN IN THE 8TH HOUSE

Having a serious and intense side to his personality, Billy is attached to the mysterious. This position makes him attracted to a lover who is considerably older or younger than himself. His intuitions and passions are strong. Sexuality, in a very physical form, makes tangible intimacy very important to this man.

MOON IN ARIES ♈

This Moon sign overpowers his Sun sign, creating a rugged, made of iron individual, who is not swayed by the opinions of others. With a desire to get at the truth, which is sometimes abstract, Billy periodically finds that the truth is out of reach. Not easily discouraged, he will always continue his quest. Highly responsive to love interests, he makes lightning decisions. With him, an affair begins full force and continues with high intensity. He enjoys nonstop emotional involvement and is most comfortable in environments where there is a lot of action and stimulation. His other needs are; adventure, being first in everything, competitiveness, directness, enthusiasm, and seeking challenges. This man feels cared for when he is given room to move, dealt with directly, and made to feel unique.

MOON IN THE 12TH HOUSE

Billy's domestic affairs can be confusing. Having very deep emotions, there are times when he finds them difficult to cope with. Intuitive, imaginative, lonely, misunderstood and highly secretive, he travels life's highway in his own way.

SAGITTARIUS SUN ♦ ARIES MOON COMBINATION ♐ ♈

Having the ability to control others, Billy likes to have his own way. He will only compromise to a certain degree—communicating in the following ways; humorously, lengthily, wordily and zealously. Having a pioneer spirit, he is also anxious, dynamic, fearless, and philosophic. Preferring to be straight forward, he is not exactly diplomatic in his conversations and yet, has a way of saying things that doesn't really offend anyone. Having no desire to fool anyone, others find it difficult to deceive him. As long as he is in the foreground, he is capable of working for the common good. His mental powers are sharp, and he can carry intricate patterns of thought and action in his mind with extreme easiness. He has a way of making two viewpoints work together in harmony. Very interested in the underdog, he understands their viewpoints—how to live in the world as it is, without having to give up ideals of correct conduct. Ardent and sincere in love, he is intensely honorable and will not compromise the truth or the right action as he views it.

MERCURY IN SAGITTARIUS ♐

This is where Billy's swift and brilliant mind is most fixed. Bluntness comes very easily with this position. If he tells a lie, it is done impulsively and unsuccessfully, for he is not able to deceive others for any length of time. His intuition is very accurate. Being a very honest person, he would not intentionally mislead anyone. Faraway places are most appealing to him.

MERCURY IN THE 8TH HOUSE

Billy is not likely to have a shallow or lightweight affair; a casual encounter can turn into a deep and meaningful relationship. Sex to him is just one of many areas of enjoyment and communication between partners. Having strong opinions, he also tends to be secretive about them. A deep thinker, he is mystery orientated, quiet and firm.

VENUS IN CAPRICORN ♑

You will rarely find this man in an unhappy situation, for he instinctively knows what's best for him and tries to use common sense when dealing with his relationships, He becomes involved with people that he has respect for and also holds some sort of status—considering all aspects of a relationship before he gets involved. Billy makes practical choices—his partners must be able to contribute to the relationship in a material way. His sense of responsibility makes him loyal when in love. Once he makes a commitment, he will be steadfast, true, and dependable. This man feels loved when he experiences security, relaxation, and appreciation for his practical approach to life. Being very adaptable, he moves with the times—thriving on his disappointments and accepting them as challenges. His tastes are basic, classical, conservative, elegant, quality-orientated, quiet and simple.

VENUS IN THE 9TH HOUSE

Besides having a love for travel and foreign subjects, Billy is a beauty-seeking, harmony orientated, fair and poetic man. His desire for love and peace are projected outwardly and into the study of religions and philosophy.

MARS IN CAPRICORN ♑

Billy is a fanatic about doing his duty. He enjoys seeing a job well done and is able to stand firm in his convictions. He feels responsible not only for himself, but for his family members. He tends to be faithful to his lover and likes to have the situation for lovemaking under control so he can deliver all that is expected of him.

MARS IN THE 9TH HOUSE

Enjoining outdoor sports, Billy is also an adventure-seeker with a need to travel.

His energy, drive and enthusiasm are expelled through education and travel. His assertiveness and ability to influence others is strong. Being a supporter of causes, his opinions and arguments over politics and religion can cause problems. Physical satisfaction for him depends on how both partners interact with each other.

JUPITER IN GEMINI Ⅱ

Patience is not one of Billy's strong points. Requiring recognition, his interests allow him to be involved in several projects at the same time—law enforcement is a lucky field for him to work in. Sympathetic and kind, he possesses great humanitarian instincts. Having some unorthodox and unusual beliefs about religion, he wants the world to be related. Having a marvelous sense of humor, he also has a talent for singing and playing the guitar.

JUPITER IN THE 2ND HOUSE

Billy obtains financial rewards easily, especially where prosperity and real estate are involved. He has opinionated beliefs and tends to indulge and revel in the luxuries of his life.

SATURN IN AQUARIUS ♒

Aquarius here gives real wisdom and maturity to Billy. Being well known among a wide circle of friends and acquaintances, and having a true insight into human nature, he is a humanitarian first and foremost. This position also gives him a great deal of influence and prosperity, especially when working with large administrations. Having desires to learn about new things, he is subtle about getting them done his way. He also shows an interest in science and the occult.

SATURN IN THE 10TH HOUSE

Having strong career ambitions, Billy plans early in life for his career—he wants to make a mark. Although he is an authority in his chosen career, he often faces some setbacks.

URANUS IN LEO ♌

This man is eccentric, rebellious and highly effusive while making remarkable achievements in life. In relationships, Billy will probably get the most out of one that has plenty of room for growth—needing one that does not complete its development or define its direction too precisely or too quickly.

URANUS IN THE 3RD HOUSE

Billy's quick and original mind is full of creative ideas. He has so much mental energy that it enables him to have a highly inventive mind. Even though he had rebellious behavior during his school years, and was difficult to educate as a child, he became extremely bright.

NEPTUNE IN SCORPIO ♏

Extremely psychic, imaginative and erotic, Billy has deep and confusing emotions. A lack of control could lead to an impending problem with vice or addiction.

NEPTUNE IN THE 7TH HOUSE

Easily affected by the moods and feelings of others, Billy's softness, sensitivity, confusion, and escapism can make it difficult to find fulfillment within a relationship. He is attracted to weak or deceitful women, resulting in self-deception about his partner's qualities. He tends to be secretive with partners and can become involved in secret relationships. This 7th house gives him a chance for an ideal partnership, a partnership where they understand each other on an intuitive level—these partnerships must have a spiritual bond to be successful.

PLUTO IN VIRGO ♍

Although Billy is capable of great details in all areas of his life, his feelings are quite different from others in his generation. He finds the company of his elders more enjoyable and closer to what he wants in his relationships. Pluto in Virgo gives him a powerful sex-drive.

PLUTO IN THE 5TH HOUSE

There is a power struggle in this sign which makes Billy's desire to win very strong. He has a tremendous well of creative energy and a subconscious drive to create. Because of his strong sexual appeal, he has obsession for romantic affairs.

SOLAR ECLIPSE IN SAGITTARIUS ♐

Billy needs to accept the responsibility for teaching his fellow beings how to understand the connection we all have to each other. He is here to spread awareness and to teach that we are all one, heading in the same direction while at the same time, learning something on his own unique path.

LUNAR ECLIPSE IN SAGITTARIUS ♐

This man has come to break through the prejudice of mankind. In this lifetime, Billy will be exposed to many things outside his belief system. Learning to overcome prejudices, narrow mindedness, and superficiality will be very important to him. He is here to awaken the consciousness of his fellow beings. Because of habitual past life limitations, he experiences some fear when expanding beyond his horizons and tends to be a lonely soul. His journey into consciousness and awareness seems to be traveled by only a few.

ೞೞ

♍ Archie MacTavish • September 15, 1936

Ascendant inLibra · Sun in Virgo · Moon in Libra · Mercury in Libra
Venus in Libra · Mars in Leo · Jupiter in Sagittarius · Saturn in Pisces
Uranus in Taurus · Neptune in Virgo · Pluto in Cancer
Solar Eclipse in Gemini · Lunar Eclipse in Capricorn
Mode: Mutable · Element: Earth · Key Idea: The Craftsman

ASCENDANT IN LIBRA ♎

Possessing a smile that lights up a room, Mac can be the world's greatest
charmer. Because of his need to have contact with numerous people, he has a
desire for many social relationships, and works well in any situation that deals
with a number of different people. However, he has the possibility of being very
indecisive with his own self-expression.

SUN IN VIRGO ♍

Meticulous and critical, Mac's main preoccupation and reason to be alive is work
related—this reason also takes on another form of work which is art. Being
highly adaptable, this man has the intellectual capacity of finding solutions,
creating order and seeking perfection. He is great at sorting out fine details.
Possessing great fortitude and forbearance, he is the sign of service. Waking up
in middle age, he tries out all sorts of new avenues before realizing what he has
been missing all along. A very good conversationalist, he can talk endlessly. Very
proficient in the care and feeding of a lover, he goes to great lengths to provide
whatever pleases his partner and puts a high value on a lover who is aware of
what pleases him. Carrying multiple affairs is difficult for him, because he wishes
to give each woman detailed attention—he is more comfortable with a long-term
affair that gives him plenty of time to structure the relationship. Finding a

partner who is creative and mutually responsive is his way to have a continuous, exciting adventure.

SUN IN THE 12TH HOUSE

There is a strong sense of privacy and individuality with this man. Believing, that all things come to those who wait, he doesn't actively seek out new relationships and only discloses his feelings in the most intimate of circumstances. Other people view Mac's personal life as quite mysterious—which attracts speculation about his behind-closed-doors affairs.

MOON IN LIBRA ♎

Hating to do anything inharmoniously, Mac has a special talent for solving the problems of others. Intellectually, he has balance; considering every problem that is presented to him with an eminently fair mind. However, because of his impulsive feeligs, he tends to blurt things out. His security lies in his friendships with others and he only feels fulfilled when he has a partner. Even though his childhood may have been simple, he has an instinct for doing the right thing. As an artist with a beauty-loving nature, he has exquisite tastes and a true grasp for the fundamentals of line, color and design—creating works that are extraordinarily beautiful. His function in life is to criticize and judge.

MOON IN THE 1ST HOUSE

Possessing a willingness to express emotions on the surface, Mac's sense of self-worth goes through phases. This man responds quickly and strongly to the moods of those around him. Other people find security in his open appreciation. In affairs of the heart, he makes up his mind quickly and chooses his partner without hesitation. Personal involvements are always high-keyed, even if they are brief. If it can't be intense, he doesn't want it.

VIRGO SUN • LIBRA MOON COMBINATION ♍ ♎

Having a live and let live philosophy, Mac is extremely capable of taking care of himself and carrying on a private and secret life of his own. Being a self-sufficient and intellectual soul, he is easy to get along with. Always within the realm of good taste and discretion, he believes what he does is his business. Without any form of deception, he keeps issues from being raised by going his own way simply and tactfully. Being a pacifist, he doesn't like to quarrel. He will give credit where it's due and expects the same in return. People with this position generally do not marry unless they do it when they're young. By agreeing with whatever his partner wants to do, his approach lends scope and dignity to the most realistic or fanciful of themes. His appreciation of beauty in art, and pursuing it as a career, has protected him from economic worry. In matters of dress, he is fastidious and tasteful.

MERCURY IN LIBRA ♎

Because he is able to see all sides of a situation, Mac is easy to communicate with—having a natural sense of justice, honesty and harmony. His need for tasteful surroundings and his sensual input must meet a high standard of excellence. Much of his pleasure in an affair comes from constant change and improvement—seeking someone that is always reaching new levels of beauty and enjoyment. His lively imagination prefers a love affair that is constantly in motion.

MERCURY IN THE 1ST HOUSE

Mac is an impulsive mercurial person with a strong ability for verbal expression. Sexually, he's willing to try anything that might be considered fun. It spurs his feeling for creativity and variety.

VENUS IN LIBRA ♎

Being one of the true charming romantics, Mac believes whole-heartedly in love, and is a shining example of love in its purest form. Seeing the brighter side of a situation, he manages to see the best in everyone. The sincerity with which he responds to people, and the generousness of his affections, keeps him forever young and pure in heart. His attractions for others arise impulsively. That same impulsiveness sometimes draws him into unsettling relationships. Whether it be appearances, clothing or hairstyles, this man has an exceptional artistic appreciation for it all.

VENUS IN THE 1ST HOUSE

Possessing excellent artistic ability, Mac responds naturally to the needs of others with a certain social charm and grace—friendships are important to him. Having a creative and fluid sex life, problems could arrive by having too many partners.

MARS IN LEO ♌

This fun-loving romantic man has a natural ability to make an excellent impression. Even when Mac's not being so nice, people will still find him appealing. His charming and magnetic nature, gives him the ability to connect with people. This very creative and active man acts passionately for what he believes in. His aggression surfaces when he feels he's not getting the respect he deserves.

MARS IN THE 11TH HOUSE

Group activity, involvement, and a strong desire for friendships are energized in this 11th House. Conflicts with associates happen only when Mac takes an action merely to be different. Placing a high value on loyalty in his relationships, he prefers a long-lasting affair that has time to develop. Striving for excellence in lovemaking, he can create a graceful, aesthetic experience that has substance as well as form.

JUPITER IN SAGITTARIUS ♐

Mac's expansive and restless mind can handle a lot of facts. He is always on the lookout for items of interest. His intuition warns him of danger; alerting him to make advantageous moves. Having a sixth sense and an instinct for the truth, he knows what people are going to do before they do it and also knows when someone is deceitful. A man destined for wealth and to be a power in his world, he can afford to spend more freely than others. New affairs usually start out robustly, without technique or subtlety. Travel brings him new and interesting experiences.

JUPITER IN THE 3RD HOUSE

Mac's wisdom is sought through the acquisition of factual knowledge. He has the ability to express creative ideas; both verbally and physically. Preferring a lover who is stimulated verbally and physically, and one with a profuse sexual imagination, his relationships are brought on by having an intellectual foundation.

SATURN IN PISCES ♓

Mac has the power to exhibit his dreams. However, he can become excessively concerned with the past and what he views as past mistakes. Worrying too much and dwelling on the past, only makes it more difficult for him to deal with the demands of the present. His greatest security is achieved through consistent emotional attention and communication from a sensitive and devoted partner. In a way, he feels empty if he is not involved in an active love relationship. He will however, demand great sincerity and sensitivity in a partner. With the right partner, he will experience great self-sacrifice to keep their relationship going.

SATURN IN THE 6TH HOUSE

When it comes to his work, Mac has highly organizational energy. He is also a skilled and sensitive lover.

URANUS IN TAURUS ♉

This sign gives Mac a remarkable amount of energy and a desire to be constructive. It also gives a magnetic and distinctive quality to his voice. Having remarkable will power, determination, firmness, diligence, and patience, he expresses them in the most positive ways.

URANUS IN THE 8TH HOUSE

Being attracted physically to his lovers, Mac's affairs take him by storm. Any whirlwind affair becomes a special source of knowledge and sexual self-understanding—teaching him about needs and desires that he may have been unaware of. These affairs have a certain fated quality, making him feel almost powerless to stop them. This house also gives him strong psychic abilities.

NEPTUNE IN VIRGO ♍

This man has a combination of spiritual and material energy that gives him an almost psychic power. Mac doesn't have to visually see something to perceive what's happening. Having prophetic knowledge and understanding of the human race, he is able to perceive it all in his mind's eye.

NEPTUNE IN THE 12TH HOUSE

This is a very psychic position with a tremendous grasp of universal needs. Mac's most valued goals and achievements are very personal and private; however, there are times when he has problems with an excessive imagination or mental confusion.

PLUTO IN CANCER ♋

With an active subconscious, Mac can indulge in dreams and fantasies. Having a deep inner life and a talent for reproduction and reconstruction, he is a creative actor that can play many parts—relating more easily to people who are younger than him. He is very determined when it comes to spreading or gaining acceptance of a new idea. Having a phenomenal memory of his personal past, he is almost psychic when it comes to intuitively knowing other people's thoughts and feelings. He puts a premium on the security of physical possessions and the privacy of his relationships. At times, there is a certain self-indulgence and self-pity on his part. He has to step carefully when having affairs, lest he upset or offend his partner.

PLUTO IN THE 10TH HOUSE

The underlying of causes in the organization of society can be readily perceived in this 10th House revealing Mac's obsessive, political beliefs. This man values his reputation and will be extremely careful in protecting it. There's a possibility of him becoming personally, financially, and emotionally involved with someone.

SOLAR ECLIPSE IN GEMINI ♊

In this incarnation, Mac is teaching his fellow beings the value of communication—learning how to communicate with body, mind and soul. Out of fear, he may reflect too much sweetness and not enough honesty. On some levels, he is also teaching freedom of movement. Physical movement is also very important to this man. Due to his confinement in previous existences, movement accelerates his communicative skills in this lifetime.

LUNAR ECLIPSE IN CAPRICORN ♑

Mac has come to learn the value of having a good reputation in this lifetime and how to be responsible for his actions. Learning to be successful is an important lesson for him in this lifetime.

ೋೊ

♊ Red • JUNE 20, 1950

Ascendant in Leo · Sun in Gemini · Moon in Leo · Mercury in Gemini
Venus in Taurus · Mars in Libra · Jupiter in Pisces · Saturn in Virgo
Uranus in Cancer · Neptune in Libra · Pluto in Leo
Solar Eclipse in Pisces · Lunar Eclipse in Libra
Mode: Mutable · Element: Air · Key Idea: Dualism

ASCENDANT IN LEO ♌

Motivated by pride, Red has good leadership qualities and sees herself as important with a need to be noticed. Being a dramatic spirit, there is an indefinable presence about her which gets her noticed immediately when she walks into a room. Before anyone realizes it, she's taken center stage. This beautiful woman loves to sing, dance, act, and dress up—which includes bright clothes and noticeable hairstyles.

SUN IN GEMINI ♊

Red is intellectual, intuitive, receptive, logical, versatile, and adept in any argument—her personality is many sided. She is a very sensitive woman with a high-strung disposition. Having a fine mind and a good memory, she is capable of expressing a continual stream of ideas in her speech and writings. Possessing a need to travel, she enjoys diversity in every facet of her existence and is never happier than when she's leading a double life—having dual professions and dual romantic interests at the same time. Adaptable to different environments, situations and people, she works more efficiently if there are changes and breaks in her routines. Clever with the use of her hands, she often has several hobbies or other diversions.

SUN IN THE 10TH HOUSE

This aspect brings early fame to Red. Her self-esteem stems from a career that receives status in society and having people believe the best about her. Having a strong drive to succeed, and a need to operate before the public, she directs herself to be prominent within her career. Although this woman's ambitions may be everything, her career could drain her energies. The people she becomes personally involved with are usually fond of her. She has a reputation of being a good lover and prefers the company of others like herself.

MOON IN LEO ♌

Red has an optimistic approach to life—sight is her most developed sense. Being a positive woman, she is able to maintain her vitality, confidence, strength, initiative and generous personality. She is also very independent and loves her freedom. Once this womqn makes a decision, she sticks to it firmly and resolutely. The first appeal must be made to her heart, not her head. Having great vigor and self-reliance, she makes an inspiring and capable leader. She may even feel she has a mission to perform.

MOON IN THE 1ST HOUSE

Red's emotional state plays a prominent role in her decisions. She is impressionable, likeable, emotional, and impulsive. Her sense of self-worth goes through phases—responding strongly and quickly to the moods of those around her. This woman is usually at the top of any social situation and her personal affairs are chosen quickly and without hesitation. Others find security in her open appreciation of them.

GEMINI SUN • LEO MOON COMBINATION ♊♌

An apparently happy-go-lucky nature conceals this woman's good sound sense.

A19

Red's deep-seated loyalty and fidelity is concealed by her apparent fickleness. Clever and quick intellectually, she also has the ability to maintain facts and information about people. Having great staying power, she can master anything she sets her mind on—she will probably go on learning and studying all her life. Disliking quarrels, she keeps the peace for a long time, even under trying circumstances. Because of her sunny, lively disposition and witty humor, this ardent and demonstrative woman is popular and sought after socially. She is able to use her popularity to good practical advantage and could become a good social or political leader. When aroused, she is capable of a hot temper and speaking her mind. Her love life is extremely important to her—giving everything to have peace, security, and love around her.

MERCURY IN GEMINI ♊

Besides being an excellent singer and actress, Red has intellectual abilities. Being a quick thinker and logical, she has a good knowledge of mathematics and other languages. This makes her an excellent spokeswoman and legal representative. However, when in any debate, she can come to false conclusions.

MERCURY IN THE 11TH HOUSE

Red's knowledge of the occult and science gives her the ability to work for humanitarian organizations. She is lively, versatile, and chatty with her friends. An optimist in love matters, her love life improves continually. Those that she has been intimate with always remains a friend.

VENUS IN TAURUS ♉

All love is sacred to this woman and she tends to worship the one she loves by placing him on a pedestal. Loving with mind and spirit, Red is repelled by anything coarse and crude. Love and courtship are a very important ritual in her eyes. Her love must be absolutely free and cannot be chained to material expressions. Loving beauty, simplicity, and harmonious surroundings, she has a superb sense of proportion, color and line. She also loves to dance and is fond of the Ballet.

VENUS IN THE 10TH HOUSE

Red is an artistic, attractive and charming woman with high standards. Her desire for love, peace and harmony is expressed in her career. To have any sense of satisfaction, her career must operate harmoniously. She is drawn to individuals who are well known in their professional fields.

MARS IN LIBRA ♎

Liking fair play, Red's sense of justice is frequently outraged. However, life is so often arbitrary and fate capricious that she often finds herself protesting its inequities loudly and clearly. Acting prudently as a judge, and with careful consideration and balanced judgment, she will fight to the bitter end for what she considers fair. She can also be a well disciplined woman maintaining a great deal of self-control. Always forceful and never violent, she conserves her energies and power of endurance by doing just enough. Her means are admirably well suited to her ends. Expressing herself in the artistic and literary fields is where she excels.

MARS IN THE 3RD HOUSE

This sign represents one who travels frequently. While Red's intellectual energy is strong, she has the basic traits of being very congenial, energetic, enthusiastic and driven. When it comes to romance, she is a conversational lover who knows how to communicate with her romantic partners.

JUPITER IN PISCES ♓

Being very co-operative, Red gets along well with her associates. Other people responding to her are usually of great importance. In government and other forms of public life, her wisdom and high ideals can prove a source of inspiration to her admirers. Sooner or later she can expect to be very fortunate by being well liked and popular. Although she is kind and generous in her relationships with others, at times they may not appreciate her. She actually benefits spiritually through the good she does for them. Somewhat psychic, she senses the needs and feelings of others. This woman loves the dramatic and all theatrical endeavors—whether it is a classical tragedy, or the simply drama of everyday life. Deeply religious in her own beliefs, a Western version of Eastern philosophy, she benefits greatly through travel, especially when it is across water.

JUPITER IN THE 8TH HOUSE

Having good investigative powers and holding an interest for the occult and reincarnation, Red tends to gravitate toward affairs that seem to have deep undercurrents and share a mysterious nature. In some circles, her sexual life could be exaggerated.

SATURN IN VIRGO ♍

Combining the wisdom of age with the mental vigor of youth, Red is refreshed and nourished by her own moments of solitude. There is a tendency to be something of a lone wolf while keeping her own counsel. Earthy and practical, she has mental strength and stability, which includes the power to analyze, criticize and organize.

SATURN IN THE 2ND HOUSE

Red's love is free of personal surroundings and is based on personal communication. Wealth and material possessions are not important when she chooses a partner.

URANUS IN CANCER ♋

Red's motherhood takes precedence in this sign. Having a highly developed psychic plane, and obeying the dictates of her subconscious, she a sensitive and receptive being who keeps her personal life very private.

URANUS IN THE 10TH HOUSE

Red demands the best of partners in her love relationships. Her political beliefs are likely to be humanitarian and there may be rebellious behavior directed against authority. Disruption, changeability, and eccentricity are channeled into her career, of which, there may be more than one.

NEPTUNE IN LIBRA ♎

Expressing herself through the arts and dance, Red's concepts of peace and equality could change the world. Old concepts for her will come under scrutiny and be discarded. Neptune in Libra is the sign of marriage or any commitment to be with someone.

NEPTUNE IN THE 3RD HOUSE

Softness, sensitivity, confusion and escapism bring about strange events during Red's daily activities. Again in this sign, she possesses artistic and musical talent.

PLUTO IN LEO ♌

Red is a daring woman with a sense of adventure and a high-minded masterful nature—destroying the old to make way for the new. Having a strong creative urge, and possessing a dynamic energy, she has a distinct talent for entertainment in every form, including acting. This is the sign of leadership, rebellion and revolution—bridging the gap between the present and the past.

PLUTO IN THE 1ST HOUSE

Having a desire to be in control, and possesseing a great deal of magnetism, Red is powerful and authoritative. Her determination, combined with the intensity of her features, especially her eyes, sets her apart from everyone. Her relationships tend to be extreme and intense. This woman goes through a series of different lifestyles. Earlier ways of living were suddenly overthrown.

SOLAR ECLIPSE IN PISCES ♓

Red has a natural gift of inborn intuition and is here to help her fellow beings develop their sensitivities. This woman needs to teach others how to follow their intuitions and hunches—helping them to sense, feel, and get in touch with their spiritual side. Hers is the gift of illustrating the principle of surrender in its highest form.

LUNAR ECLIPSE IN LIBRA ♎

Red is learning how to be fair in all areas of life, which includes, sharing her mind and expressing her thoughts by communicating with others. In relationships, she is learning the proper balance between giving and taking. Her pioneer attitude comes from a previous existence of just going after what she wanted with no regard for anyone. She must learn to develop a balanced sense of commitment in all areas of her life.

☽☾

♉ Sarina Montez • May 10, 1971

Ascendant in Gemini · Sun in Taurus · Moon in Scorpio
Mercury in Aries · Venus in Aries · Mars in Aquarius
Jupiter in Sagittariuss · Saturn in Taurus · Uranus in Libra
Neptune in Sagittarius · Pluto in Virgo
Solar Eclipse in Pisces · Lunar Eclipse in Leo
Mode: Fixed · Element: Earth · Key Idea: The Material Plane

ASCENDANT IN GEMINI ♊

This ascendant has the Peter Pan personality of the zodiac. Sarina's first
response to a new situation is to communicate. Easily bored and restless, she's
flexible, changeable, and hates to be confined.

SUN IN TAURUS ♉

Enjoying the good life and hungry for the various experiences life has to offer,
Sarina is willing to give as well as take. Needing a man in her life; her earthy
temperament can appease, attract, magnetize and hypnotize. Although
troublesome at times, she's well worth the trouble, for she is charming,
seductive, and obstinate. Refusing to be taken advantage of, she prefers you tell
her where you stand and what you want. The secret is to simply be overboard
and do not try to force issues with her—she responds to good taste and
understanding. Any nonsense draws her fire as well as her annoyance. Her
lovers must know when and where to draw the line, because she will run them
through a gamut of emotions—testing them to see how much she can get a way
with.

A25

SUN IN THE 12TH HOUSE

This House is associated with mystery, undercover pursuits, and behind-the-scenes activities. Others see Sarina's personal life as quite mysterious and there is speculation about her *behind-closed-doors* affairs—making her seem more attractive and desirable to the men who are interested in her.

MOON IN SCORPIO ♏

Sarina experiences intense and deep feelings. Her intuitive and probing nature makes her an excellent psychiatrist, detective and clairvoyant. A self-reliant, serious, and penetrating person, she is attracted to the occult way of life. Extremely fond of mysteries and the solution of crimes, she possesses extrasensory perception along with a highly intuitive consciousness. She speaks out for her principles and fights for the underdog, while inspiring confidence and creating solutions to touchy problems. When misfortune hits, she takes it personally. This woman is energetic, abrupt, and impulsive, especially when it concerns her great attraction for men. Having a great capacity for sexual enjoyment, she also enjoys sexual variety. Once she starts, there's no stopping her. It's all the way or nothing at all. She moves forward, digging deep and leaving behind broken hearts and disillusionment. Her expertise is in making others lose control. Having strong convictions, she has a tendency to go to extremes with food, drink and affairs of the heart. Her monetary position in life may be gained through inheritance, marriage, or partnerships.

MOON IN THE 6TH HOUSE

Because Sarina is very interested in suicides, causes of death, and burial information, forensic work is an ideal occupation for her. She is also good at creating fantasy structures for lovemaking.

A26

TAURUS SUN • SCORPIO MOON COMBINATION ♉ ♏

Sarina's nature is strong, impulsive and passionate—knowing what she wants and acquiring it. Intensely dramatic, her charm is instantaneously established. She thinks with one part of her brain and feels with another; self-willed, headstrong, independent, and capable of running away on a moment's notice— reason has no effect on her emotions.

MERCURY IN ARIES ♈

Fluent in speech and attracted to music, Sarina has an active imagination. She quickly reacts to those who have skill, talent and creativity. Her sensitivity perceives artistic values while appreciating their originality.

MERCURY IN THE 11TH HOUSE

Sarina is a lively woman—versatile, and chatty with friends. She also has a great freedom when expressing her sexual side.

VENUS IN ARIES ♈

This woman's appetite for love is quickly whetted because her style of loving is very intense. Sarina wishes to possess the object of her affections without delay. Needing constant stimulation, she enjoys excitement and danger and finds it difficult to be loyal or faithful when her sense of adventure is aroused. She's an emotional antenna that wants to love and be loved.

VENUS IN THE 11TH HOUSE

Sarina's desire for love, peace, and harmony is channeled into friendships and group interests.

MARS IN AQUARIUS ♒

This woman has an abundance of mental energy combined with physical proficiency. Sensitive, yet impatient with the failure, Sarina has the fire to inspire people and would rather hurt herself than injure others.

MARS IN THE 9TH HOUSE

This house gives Sarina assertiveness, drive, energy, enthusiasm, and strong influential ability.

JUPITER IN SAGITTARIUS ♐

Optimism, faith, humor, and love of higher learning, are all strongly featured in this sign. Sarina possesses keen insight about what is occurring and why—her intuitive intellect is sharp. Without any technique or refinement, her new love affairs start out robustly.

JUPITER IN THE 7TH HOUSE

Relying heavily on a lover as a source of creativity and inspiration, Sarina prefers an active relationship and may go through a number of affairs until finding the right partner. Relationships are a major source of education for her.

SATURN IN TAURUS ♉

Having firm convictions, Sarina will fight to preserve them—she is a stubborn and determined woman that maintains a fine sense of responsibility. She overcomes any difficulties that come her way and achieves success in any occupation where patience and perseverance is required.

SATURN IN THE 12TH HOUSE

Often feeling obligated and responsible for the actions of others, Sarina can withdraw emotionally at the most inappropriate times.

URANUS IN LIBRA ♎

Sarina has a deep-seated urge to be an instrument of justice. Besides possessing a flair for design and form, she has an inner longing for partnerships and other attachments. Romantic and un-conventional, her unique charm can be distant and cold with a sudden change of opinions. Her partners are also likely to be active and changeable. Everything around her is made more entertaining and unusual.

URANUS IN THE 5TH HOUSE

Mentally astute, rebellious, and unusually gifted, Sarina maintains an erratic physical stamina and is quite inventive and spontaneous in her lovemaking. Her disruption, changeability and eccentricity are channeled into creative outlets—sometimes of a bizarre nature.

NEPTUNE IN SAGITTARIUS ♐

Sarina feels something is amiss in an affair that gets too tricky or involved. Although this woman is amorous, there are times when she is unsettled mentally and physically. If her enthusiasm is diffused, she can end up as a loner or a wanderer.

NEPTUNE IN THE 7TH HOUSE

This woman yearns for recognition yet shuns the limelight. Softness, sensitivity, confusion, and escapism are the cause of Sarina's indecision and self-assertion problems. In romantic endeavors, she makes an ideal partner by idealizing her lovers.

PLUTO IN VIRGO ♍

While maintaining a powerful sex drive, Sarina looks at sex as joyous and sportive. However, problems with her peers could arise from her carefree sexual attitude—hers is more of a Pluto in Leo attitude. Committing herself to an affair can be usually difficult because they require a great deal of attention.

PLUTO IN THE 4TH HOUSE

Power, authority and magnetism are used within Sarina's home life—she likes to rule the roost. Obsessive about her home and emotions, she derives great comfort from the security of her most intimate surroundings—especially in her bedroom.

SOLAR ECLIPSE IN PISCES ♓

Sarina is here to help her fellow beings develop their sensitivities and their feelings. Her natural inborn intuition can teach others the value of following hunches and the usefulness of this awareness. She needs to follow her intuitions and not her mind. Following these insights is extremely important to the life process of those she touches. Her Karma is to help others accept the complexities of life—teaching them to get in touch with the spirit inside themselves and how to become one with the universe. This requires trusting the universal guidance and letting go of attachments to the ego. Others are inspired by her principles of surrender to operate in their lives and go with the flow.

LUNAR ECLIPSE IN LEO ♌

Sarina needs to learn lessons relating to her value system. These lessons include; not being swayed in her values, learning to share values, overcoming negative manipulative traits, respecting others, and taking care of her sexual behavior. She is learning appropriate spirituality, understanding that what goes around comes around, and how to plant positive ideas. This woman also needs to know about boundaries, for she has a tendency to push others to their limits because she wants to know their boundaries. First, she must know her limits to become totally content. When her energy is silent and reserved it is because she's angry inside. Her energy desperately needs a focus and a cause. In other lifetimes, she has let her values slip through a misuse of power. She's here this time to believe in her own goodness, while learning the proper use of power radiant expression.

౭ೲಐ

Compatibility Charts

Billy • MARS IN CAPRICORN ♑

Sarina • VENUS IN ARIES ♈

Representing vintage maturity, Billy is highly ambitious and able to put off immediate gratification until a goal sought is grasped. He may have to indulge in Sarina's tantrums because she wants plenty of attention. Her attractive blend of youthful foolishness has the persona of living in the moment.

Billy • VENUS IN CAPRICORN ♑

Sarina • MARS IN AQUARIUS ♒

Neither will change the other, but they will continue trying. He will need extraordinary patience to maintain a balance in this relationship, while she is subject to changing plans.

Mac • MARS IN LEO ♑

Red • VENUS IN TAURUS ♉

Both Mac and Red believe that there is someone created just for them. Their liaison will have the feeling of *this is it* when they meet. Mac, possessing a fair measure of "Divine Right of King," mentally believes that what is loved in a sense is owned. Both being sexually powerful, they will be compatible bedmates. It can mean a strong and long commitment when these two begin their relationship—

knowing, that their relationship is permanent and not a sexual fling. They both have similar drives and ambition is one of them. While each one is interested in material comfort and security, both parties highly respect their accomplishments and financial achievements. The most compatible thing about this relationship may be its horizontal (rather than its vertical) moments.

Mac • VENUS IN LIBRA ♑

Red • MARS IN LIBRA ♎

In dance, they would be Fred Astaire and Ginger Rogers—no one else has quite the same synergistic movements as these two together. They find the depth of their bond through music, movement, and other artistic forms of expression. Having a potentially blinding allure for each other, these two charmers turn heads when they are together.

ജ౭

♋ Vickie Keaton • July 4, 1976

Ascendant in Pisces · Sun in Cancer · Moon in Libra
Mercury in Gemini · Venus in Cancer · Mars in Leo
Jupiter in Taurus · Saturn in Leo · Uranus in Scorpio
Neptune in Sagittarius · Pluto in Libra
Solar Eclipse in Taurus · Lunar Eclipse in Scorpio
Mode: Cardinal · Element: Water · Key Idea: The Mother

ASCENDANT IN PISCES ♓

Although Vickie has the ability to be highly creative and artistic, she often lacks the confidence to develop these skills. This easily hurt woman tends to be afraid to project herself onto life's stage. Extremely impressionable, she soaks up the environment. Periods alone, providing a mental and psychic healing time, are necessary for her well-being.

SUN IN CANCER ♋

Being in the most emotional sign of all, Vickie is the most caring of people. Having a deep well of energy that provides nourishment, sustenance, and love to the world, she views everyone as babies to be looked after, fussed over, and cared for. This also applies to her job, home, organizations, and everything else she is involved in. This lovely, but often lonely woman can be quite fickle and extremely emotional. A valuable ally with a highly developed intuition, she should never be taken for granted or deceived. What she hangs on to most of all is the past.

SUN IN THE 5TH HOUSE

A strong, creative will is indicated in this 5th House. Having a generally sunny and fun loving disposition, Vickie's self-confidence and energy are pursued and

A34

promoted through her artistic pursuits and achievements. Working with children can also build her self-confidence.

MOON IN LIBRA ♎

Vickie finds her greatest expression through working in public relations, advertising, and especially the law. Her vision can see beyond the immediate evidence. Because of her gentle and understanding way, she tends to attract people with problems. This woman wants to be involved in all communications, including any procedures, information and rumors. She possesses the charm to win her way into select circles by convincing investors that she has found the pot of gold at the end of the rainbow.

MOON IN THE 8TH HOUSE

Vickie possesses a psychic ability along with deep and powerful emotions. She is good at handling other people's finances and possessions. Sexual desires may be subject to the changing influence of the moon.

SUN IN CANCER • MOON IN LIBRA COMBINATION ♋ ♎

Vickie's charming manner is a curious combination of independence, dependence and self-sufficiency—satisfaction is derived from watching the reactions and temperments of others. This woman loves flattery, attention, and having people around her. Having the ability to make other people respond to her, she finds great satisfaction in her powers of observation and her ability to detach makes her well-fitted for an artistic, scientific, or investigative career. This woman is also a gifted writer. Being sensitive and a little introverted, she doesn't give a great deal of herself, but likes to absorb the people around her. Afraid of her own emotions, this woman remains a romantic who constantly reaches into the world for companionship. Being hurt and deceived in the past has made her somewhat suspicious. An elusive person, and not especially constant in love matters, she maintains a high degree of self-protectiveness. Her admirers have a tendency to make her feel like she is being analyzed. This woman will have an active career in the romance arena before she settles down.

MERCURY IN GEMINI ♊

Vickie is inventive, witty, and humorous. An agile and intellectual woman, she has a curious mind that enables her to find out the facts. In love affairs, she finds it difficult to remain faithful and there's a possibility for her loving more than one man.

MERCURY IN THE 4TH HOUSE

In this House, Vickie's security is sought through the application of logical thinking. Her home is viewed as a base for study and reflection on experience. Her father was a communicative and intelligent man.

VENUS IN CANCER ♋

Vickie is a sentimental and sincere woman with high standards. Becoming very attached in her relationships, she is capable of holding on for too long. Wanting security in all her personal relationships, she can also be extremely strong emotionally and difficult to handle by being cold and aloof.

VENUS IN THE 5TH HOUSE

This is a very artistic position. Needing romantic liaisons and a lot of social activity, Vickie has a risk of possessing vanity along with excessive romanticism.

MARS IN LEO ♌

Having great creative energy, Vickie is also restless, anxious, dynamic and forceful at times. Although her opinions are stubborn, and her acts impulsive and swift, she does well in supporting personal causes. She can frighten the opposite sex through personal magnetism that both repels and attracts. There may be battles with loved ones and the danger that this excitement fills could develop into a psychological disorder.

MARS IN THE 6TH HOUSE

This is a workaholic position. Vickie's activities are easily channeled into her work and are accomplished in any work that involves details or the use of sharp tools.

JUPITER IN TAURUS ♉

Vickie attracts material wealth and possessions more readily than other people. She gains strength through her friends and her hobbies. Eating, drinking, socializing, spending, and sex, could all become obsessive issues for her.

JUPITER IN THE 3RD HOUSE

Vickie's expansiveness and optimism are directed at others. Relationships will be sought out on an intellectual basis, and important details concerning those relationships may be overlooked. This woman benefits from short-distance travel and the encouragement of others.

SATURN IN LEO ♌

This House could present complications for Vickie. Creative abilities may be suppressed through lack of confidence. Her sexual issues could present themselves. These issues may be the result of religious teachings, circumstances, mental issues, or a physical disability.

SATURN IN THE 6TH HOUSE

Even though Vickie has organizational energy, fears and lack of confidence may be experienced in her job situations. She needs to be careful of having a weak constitution and being a workaholic.

URANUS IN SCORPIO ♏

Vickie possesses hypnotic physical appeal and can be a dynamic natural leader. She can also be cruel or vindictive. Her behavior includes; being moody, puzzling, obsessive and compulsive. Although she may take some risks to obtain clarity and understanding, she is direct and sometimes adventurous. Her drive for achievement is in the art and scientific fields. Wanting to change the world, she may have an absolute dedication to a high purpose or worthy cause. Searching for this knowledge too actively and indiscreetly can cause personal and social damage. This woman may invent and/or discover new ways of healing—intuitively knowing that mind and body are one. Sexual experiences are probably a key to her emotional and personality development. Being magnetically attractive in the physical sense, there is also a certain combination of passion and subtle fascination that makes her a force to reckon with.

URANUS IN THE 9TH HOUSE

Freedom-seeking Vickie has a brilliant mind. In her lifetime, she will experience changes of religious beliefs. There is a love of travel and education about exotic, far-away places. Disruption, changeability and eccentricity can occur during her travels.

NEPTUNE IN SAGITTARIUS ♐

Vickie's generation will explore the mysteries and powers of the mind. Personal and mystical experiences will become routine for her. Instead of looking for God above, she will realize the God within. If her enthusiasm is diffused, she can become a loner or wanderer—unsettled both mentally and physically.

NEPTUNE IN THE 10TH HOUSE

Vickie's softness, sensitivity, confusion, and escapism can cause; indecision, lack of attainment and self-assertion. However, her escapist tendencies shun the limelight. Yearning for recognition in careers of an artistic nature, she will realize it is where she is best suited.

PLUTO IN LIBRA ♎

Charming and aggressive, Vickie is in the pursuit of justice. She has a powerful, hypnotic manner that thrives on admiration from others.

PLUTO IN THE 8TH HOUSE

Power, authority and magnetism are well controlled in this House. It does however, manifest some strong sexual urges. In Vickie's lifetime, she will have immense gains or losses through inheritance. She also has an innate fascination for the birth, life, and death process.

SOLAR ECLIPSE IN TAURUS ♉

Vickie's role is to teach proper prosperity consciousness and the importance of strong spiritual values. She is here to be an artist and express the earth's natural beauty.

LUNAR ECLIPSE IN SCORPIO ♏

Vickie's lessons are related to her value system; realigning, readjusting her principles, the proper use of power, that there is good in the world, and, that it's okay to be successful.

☽◯☾

A39

II Marc Matthews • June 6, 1965

Ascendant in Aries · Sun in Gemini · Moon in Virgo
Mercury in Gemini · Venus in Cancer · Mars in Virgo
Jupiter in Gemini · Saturn in Pisces · Uranus in Virgo
Neptune in Scorpio · Pluto in Virgo
Solar Eclipse in Gemini · Lunar Eclipse in Gemini
Mode: Mutable · Element: Air · Key Idea: Dualism

ASCENDANT IN ARIES ♈

This ascendant urges Marc to get to the forefront of whatever he's involved in. His inherent bravery often comes from innocence, impulsiveness, and having the courage to take charge when others don't. He is courageous and accomplishes a lot by helping other people. There are times however, when he can be oblivious to what people around him want. It's very easy for this Gemini man to take on too much.

SUN IN GEMINI ♊

Marc doesn't like to complain or nag. This usually popular man is; versatile, alert, charming, filled with ideas, and blessed with lots of energy. He is also idealistic, adaptable, elusive, and quick with his hands. He can talk his way out of almost anything and tends to think of himself as a cute kid. No matter what the weather is like; he is willing to go out in it, be on the move, experiment, and satisfy his own curiosity. Marc spends all of his life thinking, seeking knowledge, and discovering the truth. His brilliant mind needs constant stimulation. He can be deceptive when he is testing, probing and trying to seek sincerity in someone.

SUN IN THE 3RD HOUSE

Marc's basic drive is to attain factual knowledge and figure out how things work.

MOON IN VIRGO ♍

Marc is a wonderful detective and an excellent analyzer. He is practical at finding solutions to everyday problems by working things out in detail—never asking others to carry out something that he himself would not do. His need to understand gives him the desire to be of use, overcome obstacles, and arrive at goals. Insecurity sets in if he is not doing something he believes is useful. This man feels tremendously gratified when others ask him questions, inquire his opinion, and shown appreciation for his efforts. He prefers things around him to be clean, tidy, and items to be in their proper place—his fussiness can also extend to food. Although he is interested in a healthy diet, he can be too particular about what he eats. This man needs to loosen up, for he can be too overcritical.

MOON IN THE 6TH HOUSE

Work issues could occur through Marc's changeable attitudes. Problems of health are likely to go through various stages for this man.

SUN IN GEMINI · MOON IN VIRGO COMBINATION ♊♍

Marc can be moody and temperamental, and under a sprightly and happy exterior hides a world of woe. He may look upon himself as a palace clown sort of person with a smile that hides the breaking heart. Feeling intellectually above others, there's a good deal of self-dramatization here with a tendency to feel misunderstood and unappreciated. His romanticism is a worship of the mind. For him, the grass is always greener on the other side.

MERCURY IN GEMINI Ⅱ

Marc deals with facts and solutions and is knowledgeable on many subjects. He is an inventive, versatile, and humorous man with an inordinate intellectual curiosity. Having an agile mind, he has the potential to be an impartial arbitrator with the ability to grasp opposing viewpoints. Nervousness sets in when he takes on the problems and quirks of those around him.

MERCURY IN THE 6TH HOUSE

Marc's acute thinking abilities result in attracting jobs that involve communication. Much of his energy is expended in the pursuit of knowledge and a desire to travel.

VENUS IN CANCER ♋

When it comes to love, Marc wants some security. His needs are basic and he wants the best for his loved ones. Sentimental and sincere, he can be very attached to others. Although he is extremely sensitive and easily hurt, he manages to hide his feelings behind a dignified façade. Even though his standards are high; his drive, fire, and ambition, at times can be lacking.

VENUS IN THE 4TH HOUSE

Possessing the ability to calm others, Marc finds arguments unpleasant and has a strong desire for tranquility.

MARS IN VIRGO ♍

Marc, who worries unnecessarily about his health and diet, is a systematic man—planning his actions carefully and trying not to act without good reason. His excellent attention to detail enables him to achieve in any field where physical precision is required. This man can bring a meticulous and analytical approach to anything he is involved in. Shrewd actions are well planned and designed to bring about greater security. He needs to avoid spectacular actions that lead to embarrassment and loss.

MARS IN THE 6TH HOUSE

Marc is easily channeled into any kind of work that involves detail.

JUPITER IN GEMINI ♊

Sympathetic and kind, this man is a great humanitarian. Patience is not one of Marc's strong points. He is however, a true diplomat. The luckiest field for him is the law or on the lecture platform.

JUPITER IN THE 3RD HOUSE

Marc's expansiveness and optimism are directed toward others.

SATURN IN PISCES ♓

Unfortunate in a material sense, Marc is disappointed because of the position he occupies in life. His existence can demand more than the usual amount of self-sacrifice. His popularity could suffer from the attacks of others. Fascinated by Mysticism, this man can learn to accept the conditions of his life through philosophy. His vulnerability is his feet and the impurities that are found in the fluids of his system.

SATURN IN THE 11TH HOUSE

Although Marc finds it difficult to relate closely to friends, he still remains loyal and responsible towards them. In-group situations, circumstances may cause him to experience a sense of seriousness, limitation, fear, and lack of confidence.

URANUS IN VIRGO ♍

Being a bit neurotic, and falling subject to an overloaded mental system, Marc has difficulty in controlling his mental and practical outlets.

URANUS IN THE 6TH HOUSE

Marc's disruption and changeability occurs within his working environment. Sudden health problems could arise in this 6thHouse. This man is also a lover of large animals.

NEPTUNE IN SCORPIO ♏

Marc is very imaginative and his deeply confused emotions are a potential for vice or addiction.

NEPTUNE IN THE 8TH HOUSE

Highly emotional and warmly passionate, Marc has powerful intuitive faculties. However, softness, sensitivity, confusion, and escapism do not blend well with Neptune in the 8th House.

PLUTO IN VIRGO ♍

Marc is capable of handling great detail; unfortunately, he tends to worry about the life's minor details.

PLUTO IN THE 6TH HOUSE

This man desires to hold positions of respect. His work situations are projected into power, authority and magnetism. He is extremely competent in the caring of animals. Intense about his health, Marc is likely to suffer from sexual transmitted diseases and growths.

SOLAR ECLIPSE IN GEMINI Ⅱ

Marc is teaching his fellow beings the value of communication, freedom of movement and lightheartedness. He helps to set people free by teaching that there are more places to go, further knowledge to be gained, and additional information to pass on.

LUNAR ECLIPSE IN GEMINI Ⅱ

Marc is learning the correct use of language and appropriate protocol. Having respect for his needs is important to this man. He will master the art of communication by facing his desires honestly and communicating those needs to others. Coming from a previous lifetime where he walked a spiritual path and had a monastic mind, he must now share his knowledge with others. In that previous lifetime, he meditated in the mountains and integrated a multitude of psychological and philosophical studies.

ଔଔ

♍ Ricco Gambino • September 11, 1951

Ascendant in Scorpio · Sun in Virgo · Moon in Capricorn

Mercury in Virgo · Venus in Virgo · Mars in Leo

Jupiter in Aries · Saturn in Gemini · Uranus in Cancer

Neptune in Libra · Pluto in Virgo

Solar Eclipse in Virgo · Lunar Eclipse in Aquarius

Mode: Mutable· Element: Earth · Key Idea: Transformation

ASCENDANT IN SCORPIO ♏

Having a soft and pleasant voice, Ricco can be meek, mild, and charming, until you disagree with him. By doing things his way, he will provide you with as much assistance as possible. Having tremendous will power, this man can be very helpful and motivating. His do or die approach has the ability to transform other people's lives. Being a private person with deep emotions, he doesn't like to express his feelings publicly.

SUN IN VIRGO ♍

A practical and down to earth man, Ricco is scientific, perceptive, and very alert. Always gathering knowledge from every conceivable source, he has the ability to memorize and retain everything he learns. One can depend on him for security issues. He judges things by their practicality. Usually very modest, he is unassuming and content to be in the background. He is an evenly balanced man that almost never loses his temper.

SUN IN THE 11TH HOUSE

Attractive to the opposite sex, Ricco also attracts celebrated friends. In his lifetime, hopes and wishes become challenges.

MOON IN CAPRICORN ♑

Having a strong sense of duty, Ricco is always alert and eager to learn. Because of his power to make quick decisions, responsibilities are thrust upon him. Perceiving a problem, and correct about its solution, he has the ability to resolve it in a split second. There's an undefined coldness in his make-up that can make him a solitary soul.

MOON IN THE 3RD HOUSE

Impressionable and receptive to learning, Ricco has a healthy and intellectual curiosity. He finds security through family relationships. In affairs of the heart, he expresses his feelings verbally, and won't hesitate to let his lover know just how he feels.

VIRGO SUN • CAPRICORN MOON COMBINATION ♍

Besides haing a keen sense of good taste, Ricco is a very well integrated personality, drawing people to him steadily and permanently. Although he is a fundamentally serious man, strain underlies his sense of humor. He will rise to a position of influence, authority and worldly security and does his share to improve others intellectually. This man, conscious of the frailties of human nature, will leave the giving of tangible charity to someone else while he works on the human mind. Ricco speaks his mind frankly, even brutally sometimes, especially where an idea is in question. His passions tend to be of the mind rather than flesh. This man can quietly become magnetic and restrained. Extremely persuasive, he delights in taking the unpopular side of a question and making it the popular side. Unfailingly considerate of other people's feelings and supplies, he is the milk of human kindness.

MERCURY IN VIRGO ♍

Having a fine mind and an approach of pure reasoning, Ricco is able to handle people in practical and impersonal ways. Because he learns so easily, his detachment from emotional considerations makes him an excellent worker in the scientific field.

MERCURY IN THE 11TH HOUSE

Ricco's urge to communicate is focused upon his friends and group activities. Being an optimist in love, and remaining friendly with his past relationships, his love life seems to improve continually.

VENUS IN VIRGO ♍

Dedicating himself to a worthy cause that enlists his mind more than his emotions, Ricco can also be cold and materialistic when it comes to love.

VENUS IN THE 11TH HOUSE

Because this House gives Ricco a desire to mix with many people on a non-intimate basis, he could end up having very advantageous friends.

MARS IN LEO ♌

A genial leader, noble in his actions and by his examples, Ricco is enterprising, courageous, forceful, and proud. While admired and inspired by his equals and followers, his appeals are from the heart. When this man speaks, he can be quite persuasive.

MARS IN THE 10TH HOUSE

Career matters benefit from the energy input of Mars in this House. Because of being so pre-occupied with his career, Ricco may have little or no time for personal intimacy.

JUPITER IN ARIES ♈

A natural leader, Ricco has a pioneering instinct. Generous and idealistic, he does well in any field where he rises to authority or be in top command. Having the confidence and ability to run the show, people just naturally follow his direction. His enthusiasm is contagious. Gaining material and good fortune, he will be very successful. In matters of love, he uses the direct approach.

JUPITER IN THE 6TH HOUSE

Ricco knows how to keep morale high. He is a good advisor to his working companions—a generous man who offers everyone the benefit of a doubt. His health is good for he maintains strong recuperative powers.

SATURN IN LIBRA ♎

Having extraordinarily good judgment and patience to wait out any emotional storms, Ricco maintains a strong awareness of the need to co-operate. He is aware of exhibiting fair principles when using his authority. Because of his desire for the world to hand out justice rather than punishment, he works to bring harmony into his environment. He is sought after for his knowledge and advice and is truly a religious man in the deepest sense. There is a possibility of more than one marriage for him.

SATURN IN THE 12TH HOUSE

Ricco has a deep fear of any kind of restrictions and often feels responsible for the actions of others.

URANUS IN ARIES ♈

This man's deepest inner urges tend to be passive, not active. Having a highly developed psychic plane, Ricco obeys the dictates of his subconscious.

URANUS IN THE 9TH HOUSE

Having a brilliant mind with unusual drives, ideas, and desires, there are always surprises in Ricco's life, especially where legal, religious, and travel matters are concerned.

NEPTUNE IN LIBRA ♎

Ricco has an inborn sense of justice, aspiration and high ideals. Put into practice, his concepts of peace and equality could change the world.

NEPTUNE IN THE 12TH HOUSE

Considered as a man of mystery, Ricco is regarded as an old soul. Once finding a cause, organization, or ideal to fight for, he is difficult to stop. He will probably become a member of a secret organization because he adores the romance of mystery.

PLUTO IN LEO ♌

A magnetic and strong-willed man, Ricco has leadership qualities. In sexual matters, he approaches sex as fun.

PLUTO IN THE 10TH HOUSE

Ambitious, and with a need to control others, Ricco's power, authority, and magnetism are used in his career. Having good business sense, careers involving stamina and dedication are suitable for him. His mother is a powerful and dominant woman.

SOLAR ECLIPSE IN VIRGO ♍

Ricco has incarnated into this lifetime in order to teach people how to use their analytical faculties. His contract with the universe is to point out flaws in the world, relationships, and life in general. This way, things can be put back in proper alignment.

LUNAR ECLIPSE IN AQUARIUS ♒

Ricco's lesson in this life is detachment—nothing is allowed to crystallize. He needs to experience a great deal in this lifetime. One thing he needs to achieve is the transition from thoughts of himself and his family, to thoughts of humanity. He is the true humanitarian, and comes into this lifetime feeling that something inside must be set straight. His strong character frees him to achieve his heart's desire—this is his most important lesson. In past incarnations, he had an overdeveloped ego that caused him to believe he was better than the people around him.

80C3

♉ Louie Petticelli • May 10, 1952

Ascendant in Gemini · Sun in Taurus · Moon in Scorpio
Mercury in Aries · Venus in Leo · Mars in Scorpio · Jupiter in Taurus
Saturn in Libra · Uranus in Cancer · Neptune in Libra · Pluto in Leo
Solar Eclipse in Leo · Lunar Eclipse in Scorpio
Mode: Fixed · Element: Earth · Key Idea: The Material Plane

ASCENDANT IN GEMINI ♊

Because this is a talkative rising sign, Louie has the gift of gab. He can persuade people to do things they don't want to do. This witty man has a hard time being still and appears to be constantly in motion and on the go. Maintaining an immeasurable amount of knowledge, he is also very observant of everything that's happening around him.

SUN IN TAURUS ♉

Louie is a good-natured, domestic, and very affectionate man. Unafraid of hard work, he has countless reserved energy—obstacles only make him more persistent. Having a tendency to overeat, it's hard for him to deny the pleasures of food and drink.

SUN IN THE 12TH HOUSE

Having a strong sense of privacy and individuality, very few people really know Louie. He doesn't actually seek out new relationships. Idealizing his sexual state of affairs, he feels that all things come to those who wait.

MOON IN SCORPIO ♏

Louie is a passionate, emotional, sensual, shrewd and accurate man. His powers of observations are phenomenal, sharp and precise. His conclusions are usually based on noteworthy information. Having a mother who ruled their home in a very controlling way, he has little to do with women—they have a very weak influence in his life.

MOON IN THE 6TH HOUSE

Emotions and responses are expressed through Louie's work. He's had numerous job changes and is very considerate of those he works with. Siding with the underdog, he is not afraid to stick his neck out. This man is able to create first-rate fantasy escapades and is a very thoughtful and considerate lover.

TAURUS SUN • SCORPIO MOON COMBINATION ♉ ♏

Being a good analyst of people and situations, this intensely dramatic man has an instantaneous charm about him. A realist with a sweet and gracious exterior, Louie could be a successful actor or speaker.

MERCURY IN ARIES ♈

A quick thinker with a warm and friendly voice, Louie is always able to come up with a clever answer and quick repartee. Having a way with words, he gets right to the point. Louie, loving original ideas and intellectual adventures, is brilliant, witty and entertaining.

MERCURY IN THE 11TH HOUSE

In matters concerning the heart, Louie is an optimist—viewing his friends as intellectual challenges.

VENUS IN LEO ♌

Being a theatrical person, who likes to put on a show, Louie is also a humanitarian. Popular, generous, and loving, this man is loyal in his relationships and has a romantic spirit with a healthy sexual appetite. All his affairs tend to go all the way.

VENUS IN THE 3RD HOUSE

This charming man has a desire for knowledge and is an excellent communicator. Louie's yearning for love, peace and harmony is expressed through conversations and artistic endeavors.

MARS IN SCORPIO ♏

Detective Petticelli has a crusading spirit and the ability to persevere when others give up. Having a fixed determination, he commits himself emotionally and passionately in all endeavors.

MARS IN THE 6TH HOUSE

Louie is a quick paced workaholic.

JUPITER IN TAURUS ♉

An extravagant man, Louie attracts material wealth and possessions more readily than others. He is successful wherever money management is involved. Generally domestic and devoted to his home and family, he is not likely to enter a new relationship hastily. He loves to sing and has a very good voice.

JUPITER IN THE 12TH HOUSE

Being very emotional and compassionate, Louie is also capable of having a secret life. In his lifetime, financial situations tend to increase at diverse times.

SATURN IN LIBRA ♎

Louie's strong awareness, his organizational efforts, and the need to cooperate, are very powerful. He understands the need to be fair when using authority, and desires to bring harmony to all relationships. Being diplomatic and impartial, he is very aware of the law and its principles—believing that there are things of lasting value that have to be achieved.

SATURN IN THE 5TH HOUSE

Louie is slow to form romantic relationships, however, when one does come into his life, he takes her and their relationship quite seriously.

URANUS IN CANCER ♋

Louie has had a disrupted home and family life.

URANUS IN THE 2ND HOUSE

Having brilliant and unusual ideas on how to make money, Louie also enjoys giving lavish gifts and possessions to his friends and lovers. However, he is inclined to lead an unhealthy lifestyle.

NEPTUNE IN LIBRA ♎

This creative and artistic man, who is a lover of peace and harmony, searches for the ideal love.

NEPTUNE IN THE 5TH HOUSE

Louie's sexual encounters do not always give him as much as he desires—the jaded world of the swinger is not for him. Possessing an innocent and childlike quality, he looks at sex with humor and fun. There is self-deception where love is concerned, for he idealizes and seeks perfection in his romances—wanting the kind of love that is often found in cheap motion pictures and where no powerful feelings come into play. Softness, sensitivity, confusion and escapism are all projected into imaginative thoughts for this man. He is endowed with artistic, musical, and theatrical talent, and has a love of water and liquids, which include alcoholic beverages.

PLUTO IN LEO ♌

Louie has magnetic leadership qualities.

PLUTO IN THE 3RD HOUSE

This man's daily activities are undertaken with serious and intense concentration. He absorbs information slowly and deeply. Bearing a talent with words, he can speak effectively. He has unfortunately, had a traumatic loss of siblings.

SOLAR ECLIPSE IN LEO ♌

Louie is the true teacher of the zodiac. He teaches others to lighten up and get in touch with their own creative sources—helping them to find their own motivation and self-worth.

LUNAR ECLIPSE IN SCORPIO ♏

Vickie and Louie have the same path here—discovering boundaries for themselves and others. The lesson here is to have a respect for other beings. Louie has come to learn there is good in the world and that the universe will support him while also learning what goes around comes around. He must be taught that he cannot control everything around him. He is gaining the knowledge and lessons of joint expressions and trust. Coming from previous incarnations of having cracked foundations with his value systems, moral, financial and spiritual values were shattered through abuse. In this lifetime, he must strengthen their values by trusting not only himself, but also other people.

♈ Shawn O'Hara • April 8, 1958

Ascendant in Scorpio · Sun in Aries· Moon in Sagittarius
Mercury in Taurus · Venus in Pisces · Mars in Aquarius
Jupiter in Libra · Saturn in Sagittarius · Uranus in Leo
Neptune in Scorpio · Pluto in Virgo
Solar Eclipse in Aries · Lunar Eclipse in Libra
Mode: Cardinal · Element: Fire · Key Idea: The Individual

ASCENDANT IN SCORPIO ♏

Shawn can be meek, mild, and charming, until you disagree with him. He can also be very helpful, as long as you do things his way. His main problem is that he constantly feels threatened. If he senses you are going against his wishes, he puffs up and tries to force matters. Once the perceived threat appears, his soft, pleasing voice rapidly turns into a hectoring harshness. Expecting you to eventually stand on your own feet, this man will provide you with as much assistance as he can give—his is a do or die attitude. Having tremendous will power, he can actually transform the lives of others by motivating them to new heights. This emotionally deep and private man does not like to express his feelings in public.

SUN IN ARIES ♈

Shawn is a natural leader possessing dynamic energy, determination and faithfulness. He is driven to prove himself. This man loves competition and desires to be first and best at everything he tries. He is the great investigator in life who gets things moving. Displaying actions and thoughts on a whim, and without any regard for protocol, timing, and wishes or opinions of others, he does as he pleases. Although he has a tendency to be self-centered and selfish, he is usually open and prepared to discuss himself.

SUN IN THE 6TH HOUSE

Shawn's ego, individuality, determination and faithfulness are directed toward his work. His love relationship needs a set of reference points and a definite framework to work. He is better off with one steady partner.

MOON IN SAGITTARIUS ♐

Unconsciously, Shawn searches for the perfect solution. He seeks the ultimate vision that will empower him to put his physical universe in order and furnish him with proof of his righteousness. He is strongly influenced by his parents' beliefs and does not enjoy being tied down to a routine job. He often daydreams about some person, place or object, and then actually feels as though he's had that particular experience.

MOON IN THE 2ND HOUSE

Shawn will be the happiest with someone who is faithful. No matter how romantic the liaison is, he will not be happy in a money-starved love relationship.

ARIES SUN • SAGITTARIUS MOON COMBINATION ♈ ♐

Shawn's thoughts, actions, and speech are of an independent nature. He is in many ways a pioneer, a fighter and a self-starter. This man is a strong individual with a powerful desire to bring the world—great or small—to his way of thinking. He is a pleader of new doctrines, philosophies, abstractions and lost causes. Instead of using the power of position or authority, he derives great satisfaction utilizing the power of their minds. His executive powers take the form of controlling others with ideas, thoughts, and principles. The truth is so evident to him that he sees no sense in mincing words. Emotionally intense, he is not especially aware of the feelings of others, but is acutely aware of his own. This attitude can be difficult for those around him.

MERCURY IN TAURUS ♉

Obstinate, loyal, with excellent powers of concentration, Shawn gains more knowledge from sight than from sound. He profits from reading, observing, absorbing knowledge, and visual demonstrations. Generally diplomatic, this man has strong likes and dislikes. Once he has decided on an idea or course of action, he is almost never persuaded to change his mind. While demonstrating patience and practicality, he stubbornly sticks to his opinions and puts his ideas into practice based on sound practical sense—not recognizing anything he doesn't regard as important.

MERCURY IN THE 7TH HOUSE

This man is attracted to everything that is law orientated. His urge to communicate is carried over into his relationships. Shawn is happiest with an active and very talkative lover.

VENUS IN PISCES ♓

Charming, romantic, poetic Shawn has a very good singing voice. In romantic endeavors, he depends on an invitation where his affections are concerned. Never earthy or crude, this man loves so wholeheartedly that he asks little for himself in return and is truthfully devoted when he is in love. Being very considerate, soft, and tender—with an unequalled capacity for dedication and self-sacrifice—he intuitively knows how to please his partner. Longing for an ideal union where he can give himself completely, his pleasures lie in giving rather than receiving. Although this emotional man's love is always pure, he is not very particular about the kind of person he gives his heart to. He may even feel greater nobility in loving someone inferior—one who depends on him and truly needs his love.

VENUS IN THE 5TH HOUSE

Shawn has a desire for peace, love and harmony. Personal communication with his partner is more important than sex. Needing romantic liaisons, his lover should be active and energetic enough to provide the variety and delight he desires. Lovemaking and sex for him can be a source of limitless entertainment.

MARS IN AQUARIUS ♒

This man challenges authority and tends to alienate others by his assertiveness. Being a humanitarian, Shawn's desire is to reform existing systems. He can become coldly dispassionate toward others in order to act freely on those ideals. Although he is forthright, freedom loving and candid, he has to do things his own way. His anger is aroused by any establishment and bureaucracy that break others down. He channels his personal energy into humanitarian work, the occult, scientific, and technical channels. Love relationships must always have the purity and beauty of a flower, for he is happiest with a lover who doesn't beat around the bush.

MARS IN THE 4TH HOUSE

Willing to fight for country, home, and possessions, Shawn attracts people with fiery ideas, and creative individuals who are full of life. He has stormy sessions in his domestic life which included a powerful, aggressive father and a difficult upbringing. Assertive and dominant in private matters, there are times when he needs to get away from it all. There have been many changes and dangers in his lifetime—including fire related situations. Romantically speaking, he is a carefree and thoughtful lover, while creating an all-encompassing sexual experience for his partner. Although his manner of loving has considerable strength, the feeling behind his love may be quite parental. This can be very comforting and reassuring to his partner.

JUPITER IN LIBRA ♎

Shawn has an extraordinary talent for spotting opportunity, swaying public opinion, winning friends, and influencing people. He is prepared to share his knowledge so that it can be used for the greater benefit of others. His luck comes through his deep sense of justice. He also profits from the exercise of abstract reason. This man has the ability to weigh the pros and cons of any situation. His achievements are manifested through marriage, partnerships and projects. Marriage could be very fortunate for this man— his mate would be a blessing in his life.

JUPITER IN THE 2ND HOUSE

Shawn has a tremendous capacity for a secret life. Resourceful and charitable, he is willing to take chances by trusting less fortunate individuals. His best performances are behind closed doors and his favorite audience is his lover. This man is likely to pursue a single relationship for a fairly long time.

SATURN IN SAGITTARIUS ♐

This position doesn't make it easy for success. However, Shawn is able to reach more profound conclusions than most people. Although he achieves success, he will have sobering experiences in his lifetime. He may suffer some early setbacks and have more than his share of disappointment before he accomplishes what he sets out to do. It's this kind of adversity that teaches him the philosophy and wisdom that makes his contributions so valuable later on in life. It also gives him the compassion and understanding of human nature. Because of his generosity, he will go far mentally and physically. Being an idealist, his vision shows true dedication to a cause. He has very opinionated religious and philosophical viewpoints. Travel and his occupations are usually connected with his causes. This position has a high incidence of deaths that relate to political reasons.

SATURN IN THE 2ND HOUSE

Shawn has rigid values and builds for the future. Even though this House can also represent frustration for him, it also brings him great appreciation for what he gains in life.

URANUS IN LEO ♌

Shawn is magnanimous, eccentric, highly effusive, and rebellious. He is a man of remarkable achievements and will gain the most out of any personal relationship that moves slowly and leaves room for growth.

URANUS IN THE 10TH HOUSE

Disruption, change, ability, and eccentricity are channeled into the many careers of Shawn O'Hara. He settles for nothing but the best. This man has acquired a reputation for being original in all areas of life, including lovemaking. He needs a fairly adventurous lover.

NEPTUNE IN SCORPIO ♏

Shawn is extremely psychic, imaginative and erotic.

NEPTUNE IN THE 1ST HOUSE

Shawn's features have a dreamy, far-away look. Softness, sensitivity, confusion, and escapism, render him; magnetic, ethereal, and extremely difficult to understand. This intangible quality adds to his romantic appeal. He needs to make sure that his lover is aware of who he is and what he wants.

PLUTO IN VIRGO ♍

Having a powerful sex-drive, Shawn is capable of great detail in that specific area.

PLUTO IN THE 11TH HOUSE

Practical in his approach to people, friends, and ideals, Shawn is also loyal to various causes and movements. Although he is very harmonious in his love affairs, he will be the first to break up a relationship—remaining to be friends with his previous lovers. The sexual feelings and the emotional hunger he experiences are the part of his chart that requires great care and attention.

SOLAR ECLIPSE IN ARIES ♈

Shawn is teaching his fellow beings the lessons of assertiveness, independence, courage of convictions, and overcoming the fear of new beginnings. He is clearing the path for others to follow. This man is sharing that it's all right to move forward with change and that nothing can survive in a static environment.

LUNAR ECLIPSE IN LIBRA ♎

Along with possessing strong sensitivities, Shawn is also psychic. He works hard physically to keep things together so that as spiritual beings will have a safe and healthy environment in which to manifest. He is learning the proper balance between giving and receiving. Accustomed to doing things himself, it is difficult for him to learn and depend on someone else. He needs to learn the social graces which include; consideration, tact, sensitivity and teamwork. His emotions are raw with emotional gut instincts. He is here to teach those of the physical world how to see the role of the spiritual realms, and the role that the earth plays in the universal plan.

☙❧

♒ Francoise Luc Joubert · February 4, 1960

Ascendant in Capricorn · Sun in Aquarius · Moon in Taurus
Mercury in Aquarius · Venus in Capricorn · Mars in Capricorn
Jupiter in Sagittarius · Saturn in Capricorn · Uranus in Leo
Neptune in Scorpio · Pluto in Virgo
Solar Eclipse in Aries · Lunar Eclipse in Virgo
Mode: Fixed · Element: Air · Key Idea: The Innovator

ASCENDANT IN CAPRICORN ♑

Joubert, a person of conventional methods and conservative ideas, has periods
of using new and alternative ways. Although he gives out the impression of
being cool and aloof when first introduced, he is a loyal man with new ideas on
how to improve the world. Social and spiritual issues are important to him.

SUN IN AQUARIUS ♒

Joubert is a noble, well-balanced, strong, and very scientific being, who believes
in helping others. Having a dislike for human suffering, he will go to any lengths
to help those in need. This man has an instinctive understanding of human
nature that is coupled with a great tolerance for human weaknesses. His sound
and practical approach to problems is always taken with a fair and open mind,
making him the ideal person to consult for safe, sane, and well-considered
judgments. Not influenced or affected by his environment and public opinion, he
realizes that the mistakes people make in the course of a lifetime is for the
growth of their souls and their own eventual good. Being a profound student of
human behavior, he is a mastermind when it comes to the powers of
observation, and is able to theorize them accurately. Because he is aware of
every factor, he sees into the heart of all situations. He believes in the

Brotherhood of man and in an eventual world order where race and nationality will be transcended by international unity. A firm believer in astrology and psychic research, he relies on his spiritual and mental powers to solve problems. His friends are sensible, intelligent, well-educated, and spiritually minded.

SUN IN THE 2ND HOUSE

Strength of purpose emanates from Joubert. His energy is applied to anything that brings him stability. He often attracts money through his excellent business ability.

MOON IN TAURUS ♉

Because of Joubert's conservative outlook and deep powers of concentration, he reacts very slowly and fully. This man's loyalty is unquestionable and the women he gets involved with are faithful and domestic.

MOON IN THE 5TH HOUSE

This House brings early success and publicity to Joubert. He has an excellent sense of drama and is good when it comes to dealing with children and educating others. Having strong emotional attachments to his creative output, his security is sought through the respect he receives from those around him.

AQUARIUS SUN • TAURUS MOON COMBINATION ♒ ♉

Joubert has a nice blend of emotional and intellectual natures. His mind is efficient, purposeful, reasonable and logical. Willing to live and let live, he has fixed principles and is prepared to wait for their results. This man knows the futility of forcing issues. Being an avid lover of peace and harmony, he will use his diplomatic and affability skills to avoid any harsh disputes.

MERCURY IN AQUARIUS ♒

Joubert's power of observation is incredible. He is an excellent judge of human nature and loves to analyze everyone, which include; total strangers, casual acquaintances and those close to him. No matter how superior his idea, it sounds ordinary when he expresses it. Having a driving passion for the truth, he intuitively understands people and their behavior. This logical, analytical, resourceful and ingenious man has a fine mind with a strong ability of concentration. His interest in astrology gives him psychological insights to those around him. He can predict the outcome of actions and situations with astonishing accuracy.

MERCURY IN THE 2ND HOUSE

References that prove Joubert's intellectual beliefs to be accurate only strengthen him. He desires honesty and consistency in all of his relationships.

VENUS IN CAPRICORN ♑

Having a somewhat of a suspicious nature, Joubert expects others to make the first move. Moral beauty, instead of the physical kind, is what appeals to Joubert. However, he can be lusty, earthy, detached and cold—all at the same time. This man needs encouragement before he can relax and love.

VENUS IN THE 1ST HOUSE

Joubert has a great deal of social charm and is naturally responsive to other people's needs. People often turn to him for sympathy and understanding.

MARS IN CAPRICORN ♑

This excellent position for success is perfect for the strong-willed Joubert. He doesn't beat around the bush. Direct and persistent, this capable leader combines mastery and technique with great strength and endurance. His personal magnetism inspires others to follow.

MARS IN THE 1ST HOUSE

Joubert has a strong desire to experiment and test the waters for himself. He also has excellent leadership qualities combined with the strength to fight on the behalf of others.

JUPITER IN SAGITTARIUS ♐

This is the best sign for financial success and Joubert's destiny is to be wealthy and possess power in the world—spending brings him luck. He will do well in any field where intellectual sharpness and precision is needed. His sixth-sense ability seems to know what people are thinking. He has an instinct for uncovering the truth.

JUPITER IN THE 12TH HOUSE

Compassionate and emotional in all relationships, Joubert will have sudden and unexpected boosts of fortune in his lifetime.

SATURN IN CAPRICORN ♑

This man is ambitious, determined and tends to do everything himself. He'll utilize everything within his power to give configuration to a problematical situation. His talent for organization and working hard brings forth an excellent chance for success. He may have to contend with more than his share of obstacles and hardships in life. He handles living in a steady and practical way and rarely allows problems to upset him. In romantic relationships, this man is a steady and dependable lover.

SATURN IN THE 1ST HOUSE

Responsibility was put on Joubert early in life. His parents most likely were separated and childhood problems would have forced an early assumption of responsibility on him.

URANUS IN LEO ♌

Having attained remarkable achievements in his life, Joubert remains magnanimous, eccentric, highly effusive, and rebellious.

URANUS IN THE 8TH HOUSE

Having strong psychic abilities, Joubert is attracted to the mystic arts. He investigates the occult, astrology, alchemy, science, and technology with inspiration. He also has windfalls of money that increase his financial income.

NEPTUNE IN SCORPIO ♏

Having immeasurable emotions, Joubert is extremely psychic, imaginative and erotic.

NEPTUNE IN THE 11TH HOUSE

Unknown enemies, and being deceived by friends, could become a problem for Joubert. His compassionate ideals can be put to work in-group activities, especially if humanitarian causes are being pursued.

PLUTO IN VIRGO ♍

Although Joubert's professional life involves great attention to detail, his personal lifestyle is rather relaxed and undemanding.

PLUTO IN THE 9TH HOUSE

Joubert has the ability to get to the root of social problems. His power, authority, and magnetism are concentrated into a higher learning of religion and traveling. Intense about foreign concerns, his life could end in a foreign country.

SOLAR ECLIPSE IN ARIES ♈

Joubert is teaching his fellow beings assertiveness, independence, the courage of their convictions, and how to overcome the fear of new beginnings.

LUNAR ECLIPSE IN VIRGO ♈ ♍

Joubert, possessing strong sensitivities in this lifetime, has been psychic since birth. In this incarnation, he is learning physical integration on a multitude of levels. Another major lesson is finding a balance between the spiritual and the physical worlds. He needs to comprehend that while we are in physical bodies, we also have physical desires. He also needs to be allowed to satisfy his own curiosity. In past lives, he was overly involved in the spiritual realm. This time he must adjust with his feet back on the ground.

ෂ☾ß

ACKNOWLEDGEMENTS

CELEBRITIES:

Armani · Antonio Banderas · Warren Beatty · Willie Best · Jerry Bruckheimer · Nicolas Cage · Darby Conley · Sean Connery · Rodney Dangerfield · Robert De Niro · Stephen Dorff · Faye Dunaway · Peter Falk · Sean Patrick Flannery · Jeff Foxworthy · Kay Francis · Mel Gibson · James Gleason · Cary Grant · Hugh Grant · Mariska Hargitay · Richard Harris · Alfred Hitchcock · John Larroquette · Larry the Cable Guy · Christopher Lee · Jennifer Love Hewitt · Groucho Marx · Miami Dolphins · Kim Novak · Eleanor Parker · Joe Pesci · Vincent Price · Edward G. Robinson · Otis Rush · Kurt Russell · Robert Ryan · Arnold Schwarznegger · Zachary Scott · Bob Steele · Donald Sutherland · Kiefer Sutherland · Kathleen Turner · Lee Tracy · Bruce Willis · Whitesnake ·

ENTERTAINERS, MUSICIANS AND MUSICAL GROUPS:

Marc Anthony · AC DC · Bad Company · Bon Jovi · The Chimes · Patsy Cline · Fats Domino · The Drifters · The Eagles · Ella Fitzgerald · Clarence Gatemouth Brown · Gloria Gaynor · Jerry Goldsmith · Buddy Guy · Billy Holiday · Engelbert Humperdinck · Etta James · Alan Jackson · David Letterman · Delbert Mc Clinton · Metallica · Cole Porter · Lloyd Price · Paul Rogers · Lynyrd Skynyrd · Joe Turner · Joe Walsh · Barry White ·

FICTIONAL CHARACTERS, LEGENDS, AND PLACES:

The Abominable Snowman · Armageddon · Athos · Camelot · Carmen · Daffy Duck · Detective Benson · Esmerelda · Get Fuzzy · Gumby · Hannibal Lechter · The Ice Queen · Inspector Clousseau · King Arthur · The Knights Of The Round Table · Mr. Magoo · Mrs. Robinson · Muarte · Peter Pan · Phantom Of The Opera · Pied Piper Of Hamlin · Porky Pig · Pluto · Rob Roy · Roger Rabbit · Santa Claus · Satchel · Shangri-La · Superman · Thelma and Louise · The Three Musketeers · Treasure Island · Tweety · The Yeti · Zorro

FILM AND TELEVISION:

Alien · Animal Planet · Arsenic And Old Lace · Bonnie And Clyde · CSI NY · Camelot · Columbo · Comedy Central · Con Air · Conspiracy Theory · CMTV · David Letterman · The Discovery Channel · Dracula · Dragonwyck · Escape From New York · The Exorcist · Foreign Correspondent · The Godfather · Hannibal Lechter · His Kind Of Woman · House of Wax · In Name Only · Jaws · The Lady Vanishes · Law And Order · Law And Order SVU · Medicine Man · Mildred Pierce · Monty Python · Night Court · NYPD Blue · Thelma And Louise · Twelve Monkeys · Twilight Zone · Vertigo · X Files ·

HISTORICAL FIGURES AND PLACES:

The Alamo · Billy the Kid · Butch Cassidy and the Sundance Kid ·
Bob Ford · Bonnie Parker · Clyde Barrow · Colonel George
Armstrong Custer · Frank James · The James Gang · William Kidd ·
John Kennedy · Picasso ·

LOCATIONS:

Brooklyn On The Bay · The Brooklyn Bridge · Central Park · Devils
Island · Disneyland · FATBURGER · Forest Lawn Cemetery · The
Hyatt Regency · Knott's Berry Farm · L'Ermitage, Paris, France ·
Martoni's · Mickey D's · Pelican Bay · Pershing Square · The Plaza
Hotel · Ritz Carlton Hotel · Rue De Mouffetard · 7-11 · 24 Rue
Lamarck · San Diego Zoo · Sea World · The Water Club, New York
City · WAXQ ·

POLICE PRECINCTS IN NEW YORK CITY:

13th · 15th · 19th · 20th·

MUSIC:

A Man Without Love · After The Lovin' · Am I That Easy To Forget ·
As Time Goes By · At Last · Bad Company · Blueberry Hill · Born
Under A Bad Sign · Corrina, Corrina · Don't Think Twice · Everyday
I Have The Blues · Faithfully · Feel Like Makin' Love · Feels like Rain
· The Fishing Song · Funk #49 · Going Back To Louisiana · Here I
Go Again · I Need To Know · If You Love Me, Really Love Me · I
Will Survive · I Drink Alone · Just One Of Those Things · The Last
Waltz · Les Bicyclettes De Belsize · Let The Music Play · The Man I
Love · Movin' On · Please, Please, Please · Pride And Joy · Night
And Day · Northern Lights Of Aberdeen · Once In A While · Release
Me · Ruby Baby · Someone To Watch Over Me · Take It To The
Limit · Tragedy · Unforgettable · Victim Of Life's Circumstances ·
You Give Love A Bad Name · The Way It Used To Be · Winter World
Of Love · Who's Cheating Who ·

BIBLIOGRAPHY:

Abadie M.J. (1994). *Child Signs*
Connecticut: Longmeadow Press.
Atheneum Books for Young Readers *Pirates Most Wanted*
Simon & Schuster, New York, London, Toronto
Grant, Lewi (1977). *Heaven Knows What*
St. Paul: Liewellyn Publications.
Lee Christopher (1990). *Astrology*
Great Britain: Self Publishing Assoc. Ltd.
Martin, Paul (1991). *How To Find A Perfect Partner*
New York: Channel Media Inc.
Michelsen Neil F. (1992). *The American Ephemeris For The Last 20th Century*

San Diego: ACS Pub.
Omarr Sydney (1965). *My World of Astrology*
California: Wilshire Book Co.
Quigley, Joan (1969). *Astrology for Adults*
Canada: Holt, Rinehartand Winston.
Spiller, Jan and McCoy, Karen (1988). *Spiritual Astrology*
New York: Simon and Schuster Inc.
Townley, John (1987). *Planets In Love*
Pennsylvania: Schiffer Pub. Ltd.
Zolar (1989). *Starmates*
New York: Simon and Schuster.

MUSIC BIBLIOGRAPHY:

After The Lovin' · Silver Blue Music (Alan Bernstein and Richie Adams)

Am I That Easy To Forget · Parrot Records / London Records / BMI (Carl Belew and W. S. Stevenson)

Baby What You Want Me To Do · Jimmy Reed, © Seeds of Reed Music and Conrad Music (BMI)

Born Under A Bad Sign · Irving Music BMI (Jones and Bell)

Damn Right I Got The Blues · Mic-Shau Music Co. (adm. by Zomba Songs) BMI (B. Guy)

Don't Think Twice · Special Writer Music ASCAP (Bob Dylan)

I Need To Know · Sony / ATV Music Publishing (Marc Anthony and Cori Rooney)

I Wanna Be Just Like You · Richard and Robert Sherman / Disney

If You Love Me (Really Love Me) · Capital Records Inc. (Marguerite Monnot and Jeffrey Parsons)

I Will Survive · Copyright © 1978 PolyGram Int. Publishing and Perren Vibes Music Inc. (Freddie Perren and Dino Fekaris)

Just One Of Those Things · Copyright © Warner Bros. Music ASCAP (Cole Porter)

Keep Your Hands To Yourself · Dan Baird/ No Surrender Music/Warner-Tamerlane Pub Corp/Elelsylum Music Inc. BMI

Let Me Be Your Lover · McClinton / Cotillion / McClinton Music, BMI/RSO Publishing

Lone Star Blues · McClinton / Nicholson / Nasty Cat Music, LLC BMI

Lovey Dovey · Memphis Curtis/Ahmed Ertegun

Please, Please, Please · Polygram Records Inc. (James Brown and Johnny Terry)

Night And Day · Copyright © Warner Bros. Music ASCAP (Cole Porter)

Once In A While · Vee Jay Records Pub. Miller Music (Edwards and Green)

Release Me (And Let Me Love Again) · © '54 Roschelle Publishing BMI / Acuff-Rose Music, BMI (Eddie Miller and W. S. Stevenson)

Someone To Watch Over Me · Copyright © Warner Bros. Music Corp. ASCAP (George and Ira Gershwin)

Stagger Lee · L. Price / H. Logan, 1985 Sony Music Entertainment Inc.

www.ingramcontent.com/pod-product-compliance
Lightning Source LLC
Chambersburg PA
CBHW020245030726
47499CB00001B/59

9780578001500